DUPLICITY

PETER CRUSKALL

Printed in Australia

Internal design by Book Burrow

www.bookburrow.com.au

First printing: April 2025

Paperback ISBN 978-1-7638557-0-0

eBook ISBN 978-1-7638557-1-7

www.petercruskall.com

Distributed by Lightning Source Global

A catalogue record for this work is available from the National Library of Australia

Also by Peter Cruskall

Uncharted Waters

Principal Characters

Julie-Anne Granger	Investigative journalist – Sydney Daily News
Jack Wagner	Senior detective with Australian Federal Police
Michael Sanderson	Detective with New South Wales Police Force
Danielle Mortimer	Jack's girlfriend
Ben Chandler	New South Wales Minister for Education
Melissa Wu	Social justice lawyer
Zhang Xiao	Chinese Consul General to New South Wales
Paul Gao	Special Emissary of the Chinese Consulate
Sophie Zhao	High class escort and psychology student
John Robertson	Deputy Commissioner with the AFP
Wie Ping Lie	Head of Chinatown based drug syndicate (Triad)
Lucie Chan	Drug courier for the Chinatown based Triad
Chris Russell	Editor, Sydney Daily News
David Bedford	Proprietor, MPS Security Services

Acronyms

AMSA	Australian Maritime Safety Authority
MBC	Maritime Border Command
AFP	Australian Federal Police
CRV	Compact Recreational Vehicle
ANPR	Automatic Number Plate Recognition
KALOF	Keep A Look Out For
CI	Criminal Informant
SRG	Special Response Group
COPS	Computer Operational Policing System
COD	Chief of Detectives
DPP	Director of Public Prosecutions
DFAT	Department of Foreign Affairs and Trade

Prologue

Wednesday 18th March

Julie-Anne ventured back out onto the balcony, leaned against the railing next to Jack and stared into the dark bushland beyond. As if on cue she heard the hollow hoot of an owl. The aroma of the small eucalypt forest reminded her of the days she had spent sunbaking on this very balcony back when they were in a relationship. Well at least she thought they were. She took a sip of her champagne. 'That was a wonderful day and a great call on the restaurant too, Jack. Most of the good guys involved in our investigation were there and everyone seemed to have a good time.'

'Well, we had quite a bit to celebrate, JA. Li and Woodard have been charged with money laundering offences, Wang Wei is being extradited to Queensland, Li Jun was taken out in the SRG raid and we exposed and charged a corrupt cop. And let's not forget, we retrieved Michelle Ironside safely.'

'Yeah, I know, and that's all great, however we didn't get close to exposing Wie Ping Lie's illicit activities and no one was held accountable for the attempt on my life. And I just know the Chinese Consul General is indirectly linked to Wie and to Melissa's failed recruitment. Which means the Chinese government must be involved at some level. I'm going to go after them all with a vengeance in my next investigation.'

'Good for you, but I've warned you before, be careful. Wie won't take the loss of his two lieutenants lying down. Speaking of Melissa, what happened with you and her tonight?'

'Other than me becoming slightly melancholy after a few glasses of champers.'

'What were you getting all melancholy about?'

Julie-Anne knew exactly why. Her and Jack had both been focused on their respective careers and she often wondered what might have been had they been less so. 'It doesn't matter now, but I'll call her tomorrow.'

'Yeah, you should, she's been through the ringer these past few weeks, and she is obviously disappointed at having her political dreams crushed.'

'While we're on the subject of missing persons where did Danielle disappear to?' she asked Jack, knowing all too well what the answer would be.

'Well, she didn't say a lot really, she was uncomfortable that I was spending so much time out here talking to you. It was pretty full-on and potentially confronting spending the day in the company of your partner's ex-girlfriend even though I thought she handled herself spectacularly well. Anyway, I'm guessing she didn't want to make a scene, so she slipped quietly away.'

'That's a very adult way to handle an awkward situation. You should check on her though, Jack.'

'I have, and the call went straight to voicemail, so I left her a message. She sent a text saying that she's home safe and sound. Everything seemed to be so going well until we arrived here,' he said ruefully.

'Aah, well, weird and wonderful things typically happen when alcohol is involved,' Julie-Anne offered by way of consolation.

'Do you remember the last time we were out here on the balcony?' she teased.

'I reckon I'll get this. Hang on, it's on the tip of my tongue.'

After a wonderful evening of wining and dining at Alegrias, their favourite Spanish restaurant, they were consummating the evening on his balcony when, much to Julie-Anne's chagrin, Jack started humming a Diesel song of the same name. 'You're still a funny man, Jack Wagner.'

They had both consumed considerable quantities of alcohol throughout the afternoon and evening, and if Jack felt anything like her, he would be well on his way to cultivating a hangover. They were both quiet for some time, leaning over the railing, staring out into the darkness and enjoying the serenity. After a while Jack broke the silence. 'I could stay out here forever, but it's getting a tad on the chilly side, and anyway, I've had enough to drink for one day, so I'm going to hit the sack. Do you want me to book you an Uber?'

This was the moment. Julie-Anne had become aroused at the memory of their last interlude on the balcony and was wondering if Jack would ask her to stay the night. He looked good in his fitted linen shirt and dress jeans and her insides were stirring again. He had offered to book her an Uber, so his thought process was obviously heading in a different direction. Unless of course he was just being a gentleman. Which was it? She couldn't tell by his expression, or lack of it. Did she risk it and ask him if she could stay or should she just respond in the affirmative. She opted for the middle ground and subtly deflected the question for him to answer. 'Yeah, I suppose you could,' she replied coyly.

Jack turned to face her and noticed what he thought was an expression of yearning. He paused for a moment. God she was sexy. He breathed a heavy sigh. 'JA, it would be unfair to both Danielle and Melissa if I were to do anything other than book you an Uber.'

'Yeah, I'm sure you're right,' she said. Julie-Anne heard the hoot again. The wise old owl obviously agreed.

While sitting in the back of her Uber for the short ride home to Newtown Julie-Anne mulled over her friend Sophie's damning revelation from earlier this evening regarding Danielle. If it was true it would heap a world of pain on Jack, but at the same time, it might just kickstart Julie-Anne's next investigation. However, at what cost?

1. AMSA Headquarters Canberra

Two Months Later - Thursday 14th May

Three hundred kilometres to the south of Sydney, James Fairweather was ensconced at his desk in the secure monitoring room of the national headquarters of the Australian Maritime Safety Authority. Months after having proved his worth as an analyst by alerting his boss and the Maritime Border Command guys to the illicit activities of the Chinese Horizon, he was still the only operator in attendance on the night shift. He remembered a thought from that time. *Analysts used their brains, monitors used their eyes.* James was hoping that an analyst opportunity would open up within AMSA following his Chinese Horizon success, yet he also knew the wheels of government turned slowly. Too slowly, especially so in Canberra. So, here he was again, deskbound in front of the seven screens that showed the location and movements of over four hundred commercial vessels operating within Australia's Exclusive Economic Zone. Given the China Shipping Company was the owner of the Chinese Horizon, all staff had been instructed to closely monitor all ships owned by the CSC. James had flagged all five CSC vessels currently in Australian waters from the time they each had entered Australia's EEZ and he was now monitoring their progress diligently.

'What is she doing so close to the coastline?' he murmured

to himself. One of the CSC vessels was now stationed approximately ten nautical miles off the coast of Townsville in northern Queensland. The Marine Traffic website had the Chinese Panorama listed as travelling from Qingdao in north-eastern China to Brisbane. She was now inside the Great Barrier Reef and stationed on the seaward side of Magnetic Island. If she was heading for Brisbane via the traditional navigational routes, then she should have been about three hundred nautical miles further east.

Not twice in six weeks surely. Here we go again…

2. Maritime Border Command

Thursday 14th May

After his experience with the Chinese Horizon in March, James Fairweather was clear on the course of action he would embark upon following his latest discovery. The Chinese Panorama, just like its sister vessel, the Chinese Horizon, had been previously, was now positioned in an area well outside its intended course. He didn't believe in coincidences and alarm bells were ringing. He'd been watching the ship for a while, but she hadn't moved. *What is she waiting for?* He knew the answer.

It was now late in the evening and time for James to follow through on his suspicions. Unlike the preceding occasion, he didn't bother to contact the ship's captain. Given his previous interactions with the Chinese Horizon's captain he knew precisely the lame excuses that would be offered up. Rather, he drafted a succinct email to his superior, Jonathan Caldwell, and as he had been instructed, copied Shane Williamson, the Operations Manager at Maritime Border Command. He had simply outlined the similarities between the two incidents and hit the send button. There would be no lengthy interrogation surrounding his suspicions this time.

As was always the case, Shane Williamson was at his desk at the MBC Headquarters in Canberra at sunrise. He was now reading an email from young Fairweather at AMSA. Maritime Border Command is responsible for countering civil maritime security threats to Australia's borders. These threats can range from illegal arrivals, people and drug trafficking, prohibited imports, piracy, and even attacks on environmental and commercial infrastructure. Just like her sister ship before her, Williamson was acutely aware that the Chinese Panorama could have been involved in any of these illicit activities. His best guess told him that it would most likely be drug importation again. Williamson forwarded Fairweather's email to Damian de Vries with an instruction to call him ASAP. De Vries was the Brisbane based Operations Manager for Queensland.

Williamson's mobile phone rang. He thought it would be de Vries. He recognised Jonathan Caldwell's number, so he let the call go through to voicemail. Fairweather's immediate superior was your typical arse covering, procrastinating Commonwealth public servant. He wouldn't add any value to the kid's report, rather he would seek to take some of the credit for himself. Next the desk phone rang and the Brisbane office number was displayed on the screen.

'Damian, good morning, did you get Fairweather's email?'

'Yeah, he's on the ball that kid.'

'Yes, he is and I want to move on this expeditiously. How soon can you get Benson and Harvey up there?'

'It's not that simple in these times of the pandemic, Shane. Virgin only fly once every few days and Qantas are down to only one flight per day. Luckily, the flying kangaroo flight doesn't leave for a couple of hours. I have already forwarded the email to Harvey and Benson, so they will be up to speed and ready to go as soon as they arrive for work.'

'Okay, that's great. A few more things, Damian. We lost valuable time with the Chinese Horizon case, time that we won't have on our side if this plays out the way I think it will. Secondly, tell your guys to wear masks and maintain all appropriate precautions. We don't want them out of action, especially now. And just so you're in the loop, I'm going to contact that AFP detective in Sydney that we worked with on the Chinese Horizon case and give him a head's up.'

'The guys won't be happy about that, but I understand the bigger picture, Shane.'

Williamson replaced the handset and scrolled down his Outlook contacts list. He picked up the handset once more and punched in Jack Wagner's mobile number.

'Jack, it's Shane Williamson, Maritime Border Command here. We gave you the head's up on the Chinese Horizon case back in March.'

'Yes you did, and thank you again. What can I do for you?'

Williamson gave Jack an overview of Fairweather findings and suspicions and advised that Harvey and Benson would be in Townsville early this afternoon.

'That's great, let's hope they turn up something useful. I would dearly love to catch the local head of the syndicate down here in Sydney. Given it's the same shipping company involved, a similar location and just like last time the ship is way off its scheduled course, then I assume the Chinese Triads are still at their importation game.'

'Let's not get ahead of ourselves, Jack. My boys aren't even on the ground yet, let alone discovered any useful intel. There may be a simple explanation for the ship captain's unusual behaviour. And at this stage, it remains an MBC operation.'

Jack remained calm, wanting to avoid a jurisdictional pissing match. 'I hear you clearly, Shane. But, you wouldn't have reacted so expediently if you didn't have your own suspicions. With the timely warning this time we may have a golden opportunity to finally implicate the head of the Triad here in Sydney.'

'I am well aware of the bigger issue that you are implying

may be in play here. For fear of repeating myself, let's not get ahead of ourselves. As soon as my guys have something to report, and if it's indicative of what you are suggesting, then we can have another chat and reassess the situation.'

'Okay, that works for me. For now.'

3. Townsville North Queensland

Friday 15th May

'Scott, I'm not sure what we're exactly supposed to do up here,' Benson said as they drove away from Townsville Airport in their hire car.

'Yeah, I know, we don't have much intel to work with, so we'll have to be creative and use our imagination. We're heading to the port and we'll start by asking around and see if anyone has seen or heard of anything suspicious in the past twenty four hours. Then we can take it from there, dependent on what we find out, Sam.'

Harvey navigated the car around the monolithic Castle Hill, continued along Ingham Street and through the sparsely populated downtown of Townsville. He turned right at Denham Street, left into Palmer and continued all the way down into the heart of the Port of Townsville. They parked at the entry to Suter Pier, exited the car and strolled out to the Mission to Seafarers building.

'What a spectacular day,' Harvey said as he looked out across the turquoise waters.

'I lived up here for a couple of years in my early days at the agency and the weather's like this from May until August, twenty seven degrees and blue sky every day.'

The two agents walked through the entry alcove which

was occupied by a snack vending machine, notice board, wall maps and a guard of honour of large, flourishing, potted tropical plants.

'Well, we can't get a return flight until tomorrow afternoon, so depending on our progress, we might be able to make the most of it. Maybe even take a ferry ride out to Magnetic Island.'

'This looks ominous, what can I do for you gents?' asked a stern faced man eying the men in uniform standing before him in the foyer.

Harvey and Benson introduced themselves to Gavin Muller the Mission's manager and outlined the reason for their visit. 'In particular, we're interested in a cargo vessel that may have anchored on the seaward side of Magnetic Island last night. Name of the Chinese Panorama,' Harvey said.

'There's a lot less activity out here at the port since the nickel refinery closed four years ago, so any unusual occurrences would certainly be spotted,' Muller offered. 'And nothing's been reported to me. You should try the Sportfishing Club. Their members would pass by Maggie on their way to and from the fishing grounds out on the reef. The address is 266 Boundary Street over in South Townsville.'

'Okay, we'll do just that, thank you, Mr Muller.'

'I'm going to call into the Port of Townsville office and see if anyone there knows anything. It's on the way, Sam.'

Fifteen minutes later they were back on their way to South Townsville. The duty officer had confirmed that they had no record of any unusual activity in and around the Port. 'I can't believe that they weren't aware that a twenty thousand tonne cargo ship was moored a few kilometres off of their coastline, Scott.'

Harvey chuckled. 'Queenslanders. Too busy fishing.' He navigated through the dusty precinct of South Townsville and past too many tired looking workers cottages and large verandahed houses until he reached their destination. 'This area's definitely seen better days. Times are obviously tough up here.'

'Eight hundred workers lost their jobs at the nickel refinery, so it's no surprise.'

Harvey pulled up next to the double story, nineteenth century built, Victoria Park Hotel. The lack of any promotional signage, the grimy windows and dusty footpath told them that the pub was closed permanently.

'Just imagine the history and wild stories that would be linked to old hotels like this,' Benson marvelled.

Harvey checked the address again. It was correct which meant that the Sportfishing Club was situated in a private house directly next door to the hotel. 'I could live right here, Sam. Staggering distance.'

'Not any more, Scottie.'

The men arrived in the front yard of a renovated Queenslander where a well-tanned man in board shorts and work singlet was hosing down a small motorboat resting atop a trailer. As they drew nearer Harvey discerned a panicked expression develop on the man's face. Their dark blue uniform replete with its epaulettes, badges and logos could do that. 'It's okay, we're just here to ask you a few questions, sir,' Harvey called out while holding up his hands to placate the man. 'You've done nothing wrong.'

The men introduced themselves and Harvey explained the reason for their visit. 'Essentially, Mr Williams, we want to speak to anyone who may have witnessed anything unusual out on the water in the past twenty four hours.'

'You're kidding! Nice timing guys.'

'Not at all, Mr Williams, why?'

'On the way back from the reef last night about halfway between Maggie and the port I heard an unusual buzzing sound.

When I looked up I was surprised to see two flashing lights, one red and the other white, passing overhead. The lights were well spaced so whatever it was, it wasn't small, but it was definitely too small to be a plane. I'm guessing, but I reckon it was about fifty metres above me and moving steadily towards town. It was quite spooky really.'

'Were you able to see precisely where it was heading?' Benson asked.

'As we were entering Ross Creek I could see the same two lights backdropped against the shadows of the entertainment centre, so it must have landed somewhere near there.'

'By chance, did you notice anything else?'

'There's always a few guys fishing behind the centre. Maybe talk to them. If they were there last night then they ought to have seen or heard something.'

'What time was this, Mr Williams?'

'About one o'clock this morning.'

'You've been very helpful. Thank you for your time.'

Harvey drove northwest back into the centre of Townsville and the District Police Headquarters. There the two agents spoke to the desk sergeant and he searched his incident logbook, to no avail. They considered visiting the yachting and sailing clubs, but they couldn't imagine sailboats venturing out to sea in the dark of the night.

'Okay, Sam, let's go find a hotel. We've got a few hours to kill.'

Benson Googled Townsville hotels and was pleased to see there was a hotel conveniently located directly adjacent to the entertainment centre. They checked into the Ville Resort-Casino and settled into their rooms. Harvey called Williamson and informed him of their activities to-date and their intended course of action later this evening. Benson went for a swim in the large infinity edge pool that afforded a panoramic view across Cleveland Bay to Magnetic Island.

At ten o'clock in the evening Harvey and Benson met in the foyer of the hotel. They were frustrated by their lack of success earlier in the day. 'This is our last opportunity to gain some traction, Sam. We know the vessel was moored out there behind the island last night, so let's hope we can find these fishermen and they have something useful for us. Otherwise, we're going back to Brisbane empty handed.'

They walked out of the hotel and across the vast carpark it shared with the entertainment centre. They navigated Entertainment Drive around to the rear of the centre where they came upon two men in overalls and floppy hats who were unloading fishing equipment from a flattop utility vehicle. 'Gents, good evening, do you have a minute?' Harvey asked as they approached the men.

'Who are you guys, fisheries inspectors?' the nearer of the two men asked warily.

The uniform again. 'Not at all, we are with Maritime Border Command and we would just like to ask you some questions,' Harvey responded in a placatory manner. 'I'm Agent Harvey and he's Agent Benson. In particular, we would like to know if you guys were fishing here last night.'

'As a matter of fact we were. We fish most nights, why?'

'Did you see anything unusual?' Harvey wasn't going to mention the drone that Williams had spotted, rather he wanted the men to raise it, unprompted, if they were so aware.

'I'm guessing you already know we did otherwise you wouldn't be here asking questions,' the man replied smugly.

Harvey smiled. 'You're a clever guy. Continue please, sir.'

'We were fishing at our usual spot behind the centre not far from the rock wall when we heard a buzzing noise. It was getting louder, so it was obviously coming towards us. We thought it might be a UFO. We began to worry and started packing up our gear.'

'Go on, what happened next?'

The fisherman stopped unpacking and turned to Harvey. 'Two things. Firstly, a grey SUV pulled up not far from where we were fishing. Just along there,' he said gesturing over his shoulder to a grid of marked parking bays by the rock wall. 'Two Asian guys got out and stood next to their vehicle. We were only maybe thirty to forty metres away, yet they completely ignored us.'

'You said two things, what was the other?' Benson asked, inserting himself into the conversation.

'Oh, yeah, sorry. Then the buzzing noise got really loud and we looked up to see this UFO thing with its flashing lights slowly coming down from the night sky.'

'One red and one white?'

'How did you know that?'

'Lucky guess. And you didn't think that seeing a "UFO thing" was even just slightly unusual?' Benson suggested using finger quotes to accentuate his point. 'Never mind, continue please.'

'A large white box was strapped underneath the UFO, like those polystyrene boxes the produce market guys use. The chinks unstrapped the box, put it into the back of their SUV and drove away. At the same time the UFO rose up into the sky and disappeared seconds later.'

'Which direction?'

'Back out into the bay. Towards Maggie.'

'How big was this UFO thing?'

'It wasn't small. It had to be over a metre wide.'

'Did you get a good look at it in the dark?'

'Sort of. The thing was black, H shaped with four rotors at the end of two arms. And the whole contraption sat on top of two supports, similar to a sawhorse like I use at work.'

'Thank you. I'm assuming the men were local, so did you recognise them or their vehicle?'

'Never seen them before, but we did see them again.'

Just when he thought there wasn't more to be learned from these guys that refocused Harvey's attention. 'Really, when?'

'We got our gear back out and resumed fishing. They came back about an or so hour later.'

'What happened this time?'

'Exactly the same thing as the first time, like clockwork, you could say.'

'Didn't they say anything to you?' Benson asked.

'No, they didn't even look at us; just ignored us the whole time again.'

'Can you describe the vehicle, sir?'

'I can do better than that. When they came back the second time I realised something dodgy was going on. As the vehicle turned around to leave I saw the rego plate, so I decided to memorise it. If they were doing something illegal the dumb bastards didn't have the smarts to remove the globe above the plate.'

Harvey was surprised at this guy's initiative and wrote down the registration details of the Mazda CX9.

'Did you report the incident to the police or port authorities, sir?'

'I considered it, but I didn't want to get involved and I get nervous around the police.'

'Is there anything else you can tell us?'

'Nah, that's all I saw.'

'Okay, thanks, you've been very helpful, sir.'

4. Queens Park

Friday 15th May

Lucie Chan was rather chilled and lost in a world of her own as she drove her black Honda CRV along York Road on the edges of Bondi Junction. Even though the car's windows were tinted she could still revel in the sight of the setting sun turning the falling autumn leaves of the adjacent Centennial Park into a golden hue. She was singing along to Beyoncé's Blow, the title which, she tittered to herself, was fitting given her activities this evening. This was her last delivery for the day and to celebrate she would head to Isabel's on Bondi Beach afterwards and treat herself to a Blossom or Miso cocktail. She was wearing a backless, black lace, mini cocktail dress and matching heels, so she would be comfortable among the stylish Bondi set. It was Friday night and maybe she would even get lucky. *Lucky Chan*, she laughed to herself. Of course, that was assuming the bar wasn't locked down due to the virus her country of ancestry had given the world.

Lucie flicked the indicator upwards, made the left hand turn into Birrell Street and spied the entry to Birrell Lane up ahead on her right. The lane was about three hundred metres long and had a dog leg to the left at the end which prevented her having a view of her exit. The lane was predominantly bordered by the roller shutters that provided rear access for the occupants vehicles. Each had an assortment of two hundred and forty litre wheelie bins placed adjacent to the shutters. She paused at the kerbside bordering the entry and scrutinised the full length of the laneway. Comfortable that it was devoid of activity she turned off her radio, locked her doors and texted her contact. Lucie, with her senses now heightened, proceeded cautiously to her destination. This client's house actually fronted Ashton Street, but given the nature of the transaction and the snobby local elite, it was safer to conduct the deal in the rear laneway out of his neighbour's prying eyes. She brought the Honda to a stop adjacent to the shutter that her client would exit from and waited. She was disgusted to see that there were piles of rubbish and recyclables lying next to two of the wheelie bins. *These people.*

After five long minutes her client still hadn't appeared, so she turned off the ignition and exited the car. Normally with a no-show she would just leave, however, this was a long-term client, so she would cut him some slack and bang on the shutter. As she closed the car's door she heard loud flapping sounds behind her. It only took her a split second to put two and two together. She was in serious trouble. Quickly turning on her heels she reached for the car door handle. She was halted in her tracks by a strong arm that looped around her neck cutting off her breathing. Lucie was pulled backwards and away from the relative safety of her Honda. A second thick-set man of swarthy appearance then appeared in front of her.

'This is our turf bitch and we are going to teach you a lesson for stealing our customers. Then you need to go back to Chinatown and stay there. If you're still alive of course.' He punched her hard in the stomach.

She anticipated the blow and tensed her abdominal muscles at the last second to minimise the impact. Remaining upright, Lucie's right leg lashed out with considerable force and caught the man squarely in his genitals. He cried out in pain and went down on his knees, clutching his groin. 'You fucking bitch.'

The first man momentarily stunned, stopped pulling her backwards and she seized the opportunity to stamp down on his foot with the chunky heel of her slingbacks. Then she pivoted on the ball of her foot and swung her elbow hard into the man's jaw. He fell heavily to the ground and she stood over him and began to kick him hard with the toe of her shoes. She was panting hard. 'You miserable bastard,' she shrieked.

Lucie needed to calm herself and gather her thoughts. The men had obviously been hiding in the wheelie bins, which explained the strewn rubbish and the flapping sound she heard as they flipped the lids back. A rookie mistake, Lucie, she lamented. As she turned back to the first man she was caught by a crunching blow to the side of her head. She immediately felt the warmth of blood trickling down the side of her face. *The lowlife's wearing a knuckle duster.* She was losing consciousness, so she breathed deeply, endeavouring to get some oxygen back into her brain and compose herself. That idea was rapidly laid to waste by a second blow to her head. She wobbled momentarily and then everything went black.

The men, both sufficiently recovered, rolled her over and proceeded to cable tie her arms and legs together. They then lifted her up, carried her over to one of the wheelie bins, unceremoniously dumped her headfirst into the receptacle and closed the lid. Calmly walking to the dog leg at the end of the laneway, they turned the corner, climbed into their car, and drove away.

Lucie was startled awake by what sounded like a heavy goods vehicle further down the laneway. She had no idea what time it was, but given the sounds of birds chirping cheerily, it had to be around dawn. The vehicle was drawing nearer, and she could hear a loud secondary crunching sound, the source of which suddenly became abundantly clear. It was the heavy-duty hydraulic system of a garbage truck as it compacted rubbish from the laneway's wheelie bins. *Think Lucie, think.* Her head was protesting with pain and thumping incessantly, her abdominal muscles were sore from when she had tensed up, and she sensed the scabs of dried blood sticking to her cheek and neck whenever she grimaced. And the stench was overpowering. She had no time to worry about any of that now; she needed to get out of her predicament before being crushed into oblivion.

Being inverted and confined in the narrow space she had no leverage with which to manoeuvre her battered body out of the bin. The sounds of the garbage truck's engine and hydraulics were becoming louder, and she knew that it couldn't be more than two or three houses away now. Blood had rushed to her head during the night, but she had no time to worry about that either. She considered herself to be resourceful and needed a plan. Now. An idea came to her. Even though she was stuck in the inverted position she found that she could move her body from side to side. She began to do just that, repeating the process time and again, and within a few long seconds she managed to gain some momentum, rocking the bin like a pendulum. Lucie could tell by the heightened growl of the truck's engine that it was drawing alongside her position. This was the moment of truth. She flexed her legs tighter, made her body even more rigid, and putting in one final concerted effort, the wheelie bin came back through its apex and continued past the point of no return. It tumbled and crashed to the ground just as the garbage truck pulled to a halt next to her.

'Oh, my golly gosh?' she heard a man exclaim.

A turbaned man alighted from the truck and was astonished at what he saw. A woman in a party dress had spilled out of the wheelie bin. She was now sprawled on the ground, her dress riding around her waist. Even though it was still dark, through the truck's flashing amber, warning light, he could see that the woman's arms and legs were bound with cable ties. There also appeared to him to be dried blood down her face and neck and she smelt like she had been swimming in the Ganges. This was the last thing he expected to see on his rounds, especially at five o'clock in the morning. He climbed up into his truck, took a pair of snips from the glove compartment, and returned to the woman.

'Please roll onto your stomach,' he quietly told her in his high pitched, sub-continental accent. He held his breath, helped turn her body, cut the cable ties, and assisted the smelly woman to her feet. 'Are you okay? What happened to you, miss?'

Lucie leant against the roller shutter and breathed deeply, waiting for the head rush to abate. Slowly, but surely, her dizziness evaporated. She had learnt as a child, that when performing handstands the best way to minimise blood rushing to her head, was continually wiggling her toes and breathing into her abdomen instead of her chest. She had done this throughout the night to lessen the inevitable blood rush.

'Never mind, I'll be fine,' she snapped.

'What do you mean, you'll be fine? I am only trying to help. Two more minutes and you would have been flatter than a piece of naan.'

Lucie noticed the man's concerned expression and softened. 'Thank you for your help; I really do appreciate it,' she replied as she turned and headed for her car.

'You need a doctor and you should contact the police,' the driver called out.

Lucie ignored him, started the engine of her CRV, and drove away. *She really was Lucky Chan.*

5. Julie-Anne's Apartment

Friday 15th May

Julie-Anne was fussing around, ruffling cushions, straightening chairs, and adjusting the multicoloured arrangement of hybrid LA Lilies for the fourth time. Her apartment was always tidy, but she felt it needed a little more fluffing. *Who says I'm fussy?* It was light filled with timber flooring, soft grey horizontal blinds, stone benchtops and stainless steel appliances. And it had a north facing balcony. Best of all, it was only a short walk from the heart of her vibrant and eclectic suburb of Newtown. It had been nearly two months since the celebratory lunch at The Boathouse and the less than successful post lunch drinks at Jack's. With all the restrictions imposed due to the coronavirus pandemic, people across Australia had been in various stages of lockdown since the end of March. The New South Wales government had loosened the restrictions somewhat and you could now have minimal visitors to your place of abode. Having not being able to catch-up with Sophie since the evening at Jack's, she had taken the first opportunity to invite her to dinner. Julie-Anne had originally met Sophie Zhao through her investigation into political interference and money laundering by Chinese government sponsored operatives. She had grown fond of Sophie, however she knew in the deep recesses of her mind she also had an ulterior motive for the invite. The last time she had had a visitor at her apartment was months ago when Melissa had arrived for dinner and Julie-Anne had opened up on her investigation into Li Qiang and his illegal activities. Li was to be her financial sponsor for the state's parliamentary elections due later in the year. The revelations had ruined Melissa's evening and her political ambitions. The next morning hadn't unfolded any better when Melissa had discovered a none too subtle, intimidatory message pinned to Julie-Anne's front door. The subtext was aimed at encouraging Julie-Anne to back off from her Chinese interference investigation. *Not a chance.*

Her thoughts were interrupted by the chiming of the doorbell. She opened the door and greeted Sophie with a hug and side to side cheek kisses. 'Wow, you look great, girlfriend.' Sophie was tall and lithe, yet shapely, with lustrous, black hair and dark almond eyes. She was dressed smart casual in distressed denim skinny jeans, a white tee shirt, a lightweight black leather jacket and black pumps.

'Where did you get the jeans?'

'DJ's. They're by Citizens of Humanity, an LA based company. I love them. And you probably guessed that is Brigit Bardot on the front of the tee shirt. She was one of my favourite actresses. That's the famous image of her smoking a cigar on the set of Les Petroleuses in 1971.'

'I love it. Now, come in, come in.' Julie-Anne ushered Sophie into the living area. 'Make yourself comfortable and I'll grab us a champers.'

'Wow, I love your hair. Why the change and what do you call the colour?' Sophie asked.

'Thanks. I just wanted a change for winter and to celebrate the end of the lockdown, so I decided to go for a rich colour. Believe it or not it's called Raspberry Bourbon. Apparently, according to my hairdresser at Dolce Vita, it's an evolution of the cherry red colour, whatever that is.'

'Haha. I think it looks like a rustic mahogany and definitely highlights those piercing blue eyes of yours.'

'Thank you, that's very sweet.'

'I've missed you, Julie-Anne. How long has it been?'

'Two months, yet it seems so much longer.'

Sophie was checking out the open space living area. 'I love these, Julie-Anne. Where did you get them?' She was admiring two prints, one featuring colourful parrots flying through woodland and the second of a forest wetlands scene.

'They're by Philip Adams and I picked them up at a framing shop around the corner in Newtown. I used to lay out on Jack's deck getting some rays and listening to the birds singing in the bushland behind his apartment. Subsequent to our break up I missed being close to nature, so I thought I would bring the bushland to me. Now, what have you been up to since our lunch at The Boathouse?'

'Given the lockdown and our inability to venture out anywhere, I've mainly focused on my studies. There's certainly been no work in the escort field unless I wanted to undertake work as a private escort and I certainly wasn't entertaining that, especially after the Li Qiang fiasco.'

'Speaking of Li Qiang, did you know he has had his Business Electronic Travel Visa cancelled? So, assuming that he's convicted, when he's eventually released from prison he will be deported. He's out of your life forever, Soph.'

'That's wonderful news and such a relief.'

'I can imagine. Now, what are you studying?'

'A Bachelor of Psychology at Sydney Uni. I'm not sure what I will do with it, but I am really enjoying the course. It's challenging, yet mentally stimulating at the same time.'

'Good for you.' Julie-Anne passed her friend a bubbling

glass of champagne. 'Here's to the easing of the lockdown and rejoining the citizens of humanity,' she said, laughing at her double entendre. 'Cheers, Soph.'

'You're a crack-up. I've missed you. Cheers to you and thank you for the invite. It's lovely to see you again.' Sophie took a sip of her bubbles and sat forward on the sofa. 'Now, what about you. What's happening in your world?'

'Not a lot really. I wanted to start the next stage of my investigation into Chinese interference in Australia, but with the coronavirus pandemic dominating the headlines, there wasn't the spare column space within the paper nor the appetite within the organisation for a full-blown investigation. So, I took some me time and just chilled out.'

'Good for you. You would have needed some time-out after the attempt on your life.'

'Yeah, it took me awhile to recover from that, however, I'm fine now.'

Julie-Anne had begun a relationship with Melissa Wu who had been handpicked by Chinese business interests and consular associates to be their independent candidate in the seat of Burwood for the upcoming state elections. Unfortunately they were displeased with their candidate having a relationship with an investigative journalist. Julie-Anne was shot at while driving to work, her vehicle had run off the road, hit a fence and she ended up in hospital being treated for concussion and severe bruising. She was incredibly lucky.

'Sophie, are you okay with me referencing Chinese interference in front of you? I feel uncomfortable about it sometimes.'

'I've been in Australia for a number of years now and consider myself an Australian. I would hate to think that the country of my ancestry was interfering in Australian political, economic or public life, so knock yourself out,' she laughed.

'Now, who's the comedienne? How about we start dinner, shall we?'

'That was quick.' Sophie's eyes lit up as her host placed the entrees on the table. 'Wow, what's this exotic looking treat?'

'Rockmelon bruschetta with goat's cheese and prosciutto. It's my cooking with colours recipe,' she replied with a laugh and a flourish of her arm.

'Well, you've certainly succeeded.' Sophie forked a piece of each. 'And it tastes great too. The three ingredients work really well together.'

'Try a glass of this which hopefully works just as well. It's my favourite, a Shaw and Smith Sav Blanc from the Adelaide Hills.'

'It's got a floral aroma and a zingy taste. I like it.'

'With this damnable virus hanging around how have you been able to continue your studies, Soph?'

'All courses are pretty much available online now, so it's just a matter of adapting, and being disciplined when studying at home. If I get stir crazy I can still utilise Sydney Uni's libraries and study spaces. We just have to be masked up and maintain physical distancing.'

'Now that the lockdown restrictions are easing do you have any work on the horizon?'

'Surprisingly, I have a job coming up this week. It will be my first for ages. All I know is that the client's apparently some sort of politician from the country and just wants company for a few hours. I'll dress conservatively just in case he's roaming, both literally and metaphorically.'

'That's funny, Soph. I like it.'

'All clients are heavily vetted, so it should be okay, and it will be nice just to go out again. I'm meeting him at the Rooftop Bar at the International.'

'Wow, go girlfriend.'

'And what's more, I get paid for going there too, how good is that? Now, what about you? Jack – Melissa – Jack – Melissa - Jack?' Sophie was teasing her now.

Julie-Anne laughed. 'Oh, stop it. I have caught up with both of them since the debacle on Jack's balcony. Given my conduct that day and night I needed to clear the air with them. I rang Melissa the following day and I apologised for the uncertainty I created in our relationship with my lingering feelings for Jack. We agreed to take a timeout until I cleared my head.'

'That will be good for both of you. And what about you and Jack?'

'He's a good fun guy, I really enjoyed his company, we were good together, and wow, the sex was great. I would have stayed with him that night, but for once he was the strong one and ordered me an Uber instead. Unfortunately, I realised with some clarity, that Jack's job will always be the dominant focus in his life. I'm a very giving person, and whilst I'm not needy, I would like a partner who reciprocates the energy I devote to a relationship.'

'Great sex, hey? What I would give for that. It's been so long I have forgotten what that is,' Sophie said with a sigh of exasperation.

'Maybe your politician will turn out to be prince charming and sweep you off your feet.'

'Huh! With my luck it would be more like, I kiss him, and then he turns into a frog.'

'What about a woman, Soph?'

'I've never really considered it. I wouldn't necessarily be against it, but I do like the feel of a strong man wrapping his arms around me and making me feel special. Maybe if the right woman came along I might be tempted.'

'I was one of those women who, never for one minute, thought I would end up in a relationship with another woman. And then Melissa moseyed into a cocktail party I was attending, and I was blown away by this vivacious, intelligent, stimulating woman. It was quite funny. She was flirting with me and I, surprisingly I might add, found myself reciprocating. Intellectually, emotionally, and physically we had a wonderful, mutually interactive relationship, until of course, I mucked it up,' Julie-Anne lamented. She went quiet and was staring out the balcony window, so Sophie remained silent and gave her a moment.

Julie-Anne sprung up from the table. 'Okay, enough of that reminiscing, I've got more cooking with colours to do. Grab yourself another wine and I'll be with you in a moment.'

Sophie wanted to lift Julie-Anne's spirits and there was her opening. 'You are too funny. You make it sound like Ken Done is in the kitchen.' *No reply.* 'Well, I thought it was funny.'

'It was. Sorry I was focused on finishing off the dish. I have never cooked it before.'

A few moments later Julie-Anne walked across to the dining table carrying a large wok.

'Wow. What is that wonderful looking creation?'

'I saw the recipe in a Spanish cookbook and thought, why not, let's have a crack at this. It's called Fideua, a seafood dish from the Valencia coast. The name is derived from the word fideo, which means noodle. It's like Paella, but with noodles instead of rice.'

'Cheers, Julie-Anne, here's to Spanish cooking ala Ken Done.'

'Now you're cracking *me* up, Soph.'

'This is just delicious, such wonderful flavours.'

The two women were quiet while they twirled forks through the noodle dish and sipped their wine. To Julie-Anne this was as good a time as any. 'Do you mind if I ask about a topic you mentioned once before?'

Sophie stopped twirling and stared at her host. 'With respect, Julie-Anne, I think I know where you're going with this, and no, I don't mind as long as you're asking for the appropriate reasons.'

'I promise, it only relates to my investigation and has nothing whatsoever to do with Jack.'

'Okay, ask away.'

'Do you remember what you told me that night when we were chatting away on Jack's balcony?'

'We had consumed quite a lot of champagne by that stage, but yes, I remember.'

'You told me that you thought you saw Danielle Mortimer exiting the Golden Phoenix Restaurant in Chinatown one day when you were walking in with Li Qiang.'

'Yes, I did. I recognised her at lunch that day, however, it took me a while to remember from where. Eventually I remembered. And given the direction from which she was walking, I was wondering who she had been with. As you know, she's a vibrant young woman and hard to miss. She was walking by herself, and I didn't know who she was then, so I never thought anything of it. Then Li and I walked in a similar direction over to a table where a smartly dressed, Asian man was dining.'

'Wie Ping Lie.'

Sophie took a sip of her wine. 'Exactly. I think she might have been his lunch guest.'

'Jesus, Sophie, that would open a whole new can of worms, especially for Jack, both professionally and personally.'

'I know, yet unfortunately, or fortunately, I can't definitively say she was actually with Wie Ping Lie. She could have been lunching with anyone, but my gut feeling is that she was with him.'

'Now that the lockdown restrictions have eased I want to start work on a postscript to the earlier story we published about

Chinese interference in New South Wales. As we have discussed before, I'm certain that some of Wie Ping Lie's profits from his drug distribution empire were laundered by Li Qiang and were intended to be redirected to funding Melissa's proposed election campaign.'

'Well, I for one am delighted and relieved that at least Li Qiang is now behind bars. I feel free for the first time in three years,' Sophie said as she allowed her mind to wander.

'I imagine you do. Good for you girlfriend.' Julie-Anne paused and allowed her friend a moment for reflection. 'My investigative mind is wondering whether Danielle was complicit in Li and Wie's illicit activities all along. I'm now speculating whether she was inserted into the operation by Wie to keep an eye on Li Qiang and Tony Woodard and ensure the money laundering went according to plan. I can't think of any other reason why Wie would need to plant her inside the casino.'

'There's another possibility,' Sophie suggested. 'Maybe she became aware of what was occurring, calculated the potential to make some good money, and somehow managed to insinuate herself into the operation. That would have to have been through Wie because I know from experience she wasn't involved with Li Qiang and I doubt she would have had anything to do with that weasel Woodard.'

'That's a thought, I hadn't considered that, but either way she would be complicit. It now also raises questions about what else might not be as it seems when it comes to that woman. And I have some ideas about that too,' Julie-Anne said.

'If any of that's true, where would that leave Jack?'

'When I spoke to him recently he mentioned Danielle in passing, so I imagine they are still in a relationship. I am now wondering whether she realised Jack was investigating Li Qiang and came onto him, so she could glean any information about his investigation from inside their relationship.'

'Judging by their interaction at lunch he does seem smitten with her, and if that's the case, it certainly worked out to her considerable advantage.'

'Yeah, I know, Soph, and with the AFP's Deputy Commissioner deciding not to press charges for her involvement, it looks like she got away with it. I'll have to be careful how I go about my investigation, though. I don't want to cause Jack any unnecessary angst and possibly ruin their relationship.'

'That will be a tightrope walk if ever there was one.'

'Anyway, I have unfinished business with Wie Ping Lie after he had his enforcers try to kill me. So, if they are involved in this together, I will go after them both, with a passion.'

'Yes, and you should too, Julie-Anne.'

'Alright, enough of that doom and gloom, let's have another glass of bubbles.'

6. Townsville North Queensland

Saturday 16th May

'Those market boxes hold about twenty kilos Scott, so that would be a lot of trouble and expense for only forty kilos. They must have made more flights.' By midnight Harvey and Benson were back in Harvey's room planning the next steps in their investigation.

'Scott, there's only a couple of non-military drones available in the domestic market that could lift twenty kilos. It would have to be something like the Vulcan UAV Airlift which has a payload of twenty five kilos and the range to be able to fly the thirty kilometres from the vessel to the drop and back again. Those Vulcans aren't cheap, so if that's what they used then the drone would probably have made at least four or five return trips to make it worthwhile.'

Harvey remembered the conversation back in March with the ill-fated captain from the Chinese Horizon. 'That would be consistent with what Captain Liu told us. He said there were twenty, five kilo packages in his shipment. If that's the case again, and given the Vulcan's payload capacity, they would have to have made five return trips. That would have taken most of the night which would explain why the fishermen only saw it twice.'

'Scott, with the ramped up border security and increasing COVID-19 restrictions in-place, it's becoming more difficult to bring coke into the country. As a result the price is sky rocketing, hence how they can afford to utilise an expensive drone like the Vulcan.'

Given the lateness of the hour there was no point in calling de Vries, so Harvey was composing an email that their boss would receive first thing in the morning.

'Scott, we need to move on this,' Benson said.

'You're stating the bleeding obvious,' Harvey said abruptly.

Benson ignored the gibe. 'Townsville to Sydney is just under twenty one hundred kilometres via the coast which would normally take at least twenty four hours to complete if the two guys took turns in driving. They can't afford to get pulled over by the police or highway patrol, so they'll have to adhere to the speed limits.'

'You're stating the obvious again.'

'Okay, what's got into you, Scott?'

Harvey turned to Benson. 'Sorry, I'm just frustrated that it's now the middle of the night, we have so much information to follow up and everyone we need to speak to is asleep.'

'I know.' Benson continued. 'I've been checking on possible routes on Google Maps. Given they have to adhere to the speed limits, and the large number of towns they have to pass through, their journey could take up to thirty hours. They couldn't have left Townsville much before dawn, so as of now they should still be at least eight hours from Sydney, assuming that's where they're heading. If they've taken the coastal route they will still be north of Coffs Harbour and if they went the inland route then they should still be north of Narrabri. I think we have some time to come up with a plan, Scott.'

'Okay, I'm listening,' Harvey said.

'Either way they will have to pass by Newcastle and that shouldn't happen before ten o'clock in the morning. We just need to contact the Highway Patrol and Transport New South

Wales and we should be able to pick them up on the Pacific Motorway cameras between Newcastle and Hornsby.'

'Good work, Sam. I'm going to grab a couple of hours of shuteye. You should do the same. We've got work to do in the morning.'

Harvey's mobile phone alarm rang far too loudly, bringing him out of his all too brief slumber. It was already six o'clock, so he had a two minute shower, readying himself for a busy morning. As he re-entered the hotel room proper he noted Benson already Googling on his laptop. 'What are you up to, Sam?'

'Good morning. I am just rechecking my calculations from last night to ensure I have the suspects anticipated travel times correct.'

'If you are comfortable with what you told me a couple of hours ago, I'm going to ring Damian and get a plan enacted ASAP. He should be awake by now, even on a Saturday.'

'Yep, I'm happy. Go get 'em Scott.'

'Damian, I'm sorry to call so early, but have you had a chance to read my emails?'

'Yes. What do you need from me?'

'We need to find and track the suspect's vehicle as soon as possible. Benson has calculated their probable movements and they should be passing by Newcastle on the Pacific Motorway somewhere between nine and eleven this morning. We need the Highway Patrol to find the vehicle or Transport New South Wales to locate it on their motorway cameras. After we do that, it will obviously be up to you and Shane as to what the next steps are.'

'Okay, Scott. I'll get busy finding your suspect vehicle for you. Let me warn you and Benson though, this could end up being a federal case just like last time, so you better get your heads around that possibility.'

Like his agents, de Vries ideally wanted to keep this investigation in-house, however, Williamson would look at the bigger picture, and that would mean getting the Feds involved.

'Hi, Damian. It's early Saturday morning, so this must be important.'

'Yes, it is.' De Vries provided Williamson with an update on Harvey and Benson's progress to date and the next actions they wanted undertaken. 'I need to get onto the New South Wales Highway Patrol and Transport Departments and find this vehicle.'

'Yes, you do, but you need to instruct them to just follow, not to intercept at this point. Given the history behind this investigation, I'm also going to call that detective at the AFP in Sydney again. I don't want to find out after the fact that there was a bigger picture at play and we blew it. But, if that's not the case, then you and your boys are welcome to go grab these guys.'

'Okay, I know how this works, Shane,' de Vries said reluctantly.

7. North Sydney

Saturday 16th May

Williamson scrolled through the contacts on his mobile until he found the AFP detective again.

'Jack Wagner.'

'Hi, Jack, it's Shane Williamson.'

'How did your boys get on up in Townsville?'

'We may have another case involving our Chinese friends. It turns out that the Fairweather kid at AMSA might have been on the money again. As I mentioned yesterday, Harvey and Benson have been following up on his intel in North Queensland. It seems this case is based on a similar modus operandi as the one that we encountered back in March with the Chinese Horizon.'

Jack was excited at what he was hearing. They had wrapped up the previous investigation without getting close to the principal, which he knew to be the head of the notorious Chinatown based Triad in Sydney. 'This gives us another opportunity to finally nab Wie Ping Lie. This is great news, Shane.'

'Don't get ahead of yourself just yet, Jack.'

'Why, what are you saying?' Jack was concerned that this could turn into the interagency tug of war he desperately wanted to avoid. 'The last time we spoke you offered to reassess the situation if more evidence came to light, which appears to be the case. Otherwise why would you be calling?'

Williamson was reluctant to hand over responsibility to the AFP, but he realised the wider implications of not doing so. 'Yes, you're correct. It seems that the Chinese are moving with the times and are now using heavy lift drones to bring their product ashore.' He provided Jack with an overview of what his guys had ascertained to this point and the course of action they were proposing. 'And if my agents are correct in their calculations, then the couriers transporting the contraband will be on the outskirts of Sydney in the next couple of hours.'

Jack was concerned at this revelation. 'The closer they get to Sydney the easier it will be for them to disappear into the web of Greater Sydney's back streets and we'll lose them. We need to find them before they get off that motorway, Shane.'

'De Vries is working on that now and I'll know more within the hour,' Williamson said, sounding hopeful. 'I'm going to allow de Vries to keep trying to track these guys for now, Jack.'

'Yeah, I agree, but I want to pick up the tail if and when they come off the motorway at Wahroonga. We don't want to engage them at that point, yet we can't afford to lose them either. I just want to track the drugs to their final destination and with a bit of luck that will lead us straight to Wie. I have to get to Wahroonga within an hour or so before they disappear off our radar. Can you put me in touch with de Vries ASAP and also give me the suspect's vehicle details?'

'Yes, of course, write this down and then I'll call de Vries.'

'Just so you're aware, Shane, I only want Wie and Michael Sanderson only wants to shut down his dial a dealer network, so the maritime component is all yours.'

'That should work for everyone, Jack. Cheers.'

Jack disconnected the call and immediately rang Sanderson. 'Michael we have a new lead on Wie's drug business from Williamson at MBC. I'm about to head towards Wahroonga; where are you?' Detective Michael Sanderson was stationed at the Day Street Police Station in Chinatown and he had worked cooperatively with the AFP, and Jack in particular, on an earlier related investigation.

'Watching my son play football in Lane Cove.'

'Okay, I can pick you up in about twenty minutes.'

'Whoa, Jack, hold up; this is my family time.'

'Do you want to bring an end to Wie's drug distribution network, or not?' Jack heard a resigned huff before the call was disconnected.

Jack headed up Victoria Road in his Holden Commodore and continued over the Iron Cove, Gladesville and Fig Tree Bridges into Lane Cove. He drove down Little Street to Pottery Green Oval and saw Sanderson waiting on the kerbside.

'Michael, how are you?'

'Okay thanks, but, I'd be a helluva bloody lot better if you hadn't called me,' he said sharply.

'I know, and I'm sorry.'

'Well, with the populations movements being restricted, crime has been on the decrease. As a result I have been able to grab some quality family time. Well up until now of course. Somehow I think I'm about to be thrown back into the fray,' Sanderson said while staring blankly out the window.

'Yes, you are, although you'll be pleased with what's about to go down.'

Jack called Damian de Vries and placed the call on speaker. 'Damian how is your tracking going?' he asked without indulging in pleasantries.

'I've got direct links into the Highway Patrol and Transport New South Wales control rooms, but so far they haven't found the suspect's vehicle. Highway Patrol has confirmed that the vehicle is listed as stolen, so our targets are taking a big risk driving over two thousand kilometres in a hot car.'

Jack knew that the ANPR cameras fitted to the state's

Highway Patrol cars had the capacity to scan and identify over three hundred licence plates per minute, so if his target vehicle was on the motorway, they would surely find it. 'Bugger. Can we ensure the KALOF is listed as do not intercept, just to follow and to contact their control room if they spot the suspect's vehicle? If they intercept it, the occupants will simply clam up and we won't get to the head of the syndicate and this whole drug importation will continue, unabated.'

'I'm all over it, Jack.'

Twenty minutes later Sanderson was waiting with Jack in his Commodore watching the three lanes of heavy traffic coming down Pennant Hills Road from the motorway. Jack's mobile phone rang. He answered it in hand's free mode. 'Damian, what have you got for me?'

'Nothing at all at this stage, Jack.'

'You're kidding.' He heard Sanderson sigh in the seat alongside him. 'Are you saying that not one traffic camera or Highway Patrol Officer has spotted the suspect's vehicle in a one hundred and forty kilometre stretch of motorway?' Jack was exasperated. 'How can that possibly be?'

'I know you're disappointed, but that's the situation as it stands.'

'Damian, have your guys got their calculations correct?'

'Of course, they know what they're doing,' he replied snippily. 'Maybe the suspects are being very cautious and are taking their time. Or, they could have taken another route further inland than we thought.'

'Okay, thanks. We have eyes on the motorway exit, so we'll sit tight for another hour.'

It was now after one o'clock in the afternoon and the two detectives were still in the Commodore on the lookout for a vehicle which seemed increasingly likely wasn't going to show.

'Come on, Jack, let's go, we've drawn a blank here,' Sanderson urged.

'Not yet. Let's give it another half an hour and then we'll pack it in.'

'This is a bust. I could have stayed and watched my son's football match rather than sit here for hours twiddling my bloody thumbs,' Sanderson whinged.

'Yeah, I know, stakeouts aren't much fun for anyone, but they're a staple of investigations and we do what we have to,' Jack reasoned.

The dashboard clock ticked past one thirty in the afternoon and the suspect's vehicle still hadn't been spotted. 'It seems that somehow they've slipped through, so let's call it a day and regroup when we have some more information.' Jack proposed. 'We'll get another opportunity somewhere down the track and when we do, we'll be ready for them.'

'You hope.'

8. Chinatown

Saturday 16th May

Wie Ping Lie was having lunch at his favourite restaurant in all of Sydney. Of course it suited him that the restaurant was located in Chinatown, right in the heart of his territory. He had been introduced to the Golden Phoenix and its signature dish of Pipis in XO Sauce by his previous business partner. Unfortunately, Li Qiang had overindulged in the western excesses available in the Emerald City and this had compromised his judgement, much to his detriment. As a result, he was now a guest of the New South Wales Government at the Metropolitan Remand Centre in Silverwater. Li's activities had exposed a link between their business activities and had drawn unnecessary attention upon Wie. He was fortunate to have escaped serious scrutiny, but had lost two of his best men in the investigation. And he still had unfinished business with that female reporter that Li had underestimated. For now though, he would bide his time before exacting retribution for her role in exposing their illicit activities. He was shelling more pipis when his mobile phone vibrated.

'Wang, what's up?' Wang Yong was his lieutenant, newly promoted after the unfortunate demise of Li Jun at the hands of the Federal Police's SRG Unit. *More unfinished business.*

'Lucie has finally reported in and she is not very happy at all, Master.'

'Why, what has happened?'

'She was conducting a delivery near Centennial Park when she was ambushed.'

'Tā mā de. What happened exactly?'

'Lucie was attacked by two men, knocked out, bound, and dumped in a garbage bin directly behind her client's house. She could have been killed. They were waiting for her, so somehow, somebody knew of her movements.'

'Is she okay and do we know who was responsible, Yong?'

'She has some cuts and bruises, but she says that she's fine. Her attackers were both stocky men of leathery appearance with Middle Eastern accents. I'm guessing they were the local Lebo dealers.'

'Where did it happen?'

'In a laneway behind her client's house.'

Wie was furious that someone would do this to his Lucie. 'Okay, this cannot be allowed to happen without a consequence for them. Contact the client and have a serious talk with him about how these guys found out about her delivery schedule. And Yong, don't take *I don't know* for an answer.'

'Yes, Master.'

'Don't forget we have a delivery arriving today and you are to handle it personally.'

'Yes, Master.'

Wie had been able to source a higher purity product through his connection in China and the financiers, stockbrokers and their entitled, snotty nosed kids of Sydney's exclusive eastern suburbs were more than happy to pay upwards of four hundred dollars a gram for the stuff. He was a businessman and had identified a gap in the local market. He was offering a better product, not one cut with baby formula, so he didn't see it as competition at all. Obviously, the lowlife Lebos had other ideas on the subject.

Xiǎodòng bù bǔ, dàdòng chī kǔ. He would fix this small problem before it grew larger and he lost control of the situation. And that would start with sending a message to the men who had attacked his Lucie. Out of the corner of his eye he spied a leggy, attractive woman swanning through the restaurant towards him, her blonde hair bouncing off her bare shoulders. She was wearing a silver sleeveless and backless mini dress with a deep vee neck that highlighted her tanned skin and revealed more than he thought appropriate. She was wearing black pumps and carrying a black leather jacket folded over her arm.

Wie stood and kissed her cheek. 'Surely you are cold in that dress. And you shouldn't be seen here with me anyway, it could be dangerous, for both of us.'

'Well, hello to you, too, Mister. It is a surprisingly warm day for this time of the year, so I dressed for the weather, and I wanted to see you. Don't you like my dress?'

'I don't like it when you dress like that as it attracts the attention of many men and they stare at you.'

'Aah, you're jealous. That's cute.' He was handsome, in an Asian kind of way, had a chiselled body covered with sexy tattoos, both of which she loved navigating her way around. She adored his muscular arms, particularly when they were wrapped around her. He had a dragon tattoo on his neck, and she liked that he was a bad boy. Her reflections were making her moist.

Huang, the maître 'd brought over her usual. She loved a Cranberry Mimosa, especially on a warm day. 'Thank you Huang.'

She turned back to Wie. 'How about I finish my drink and then let's get out of here?'

'You have only just arrived, and where do you want to go anyway?' He kept a straight face, but he knew exactly where she wanted to go, and why.

She leaned forward and discreetly placed her hand between

his legs. 'Does that give you a clue?' She was doing her own teasing now and it was working.

It was only a short walk along Sussex Street in the sunshine to his apartment and she looped her arm inside his and bounced along the footpath. He was mesmerised by her breasts swaying as she walked, and she caught him ogling her. 'Put your eyes back in your head, mister,' she said while offering him a cheeky wink.

'You're very excited about something,' he said.

'We're here, so if you're lucky you might find out,' she said as they exited the elevator.

'Today is the sixteenth and it is a lucky date for those born in the year of the tiger. I was born in the year of the tiger?'

'Then my timing is perfect. Open the door.'

Wie swiped his access card. She turned his body, rapped her arms around him and kissed him hungrily. They crashed through the doorway to his apartment, she pushed him hard up against the hallway wall and ripped his shirt open, buttons popping and fabric tearing as she went. She wanted him badly and sucked hard on his tattooed pectoral muscles while undoing his belt. Unzipping his trousers, she slipped her hand down inside his boxers and gripped him firmly. 'Oh, yes, you're definitely a tiger.'

He spun her around and lifted her dress up over her head. He marvelled at her magnificent, tanned body amongst her other attributes.

She gripped him by the shoulders, lifted herself up into the air, rapped her legs around his body and then slowly lowered herself. 'Okay, take me now tiger.'

He gripped her by the hips, pushed up into her, and she leant back against the wall and groaned deeply.

'Harder.' She aggressively rode him up and down in time with his thrusting and then began gyrating wildly. 'Don't stop, I don't want this to end,' she cried out. She grabbed his hair and pulled his head down onto her breasts and held him in place. He teased her firm, erect nipples with his tongue. She knew he was close when he kissed her enthusiastically and she sucked hard on his dragon tattoo. He gave her one final deep thrust; she was at her destination and pulled him in tight. 'Oh, yes, yes, yes,' she cried as her body began erupting.

'Oh, my God, I so needed that. You certainly are a tiger, and you're my tiger,' she crowed as they lay on the hallway floor. What is your word for tiger?'

'Hǔ.'

Her plan had worked a treat, and she wouldn't have him in a better headspace than he was now, so she would dive headlong in. 'Well, Hǔ, we need to talk about something important.'

'What?'

'Do you know how hard it is playing the pretend dutiful girlfriend to the detective. It is becoming dull and boring and we should end that arrangement, and soon.'

'We will end it when everything is back to normal and we are safe from your friend's activities, and not before,' he replied staunchly.

'How long will that take?'

'As long as it takes nǔ rén.'

She stared at him, puzzled. 'Nǔ rén?'

'Woman.'

'Well this nǔ rén has had enough of leading a double life. The longer it continues, the more likelihood there is of me being exposed.'

Wie bounced up from the carpet. 'I have important business to conduct and I need to know what that detective is doing at all times. We will end the arrangement when I say so and not before. Is that clear nǔ rén?'

9. AFP Headquarters

Monday 18th May

Jack was driving over the Anzac Bridge in the gloom of the autumn morning heading into the AFP's head office in Goulburn Street in the heart of the city. The seasons were changing and he was missing the blue sky mornings and the shimmering waters of the various bays that dotted the inner reaches of Sydney Harbour. Having little of interest to look at, he used the time to plan his day and the week ahead. He was disappointed at the lack of success on Saturday and was wracking his brain for another avenue in which to progress the investigation. An idea formed in his mind and he called Damian de Vries.

'Damian, it's Jack Wagner.'

'What's up?'

'I have an idea. I'm not sure if it will advance our investigation, however, it will provide corroborating evidence if we get these guys to trial one day.'

'I'm listening.'

'Shane mentioned that your guys thought our suspects were utilising a drone to ferry the coke ashore.'

'Yes, they have two witnesses up in Townsville that either saw or heard a drone in operation.'

'It would have to be a heavy lift UAV with a decent range to get the volume of drugs from the vessel to the coastline across one night. I don't suppose your guys know the make or brand by any chance?'

'Benson did some research while in Townsville and he came to the conclusion that it was probably a Vulcan UAV Airlift. In his opinion it was the best non-military UAV available on the open market. Why are you asking, Jack?'

'I realise the drone market is growing exponentially, but not necessarily in the commercial sector in this country. So, I'm thinking it can't be too difficult to track down the ownership of drones that match the specification that our suspect's drone would need.'

'I like your thinking. Benson has an understanding of UAV's, so I'll get him to undertake some more research and let you know what he finds.'

'And I'll do likewise. Cheers, Damian.'

Jack parked his car in the basement carpark and rode the elevator up to the tenth floor detective's office. He had a plan, however he needed to do some serious research first. Awakening his desktop he went straight to the Google search engine and typed in Vulcan UAV Airlift. He clicked on the Vulcan UAV company's webpage and scrolled down until he found what he was seeking out. The specs of the Vulcan D8 UAV fitted the criteria the suspects would need to ferry the quantity of drugs from ship to shore as described to him by de Vries. He then clicked on the Contact Us link and saw the company's address listed as Ground Floor Building 11, Vantage Point Business Village, Mitcheldean, Gloucestershire GL17 0SZ. That was good news to Jack as he had a colleague at MI5 in London that he had worked with on a previous investigation into cross border people trafficking. Given the controversy in most western countries surrounding the use of drones he knew there would now be a registration system in place. This wouldn't necessarily apply to a UAV not intended for use in the UK though. Therefore he would need to ascertain purchaser information from the Vulcan UAV company. His MI5 contact should be able to help with that. He began composing an email to Stephen Bainbridge detailing the reasons behind the information he was seeking. Bainbridge could easily access registration records, but Jack would need his man at MI5 to obtain access to Vulcan UAV's purchase records. He nominated the China Shipping Company and Wie Ping Lie as potential purchasers of interest. He also asked Bainbridge to widen his search to include any purchases from China or Australia. He also provided a comprehensive summary of both the previous and current investigations to support the search warrant Bainbridge would be required to apply for. It had taken Jack nearly two hours to draft the summary and it was now three o'clock in the morning in London. He wouldn't receive an acknowledgement until late afternoon at the earliest. It would take even longer to achieve a result. He pressed the send icon.

The rest of his day had been largely unproductive, so he was thinking about leaving early and going for a lazy jog around Hyde Park. As he was about to leave his mobile rang. He saw the +44 area code followed by a long list of numbers displayed on the screen. He assumed this would be Bainbridge. 'Hi, Stephen, you're up early.'

'Unfortunately, there's a wide range of hostile actors using cyber to target the UK these days, so there's no rest for the wicked. How are you, Jack?'

'I'm good, but I've become bogged down in my latest investigation and it's going nowhere fast, buddy.'

'I figured as much if you're having to reach out to me on the other side of the world. I've read your email, but can you just walk me through your thought processes, so I'm clear on what you want?'

Jack provided Bainbridge with more history of the first investigation into Wie Ping Lie's drug business, the Chinese

Shipping Company connection, money laundering links, Captain Liu's murder and the SRG raid that neutralised Wie's lieutenants. Then he linked the current investigation to the previous one through the similar modus operandi that AMSA and the MBC had identified. 'I realise some of that is circumstantial, however, I am confident we can further progress this investigation with your support.'

'It won't be easy obtaining a warrant to access Vulcan's records, nonetheless I will do whatever I can, Jack. It's only Monday morning, so I have a whole week to work some magic. I'll get back to you one way or the other by Friday.'

The British were sticklers for process and procedure. They were also known for their due diligence, so Jack wasn't expecting a timely response anyway. 'Thanks, Stephen, I appreciate it.'

He had another idea. He picked up the handset again.

'Damian, it's Jack. Is it worthwhile interviewing the captain of the Chinese Panorama? It should have arrived in Brisbane today, so it's in your backyard, so to speak.'

'I considered that too. While Captain Liu led us to the Midnight Express launch last time, he didn't have anything to offer in regard to the source of the coke nor who was heading up the whole operation in China. I will get Harvey and Benson to have a word with the Panorama's captain though, just in case.'

'Okay, thanks, Damian.'

10. Sydney Daily News

Monday 18th May

Julie-Anne was refreshed after having the weekend to herself. She had window shopped up and down King Street in her beloved Newtown, had the best breakfast stack ever at Either Or Café, burnt off the calories in boxing and high intensity classes at the gym and then pampered herself with a spa and massage treatment at Dolce Vita. She arrived at her Surry Hills office early on Monday morning with a bounce in her step. With the lockdown easing and the state's commerce returning to something that resembled normality, there would be pressure on the senior team to start sourcing public interest stories that would drive circulation of the broadsheet back to pre-pandemic levels. She went to her desk, got herself sorted and mapped out her day. As a senior journalist she was afforded the opportunity to attend the morning editorial meeting, which was where she was heading next. The boy's club of the previous century was diminishing and there were now four women invited to attend the daily meeting. Rather than sit with the female editors, and to avoid any appearance of a sisterhood developing, she sat between the finance and political journalists, both male. She was also afforded the opportunity to work independently of the editorial team and reported directly to the Editor in Chief, Chris Russell. Unlike many publications of the digital age that just focused on clickbait stories and unchecked sensationalism to drive readership, the Sydney Daily News was still committed to investigative journalism and reporting. Earlier in the year she had investigated a money laundering operation that was linked to a drug importation syndicate. She had also loosely connected the Chinese Consul General to the principals of both operations as well. It had been the lead story and she would write a follow-up once the court cases began. Unfortunately for Julie-Anne, she hadn't been able obtain definitive proof of Wie Ping Lie's activities as the head of the syndicate, nor for his involvement in the attempt on her life. With the coronavirus lockdown in-place there hadn't been much action on the streets of Sydney and criminal activity was at a minimum as a result. Now that the lockdown was being progressively eased the criminals would come out of their collective gutters and she could start investigating again. And her friend Sophie had given her just the place to begin.

Chris Russell called the gathering to order and one by one the departmental editors provided an update on the stories they were developing for the following day's edition. The majority were related to the coronavirus pandemic and its effect on the various aspects of society. The finance editor was focussed on the banks supporting the community with deferred loans and repayments, the political editor was comparing the various state government's responses to the pandemic and the health editor was focussed on the daily numbers and coronavirus hot spots. Julie-Anne felt for the environmental editor. The environment and climate change was the last thing the general public was thinking about during this challenging time, and as such, his news stories had been pushed far back into the paper's general news section. Russell turned to Julie-Anne.

'Can I take a raincheck and take my investigation offline for now, Chris?' She had done this once before and it hadn't been well received by her peers. The murmurs started reverberating around the room.

'JA, nothing is off limits amongst the senior editorial team here. You know that.'

Same response as last time. Julie-Anne was hellbent on sticking to her guns. Again. 'I need some advice from you before I proceed, Chris. It's important and it's not for public consumption,' she said doggedly. *More murmurs.*

After the meeting concluded Julie-Anne made her way straight to the Editor in Chief's office, shadowing her boss the entire way.

'That's twice now, JA. What's so damned secretive that we need a cone of silence?'

She noticed him holding back a smile at his Maxwell Smart reference. *That's better,* she thought. *He's coming around.* 'A friend of mine has provided me with information about Wie Ping Lie's operation that I want to follow up.'

'And that's what exactly?'

'You remember Danielle Mortimer, the woman who was in the middle of Li Qiang and Tony Woodard's money laundering operation at the Oceanic?'

'Yes, of course. She assisted the AFP with their sting at the casino that caught Woodard and Li red-handed, and in return they decided not to charge her for her involvement in the money laundering. What about her?'

'She was seen leaving the Golden Phoenix restaurant in Chinatown a while back and my friend thinks she had been lunching with Wie Ping Lie. My friend was walking in with Li Qiang.'

'Gee, that's a bit skinny.'

'Yes, it is, but I also don't believe in coincidences.' Julie-Anne continued. 'Chris, in a city of over five million people what are the chances that they would be in the same restaurant at the same time. And with Li Qiang in the house as well. That couldn't have been by chance.'

'So what do you want to do, JA?'

'I want to place Danielle Mortimer under surveillance for a few days.'

'Jesus, do you realise how much that would cost? And based on what? Someone saw someone leaving a restaurant where someone else was dining,' he replied, sounding exasperated.

Julie-Anne understood her bosses' position; he had a budget to consider. 'Okay, I'll do it myself for a couple of days and see what I can find out.'

'JA, this is not an episode of Law and Order. You've been told numerous times to be careful around Wie, so start listening to that very sound advice,' he offered empathetically.

'There's more, Chris,' she said hesitantly.

'Why am I getting nervous about what's coming next?'

'Danielle Mortimer is in a relationship with Jack Wagner.'

'Your Jack Wagner?'

'Yes, my ex-boyfriend.'

'And I'm guessing that you think that's not a coincidence either.'

'Where some people see coincidence, I see collusion. That's my job,' she replied dogmatically. 'What if she deliberately targeted Jack once she realised he was a detective snooping around the Bennelong Room in the Oceanic. And she's a stunner, so it's not a stretch to imagine Jack being taken in by her.'

'Give me a couple of hours to think about it and I'll get back to you.'

'Now can you see why it's not for public consumption, Chris?'

Russell sighed begrudgingly. 'Okay, I think you've made your point.'

11. Chinese Consulate General

Monday 18th May

The Consul General to New South Wales encrypted mobile rang. Only one person was aware of this phone number, so he knew all too well who was calling and he didn't like it. It was never good news.

'Good morning, Master Tan.' Tan meant "magnificent" in his native Mandarin, but there was never anything magnificent about this man calling.

'Xiao, nine months have passed since the Confucius Institute was removed from schools within your jurisdiction. This has brought immense shame on our great country and you have made little progress to have it reinstated. This cannot be allowed to continue and must be addressed immediately.'

'Yes, I agree and I am taking the appropriate measures to remedy the situation, Master.'

'What are these measures you speak of?'

'I am soon to meet with an operative who is as committed to the advancement of the mother country's magnificent objectives as I am. I will rectify this unsatisfactory state of affairs as a priority, Master.'

'I hope you are true to your word. I don't want to have to contact you again about this matter. That will not be beneficial for your career, Xiao.' The call was disconnected.

The intercom on the desk phone rang.

'Yes, Mei Lin.'

'Mr Zhang, Mr Gao is here for his appointment.'

'Send him in please, Mei.'

'Paul, thank you for coming. Please sit,' the Consul General said, gesturing to a black leather chair across the desk from him.

Zhang Xiao had known Paul Gao for many years through various overseas postings. Whilst Gao would never attain a formal diplomatic posting, he was a man who could be trusted to get things done. He was early middle age, quite a tall man by Chinese standards, athletically built, university educated, articulate, and had proved himself to be an influencer of note in the past.

'Paul, now that the media attention surrounding the Li Qiang fiasco has abated, it is time for us to revive our program of influence. Our remanded friend failed to realise our political ambitions and source a suitable candidate to contest the New South Wales election in three months' time. Unfortunately, we now don't have the time to achieve that, and soft diplomacy isn't working, so we must find another way to influence the government's policies. We need to be more forceful in encouraging them to overturn their cancellation of the Confucius Institute Program.'

'Mr Zhang, I read about that unfortunate situation last year and I knew you would be concerned. How can I be of assistance?'

'We can't allow these ideological prejudices against China to progress, Paul. We must act and have the Program re-instated, as a priority. If this program expulsion is not overturned then other states within Australia may be encouraged to do the same. That cannot be allowed to happen. So, I would like you to handle this first stage of our program of influence personally. You will report to me only and I think Special Emissary would be a most suitable title to ensure everyone's cooperation, both inside and outside the Consulate.'

'How do you propose I should go about achieving your ambition, Consul General?'

'Firstly, it is not my ambition alone. It is mandated by the masters of the Party, so you should realise the importance of your task.'

Xiao had just been talking to the Chairman of the Confucius Institute Headquarters Council in Beijing, himself. Tan Chailun was displeased with the lack of progress in overturning the state government's decision and had made his concerns known to Xiao in no uncertain terms. He had made a passing comment about the vacant Consul General's position in Kazakhstan. Xiao took it for what it was. A not so veiled threat. Tan Chailun was previously responsible for the United Front Work Department, which leads the Chinese Communist Party's foreign influence efforts abroad. He was not someone to be disobeyed.

'Of course, Mr Zhang.'

'I am meeting with the New South Wales Minister for Education tomorrow morning where I will once again encourage him to review his government's decision. I already know what his response will be, but I will go through the formalities regardless.'

'That is very wise of you, Mr Zhang.'

'Yes, it is important that we are perceived to be adopting soft diplomacy in our quest. In the meantime, Paul, how you achieve the Party's ambition is up to you, however, you should use all means necessary, at your discretion of course. This is just the first task, if you succeed there will be other worthy causes for you to become involved in. We have much that needs to be addressed in this country, so it is important that this cannot be traced back to me or the consulate. Westerners call it plausible deniability. That would be a disaster for this office, our diplomatic relations with the state and my career. Do you understand?'

'Yes, Mr Zhang. Thank you for trusting me with this mission of noble standing.'

12. Sydney Daily News

Monday 18th May

Julie-Anne was back at her desk researching Danielle Mortimer when the desk phone intercom buzzed. 'It's JA.'

'JA, it's me, Chris. Come and see me at midday and I should have a response for you by then.'

'That's great, thank you, thank you,' she replied effusively.

'You wouldn't be you if you didn't get ahead of yourself. Nothing's decided yet,' he said, taking the wind out of her sails.

Two hours later Julie-Anne bounced into Chris Russell's office. She was surprised to see that David Bedford was seated across from her boss. Bedford was mid-fifties, thick set, sported close cropped hair with the salt beginning to intrude on the pepper. He was wearing a navy blue suit complemented by a red tie. On two previous occasions his company, MPS, had been engaged to provide protection for Julie-Anne. 'Hi, David, how are you?' she asked while shaking his hand.

'I'm well thanks, Julie-Anne, how are you?'

'I'm all good thanks. I'm just about to wade knee deep into an investigation, I think,' she replied, casting a hopeful glance across to her boss.

'You wouldn't be you unless something potentially

hazardous wasn't happening in your world,' Bedford replied, while regarding her in a fatherly manner.

'I'm much more careful these days after my near miss with Wie's crew back in March, David,' she fibbed.

'Take a seat, JA,' Russell directed. 'Okay, I've discussed your request with David and he has agreed to accept the surveillance assignment that you want undertaken. I've managed to work a contra deal with him and under our agreement his company will provide us with seventy two hours of surveillance as a result.'

'That's excellent news, thanks boss and thank you too, David,' she replied, rubbing her hands together in excitement.

'Now, JA, you need to brief David and then let him get on and do what he does best.'

'Yeah, I can do that, however I would like a daily update, just so I'm in the loop if anything of importance breaks. Is that okay?'

'No promises, Julie-Anne, because my guys will be working around the clock, however, we'll do our best to accommodate your request,' Bedford replied.

'That works for me. Can you come downstairs to my office and I'll give you the information you need?'

Julie-Anne always used the fire stairs to get her daily steps up and she gave Bedford an overview of her concerns as they descended. She deliberately left out the part about the target of the investigation being her ex-boyfriend's current girlfriend. They arrived at her desk.

'Just in case you accepted the assignment I have already put together a folder containing the information your guys will need to undertake the task. I'll text you the subject's home address when I obtain it and I've included a list of likely hangouts as well.'

Bedford opened the folder and perused the information. 'I see her place of work is listed as the Oceanic Hotel and

Casino, so I'm guessing this has some relationship to your earlier investigation.'

'Yes, and obviously the current one too. I have also included various photos of the subject, David.'

'Okay, we'll get on with it and do what we do best.'

With David Bedford's company now successfully engaged, Julie-Anne went back to her desktop and continued her search. She had another suspicion that she wanted confirmed or quashed, sooner rather than later. She went to the bookmarked NSW Registry of Birth Deaths & Marriages website, where she was a registered user. She navigated to the Birth Certificates section where she filled out the online form requesting a copy of Danielle Mortimer's birth certificate. She had obtained Danielle's date of birth and full name from her Facebook page. *Why do people share so much personal information online?*

29th November 1990. She's a Sagittarius. Julie-Anne Googled Sagittarius. *Humour is Sagittarius's number one flirtation technique. You love to keep your crush entertained and surprised, and you're the most unpredictable of all the zodiac signs.* She thought that just about described the woman and wondered at the unpredictability trait, particularly in light of Sophie's revelations.

Two hours later she was surprised to receive an email from NSW Registry of Birth Deaths & Marriages with a copy of Mortimer's birth certificate attached. She opened the attachment and noted that her parent's names were James and Wendy Mortimer. Julie-Anne then switched to the Ancestry. com.au website where she was also a registered user. She didn't have access to the plethora of government databases that detectives had, so it was just as well her boss had agreed to cover the cost of her numerous subscriptions otherwise her research capabilities would be severely limited. She began searching for James, Wendy and Danielle Mortimer. Someone named Mark Mortimer had created a family tree for Mortimer family. This was what she was after. She went back to James and Wendy Mortimer's side of the tree. And there it was. James and Wendy Mortimer had only one child listed, Danielle Rose Mortimer, born 29th November 1990 at Narribri, New South Wales. She was an only child. Sadly for Jack, but also to her own relief, her suspicion had been vindicated. 'Oh, no!' she exclaimed.'

This would open up a whole new can of worms for everyone involved in the earlier investigation and for Julie-Anne with her current one. They had all bought the woman's story of innocence in the money laundering scandal and the compassionate tale about needing the money to support her brother Ollie who apparently had a congenital heart condition. Even the Deputy Commissioner of the AFP and the DPP had been convinced of the naivety of her involvement, to the extent that they had decided not to initiate charges against her. Julie-Anne needed to think carefully about how she would deal with this new revelation. And somehow she would need to find a way to tell Jack of her findings. He wouldn't be pleased at all, in fact he would be devastated. Rather than go off half-cocked, she would wait until David Bedford's company had reported on their findings, and then she could hopefully provide Jack with the complete story. She had another thought. Making her way to the newspaper's library on the floor below she retrieved the electoral roll for the Sydney electorate and flicked through the pages until arriving at M for Mortimer. Pausing to lick her finger, Julie-Anne then turned the pages one by one until she found what she was looking for. Running her finger down the listing she stopped when she found Mortimer, D.R. 37 Colbourne Avenue Glebe NSW 2037. She quickly texted the address to David Bedford. Julie-Anne returned upstairs to her desk and opened her internet browser, navigating to the bookmarked New South Wales Land Registry Services website. Under the Find Records tab she clicked on Street Address Inquiry and obtained the Title

Reference Number. Then she went to the Certificate of Title inquiry page and entered the TRN and clicked on the proceed button. She read down through the usual mumbo jumbo until she saw a name she recognised.

'Oh, no, poor, poor, Jack.'

13. Centennial Park Sydney

Monday 18th May

'Usual place, Mr Wagner?'

'No. We can't meet at Milk and Honey. The place will be packed now the lockdown restrictions have eased. Have you been living under a rock these past few months, Stevie?'

'I didn't think about that.'

'Durrr, really, you genius. Look, I'm going for a jog around Centennial Park later this afternoon, so if you want to join me, I'll see you near the Lily Pond just off Parkes Drive.'

'Mr Wagner, I can't run that far,' Stevie bemoaned.

'I was joking Stevie. I'm well aware of your lack of athletic prowess. I meant after I finish my jog. I'll meet you on the bridge over the Lily Pond at four o'clock. It's relatively quiet there, and given the dubious company you keep, I doubt your enemies frequent such a celebrated location. Do you think you can manage to locate it?'

'It's a long walk, but I'll find it, Mr Wagner.'

'It wouldn't be an issue if you didn't keep having your driver's licence suspended. I'll see you there at four,' Jack said then disconnected the call.

Jack was sweating profusely towards the end of his run around the park. It was just the workout he needed, and his Garmin tracker told him he had covered nearly eight kilometres. He had completed two laps and was now jogging down Parkes Drive through the centre of the park. He clearly saw his CI standing behind a large eucalypt tree near the Lily Pond bridge. Whenever Jack was here it reminded him of when he had first learned about Claude Monet's Bridge Over the Lily Pond in his art history class at Charles Sturt University in Bathurst. Jack had little interest in the subject, but the school hottie, Rebecca Finucane had enrolled in the class, so that was good enough for him.

Stevie was obviously trying to hide from anyone who may have followed him, but Jack had spotted his gaunt frame from some considerable distance away. 'A bright red windcheater, really?' Jack said, exasperated. 'Some criminal you are. I spotted you way back. You need to be careful, you're not particularly good at this cloak and dagger stuff, Stevie.'

'Really, Mr Wagner?'

'Yes, really.' Jack doubled over and rested his hands on his knees. 'Okay, tell me what you've got for me while I get my breath back.'

'Straight down to business again, Mr Wagner.'

'Stevie, I don't know which part of criminal informant you don't understand. You're my snitch. I'm not interested in some male bonding ritual or idle chatter and we're not exactly best mates.'

'That hurts, Mr Wagner,' Stevie said while offering a pretend sulky face.

Jack was becoming irritated and groaned with impatience.

'Okay, fair enough, Mr Wagner. Do you remember a couple months ago I told you about the chinks selling the new gear around the eastern suburbs?'

'Yeah, that's old news. What of it?'

'Well they've taken it to another level and have adopted a

dial a dealer business model which has got the locals excited, and business is booming, Mr Wagner.'

'I'm also well aware of that, Stevie. And you don't have to call me Mr Wagner all the time.'

'Okay. Well, the local dealers don't like that at all and are pushing back, and hard. Did you hear about the woman in the laneway?'

'No, what woman and what about her?'

'She was making a delivery in a laneway off Birrell Street not far from here and it didn't go well.'

'Do I have to drag this story out of you. Get on with it.'

'Okay, okay. One of the chink's drivers was apparently ambushed, beaten unconscious, tied up and then thrown into a wheelie bin. She was found by a garbage truck driver just before he was about to lift the bin into his truck's compactor. Another minute or two and she'd have been a flatpack.'

Jack stifled a laugh at the analogy. 'Finally, you've given me something I might be able to use. When did this happen?'

'Friday night. I was told the truck driver might have reported it to the police.'

'Okay, that's better.' Jack handed him a one hundred dollar note. He then set off on a jog south along Parkes Drive to his waiting car, scuffing up the carpet of autumn leaves as he went.

'What's this, a miserable one hundred dollars?' Stevie called out.

'Don't spend it all at once,' Jack called out over his shoulder.

Jack's interest was piqued by Stevie's information and given it was only four thirty in the afternoon he decided to head straight to the nearest police station. The Waverley Police Station was less than one kilometre from Birrell Street, so it was the obvious place to start. Still in his tracksuit he entered the station and approached the counter. The attending sergeant's name badge read Willoughby. He was about fifty years of age, tall and stout and already greying at the temples. A career policeman no doubt. 'Sergeant Willoughby, good afternoon.'

'What can I do for you, sir?'

'I'm Senior Detective Jack Wagner from the AFP.' Jack extracted his wallet and showed his credentials.

'How can I help you, Detective?'

'I'm following up on a lead I was given relating to a drug importation case I'm working. I'm wondering if you have received a report relating to the nearby assault of a woman a few days ago.'

'Well, that sure narrows it down,' Willoughby replied, heavy on the sarcasm. 'If you haven't noticed we're in the middle of a domestic violence epidemic at the moment and we receive countless reports of that nature every week.'

'Sorry, let me narrow it down for you then. A woman, probably of Asian appearance, was assaulted in a laneway off Birrell Street, then cable tied and dumped into a wheelie bin. The obvious intent being that the bin would eventually be scooped up and emptied into the council truck's garbage compactor. Does that narrow it down for you, Sergeant?' Jack replied with his own dose of sarcasm.

Willoughby eyed Jack over the top of his glasses and released a sigh. 'How long ago exactly?'

'Friday night or Saturday morning.'

'I've been on this desk all week and haven't received any reports of that nature. Something that disturbing I would certainly remember. What's the AFP's interest in this?'

'We're investigating the importation of a higher purity cocaine by the Triads from Chinatown that they're now distributing via their new dial a dealer network here in the eastern suburbs. I'm reasonably certain that she was one of their distributors and I'm assuming your local boys didn't take too kindly to her presence on their turf.'

'No they wouldn't. Give me your card and if I hear anything I'll give you a call.'

'Okay, thanks, Sergeant.'

The next obvious step in his follow-up of Stevie's information would be to contact the waste company, but given the time of the day, that would have to wait until tomorrow.

14. Ashton Street Queens Park

Monday 18th May

Sam Bourdain had the white powder perfectly lined up on the coffee table. With no straw handy, he rolled up a pineapple and seconds later, the snow was gone. He could feel it travelling through his body, with it's intense, euphoric sensation stimulating his brain. He was now ready to binge watch the latest series of Orange is the New Black. He was hoping for plenty of sex scenes, so as not to waste the blow. If not, Miranda will be over later to take care of his desires. His euphoria was disturbed by a loud knock on the front door. He ignored it. He wasn't about to allow anything to ruin his evening of guilty pleasure. There was the knock again, even louder this time. 'Shit.' He paused the television, rose from the sofa, put his jeans back on and walked down the hallway to the front door. He opened it cautiously. It was ajar at best, with his foot firmly resting against the base. A tall, well-built man of Asian appearance wearing a work singlet and jeans was standing on the porch.

'Hello, Sam, how are you?' The man was smiling, but Sam deemed it a sinister smile at best. And the man knew his name.

'We have some business to discuss.'

Sam detected only a slight accent, which belied the man's appearance. He didn't know the man and couldn't imagine what type of business they needed to discuss. 'Sorry, you must have the wrong house,' he replied and started to close the door. The man's smile instantly evaporated. He leant back, lifted his right leg, and slammed it into the door, all in one swift movement. The sharp edge of the door frame smashed into Sam's nose and he was sent reeling backwards across the hallway carpet. It happened in the blink of an eye. He was dazed and could feel warm blood trickling down his cheek.

'No, I definitely have the right house,' the man said as he entered the hallway and kicked the door closed.

Sam's nose was throbbing, and he could feel a lump swelling up on the back of his head where he'd banged it against the wall. He was trying to regain his composure and he sucked in some oxygen. The man was towering over him with his foot firmly planted on Sam's chest, preventing him from moving. He was going nowhere.

'Now, shall we start again?'

'I don't know you or what this is about,' Sam spluttered.

The man put his hand in his pocket and retrieved a brass object. 'Then let me clarify the situation for you. You don't need to know me, but the men you sold out my friend to bashed her and left her to die. The cowards. That's what this is all about.'

'I still have no idea what you're on about,' Sam pleaded.

The man looped his fingers through the brass object and held his hand in front of Sam's face. 'This is what they bashed her with. It's called a knuckleduster. Can you imagine what this did to her pretty face?'

Sam quickly realised what this was all about. In his greed, he had traded information for a few grams of blow. 'I don't know who they were. They threatened me if I didn't give them the information they wanted.'

'Do you understand the expression "quid pro quo"?'

Sam looked up apprehensively at this aggressive man.

'No? Well, let me explain it to you. It is when you receive favour, benefit, or a gift in return for something. That's what you did, Sam. So, you're going to do it again except this time it is me who is going to receive the favour. Do you understand?'

The man slammed his fist into the side of Sam's head. His consciousness was floundering, his head pounding in three different places now and he was doing everything not to pass out. He tried to regain his composure for the second time in as many minutes while shielding his face. 'Okay, okay, what do you want to know?'

'That's more like it. Now, I'll keep it simple for you. Just give me the names of the two men you betrayed my friend to, and I will be on my way.'

'Their names are Amir and Jasar.'

'Describe their appearance.'

'Oh, I don't know,' he whined. The man raised his fist preparing to strike out once more. Sam recoiled in anticipation of the blow and banged his head against the wall again. 'Shit. Okay, um, they are stocky and muscly, hairy, dark skinned with accents. Amir is the boss of the two.'

'What else?'

'They call their business, Deals on Wheels.'

'That's better, Sam. Alright, one last thing. Give me the contact number you use to place your orders for their cheap rubbish.'

'They will kill me.'

'You think I wouldn't do the same thing to a snivelling little prick like you.'

'Let me get my phone.' The man helped Sam to his feet and accompanied him to the lounge room.

'Thank you, that wasn't so difficult after all. Now, you keep this conversation strictly between us and I won't need to come back. If I do, the knuckleduster will be the least of your problems.' The man launched another blow to the side of Sam's head, and he slipped into the blackness.

15. Jack's Apartment Balmain

Monday 18th May

'Hi, handsome, how's my favourite detective?'

Danielle and Jack had been dating for about two months now. They had met when he was working undercover for the AFP in the Bennelong Room at the Oceanic Casino and she was employed serving drinks at the time. She had picked him for a detective straight away and they had flirted with each other, probably for similar reasons. He wanted to pick her brain for his investigation, and she wanted to know what he was up to. That first night she had invited him for a drink after finishing her shift. Danielle knew he would say yes. Just to be certain she had his interest, she had swapped her work uniform for a white sleeveless and backless short mini dress that highlighted her tanned skin, long legs and most of her cleavage. He had waited downstairs on the main casino floor for her and she had swaggered across the room towards him, her blonde hair bouncing off her bare shoulders and her breasts swaying in time. He recalled his gobsmacked facial expression. He was hooked.

'I'm really good, thanks gorgeous.' He placed his hands around her waist and embraced her enthusiastically.

'Wow, yes you are. What's got you into such a happy place?'

'Well, finally this goddamned lockdown is over, and I can

get back to some serious investigative work.' She frowned and made a pretend pouty face.

'And of course, I'm excited to see you again,' he said, realising his faux pas.

'Nice recovery, Jack.'

'Cheers, Danielle.' He passed her a glass of her favourite Pierro LTC and they toasted the end of the lockdown.

'Wait until you see what culinary delight Chef Jacques has prepared for you tonight, Ms Mortimer.'

Chef Jacques, really!

'So, tell me, how are things at the casino? Have your employment circumstances improved at all?'

Danielle had gotten herself involved in money laundering activities in the Bennelong Room which was the domain of the casino's high rollers. In an endeavour to extract herself unscathed, and mitigate any potential criminal charges, she had agreed to work with Jack to bring down the principals of the operation. She had succeeded on both counts, and managed to retain her job, albeit only in the hospitality section downstairs in the main casino. 'My three month probation ends in a few weeks' time, and fingers crossed, I'll be reinstated to my treasury role. I am grateful that at least I was able to keep my bar job though.'

'How is Michelle doing?' Michelle Ironside was the Bennelong Room's Treasury Manager who, to prevent her revealing what she had discovered, had been kidnapped during the money laundering operation. She had been found traumatised and dehydrated days later wandering in a park by the Parramatta River in Silverwater. 'Has she recovered from her ordeal?'

'Yes, she seems back to her old professional and demure self.'

'That's great news. Righto, check out my latest culinary creation,' he crowed.

'Wow, Jack, what is it, other than the obvious?'

'I'm not big on vegetarian dishes, however, this recipe is simple to cook and too good to ignore. It's mushroom and spinach gnocchi with a creamy parmesan and white wine sauce. The secret is to utilise Portobello mushrooms, they're juicy and full of flavour.'

Jack topped up their wines. 'Cheers gorgeous, it's great to see you again.'

'You too, detective.'

'Before I forget, how is Ollie's health?'

She had told Jack that her brother Ollie had a congenital heart defect and unfortunately, surgery might be necessary to repair the defect and that would be prohibitively expensive. Hence, the reason that she had become involved in the money laundering in the first place. 'The medication seems to be working and his heart's pump function continues to improve.'

'That's wonderful news. You must be so pleased.'

'Isn't it ever and I am over the moon,' she gushed.

'Did you have to repay the money?'

'No, your Deputy Commissioner eventually said that they couldn't prove the money I was given was the proceeds of crime, so under the existing legislation, I didn't have to pay it back.' She needed to change the subject. 'Now that things are returning to some sort of normality, what's your first investigation going to be, Jack?'

'If you remember back in March we temporarily halted the Chinatown based drug importation operations, arrested one of the middlemen and the other was killed in the SRG raid. Unfortunately, we didn't get close to the principal or principals, so that will be my immediate focus.'

'Where will you start and how will you go about that?' she enquired while distractedly toying with her gnocchi.

It was unusual for her to ask about his investigations. Maybe she hadn't asked before because she was actually inside the casino investigation and knew the details intimately. Or was she just being an inclusive girlfriend and taking interest in his work. Jack liked to keep his work to himself. This tenet having invariably come between him and Julie-Anne previously and inevitably ruined their relationship. He didn't want that to happen with Danielle, so he would open up. 'Well, my CI told me about a woman who was bashed, bound and left to die in a wheelie bin in a laneway close to Centennial Park.'

Her interest was piqued. 'That's just horrible, Jack,' she replied while picking at her pasta.

'I think she was dealing drugs on behalf of the Chinatown based triads and the incumbent drug gang in the eastern suburbs was just protecting their turf. If she was dealing the higher purity coke that I think she was, then that could be the link back to the drug importation investigation I mentioned before.' Old habits got the better of him, so he omitted to discuss the ill-fated attempt to snare the drug couriers last Saturday.

'That sounds promising, Jack,' she offered unconvincingly.

Later that evening they were spooning in bed, their naked bodies entwined. It had been awhile. He pulled away with the intention of moving on top of her when he spotted it. 'You've got a large bruise on the inside of your thigh. What happened? Are you okay?'

Shit, she had forgotten about that. She adapted swiftly. 'Yeah. In my haste at work I turned around and walked straight into the open door of an under bar fridge. God it hurt.'

'Is it okay now?'

It suited her to keep this tale going. 'Yeah, but I should have been more careful. Anyway, I've been thinking about resigning and finding something more interesting that will challenge me mentally and provide more job satisfaction.'

'I reckon I can provide you with some satisfaction.'

'That sounds promising, detective.' She lay down on her back and he rolled over onto her.

Danielle delighted in having sex and was normally imaginative and energetic to say the least. Unusually, she wasn't at her best tonight. Maybe she was still sore. 'Are you okay?'

'Yeah, I'm fine, Jack.'

'That's not a very enthusiastic thing to say. You know of course what the fine acronym stands for?'

She did, but would play his silly game. 'No, why don't you tell me, detective?'

'Fucked up, insecure, neurotic and emotional.'

Really!

16. Rooftop Bar - International Hotel

Monday 18th May

Ben Chandler was sipping his fifteen year old Macallan when he was distracted by the sight of a tall, elegant, smartly dressed woman walking into the room. He wondered if he were so fortunate that this could be his appointment. She paused, subtly looked around the room, and then confidently started to walk towards his table. She was aware of the eyes on her, but she brushed them away with a casual flick of her lustrous black locks.

'Hello, Mr Chandler, I'm Sophie,' she said while offering her hand in greeting.

'Pleased to meet you, Sophie.' He promptly moved around to her side of the table. 'Please take a seat.'

'Thank you.'

'How did you recognise me?'

'Discretion for our clients is important, so I do my research and that way no one gets embarrassed.'

'Thank you. That's very thoughtful. Now, would you mind if I suggested a drink for you?'

'Yes, why not, I'm game and I'm sure I can trust your taste, Mr Chandler.'

'Firstly, please call me Ben. I'm not a high profile politician or government minister tonight,' he said, while smiling self-assuredly.

She might start by bringing him down a peg or two without being too impolite. 'I'm sorry, I didn't realise you were a politician, I thought you must be a successful businessman or entrepreneur, particularly given the smart suit you are wearing and where we are inhabiting.'

'Okay, I guessed I deserved that. As a politician, and especially as a government minister, I'm never far from the spotlight. Let's start again, shall we? Hi, I'm Ben.'

She smiled playfully. 'Hi, Ben, I'm Sophie. You mentioned something about a drink.'

'Yes, I did, sorry. The hotel has created a cocktail to celebrate the one hundred and seventieth anniversary of the construction of the original Treasury Building where the hotel now stands. The drink is called the Treasury Martinez and is based on the traditional Martinez, which was the predecessor to what we now know as the martini, and coincidentally, is now also celebrating one hundred and seventy years since it was first created.'

Sophie was trying not to appear too impressed. 'That's what I call synergy. Where did you learn all that?'

'I stay here whenever parliament is in session, so I have learned quite a bit about the place over time.'

He was a handsome man with a strong face, a smooth and tanned complexion, more pepper than salt hair and piercing blue eyes. She speculated he would be popular with women. 'What a magnificent view. There's the Harbour Bridge, the Opera House and in the distance I can even see the Heads.'

'There's an outdoor terrace with even better views, although it might a bit too bracing at this time of year.'

'Bracing, that's a word I don't hear too often, however, it's quite fitting.'

'Here comes your martini. Feast your eyes on that, Sophie.'

'That is simply spectacular. What are the ingredients?'

'Apparently, the recipe is a secret, but I twisted the maître d's arm once before. It combines gin and bitters with sweet vermouth, maraschino liqueur, and dash of absinthe. The ice cube is hand-chiselled and dressed with twenty four carat gold. And on the side are sweet gold-dusted pearls of lychee caviar.'

Sophie guessed she wasn't the first woman that he had ordered this particular cocktail for. 'Thank you. Cheers, Ben.' They clinked glasses and he held her gaze longer than was appropriate. *Uh-oh*. She needed to change his focus, even if just to mitigate any extracurricular thoughts he may be having already. 'How wonderful is it to be able to socialise again? And it felt liberating to get dressed up again after living in sweatpants and lycra for the past two months.'

'So, what kept you in sweatpants and lycra for all that time?'

'I'm going to Sydney Uni and we have been restricted to studying online from home during this awful pandemic. So, it's sweatpants at home and lycra when I go for a jog. Hence, why I feel like a new woman tonight.'

'Well, you look ever so stylish. What are you studying?'

'A Bachelor of Psychology. I'm not sure what I will do with it, but I am really enjoying the course. It's mentally challenging yet stimulating at the same time.'

'Why don't you think about executive coaching in the private sector. There are far too many executives, both men and women, but particularly men, that behave unethically these days.'

'I've actually considered that. I studied a survey recently that provided an analysis of the turnover of Chief Executive Officers in the majority of the top globally listed companies. It found that thirty nine percent of the senior executives dismissed left under a cloud of being accused of ethical lapses including sexual harassment, insider trading, governance breaches and other activities that embodied misconduct.' Sophie paused as he gave her that piercing gaze again. *Maybe he's just being attentive,*

I'll give him the benefit of the doubt. 'Sorry, that might have been a bit too heavy,' she said bashfully.

He was already impressed by this intelligent woman and her thought processes. 'Not at all. I was enthralled by your passion for the topic. In my line of work I see that kind of behaviour all the time and it appals me. We have to carefully scrutinise our political donors and that especially extends to the ethical lapses by company executives that you so eloquently highlighted. We also have to be extremely careful about who in the corporate world we engage with. Apparently, it's all about the "optics" these days.' He used his fingers to emphasise his point.

She would lighten the tone and at the same time find out more about this man. 'So, is this your local haunt, Ben,' she teased.

He burst out laughing. 'You're funny. If it were, it would be an expensive local. No, I live with my family on the Central Coast.'

Tick one for honesty.

'You're correct in one sense, as I always stay here. Woy Woy is an hour and a half away at a minimum and it's just too far for a daily commute. At least by staying here I get a brisk five hundred metre walk twice a day to get the oxygen flowing. And when parliament's not in session I work from my electorate office which is close to the water in Woy Woy.'

She persisted. 'Your family must miss you, and vice versa when you're working in Sydney.'

'Well, fortunately, there are only seventeen weeks of sittings and budget estimates that require my attendance. My boys are now in their teens and have plenty of distractions in Woy Woy and my wife has her own business, which takes precedence over most things these days.'

Sophie picked up on the subtle illusion he was creating.

He obviously wanted her to think that things could be better at home. Each to their own and whom was she to judge.

'Maybe I'll be fortunate enough to find a corporate position closer to home one day when I'm done with politics. You could even be my executive coach.' He laughed at his own suggestion.

'Well, you never know, and I do like the beach. I live near Coogee and spend quite a lot of time strolling along the coastline. Sometimes I will powerwalk the Coogee to Bondi boardwalk and most days I'll bodysurf as well.'

He was listening intently, but his mind was occupied imagining her in a swimsuit. 'Aah, what I would give for your lifestyle, Sophie.'

'What, you want to be an escort?' she exclaimed while giving him a mischievous smile.

He laughed long and loud. 'Intelligent, and funny too, I see,' he replied.

'I do crack myself up sometimes.'

'I see you do. Laughter is good for the soul, so I've heard. How did you get into bodysurfing? That's an unusual pursuit for a woman.'

'Well, I do quite like the gym, however, I dislike the pretentiousness that pervade many of them these days. I prefer low impact exercise like swimming anyway. The constant repetition of strokes improves muscle endurance and because water is much denser than air, the higher resistance against the body's movements cause the muscles to be strengthened and toned. Swimming gives your body a workout akin to training in the gym without the pounding of treadmills, lifting weights and I get to avoid the pretentious, lycra clad, twenty somethings. Sorry, that sounded like a speech. I'll come down off my soapbox now,' she said apologetically.

'If I put my politician's head on, just for a split second,

I might say. Could Ms Sophie please answer the honourable ministers question?' He was smiling cheekily now.

She looked at him with innocent eyes. 'What question, honourable minister?'

'Bodysurfing.'

'Oh, sorry. I was so busy rambling I forgot what you asked. I was down at Coogee one day swimming from the rock pool to Dolphins Point and back when I saw these guys surfing without boards. This was a new phenomenon to me, I like a challenge, and the rest as they say, is history.'

'Oh, dear, look at the time. I have a meeting and press conference early in the morning, so I should call it a night. I have really enjoyed your company, Sophie. Can we do this again?'

'I am happy to, although you will need to make a booking through the agency.'

'Can't we bypass the protocols and work something out between us?'

'Not really. It's important that the agency is aware of my whereabouts and whom I'm with at all times. It is about my personal safety and security.'

They rose from the table. 'I respect that. A woman's safety is paramount, however, you do know who I am, and this is a very respectable and public place,' he said gesturing around the stylish lounge area. 'I won't ask for your phone number because I know you shouldn't provide it, but please take my card.' He handed her his business card and kissed the back of her hand. 'Hopefully, I will see you again. Can I book you a taxi?'

'No, I'm fine thanks. I have a driver waiting.'

Sophie was sitting in the rear of the taxi and reflecting on her evening. She had savoured Ben's company, found him to be refreshingly honest, especially given his occupation. He was considerate and attentive which had made her feel quite special, unlike that horrible little Chinese man she worked for previously. Ben Chandler was easy on the eye too. And after being locked down for the past two months, it was fun to be back at work, glammed up and earning some money. She hoped he would rebook her, but it would have to be through the agency.

The man was reclining in a charcoal grey armchair at the Rooftop Bar of the International Hotel. He had read somewhere that the vibe is hushed glamour, so expect do a lot of chilling. That's exactly what he was doing while admiring the stunning harbour views and sipping his cocktail made from Bulleit bourbon, spice syrup, pineapple juice, Vermouth, Campari, and Bitters. An interesting combination, not unlike the two people whose reflection he was observing in the floor to ceiling windowpane. Having followed him from his office he knew who the smartly dressed, suave looking man was, but he would need to find out who his companion was. A plan was forming in his mind and she might be useful at some point. She was tall, conservatively dressed wearing a red crepe jacket, matching pencil skirt that landed just above her knees, a beige blouse and red heels. He guessed she had come straight from work too. This extremely attractive woman of Eurasian appearance had, after pausing briefly, confidently strode across the room to the man's table. At the conclusion of their evening, once the woman had left, the man slowly followed the politician to the bar, maintaining a discreet distance. He hung back until the politician had placed his signed drinks account on the bar and turned to leave the lounge. The man then quickly stepped forward and observed his quarry's room number on the drinks account.

'Excuse me,' he called out to the barman.

'Yes, sir, can I help you?'

The man extracted his wallet from his pocket and held it up. 'My friend left his wallet behind. Is Mr Chandler still in room 2501?'

'Yes, sir, Mr Chandler always stays in 2501. It's blocked out for him whenever parliament is sitting.'

'Okay, thank you, I'll take it down to him.'

17. AFP Headquarters

Tuesday 19th May

Unusually, Danielle wasn't in the mood for a morning glory. Jack was surprised. This was the same woman who had unashamedly seduced him on their first proper date in fading light at that cute, little beach near South Head. So, drawing a blank, he rose early, shaved, showered, dressed, and drove over the Anzac Bridge to AFP Headquarters. His first task for the day was to follow-up on Stevie's lead about the woman in the wheelie bin and contact Waverley Council's waste management department.

'Good morning. This is Detective Jack Wagner from the Australian Federal Police.'

'What can I do for you detective?'

'I am following up on information provided to me relating to a potential crime that may have been committed in the vicinity of Birrell Street in Queens Park last Friday evening or Saturday morning.'

'What sort of crime?' the man enquired.

'That's confidential. What's the name of the waste contractor that services that area?' Jack asked firmly.

'It's Eastern Suburbs Waste Management and I'll give you their contact phone number.'

Jack wrote down the number, although he had no intention of using it. It was all too easy to be fobbed off over the phone, so he would visit the company in person. Half an hour later he walked into the waste company's offices in Randwick and asked to speak to the manager. Following an inordinately long delay, a stocky, slovenly dressed man with an ESWM logo on his untucked work shirt, ambled out from behind the reception counter.

'Tom Sullivan. What's up?'

Keep your cool, Jack. 'Jack Wagner, Australian Federal Police.' He held his credentials in one hand and greeted the man with the other. Sullivan nearly crushed it. *Okay, it's like that is it?* 'Mr Sullivan, I am conducting an investigation, and one of your drivers may have pertinent information relating to that. I want to talk to the driver that serviced the Birrell Street area last Saturday morning.'

'Why?'

'I can't discuss that.'

'Then why should I tell you anything?'

'Look, Mr. Sullivan, your driver is not under investigation, nor is your company, but he may have information that is vital to my case. That's all.' Jack was keeping it civil, for now.

Sullivan was quiet, so Jack maintained the status quo.

'Ravinder Singh,' Sullivan eventually replied. 'He should be finishing his rounds soon. Take a seat.' With that Sullivan disappeared back behind the reception counter, pushed through a swing door and disappeared into the back of the building.

After half an hour Jack had finished flicking through the tattered waste industry and environmental magazines and was wishing he were in his doctor's waiting room. At least there he could ogle his way through Vogue or Who Weekly. He heard the swing door bang against the wall and looked up to see a tall, lean man wearing a turban walking around from behind the reception counter.

'Mr Wagner, I am Ravinder Singh. Hello,' he said in his pronounced subcontinental accent.

'Mr Singh, thank you for speaking to me. I am led to believe that you witnessed an unusual incident when conducting your rounds in Queens Park last Saturday morning.'

'What sort of incident, sir?'

'Here we go again,' Jack mumbled. 'Mr Singh, you are not in trouble here. I just want to know what you saw, that's all,' Jack said, almost pleading.

'Oh, okay, thank you, sir.'

'Mr Singh, what did you see?' Jack asked, becoming increasingly exasperated.

'Oh, okay, sir.'

Ravinder Singh told Jack, with surprising detail of the unusual events that unfolded early on that Saturday morning, which pretty much reiterated what Stevie had already told him. Finally, Stevie's information was on the money.

'Did you contact the police?'

'I told my boss and he said I shouldn't get involved as they might be gangsters and come after me.'

'You should go to Waverley Police Station and lodge a report.'

'No, I have told you, so I am okay now.'

'Alright, that's up to you. Is there anything else you can tell me?'

'Yes, yes, I just remember. I wrote down the registration of the woman's car. He pulled out a tattered piece of paper and handed it across. Jack couldn't read it clearly, so he handed it back to Singh to read out the details. He told Jack the vehicle was a black Honda CRV with tinted windows and he read out the registration.

'Mr. Singh, will you come for a drive with me and show me the exact location where you found the woman? It's only ten minutes away, so it won't take up much of your time.'

Less than ten minutes later Singh directed Jack to a roller shutter in Birrell Lane.

'Let's get out and you can show me exactly where you were and where you found the woman, Mr Singh.'

Singh moved around the scene in accordance with how the events unfolded in the dark that morning and talked Jack through what occurred.

The wheelie bins had a stick-on number on side which Jack assumed corresponded with the house's Ashton Street address. 'And you found the wheelie bins directly behind that roller shutter?'

'Yes there were two bins, one for waste and another for recycling, sir.'

'And she spilt out of the waste bin?'

'Yes and it fell here, sir.' Singh pointed to the spot where he found the woman. 'She did not smell good.'

'And where was her car?'

'Just over there.' He pointed to a spot about ten metres away. 'I don't know how I would have got passed it in my truck.'

'Mr Singh, I need to stay here for a while longer, so please take this Cabcharge voucher and make your own way back to your office.'

'Thank you, sir,' he said while clasping his hands in front of him and tilting his head.

After surveying the crime scene Jack drove around to the front of the house at 19 Ashton Street. It was a pre-war dwelling with a second floor added recently and a newly built privacy wall at the front. Jack lifted the latch on the gate and walked up the short pathway and knocked on the front door. Receiving no response he knocked a second time and waited. Nothing. He would come back another time. This part of Jack's investigation was essentially an issue for the state police anyway, but he was hoping it would provide leads which would contribute to his wider drug importation investigation. He called Michael Sanderson from his car.

'A CI of mine provided me with a lead which I have been following up for the past day or so. It seems that your drug dealing friends in Chinatown have adapted their business operations during the lockdown to a dial a dealer distribution model.'

'Are you talking about the eastern suburbs, Jack?' Their earlier joint investigation had ascertained that one of the Triads was now importing a higher purity cocaine into the country and that had got the eastern suburb's elite all excited.

'Yeah, you got it, buddy.' Jack talked Sanderson through what he had discovered so far and suggested they widen the focus of their joint task force to tackle the issue. 'Can you run this vehicle registration through your database and then meet me at Goulburn Street and we can formulate a plan.'

'Sure, see you there, Jack.'

18. Ministerial Offices – Martin Place

Tuesday 19th May

'Consul General, it is good to see you again; how have you been?'

'Minister, I have been extremely well thanking you, and yourself?'

'You know how it is, busy as always. Please take a seat.' The Minister ushered him across to one of the two facing sofas and sat opposite the Consul General.

Ben Chandler had been in his Minister for Education and Early Childhood Learning role for a number of years now and was comfortable with his knowledge and command of the requirements of the role. There was only one reason why the Chinese Consul General would be here this morning. He knew full-well why Zhang Xiao had made this appointment, but he would ingratiate his guest with the customary small talk first and avoid the elephant in the room for now.

'How are things at the Consulate, Xiao?'

'These are busy and also challenging times, Ben. We have been swamped fielding enquiries from your exporters who wish to avail themselves of opportunities under the China Australia Free Trade Agreement. CHAFTA has been an excellent initiative for both countries and especially for New South Wales.'

'I agree. What are the challenges you speak of?'

'We have been inundated with enquiries from Chinese

students who have been stranded in China following Australia's ban on non-resident foreigners entering the country. Tens of thousands of them were in China during the university holiday break when the coronavirus outbreak occurred. The timing could not have been worse for them.'

'I know what you mean, Xiao. Our education exports have suffered dramatically due to the pandemic. Our universities and colleges are financially hurting as a result. Just so you are aware, New South Wales is fully supportive of the federal government's stance on banning non-Australians entering the country at this time. It was vitally important that we limited the spread of the virus. Hopefully, for both of us and our constituents, now the lockdown has eased, things may get back to normal in the not too distant future.' They both new this would not be the case.

'I sincerely hope so. New South Wales has in excess of one hundred thousand Chinese students enrolled in its universities and colleges which is one third of your total international student market. When you add in their spending capacity it is a significant contributor to your state's economy. The average spending of each Chinese student is over twenty five thousand dollars per year. I'm sure you can do the mathematics and calculate the benefit to the New South Wales economy yourself, Ben.'

Xiao was annoying Chandler now with his preaching, however, he would remain on the higher ground. For now. 'Education has been a significant export earner for the state, and we are particularly cognisant of the impact Chinese students have in this market sector, Consul General.' He deliberately reverted to the use of Xiao's title to show him that things were cooling slightly.

'Ben, I am glad that you recognise the benefits that Chinese students provide to your economy. Do you not agree that the

Confucius Institute could also provide considerable benefits to a multicultural society?'

There it was. The New South Wales government had removed the Confucius Institute program from their high schools at the end of 2019 due to the perception that "the Institute is or could be facilitating inappropriate foreign influence" as their internal review had found. Xiao had authored an article at the time condemning the decision and posted it on the Consulate General's website.

> *China has always been committed to developing relations with other countries based on principles of mutual respect and non-interference in each other's internal affairs. It is noted that the relevant review by the NSW Department of Education found no evidence of actual political influence through its Confucius Institute program. We hope the relevant parties will discard their ideological prejudice and view China's development and foreign policy in an objective and rational manner.*

'Mr Consul General, with respect, we have had this conversation before. The government supports the findings of the review and our position hasn't changed.'

'Minister, when handing down its report, your very own department said the review found no evidence of actual political influence. On that basis, I fail to see what the problem is.'

'Mr Consul General, there is no problem, we have simply replaced the program with our own in-house Mandarin classes run by my department. And contrary to the article you authored last year, we don't have any ideological prejudice. Furthermore, your reference to China's development and foreign policy have nothing to do with the subject we are discussing. This is about the education of New South Wales students and nothing else.'

Ben Chandler also had concerns about the governance arrangements and the fact that the program's Chinese teaching assistants were vetted for good political quality and a love of the motherland. In the interest of diplomacy he would adhere to his current explanation this time. He stood and offered his outstretched hand in an obvious sign that the meeting was over.

'Mr Consul General, thank you for dropping by.' He offered the sincerest smile he could manage.

'Thank you for your time, Minister. I will see myself out,' Xiao said, coldly.

It seemed that Plan B was the only remaining avenue available to Xiao and he would now be reliant on Paul Gao to achieve the party's goals.

19. AFP Headquarters

Tuesday 19th May

'Hi, Jack.'

Sanderson had signed-in at reception and made his way up to Jack's office on the tenth floor. 'Hi, Michael, pull up a chair.'

Sanderson sat alongside Jack and pulled out his notebook, flipping through the pages until he found what he was looking for. 'Here we go, Jack. The owner of the black Honda CRV vehicle is Lucie Chan and she resides as Apartment 1419 in the Sussex Street Apartment Building at 362 Sussex Street.'

'Jesus, Michael, is that ringing bells for you, too?' The AFP had raided an apartment on the same floor of that building two months earlier searching for two Chinese Australians who were implicated in drug importation and a related murder at the Seaman's Mission in Brisbane. The prime suspect in the murder had been killed in the raid and his accomplice arrested.

'Oh, yeah, buddy. Her apartment is only two doors down from the one we raided back in March. And what's more, I have conducted a title search on the property and it is registered to a Than Ping Lie. That is the same woman who owns the apartment we raided.'

'Who, Michael, we assume is Wie Ping Lie's mother, wife or sister.'

'The one and the same, Jack.'

'So, it's not a stretch to assume that Lucie Chan is dealing drugs on behalf of Wie then?' Jack suggested.

'You're on the money. At Day Street we know who she is and have long suspected her of involvement in drug dealing for his Triad. She has obviously moved up the dealing food chain and is fronting Wie's eastern suburbs dial a dealer operation now. Going back to the incident you mentioned in Queen's Park, that would explain why we haven't seen her in and around Chinatown lately.

'Before we get further into this, Michael, my investigation is one related to drug importation and I have no jurisdiction over land-based drug distribution. Having said that, my sense is that there is definitely a link between the two and I get the feeling that Lucie Chan could be the crucial link into both investigations.'

'No doubt.'

'Then we should pay young Lucie a visit and see what she will tell us. We just might be able to come at Wie's drug importation business from a different angle, especially given we lost the guys transporting the shipment down from Townsville. Speaking of which, I have contacted a colleague at MI5 in London and asked him to scrutinise Vulcan's UAV sales records for the last twelve months and see if anything stands out.'

'That's a good angle, Jack.'

'Well, the MBC guys are pretty convinced that the drone used for the ship to shore drug shipments has to be a Vulcan UAV Airlifter, so I'm backing their technical knowledge and experience. In the meantime I'm going to try and track Lucie Chan's movements through the state's Transport Department network. With any luck, I can place her in the vicinity of the attack at the precise time. I also have another person to interview. I'm guessing at the time she was attacked, our Lucie Chan was doing a drop in Birrell

Lane, so I'm going to interview the occupants of the house I think she was visiting.

Sanderson rose from his chair. 'Okay, see you soon, Jack.'

It was a mild twenty degrees outside, so Jack decided to walk the kilometre down George Street to the Transport NSW Head Office in Chippendale. He should have called first, but once again he didn't want to get fobbed off, which he regarded as a specialty of public servants. He signed in at reception and then rode the elevator to Geoff Richardson's fourth floor office. Richardson could see him through the glass door. Irrespective, Jack knocked anyway, just to show him some courtesy. 'Hi, Geoff, how goes things?' He knew he would have to be patient as Richardson would no doubt regale him with tales of woe about being overworked, underpaid and underappreciated.

'Hello, Jack, what brings you down the hill to the public service backblocks?'

Okay, no poor me speech, go for it, Jack, he thought to himself. 'I'm in the middle of a drug importation investigation and I need to track the vehicle movements of someone I suspect of involvement.'

'Alright, give me the location specifics and date and I'll gear it up for you.'

'Last Friday the fifteenth at around five o'clock in the evening would be the approximate time. What cameras do you have in the Oxford Street, York Road and Syd Einfeld Drive vicinity?'

'Plenty, it's a busy area, so can you narrow it down for me?'

'My best guess is that my suspect would have been driving away from the city heading for her appointment in Birrell Lane, so do you have a camera that covers the entry to Birrell Street?' Jack was betting that Lucie Chan would have driven directly from Chinatown, so she would have to turn into Birrell Street to get to Birrell Lane.

'No, but we have a camera covering the right hand turn lane into York Road from Oxford Street. Will that do?'

'Perfect, let's start with that and hopefully I'll get lucky.'

'Alright, follow me and I'll get you set-up over there and arrange a login for you.'

Five minutes later the public servant returned. 'Okay, here you go.' Richardson handed Jack a printed sheet of paper containing his login details and temporary password. 'You have a restricted login and will only be able to access the icons depicted on the home screen. I asked them to load up all five cameras in the vicinity of the junction you mentioned, so you should see five icons on the home screen when you login. Good luck, Jack.'

Richardson's IT guys had allocated the first icon to the camera covering the right hand turn lane into York Road. *Smart boys.* Jack double clicked on the icon, moved the video forward to five o'clock then tapped the play button with the cursor. Knowing exactly what he was looking for, a black Honda CRV, he quickened up the video to four times normal speed. He would have liked to speed it up even further, but Sydney was in twilight at the time, he might miss her and have to repeat the process. At the five fifteen mark he observed a black Honda CRV pull to a halt in the right hand turn lane at the York Road traffic lights. He froze the vision and zoomed in on the number plate. 'There you are, Lucie,' he said to himself. 'Gotcha.'

20. Chinatown

Wednesday 20th May

As was his habit, Wie Ping Lie was having lunch at the Golden Phoenix in the heart of his territory in Chinatown. He felt his mobile phone vibrate in his pocket. It was his woman. 'Nǐ hǎo,' he said greeting her in his native tongue.

'Hello to you too, mister. Are you at the restaurant?' she asked with a sense of urgency.

'Yes, what is wrong?'

'I need to talk to you, now. I'll be there in half an hour,' she blurted out, then disconnected the call.

Less than thirty minutes later Danielle bounded into the restaurant and strode purposefully across to his table. In her rush to get to the restaurant she hadn't had time to dress up for him, so she was just wearing jeans and a casual top.

'That is how you should dress all the time,' Wie stated earnestly.

Normally she would have made light of the subject all the while knowing he preferred her with no clothes on at all. 'Do you want to talk here or at the apartment? It's important.'

'What can be of such importance, woman?'

'I have learned some information from my other boyfriend and your antagonist,' she said with resolve.

'Okay, we will go to the apartment. Come on, let's go.'

They exited the restaurant and she looped her arm into his as they walked along Sussex Street where they entered the foyer and rode the elevator to the fourteenth floor apartment. She thought about the last time they were here and had crashed through the doorway in their lust for each other. This time he took a seat on the sofa facing the floor to ceiling window that provided panoramic views across Darling Harbour to the west. She sat down and turned to face him.

'Now what is so important that you couldn't talk on the phone?' he demanded. 'I have business to attend to.'

'Yes, I'm sure you do, however this is more important. Wagner has given me some information that should concern you. Do you have a woman dealing for you in the eastern suburbs?'

'What if I do?' he replied brusquely.

'Oh, come on, Wie, don't play tough guy with me. I've been deeply committed to this arrangement from the start,' she replied firmly while staring him down.

Wie breathed a sigh. 'Yes, I do and her name is Lucie Chan. What of it?'

'I have been told that she was bashed and left to die last week near Centennial Park.'

'This is true. How does he know of that?'

'He has a criminal informant who told him.'

'I should find that informant and deal with him.'

'My boyfriend told me that—'

'He is not your boyfriend,' Wie yelled, interrupting her. 'You will stop saying that.'

'You're cute when you get jealous. Anyway, my *non-boyfriend* thinks that she was dealing drugs on behalf of a Chinatown based triad which I assume would be your group, Wie.'

'La shi. You should have told me sooner,' he said angrily. 'When did he tell you this?'

'Monday night.'

'Today is Wednesday, what took you so long? You are well-rewarded to keep me informed are you not?'

She ignored the gibe. 'I've been busy and this is the first chance I've had to talk to you in person. I didn't want to discuss this over the telephone just in case, so here I am.' He remained silent, so she continued. 'He thinks this is all linked to a drug importation operation as well.'

'La shi.'

'You said that before.'

Wie remained quiet and she could see his anger rising. Knowing exactly what he needed, so she took a little plastic baggie out of the coffee table drawer and carefully emptied the contents onto the table. Then she crushed it with her apartment swipe card and chopped it into lines. She took a one hundred dollar banknote from her purse and rolled it into a tight tube. She loved that blow lowered inhibitions and invariably led to an anything goes attitude. This is what he needed and she handed him the rolled banknote. 'Come on, you need to relax before you start making decisions you might regret.'

She was correct. He needed to calm down, so he indulged, shook his head back and forth and then handed the note back to her. 'Aah, that's better.'

She drew nearer to him, clasped his chin and kissed him on the mouth. Strangely for him, he didn't withdraw, so she moved her hand down between his legs, endeavouring to take his mind off her disconcerting revelations. He was hardening and had quickly succumbed to the blow and her encouragement. She rose from the sofa and looped her arms around him and whispered into his ear.

Half an hour later they were laying on the carpet in silence. Her head was resting on his tattooed chest and her hand was still wandering. 'What are you going to do, Hǔ?' He appeared deep in thought and didn't reply. She continued. 'I think now is the appropriate time to dump him and end the arrangement. I don't think I can learn much more about his investigations than I already have. And it is becoming tiresome and I'm bored with it. What do you think?'

He pushed her off of him and sat bolt upright. 'Now is not the time to end it at all,' he said forcefully. 'Now, more than ever, I need you to keep to your agreement and see what else you can learn about this detective's activities. He will become trouble for me.'

'At some stage he will find out about my deception and that won't end well for me either. We should go away while we can. Winter will be here soon, so we could go somewhere warm for a while until things settle down.'

'I have new stock that I must move before we can do anything. Once that is done then we can go away for a while. But, for now I need to know everything he is doing and with your arrangement, you are the best person to do that.'

'Okay, how long will that take? I can't do this forever and he will become suspicious the longer this goes on.' She had actually quite enjoyed the relationship with her detective boyfriend during the lockdown. For once he wasn't immersed in any investigation, given the populace was stranded at home, so she wasn't under any pressure to glean information from him. She had felt relaxed for the first time. That had all changed now.

'Maybe two or three more weeks and then we can go.' If the authorities were closing in on him he himself would want to leave the country.

'La shi,' she said herself, as she sighed. She lay on the floor thinking about what that would entail. 'Okay, I can do that, as long as I know there is an end date.'

21. Queens Park

Wednesday 20th May

After knocking three times and waiting for an inordinate length of time, a scruffily dressed, unshaven man with unkempt, long mousy coloured hair opened the door.

'Good afternoon, my name is Jack Wagner and I am with the Australian Federal Police. Do you have a minute?'

'Not really, what do you want?'

'I've had a bad morning already Mr—' Jack paused waiting for the man to fill the gap. 'I think that's the part where you tell me your name, sir.'

'Sam Bourdain.'

'Okay, that's good, Sam. Now, do you have a minute? I have some questions for you about an incident that occurred in the laneway behind your house.'

'I don't know anything about any incident.'

'Judging by your appearance I'm guessing you just lied to a federal police officer.' Sam Bourdain had a badly swollen nose and cuts and bruising on the side of his head. The bruises were still reddish in colour, so the damage had been inflicted in the last twenty four hours or so. 'I already identified myself as a federal police officer, so that is an offence under Commonwealth law. Now, why don't you invite me in and we can get comfortable and have a quiet chat about what you supposedly don't know?'

Bourdain sighed disdainfully and then reluctantly led Jack down the hallway to the lounge room. They took seats across from each other on matching red velvet, two seater, antique sofas.

'Great house, Sam. It must be nice living in a large house in an expensive suburb like Queens Park?'

'It's my grandmother's house. She's on an overseas cruise around the Americas for three months, so I'm housesitting for her.'

'Good for her, and you. Now, Sam, I am investigating an incident that occurred at the rear of your house Friday evening or early last Saturday morning.'

'I have already told you I don't know anything about any incident.'

He was lying again. 'Look, we can play this two ways, Sam. You can either answer my questions now, truthfully, and I will be on my way leaving you to continue your recovery from whatever you keep saying didn't happen. Or I will arrest you, take you to AFP headquarters and place you in an interrogation room. At some stage I will get around to interviewing you.' Jack stared directly at Bourdain and waited. 'The choice is yours.'

Bourdain sighed in defeat. 'So, what do you want to know?'

'That's more like it. Now, a woman was bashed behind your house on Friday night or early Saturday morning and left to die in the laneway. Her arms and legs were bound and she was dumped in a wheelie bin. It was only through sheer luck that she didn't end up compacted in a garbage truck. Given that occurred directly behind this house, and the injuries you have so obviously sustained, I'm guessing there is a direct connection between the two.'

'What do you want me to say? I know nothing about the bashing of any woman.'

'I don't think you bashed her, but you are aware of the circumstances surrounding the incident. I know the identity of the woman, what she does for a living, and I have tracked her movements to this house,' Jack lied. 'So I'm assuming she was making a delivery to you when something went horribly wrong. How am I doing, Sam?'

Bourdain didn't respond, rather he sat with his hands clasped, elbows resting on his knees and staring at the floor.

Jack spied minute amounts of white powder on the coffee table. 'Sam, I'm not at liberty to discuss my investigation with you, but I can assure you that I'm not here to bust you for possession of a prohibited narcotic. That's a state issue. Now, tell me about the woman.'

Bourdain exhaled heavily. 'Her name is Lucie and she delivers to me every Friday. She is a dial a dealer driver. I just send a text message via an encrypted app to an anonymous number and my delivery arrives at the appointed time.'

'That much I already know. Come on, stand up, Sam, we're leaving.' Jack stood and walked across to Bourdain.

'Okay, okay. Two guys I used to buy from paid me a visit last week. Apparently they have been losing business to Lucie's dial a dealer network.'

'So they asked you to set her up. Am I correct, Sam?'

'I shouldn't have done it, but I was struggling for cash.'

Jack nodded towards the coffee table. 'And they gave you a baggie as a thank you. A woman came awfully close to losing her life, all for a gram of blow. You're a lowlife, Sam Bourdain.'

'I know and I'm sorry now,' he replied, suddenly remorseful. 'I should make this right.'

'What were their names?'

'Amir and Jasar.'

'And who bashed you, Sam? Not that I care really, however, it may be helpful to my investigation.'

'He was a tall, well-built Asian guy with short black hair who I assume is Lucie's minder or boss.'

'Did he have a dragon tattoo on his neck?'

'No.'

That told Jack it wasn't Wie Ping Lie, so Wie must have found a replacement for his previous lieutenant, Li Jun, who was killed in the SRG raid back in March.

'Did you give this guy Amir and Jasar's names?'

'I didn't have much choice if I wanted to live to see my grandmother again.'

Jack rose from the sofa. 'I'm sure she would be very proud of her lowlife grandson, Sam.' Jack left the house disgusted at the behaviour of some people, particularly their lack of respect for human life.

22. Double Bay

Wednesday 20th May

It was early in the evening and Wang Yong was cruising along New South Head Road in Double Bay in Lucie Chan's heavily tinted CRV in search of his quarry. The men would recognise the car, but he cared less, for he wanted them to be scared. One of Wie's Blue Lanterns, Johnny Chang, was seated alongside him. They both had the Chinese made Type 67 semi-automatic pistols for company. Yong also had a thick piece of bamboo laying on the back seat. It was an unusually warm twenty four degrees during the day, so the bold and beautiful brats of the eastern suburbs would be heading into their favourite pubs and bars to strut their stuff. Before they did that though, they would be taking delivery of a pick-me-up from their local dealer and Yong knew that to be Amir and Jasar. He drove past the already heaving Gilded Nugget and nothing of interest garnered his attention, so he turned around and headed back to glitzy Bay Street. He continued driving slowly down towards the harbour past the array of five star restaurants, designer boutiques and expensive cafes. He paid particular attention to the activity around the stylish and popular Bibo Wine Bar, however, once again he was left disappointed. Yong continued down Bay Street to Steyne Park where he came upon a children's playground. Surely even the immoral Lebo's wouldn't be dealing there.

Realising that no one was dealing out in the open, he headed for the backstreets. He retreated back up Bay Street onto New South Head Road. From there he turned right into Manning Road and then left into Kiaora Lane which would take him down behind the Gilded Nugget. He finally found what he was looking for. Halfway down the laneway he saw a black Subaru Impreza parked behind the dry cleaners. He edged forward and then pulled in behind a dumpster in the alcove behind Lingate House. From his vantage point he could see two men standing with their backs to him. Talking to them were two gaudily dressed young women, one of whom had lifted up her short skirt and appeared to be tucking something into her knickers. Yong waited until the women had broken off from the men. The laneway was now empty except for the two Lebos, so he and Chang quietly exited their car. They tucked their pistols in the back of their jeans and Yong collected the bamboo from the rear seat. The two Lebo's had turned around to return to their car when they spotted Yong and Chang. Unfortunately for them their car was nearer the Chinese. Yong immediately picked up on their concerned expressions. He and Chang stepped forward, positioned themselves next to the Impreza and drew their pistols. The Lebo's froze in their stride.

'Keep walking,' demanded Yong. The two men ignored him and the older man checked the surroundings, obviously seeking a safe exit route. 'I will only tell you one more time, walk forward.' The Type 67 is a Chinese semi-automatic pistol with an integrated sound suppressor, so Yong wasn't concerned about attracting unwanted attention in the quiet laneway. He switched the pistol to single shot and fired once into the ground in front of the men.

The two men flinched and then began walking slowly forward. The Lebo's were physically imposing, so Yong wouldn't underestimate them. He could see the older man's mind working overtime trying to calculate their options. 'Don't waste your time,' Yong commanded as they drew near. 'Lean up against the wall, now.' The men turned to face the brick wall and placed their hands on the brickwork. Yong moved alongside the men, so they could see the pistol clearly aimed at them. 'Chang, search them.'

Johnny Chang rifled through their pockets and relieved them of their stash of baggies, a substantial amount of cash and their mobile phones. Just then the older man swiftly swiped his left arm backwards towards Yong, trying to knock his pistol away. Yong sidestepped, and with his considerable bulk, the momentum caused the older man to crash to the ground. Yong brought his pistol down hard on the side of his head.

'Do you want to try that again, Amir? Now get up.' Yong saw the acknowledgement in his eyes. 'Yes, I know who you two camel jockeys are. You're the two lowlifes that attacked my friend and left her to die. Did you really think we wouldn't find you?'

'Ayreh feek,' Amir shouted.

Yong ignored the foul-mouthed Lebo. 'Chang, wheel that dumpster over here,' he ordered.

Johnny Chang manoeuvred the three metre dumpster across to where the two men were standing. Yong noticed an open padlock hanging from the hinge on the side. He was incensed at the thought of what these two men had done to Lucie. 'You bashed my friend with a knuckleduster and left her to die in a wheelie bin in a deserted laneway, you cowards.'

He took the bamboo pole from Chang. The one inch diameter pole was shredded at the end like tassels on a whip. 'Lean against the dumpster.' Amir sensed what was coming and resisted. Yong swung the weapon hard into the back of his legs. Amir winced, but did not move.

'Tough guy hey?' Yong snarled. He swung harder this time. Amir cried out and went weak at the knees, but didn't collapse. He glanced at Jasar who had looked away in fear. Chang kept his pistol aimed at the two men and Yong swung the weapon for the third time, the bamboo strips slashing his jeans. Amir shrieked in agony and went down onto his knees. 'You two lowlifes used a knuckleduster on an unarmed woman. Well, we're not that barbaric. Simple bamboo for you. Now, climb up into that dumpster,' he demanded.

The two men snarled at him and didn't move, so he fired another shot into the ground between them. The men scrambled to lift themselves up onto the rim, then climbed over and hesitantly lowered themselves into the dumpster. 'That's where garbage belongs. Now you know how Lucie felt. This is for her you pieces of trash.' Yong reached in and shot them both in the knee. He snorted self satisfyingly, all the while ignoring their shrieks of pain. Jasar, the younger man, passed out. 'Chang, lock it up and let's go.'

As they drove away, Yong called Wie.

'Is it done?'

'Yes.' Yong briefly explained their evening's activities and Wie was pleased with their work, especially the like-for-like punishment meted out.

'Zuò dé hǎo, Yong. I will let Lucie know of your success. She will be pleased that you have avenged her.'

'Xiè xiè, Wie.'

23. Rooftop Bar - International Hotel

Wednesday 20th May

Ben Chandler was once more sipping his fifteen year old Macallan and reading the Sydney broadsheet when, over the top of the headline, he saw Sophie walk into the bar. She seemed to be more sashaying than walking to his untrained catwalk eyes as she made her way across to his table. He loved the confidence of this stylish and attractive woman.

'Lovely to see you again, Sophie.'

She liked his welcoming, beaming smile. 'You too, Ben, and so soon after our last appointment.'

He was subtly checking her out and she wondered whether the outfit might have been overkill. 'You look spectacular, Sophie.' She was wearing one of her favourite dresses. It was a three quarter length cobalt blue number with hanging fringe bead work and a shallow neckline and open back. She wore matching coloured pumps, a cream shawl was draped over her arm and she carried a cream clutch. She always dressed conservatively on a first appointment and, depending on her opinion of the client, she would take things up a notch on the second. And maybe even earn a sizeable gratuity. The very nature of escort work and the fact that men wanted to spend time with a woman necessitated that the escort should be immaculately presented at all times. Clients always expected more on a second appointment and Sophie felt good about how she presented herself tonight.

He seated her then returned to his chair. 'Can I take you back in time and order you one of those martinis celebrating one hundred seventy years of synergy?'

'I would love one thanks, Ben. It was delicious and so was the caviar.'

'So, what has happened since I saw you last, Sophie?'

'Not a lot happens in my world these days. At least Sydney Uni's libraries and study spaces are available now, so I can study there as well, but we have to don masks and maintain physical distancing, which is just common sense anyway.'

'So, you're finally out of your sweatpants?' he asked with a cheeky grin.

'Wow, you are a good listener. Ten points to you,' she replied, impressed.

'It always helps when you are enchanted by the person you are talking to.' He let that hang out there.

Sophie was well-versed in these scenarios and quickly picked up on his choice of word, which she liked. *Enchanted.* She remembered what Julie-Anne had said about prince charming. 'It was nearly twenty five degrees today, so I walked down the hill to Coogee and went for a bodysurf. The winds were offshore from the northwest, so there was a nice break. And now I feel so invigorated.'

'It shows too. You look radiant.'

'Thank you, and you look very smart too, Ben.' He was wearing a fitted charcoal grey suit with fine pink pinstripes, an open neck lilac shirt and matching kerchief. And she could tell by the fit of the suit that there was an athletic body hidden in there.

It was timely that the waiter arrived with the round of drinks. They were quiet for a moment while he placed the drinks on the handsewn drink coasters. She caught Ben glance at her cleavage. The societal jury was always undecided when it came to men checking out a woman's breasts, however, she had chosen the dress, knowing full-well what was on display.

She sipped her cocktail and placed the glass down. 'So, what has my favourite government minister been working on these past forty eight hours?' she asked light-heartedly.

'Favourite government minister?'

Sophie picked up on his uneasy expression. He must be thinking that she had appointments with other government ministers. 'Only the Minister for Education and Early Childhood Learning. I was having a light moment with you, Ben. It is my job to entertain you, after all.' Sophie had decided that she was going to enjoy herself tonight and not think of the evening as an appointment.

'Oh, sorry. I must have taken your response the wrong way,' he replied. 'With this pandemic still hanging around I spend most of my time thinking about the safety and wellbeing of the student population under my care. It's also a juggling act trying to ensure nearly one million students successfully complete their year of learning and graduate to the following year. It can be exhausting, but I realise it's important work, especially in the current environment. And it's highly rewarding.'

'You should feel proud of your role. I imagine you will arrive at the end of the year and say, "wow, we did it,"' she said by way of encouragement. 'That must be such a gratifying feeling.'

'Thank you, that's awfully kind of you, and I sincerely hope so,' he replied. 'Would you like another one of those spectacular cocktails?'

'Oh, yes please, they're delicious. Tell me, how did your meeting and press conference go yesterday morning?'

'I cancelled the press conference as I didn't have anything of significance to announce and the press aren't interested unless you do. The meeting was slightly more interesting, though. The Chinese Consul General to New South Wales wanted to see me. I knew in advance what the subject would be, however in the interests of diplomacy and our important relationship with China, I agreed to see him anyway.' He paused. 'Do I make you feel uncomfortable referencing China, Sophie?'

'No, why would you ask?'

'There are many expatriate Chinese and people of Chinese ancestry living in Australia who remain loyal to the regime in Beijing. I just wondered—'

She cut him off before he could finish his explanation. 'Well, I'm not one of them, Ben. I abhor China's human rights record, their annexation of the islands of the East Vietnam and Philippine Seas, their treatment of Tibet, Taiwan, the Uighurs and lately, Hong Kong. And their Belt and Road Initiative is just a land grab in another guise. And don't get me started over this pandemic that emanated from China and their righteous indignation and complete lack of remorse over their complicity.'

'Wow, go Sophie,' he said while softly applauding her.

'Sorry, I was up on my soapbox again. That's twice now.'

'You're fine. I love an intelligent woman who is knowledgeable and has a passion for the moral global issues of the day.'

'Okay, I've calmed down now, tell me about your meeting,' she sighed.

'Alright. Do you know what the Confucius Institute is?'

'Yes, I do, there is a program in place at Sydney Uni.'

'Well, you may have read where the state government removed the program from all our high schools and colleges. Of course, that didn't go down well with China and the Consul General has been badgering me to reinstate it. He tried the usual soft diplomacy at first and then he reminded me how much Chinese students contribute to the state's economy. Just the usual subtle threats and intimidation that we have come to expect. I cut the meeting short and showed him the door.'

'Good for you, Ben.'

'It may still be balmy outside on the terrace, so why don't we take our drinks and go check out the view?'

'That sounds like a wonderful idea and I'd love to see whole panorama this time.'

They placed their glasses on the outdoor table, leaned on the railing, and admired the one hundred and eighty degree view. 'Everything is so much clearer from out here. An excellent suggestion, Ben.'

'It's a pity it's dark as we can't see out of the Heads to the Pacific Ocean. The compensation though is that the Opera House sails do look spectacular when illuminated.'

'It's a little fresher out here, yet not *bracing*.' Sophie had remembered his use of the word from the last time she was here.

He laughed. 'You say I am a good listener, but you're not too bad yourself.'

He removed the shawl from her arm, unfolded it, gently placed it over her shoulders then leant forward and caressed her neck with his lips. She shuddered. Was it because of the memories of Li Qiang touching her, the cool temperature or the sensitivity of Ben's touch? This was the first time she had been kissed sensitively for a long time and she wasn't sure how she should react. Plus, she was an escort, and this wasn't supposed to happen. She decided to just let it go.

Ben Chandler was captivated by this intelligent, funny and charming woman. He was a minister of the state, officially married and he would open himself up to serious scrutiny from the insatiable media if he progressed this arrangement. He didn't know if he could stop himself, anyway. He wrapped his arms around her waist, kissed her neck again and whispered in her ear. 'You are enchanting, Sophie.'

'Ben, thank you for saying that, it is lovely to hear,' she said softly.

She released his arms, turned to face him, and gazed into his eyes. *Aah, those eyes.* 'I should go.'

He thought she look slightly vulnerable. 'Are you sure, Sophie?'

'Yes.' He gave her the puppy dog look. 'We've had a wonderful evening, Ben.' She kissed him on the cheek. 'Thank you.'

'Alright, I'll walk you down to a cab.'

'It's okay, my driver is waiting.'

He escorted her to the elevator. While waiting for the doors to open, she turned to face him, took a business card from her clutch, and gently placed it in his jacket's outer pocket. She knew it contradicted agency policy, but she was certain she wasn't the first and doubted that she would be the last.

'Goodnight, Ben.'

Sophie stepped out of the elevator into the foyer. She paused and turned around. Should she go back up? She had spent a lovely evening with this charming, handsome man, and he was obviously enamoured with her. *And those eyes.* She was just about to press the elevator button when a voice in her head spoke to her. *No Sophie, not tonight.* She turned around and walked through the foyer to her waiting driver.

24. Double Bay

Thursday 21st May

It was just after midnight and Webster and Malouf were walking along Kiaora Lane in Double Bay on the lookout for any persons exhibiting suspicious behaviour. This was the time of night when intoxicated punters were spilling out of the popular Gilded Nugget Hotel, so the two young, uniformed constables were on high alert. As they ventured further down the laneway past the rear of the hotel they spotted a black Subaru Impreza illegally parked behind Double Bay Dry Cleaners. The policemen stopped and shone their torches into the vehicle. There wasn't anything to arouse their suspicion, but they noted the number plate down, then continued to walk further down the laneway.

'Did you hear that, James?' Malouf asked his younger partner.

'Hear what, Sam?'

'Quiet, listen,' he insisted.

After a long wait, Malouf spoke. 'I'm sure that I heard a whimpering sound coming from over there.' He pointed towards the collection of wheelie bins and dumpsters.' He waved his torch back and forth across the row of receptacles.

'They've all got locked padlocks on, so it couldn't have come from there,' Webster replied.

Amir Abboud was laying on the bottom of the stinking

dumpster holding his damaged leg with one hand and the other was keeping his tee shirt pressed firmly against the shattered joint to minimise the bleeding. Had he heard a voice? He knew he was right when he glimpsed a sliver of light washing across the gap created by the hinges of the dumpster's lid.

'Help, help,' he yelled again as loudly as he could muster, but with his energy levels severely depleted, it was nothing more than a whimper.

'There it is again, James.'

'You're right. It's coming from one of these bins. Let's move them one by one.'

As they moved the third dumpster they heard the sound once more. 'James, go grab the bolt cutters from the trunk and let's see who or what's in there.'

Moments later Webster returned with the bolt cutters. Malouf took three steps back, pulled out his Glock 22, and aimed it at the dumpster. 'Okay, cut the shackle and then stand aside.' Webster obliged and stood back, pulling his own Glock. The two constables stood quietly with both their weapons firmly aimed at the receptacle. Nothing happened.

'Keep your weapon aimed at the dumpster while I flip the lid,' Malouf said.

He stepped forward, gripped the hardened rubber handle, paused to check that Webster was in position, and then lifted the lid up and with a swing of his arm flipped it back. Nothing happened, again. The two constables nervously eyed each other. 'James, I'm going to shine my torch inside and have a look, so keep me covered.'

Webster moved cautiously forward, this time holding his weapon in a two fisted grip above the dumpster's rim. 'Okay, go, Sam.'

'Oh, my god, check this out,' Sam said as his torch illuminated two crumpled figures lying in the foetal position on top of layers black plastic bags. Both men were holding bloody tee shirts against their knees and the younger of the two men was sobbing.

'Where are you injured?' Sam asked the two men.

The older man spoke in a weakened voice. 'We have been shot in the knee and can't move.'

'James, call this in and also request an ambulance while I try and get these guys out.'

The ambulance arrived five minutes later and two paramedics exited the vehicle. Malouf brought them up to date on the severity of the men's injuries and advised that they couldn't move unaided. He had an idea. He climbed over the rim and lowered himself into the dumpster where he spoke to the injured men. 'I need you to sit upright against the rear panel of the dumpster. I will help you.' One at a time, he grasped the men under their armpits and levered them across the trash bags and into the sitting position. 'Okay, James, you and the paramedics need to lower the dumpster onto its back then we'll be able to slide the men onto the para's body boards.' Fifteen minutes later, the paramedics had completed their health checks, connected both men to saline drips, loaded them onto gurneys and wheeled them to the ambulance. Then they drove out of the laneway and headed to St Vincent's Hospital Emergency Department. Malouf and Webster followed closely in their patrol car.

'How bizarre was that, Sam?'

'I've never seen anything like it.'

25. AFP Headquarters

Thursday 21st May

'Hi, Jack, how goes it?'

For the second time in three days, Michael Sanderson strutted into Jack's office. He was wearing a broad grin and displayed a renewed swagger.

'Good thanks. How did you go?'

'Yep, all good. We have approval from my Chief of Detectives to continue to work together on our respective cases. He agrees that there is potentially a link between the two and is comfortable for me to pursue the domestic side of it in conjunction with your importation investigation.'

'That's good news. Let me bring you up to speed on what I've learned recently.'

Sanderson pulled up a chair, sat down and took out his pocket sized notebook.

Jack looked at him curiously. 'You really are an old school copper. You haven't heard of tablets, iPads, etc, buddy?'

'I might be an old school copper, but at least no one can hack my notebook.'

Jack laughed. 'You're a funny bugger. Alright, let's get on with it. As promised, I interviewed the occupant of the house adjacent to where Lucie Chan was bashed. After some prompting he confirmed that he had given up Chan to some local thugs in exchange for a gram of coke. Their names are Amir and Jasar. Do you know them?'

'Yeah, they're a couple of mid-level dealers from the southwest suburbs who have found a niche for themselves in the leafy eastern suburbs. I wouldn't think they'd be a match for Wie and his crew though.'

'The occupant of the house is Sam Bourdain and he was displaying some serious bruising, so I assume payback was swift in coming, Michael. Eventually he confirmed as much, but other than a loose description, he couldn't identify the perpetrator. All he offered was that he was a tall, well-built Asian guy with short black hair. I'm guessing this is Li Jun's replacement, i.e. Wie's lieutenant, enforcer and Chan's new minder.'

'My CI's tell me that Lucie Chan hasn't been seen around Chinatown for a while which could allude to two things. Firstly, as I mentioned before, she's been fronting the coke dealing in the eastern suburbs herself, and secondly, she has been out of action after her near death experience last week that you mentioned.'

Jack nodded in agreement. 'Sam Bourdain's responses are consistent with what the garbage truck driver told me and the traffic cameras verify the timing, so we now have corroborating evidence that can place Lucie Chan near the crime scene. I guess understandably, the incident wasn't reported to the police, so there has been no follow-up. Therefore, we're on our own here and it's been almost a week since the incident, so we need to find Lucie Chan.'

'How do you feel about raiding her apartment, Jack? I think we have sufficient evidence, albeit largely circumstantial, to convince a judge to grant us a warrant now. And we might get lucky and find her home if she's recuperating.'

'That works for me. You will need to apply for the warrant as it primarily relates to state based issues. My focus is finding the source of the coke, where it's stored and arrest the head of the whole syndicate. And our Lucie just might be able to help with that.'

'Alright, I'll get onto the warrant application and get back to you.'

'Before you go. I've heard back from my MI5 contact in London. He was finally able to obtain a list of all Vulcan UAV Airlifter purchases from the company, covering the past couple of years. He sent me the list. Check it out.' Jack handed the printout to Sanderson.

'You are bloody well kidding me. Wow! The MBC guys do know their drones after all.' Halfway down the list he saw the highlighted name. Than Ping Lie.

'That makes me wonder whether Wie Ping Lie is actually the head of the Triad. Maybe we have it all wrong and he's just the figurehead while she pulls the strings. There's at least two apartments linked to our investigations that are in her name and now she's listed as the purchaser of a heavy lift drone.'

'Or alternatively, Jack, everything is listed in her name to divert attention away from him.'

'We need to find out who she is.'

'Okay, that's a local issue, so I'll have my guys do some research on her while I work on the warrant application.'

26. Danielle's Apartment Glebe

Thursday 21st May

Jack parked his Commodore in Bridge Road Glebe and walked the fifty metres along the tree-lined street to Danielle's apartment complex. As he neared her building he detected a mid-twenties man in a silver Hyundai i20 reading a broadsheet newspaper. His detective's radar picked up on something unusual. The younger generation needed their constant fix of current events and self-aggrandisement from social media. They were equally fixated on their mobile phones, so why would he be reading the morning newspaper? Particularly one that was out of date already in the world of never-ending news cycles. The guy should have been scrolling through the dozens of apps he undoubtedly had installed on his mobile. *Rookie mistake buddy.* As he passed the driver's blind spot, he glanced back and made a mental note of the car's registration.

Jack entered the foyer and stood behind a support pillar in the rear corner. He pulled out his mobile and rang Sanderson. 'Michael, can you run a plate for me please? It's urgent, so I'll stay on the line.'

'I'm good thanks,' he replied good-humouredly.

'Yeah, yeah.' Jack could hear Sanderson typing on his laptop and he assumed he was logging into the state police's COPS database. It was illegal for police officers to access the database unless there was a valid reason for doing so. Fortunately, Sanderson had received approval from his COD to continue their joint investigation and had registered it in the database before they had met yesterday.

'That's interesting,' he said curiously. 'Jack, the vehicle is registered to MPS Security, David Bedford's company. Do you remember him?'

'Yeah, I do. Thanks, Michael. I will explain when I know more.' Jack entered the stairwell and made his way up to Danielle's apartment. His mind was thinking its way through the scenario. What was a private security operative doing outside an apartment building where his girlfriend lived, and he was visiting? He didn't believe in coincidences. The guy was obviously on a stakeout, so what, and whom, was behind it. And what was Bedford's involvement?

'You've dressed up for dinner. You look stunning,' he said when she opened the door.

Danielle had been distant on Monday night and had avoided his advances the following morning, so she needed to up her game tonight. She couldn't afford him to be suspicious around her. Well no more than came natural to a detective anyway. And he would be sceptical about her bruise. She had warmed up the apartment, mainly so she could wear something that would get his juices flowing. She wore her favourite tight fitting jeans and had decided on a backless and sleeveless gold tank top with a ridiculously deep vee. *That should do the trick.* For her tiger's benefit she would play the dutiful girlfriend a little longer, hence the dinner invitation. All the while, she would be counting down the days until she could extract herself from this situation and leave the country for a while. 'Thank you, handsome, that's very kind of you,' she gushed. 'Come in.'

'I've got your favourite beer for you. Here you go,' she said while handing him a cold midneck of James Squire's One Fifty Lashes.

'Do you know the story behind the name?'

'You're the detective, you tell me,' she replied with an impish smile.

'Apparently it's based on a true story about one of the convicts who arrived with the first fleet in 1788. James Squire was discovered stealing ingredients from the stores to make the colony's first batch of beer. The magistrate sentenced him to one hundred and fifty lashes. Subsequently, he became a brewer and the rest is history. By all accounts he was a bit of a lad.'

'Not unlike your good self,' she said friskily.

'Something smells sensational, what have you been cooking up?'

'Well, it's winter and I had all day to cook something, so I went for a Moroccan chicken casserole with onion, garlic, chicken, carrot and capsicum. And I'm going to serve it with my own homemade couscous. How does that sound?'

'If it tastes as good as it smells it will be sensational. And I brought along a Leeuwin Estate Art Series Shiraz which should match nicely with your culinary creation.'

'Okay, pour the wine detective. Dinner is about to be served.' Jack did so while Danielle brought across the slow cooker and placed it on a placemat in the centre of the table. Then she returned with the couscous. 'Alright, dig in.'

'This is scrumptious, Danielle. So full of flavour. Well done.'

'Thank you, I'm just glad you like it. You don't think there's too much garlic?' she asked.

'Not at all, I love it.'

She wanted to, no needed to, find out where his investigation was up to and she knew he wouldn't volunteer any information. 'How did you go finding out who bashed that poor woman that was left to die in the wheelie bin? That was just horrible, Jack,' she said while projecting a look of genuine concern.

'We are still searching for the culprits, although I'm confident that we'll find out who bashed Lucie Chan eventually. It's only a matter of time.'

Danielle recognised the name. 'Oh, so her name was Lucie Chan?' she asked, feigning naivety. 'Is she okay?'

'I don't know as we haven't located her yet, unfortunately.'

'So, do you still think she was dealing drugs on behalf of the triads? Maybe that's why she got attacked,' she prompted, probing for a response. *Don't push it too far, Danielle.*

This was the second time this week that she had asked him about his work and his detective radar was kicking in. He began thinking about the guy on the stakeout parked outside the building and was wondering what the link could be. Maybe she was in some sort of trouble and he could help her through it. Had her involvement in the money laundering operation come back to haunt her? He considered telling her about the stakeout. No, he needed to find out more information first, so he would keep his thoughts to himself, for now. Jack had no idea why David Bedford's guy was staking out Danielle's apartment building, however, not for one minute believing in coincidences, it must have something to do with her. Unless her phone was bugged, no one would be aware that he was coming to dinner, so she was obviously the target of the stakeout. Not knowing the reason behind it, Jack couldn't afford to provide them any ammunition to potentially use against him, not until he found out what she was embroiled in. He wouldn't be staying the night.

'That was an enjoyable evening and dinner was excellent, gorgeous. Thank you.' Jack rose from the table, leant over and pecked her on the cheek. 'I'll see myself out.'

Something wasn't right. *He always stays, what's changed tonight?* Whatever was going on in his head, she couldn't afford him to be suspicious around her, so she had to move fast. 'I think you should stay, Jack.'

He propped at the door and turned around, only to see that Danielle had lowered the straps of her top down to her waist. She was a captivating woman and he became aroused at the sight of her half naked body. She sidled up to him, wrapped her arms around his waist and kissed him fervently. Jack found his mouth opening involuntarily. He could feel the warmth of her full, firm breasts through his shirt. Geez, he was sorely tempted. *Be strong, Jack,* he told himself.

'Sorry, not tonight, Danielle. I have an early start tomorrow.'

Jack exited the apartment building and headed back down Bridge Road to his car. The man in the i20 was still reading the paper. Jack thought about the numerous tedious stakeouts he himself had been a part of over the years and he empathised with the poor guy. He was in for a long night. Jack drove down Bridge Road towards the Western Distributor which would take him most of the way home. He called David Bedford from his mobile.

'You make a habit of late night calls.'

Jack had called him late one night back in March when they were both involved in the case of the Oceanics' missing Treasury Manager. 'Yeah, you're right, sorry, David.'

'What's up?'

Jack didn't know whether Bedford was aware of his relationship with Danielle, and he wasn't about to reveal it now without knowing the circumstances of whatever operation MPS were working. *Get something first, then give something.* 'I was just driving down Bridge Road in Glebe and spied one of your guys obviously undertaking a stakeout. My curiosity got the better of me, so here I am.'

'What makes you say it was one of my guys, Jack?'

'I ran the plate and the car's registered to your company.'

'I would have to talk to my Operations Manager about that as I don't get involved in the day to day activities. So, what are you curious about, Jack? Do you have an active investigation in that area?'

'No, I was just curious, that's all.'

'You're a detective, you don't become curious without a good reason.'

'Danielle Mortimer lives in Bridge Road, David.'

'Is that a statement or a question?'

This wasn't going anywhere while they both played cat and mouse with each other. 'Come on, David, you and I both know you're staking out her apartment.'

'Even if we were, I wouldn't discuss an ongoing investigation with an unrelated party. You would feel the same way.'

'I'm not necessarily an unrelated party, David, especially if this is linked to her involvement in the money laundering scandal back in March.' *And I'm her boyfriend.*

'If it was, then I would probably involve you, or at least give you a heads-up.'

'Okay, this is going nowhere.'

'You rang me, Jack, not the other way around.'

'Okay. You might want to tell your guy to turn the interior light on when he is pretending to read the paper at night. Goodnight, David.'

27. Sydney Daily News

Friday 22nd May

Julie-Anne had spent the rest of the week spinning her wheels when it came to her primary investigation. While she was waiting for David Bedford to submit his final report she utilised the time going back over her case notes from her earlier investigation into Chinese interference in Australia, Wie Ping Lie's activities and the money laundering operation involving Danielle Mortimer. It wasn't anything she didn't already know, but at the very least it was a useful activity to refresh her mind on the questionable occurrences. There wasn't much more she could learn and she was closing the file folder when the desk phone intercom buzzed. 'Hello,' she answered hesitantly.

'JA, it's me, Chris. I see you still haven't worked out the phone display yet,' he said while chuckling down the line.

'You're the only person who calls me on this gadget. The younger generation call my mobile, Chris,' she replied offering a giggle of her own. 'Sorry, that was cheeky of me.'

'Yeah, you're an absolute crack-up. David Bedford will be here at two o'clock with his report. Give me fifteen minutes with him and then come and join us.'

'That's great boss. I'll be there,' she replied excitedly.

'Hi David, how are you?' Julie-Anne asked cheerfully

as she breezed into her editor's office at precisely two fifteen.

'Julie-Anne, it's good to see you again and you're still alive.'

He was referencing her near miss earlier in the year when members of Wie's drug gang fired upon her and her car veered off the road and into a fence as a result. 'Haha. With everything being locked down due to the pandemic things have been quiet around here, so I have managed to avoid bumping into any unsavoury characters.'

'I'm pleased to hear that and you should keep it that way.'

'Okay, thanks, Dad. Now what have you got for me?'

Bedford glanced at Russell who nodded his assent. 'Okay, we've spent this week doing what you asked. Primarily, we have been tailing Ms Mortimer. The first couple of days she didn't venture out save for doing some shopping and having her hair done. That all changed on Wednesday. She was seen driving erratically and walking hurriedly, so I'm guessing something must have spooked her. Ms Mortimer drove to the CBD, parked illegally near the Golden Phoenix restaurant in Sussex Street, rushed across the road and stormed into the restaurant.'

'Bingo, here we go,' Julie-Anne exclaimed.

Bedford continued. 'A short while later she exited the establishment with a man we identified as Wie Ping Lie. They followed Sussex Street northwards and entered the Sussex Street Apartment Building a short time later.'

'That's the building the AFP raided back in March when they were searching for Li Jun and his accomplice after they tried to kill me.'

'The one and the same. Interestingly, Ms Mortimer swiped them into the building, so she obviously has her own access card. They came out approximately two hours later, he returning to the restaurant and she to her car. She drove directly to her apartment in Glebe.' Bedford slid a folder across the table to

Julie-Anne. She opened it to see numerous photos taken from various vantage points that showed Danielle and Wie leaving the restaurant, walking arm in arm along Sussex Street, entering the apartment building and finally exiting together. 'That would seem to confirm your suspicions, Julie-Anne.'

'Well, that at least provides conclusive proof that they are close to each other, nothing more. A camera inside the apartment would have been a bonus, but we'll have to use our imagination instead.' Julie-Anne laughed before realising what she had said. 'Sorry.'

'Before I move on to the next activity involving Ms Mortimer there was another interesting development. On two occasions Wie was seen entering and leaving the apartment building and the Golden Phoenix with a tall woman of Eurasian appearance.' Julie-Anne's heart skipped a beat when her first thought was that of her friend Sophie. 'That would suggest that Wie is not in an exclusive relationship with Ms Mortimer. We have identified that woman as a Lucie Chan who is a known drug dealer for Wie.'

Julie-Anne sighed with relief. 'I wonder if the women are aware of each other.

'I think you know the answer to that,' Russell suggested.

Bedford resumed. 'Moving onto yesterday. Jack Wagner, the AFP detective was seen entering Ms Mortimer's apartment building last evening.'

'Oh, shit,' she blurted out.

Russell knew Jack was Julie-Anne's ex and it seemed that he was out of luck again. 'That's too bad,' he said.

Julie-Anne regained her composure. 'More than you appreciate. Her apartment is owned by a Than Ping Lie whom I assume is a close relative of Wie's. Jack will be horrified.'

Bedford continued. 'He didn't stay the night, but rather he called me later in the evening. He spotted my guy conducting the surveillance. Jack obviously did a quick rego check, identified MPS as the owner of the vehicle and made the call. I've got photos if anyone wants to have a look. He, of course wanted to ascertain who engaged us. I didn't tell him, but given our history with the Daily News and Julie-Anne, it's reasonable to assume he will come to the correct conclusion.'

'Yes, he will,' she replied. 'He surely will.' Jack had to be told about Danielle's other relationship, but Julie-Anne needed to collect her thoughts first before broaching that acutely sensitive subject. She would sleep on it over the weekend. 'Anything else, David?'

'That's all there is, I'm afraid.'

'Okay. That at least confirms my suspicions. Thank you both.'

28. The Cottage - Balmain

Friday 22nd May

Melissa Wu had met Paul Gao at one of the Chinese Consul General's cocktail parties, that for some obscure reason, she still received invites to. He was a fetching man, with dark eyes, chiselled features, an athletic body and she was attracted to him. She had been focused on her work and having some Melissa time after her brief, but intense relationship with Julie-Anne earlier in the year. She wasn't looking to jump into another relationship anytime soon and had made that crystal clear to Paul very early on. They had agreed to just go with the flow and enjoy each other's company when time permitted, without the pressure of placing a label on their friendship.

It was a cool sixteen degrees outside, so Melissa had dressed accordingly. She didn't believe in dressing dark for winter. She was a woman of colour, so she wore her favourite tight fitting white jeans, matching Gianni Versace tee shirt and a black blazer with a floral print. 'You look fabulous, Melissa.' Paul had said when he picked her up at her townhouse. He requested they be seated in a cosy nook inside the restaurant rather than the courtyard. The head waiter had duly complied. Melissa was now sipping her espresso martini, and Paul was sipping a mulled wine to warm up. She loved The Cottage with its mismatched décor, vintage furniture, rustic farm equipment and kerosene lamps, all of which reminded her of the farmhouse of her cherished grandparents.

The waiter returned to their table with menus and the wine list. 'Do you want to graze through a few entrees?' Paul asked.

She looked over her menu at him. 'Not on your life. I'm having the crispy barramundi,' she said, rubbing her hands together. 'I haven't had barramundi for ever.'

He read out the description of the dish. 'Humptydoo Barramundi, pea and zucchini vignole, parsnip puree and garlic cream. I'm not sure I understand much of that wording at all. What's a Humptydoo?' he asked.

Melissa was laughing, more with him than at him. 'It's a small town in the Northern Territory not far from the Adelaide River where they have those huge jumping crocodiles.'

'Okay, but wouldn't the crocodiles eat all the barramundi?' *Now he was playing with her.*

'I've been to the Adelaide River and seen Brutus and Dominator, and judging by their size they both appear to be very healthy, so maybe you're correct.'

'Brutus and Dominator, are they wrestlers?'

'Stop that,' she admonished while smiling. 'Let's order. What are you having?'

'I'm having the Hunter Valley free-range pork belly.'

'Please tell me you know where that is at least?' she said, teasing him.

'What, pork belly?'

'Too funny. If you had a pork belly you wouldn't be here, Mr Emissary.'

The waiter arrived to take their food and wine order.

'Speaking of Mr Emissary, what are you working on at the moment?' she asked.

He couldn't tell Melissa what he had actually been tasked to undertake. 'The Consul General himself has graciously appointed me to his most important project. He wants me to lead the negotiations with the state government seeking the reinstatement of the Confucius Institute Program into their schools. It is a noble cause and I am honoured to undertake it.'

'That sounds challenging, especially given all the media publicity and sensitivity surrounding the program.'

'Yes, it is, however, I am equal to the task,' he said confidently.

By what she understood of his role, she considered it odd that he would be appointed to such a politically sensitive task. Surely this would be a task for an official at the Vice Consul level, at a minimum. 'I'm sure you are too, Paul.'

'Thank you. It is a privilege. There is something I would like to discuss with you that I think you will find exciting too.'

They hadn't known each other for long, so she had no idea what it could possibly be. Heaven forbid it was a marriage proposal. 'Go on,' she said hesitantly.

'The Consul General is seeking Chinese Australians to undertake a study tour of China and I would like to recommend you, Melissa.'

She leant forward, mouth agape and eyes widening in surprise. 'Wow, where did that come from?'

'Well, I think you appropriately fit the nomination criteria. You have experience in local government, you are a prominent lawyer in your local area, you manage your own business, you are intelligent and articulate, and of course, you are Chinese Australian. I think you are a most suitable candidate.'

'I don't know what to say. That sounds quite interesting, although I would need to have a lot more information before I could reach such a decision.'

He was taken aback by her response. 'I am surprised. I thought you would be honoured to be offered such an opportunity, Melissa.'

'I am, but I have a busy law practice to manage and clients

that rely on me to support them in their times of need. I can't just turn my back on them without making alternative arrangements. Plus I would need more information about the content of the study tour, who is sponsoring it, the timing, expectations, etcetera, etcetera.'

'The study tour is a fantastic opportunity for young professionals like yourself to learn more about our culture, the modern Chinese economy, the amazing infrastructure we are building, our world leading technologies, our booming manufacturing industries and how our ecommerce businesses are leading the world.'

'Nice speech, Paul. You should go into marketing or promotions.' She changed the subject. 'How is your pork belly?'

'Tender and succulent, and your barramundi?'

'It's just as it should be, crispy on the outside and mouth-watering on the inside. I'm glad Brutus and Dominator missed this guy.'

'And I forgot to mention how funny you are, Melissa.'

'Now, back to your special project. Did I tell you that my friend, Julie-Anne was investigating the role of the Confucius Institute Program in New South Wales as part of her wider investigation into Chinese influence in Australia?'

He was trying to remain calm, but he felt his face flush, albeit slightly. He was incensed that anyone should seek to impugn the good name of the mother country. 'Yes, you did,' he said too quickly. A thought occurred to him. 'Why don't we have dinner with Julie-Anne? You talk about her frequently, quite affectionately at that, and I've never met her. She sounds like an interesting woman. What do you think?'

That came out of nowhere. Given they were now on opposite sides of the China influence debate, that was the last thing she expected from him. Melissa had mentioned Julie-Anne numerous times in passing conversation, so maybe it wasn't so unusual after all. And it would be lovely to see her friend again. She missed Julie-Anne. 'Okay, I'll give her a call and see whether she's available.'

'What about you, Melissa? What have you been working on?'

'My latest project is an interesting class action. A major big box retailer has been underpaying their staff. That's disgraceful corporate behaviour really, especially given the state of the art IT systems they have in place. The claimants apparently heard about another successful action I undertook a while ago and contacted me out of the blue. And I may have another one on the horizon too.'

'Two class actions, that's impressive. Good for you.' He was being polite. Privately, he recoiled at the very notion of class actions. They would never be tolerated in his country. 'What does out of the blue mean?' he asked, trying to sound engaged.

'A bolt out of the blue, it's like a sudden or unexpected event, something like a thunderstorm coming out of a clear blue sky. That's the best analogy I can provide, Paul.'

'Okay, I have my own bolt out of the blue. Why don't we get out of here and go make our own thunderstorm, Melissa?'

'That's almost funny. Come on, let's go,' she replied. They rose from the table, she looped his arm, and led him away.

29. Sussex Street Apartments

Saturday 23rd May

At five o'clock in the morning the two specially equipped Toyota V8 Land Cruisers made their way down a deserted Liverpool Street heading for the Sussex Street Apartments, just as they had two months earlier. The same SRG team headed by Oliver Campbell, and also with Jack and Michael Sanderson in tow again, alighted from the vehicles. Jack recognised one of the officers, Stephenson from their earlier raid and was pleased to see he had fully recovered from his gunshot wounds.

'Off you go, Michael,' Campbell directed. 'Remember, you've only got thirty seconds head start. The rest of you grab your weapons out of the back and we'll head in.' All five members of the SRG team were now carrying light mounted Heckler & Koch G36 assault rifles fitted with silencers. The team made their way around the Liverpool Street corner into Sussex Street. Jack had his own Glock out and pointed down at a forty five degree angle in a two-fisted grip. The team didn't anticipate armed resistance on this occasion, but they were prepared for that eventuality. As they entered the apartment building foyer Sanderson handed two swipe cards to Campbell and then removed the night manager to the back office. Campbell led his team to the elevators. The team exited the elevator on the fourteenth floor and made their way silently down the carpeted corridor to Apartment 1419. Campbell led the way with the four SRG officers in formation behind him and Jack bringing up the rear. As was previously planned, two officers took up position outside Apartment 1417. This was the apartment that they had raided back in March and was also owned by Than Ping Lie.

The remaining two officers took up a position to the right and left of the target's entry door. They weren't searching for armed assailants this time, so the battering ram wasn't required. Campbell knocked firmly on the door. After ten seconds or so he knocked again, more forcefully this time. Eventually he saw the peephole darken; someone was looking back at them. 'Okay, here we go, guys.' Nothing happened. The door remained closed. Campbell gave his accompanying two officers the thumbs up indicating they were about to enter. The SRG officers butted their assault rifles into their shoulders and then raised them into the horizontal position. Campbell swiped the access card and stepped back allowing his officers to barge into the entry hall. They were shouting "armed police stay where you are, do not move" as they moved deeper into the apartment. Campbell followed them in and called for Jack. He entered the hallway and made his way cautiously through to the living room. He was surprised to see Lucie Chan calmly reclining on a sofa with her feet resting on a coffee table. She was dressed only in a silky floral printed nightshirt that rode high up on her thighs. She was in her late twenties with smooth caramel coloured skin, shiny black hair and dark, almond shaped eyes. She was an attractive woman.

'Lucie Chan, my name is Detective Jack Wagner and we have a legally issued search warrant for these premises which we intend to execute.' He handed her a copy of the warrant. 'Do you understand, Miss Chan?' She ignored him and tossed the warrant on the coffee table. The SRG officers had searched the rooms and confirmed she was the only occupant. 'Is there anyone else here, Miss Chan?'

'Does it look like it?' she snarled.

Just then the two officers who had been guarding Apartment 1417 marched into the room with their hands firmly gripping another man by his biceps. He was of Asian descent, quite tall, possessed an athletic physique and was dressed only in boxer shorts. 'Where did you find him, Forster?'

'He dashed out of 1417 and the poor bugger ran straight into us.'

'Aah, Lucie, your lover was about to do a runner and leave you behind. Nice guy,' said Jack, goading her.

'Fuck you,' she said angrily.

Jack had a thought and he turned to Campbell. 'Did your boys notice any adjoining doors?' Campbell had his guys recheck the bedrooms.

'Sir.' Jack heard one of the officers call out and he followed Campbell into the second bedroom. The officers had found another doorway hidden at the back of built-in wardrobe.

'How did you know about that, Jack?' Campbell asked, intrigued.

'Lucie here is underdressed, even for this time of the morning and she doesn't have any crustiness in her eyes. They were sleeping together, Oliver. The pause at the door was Lucie Chan using that brief window of time to warn her friend here and he cleared out through the hidden doorway.'

'Why would he do that if he had nothing to fear? Do you know his identity, Jack?'

'Not for certain, but I have a good idea though.' Jack remembered the description Sam Bourdain had provided of his assailant and this guy closely fitted his verbal identikit. 'My guess is that these two are more worried about Wie Ping Lie finding them together than us. I think this guy's her handler and Wie might not be too pleased at them sleeping together.'

There were two door swipes laying on the coffee table and Jack could see a filmy covering on the glass top. He knew what he was looking at. They had obviously done lines of coke together before doing whatever it was they did next. Campbell had seen it too and nodded in acknowledgment.

'Okay guys, are we done?' Campbell called out.

'Good to go, sir.'

'Stephenson, make sure we have all their tablets, mobiles, wallets and her handbag. And did we find any weapons?'

'No sir, none at all.'

'Miss Chan, you need to accompany us to AFP Headquarters to answer some questions,' Jack ordered.

'I'm not going anywhere with you,' she blurted out. Jack stepped forward and attempted to grab her arm. 'Keep your hands off of me.'

Stephenson stepped forward and reached for her other arm.

'Okay, okay, let me dress.'

Campbell smiled. 'Do you want to do the honours, Jack?'

'He not coming with me,' she insisted.

'Come on Lucie, you can collect some clothes from your bedroom and change in the bathroom.' Jack grabbed her by the arm, but she shrugged him off. She rose from the sofa and he watched her body unfold to its full height. She should have been a model with that figure, especially with those long legs. He figured there must be more money to be made running drugs for Wie than modelling. He tried to imagine her tall body stuffed into the wheelie bin. *That couldn't have been much fun.*

'I have some questions for her friend, so he's coming with us too, Oliver.'

30. AFP Headquarters

Saturday 23rd May

John Robertson, the AFP's Deputy Commissioner met Jack, Sanderson and the SRG team in the basement carpark. 'Jack, we've got a full house today. I've booked Interview 1 and 2 for you, and remember, we can legally only hold your two suspects for twenty four hours without a court issued extension.'

'Let's hope that's enough for us to get some traction with our investigation, boss. Oliver, put the feisty Miss Chan in IV1 and Mr Boxer Shorts can cool his heels in IV2.'

'Okay, Jack. Then I'm heading upstairs to draft my report if you finished with us down here.'

'Yeah, we're all good thanks. I appreciate the help of you and your guys this morning.'

'It's what we do.' Campbell patted Jack on the shoulder as he and his men made their way to the elevators.

'Okay, Michael—'

'Hang on a minute Jack. I've just had a call from Day Street. It seems that your friends Amir and Jasar have had some misfortune. They're apparently all banged up and are currently residing at St Vincent's. The hospital thinks that there could be a serious threat to their ongoing health or safety, so they reported their admission to the Surry Hills police. They entered the information into COPS and my guys at Day Street picked it up. I am having the incident report sent to our mobiles now.'

'Okay, let's go pay them a visit first, shall we?'

Sanderson found a park on Victoria Street and the two detectives made their way into the reception area of St Vincent's Hospital. They presented themselves at the nurses station and produced their credentials. The nurse in charge was unmoved by their attendance. Given this was one of the country's busiest hospitals, Sanderson guessed this was business as usual for her. Eventually she acknowledged their presence. 'What can I do for you, officers?' she asked, while exhaling exaggeratedly. Sanderson stated the nature of their visit and they were advised that the two men had been moved from the ED to the HDU. They were escorted down the sterile corridor and into the elevator that would take them to the High Dependency Unit. Sanderson and Jack badged the two uniformed officers who were standing guard outside two adjacent cubicles. A doctor in a traditional lab coat appeared to be taking the vital signs of the first of the men. Jack picked up the chart at the foot of the bed and read the name Amir Abboud.

Sanderson went to the cubicle next door and did the same. 'I've got Jasar Khoury here, Jack.'

'Yeah, I guessed as much. What's happened to him, a gunshot wound to the knee?'

'You got it, buddy and I assume Amir there has the same.'

'Oh, yeah. We've got a matching pair.'

Sanderson chuckled. 'A matching pair of criminal geniuses that would be.'

'Doctor, I am Detective Jack Wagner from the AFP and I need to ask your patient here a few questions. Can I speak with you first, though?'

'Give me a minute and I'll be with you, detective.'

A moment later the doctor grasped Jack's arm and ushered him out into the ward proper. 'What would you like to know?'

'I won't take much of your valuable time, doctor. I just need to know the nature of their injuries, when they were admitted and have they mentioned how they sustained their injuries.'

'Okay. Both men arrived in the early hours two days ago suffering from gunshot wounds to the knee. The bullets have punched straight through the kneecap and exited via the popliteal fossa, completely shattering their bones and devastating the structure of the leg. The joints that connect the femur to the shin would have disintegrated and they both would have collapsed immediately. The kneecap cannot be perfectly restored, and even after intense reconstruction surgery and a concentrated bout of rehab and physio, they are not likely to walk anytime soon, if ever.'

'Have either of them provided any information related to the shootings?'

'Not a single word.'

'Okay, thanks for your time, doctor. Can we speak to them now?'

'Sure, but keep it reasonably brief please.'

Jack walked back into Amir Abboud's cubicle.

'Amir, good morning. I am Detective Jack Wagner from the Australian Federal Police. I have some questions for you relating to the cause of your injuries.'

Abboud sneered back at Jack. 'Piss off.'

'That's funny, Amir. You're the one who should be pissed off, letting yourself get ambushed in a back alley by a couple of chinks.' Jack was thinking back to his interview with Sam Bourdain. His description of his attacker matched that of Lucie Chan's minder or boyfriend that Jack had detained earlier this morning. Amir's expression subtly change in acknowledgement. 'Aah, I see that rings a bell with you, Amir. You see, my partner and I have quickly pieced this whole thing together. Do you want to tell me your version of events?'

'Telhas teeze.'

'I can only imagine what that pearl of brilliance must mean. I'm guessing it wasn't very complimentary. Shall we start again?'

'I told you before, piss off.'

'Aah, you're bilingual. Your mother must be so proud of your language skills, Amir,' Jack said sarcastically as he pressed down on Amir's knee bandage. Amir screamed as the excruciating pain shot up his leg.

'Is everything okay, Jack?' Sanderson called out from the adjacent cubicle.

'Yeah, fine buddy. Amir was just doing some physiotherapy exercises.'

Sanderson peered around the curtain and saw the agonising expression on Amir's face. 'Can we step outside, Jack?'

'Of course, this is your investigation after all.'

'Jasar has given me a description of their attackers and one of them sounds awfully like our friend from this morning. While we're in the vicinity, I'm thinking we could take a drive to Double Bay and check out the crime scene. The incident report didn't provide a lot of useful information, so I guess the uniformed boys and local detectives weren't too concerned about a couple of drug dealers being kneecapped.'

Jack eyed him dubiously. 'I like your idea of in the vicinity, it's miles away, Michael.'

'Don't exaggerate, we'll go via the back streets and be there in ten minutes.'

Before they left the emergency ward Sanderson spoke to the uniformed officers guarding the two men. 'These guys are to have no contact with anyone other than hospital staff, no phone calls and certainly no visitors until you hear the opposite from me. Is that clear?' The officers nodded obligingly.

'Alright, Jack, the incident report said our two guys were found in dumpsters so that's what we're looking for as a starter.'

'Here we go. Halfway down the laneway on the left there's a collection of wheelie bins and dumpsters,' Jack said as he pointed through the windscreen.

The two detectives exited the car and approached the waste receptacles. All the wheelie bins and dumpsters were locked and neatly lined up behind the Gilded Nugget Hotel. 'Do you have bolt cutters in your car, Michael?'

Sanderson was looking over Jack's shoulder. 'I don't think we're going to need them, buddy. Check that out behind you.' Jack turned around then tilted his head upwards. There was a CCTV camera bolted to a neighbouring building and it was positioned facing the receptacles. 'They must have seriously expensive rubbish if they've needed to install a camera here.'

'Well, Sanderson, we are in Double Baaayyy, my good man,' Jack replied, trying to sound like an upper-class toff.

'Alright you comedian, let's go talk to the manager of this fine establishment, shall we old chap?'

Half an hour later they were camped in the hotel manager's office scanning through video footage from the previous Wednesday evening and Thursday morning. 'The two guys were found at twelve fifteen on Thursday morning, so we should work back from there, Jack.'

Jack asked the manager how to speed up the video footage. 'Eight times normal speed should be fine,' he said confidently. 'This had to have occurred between sunset and the time the guys were found, Michael, so at eight times normal speed, this should only take us an hour at the most.'

The two detectives sat quietly facing the hotel manager's desktop screen watching the reversing footage and hoping they wouldn't miss the crucial moment. 'My eyes are blurring and I'll need a break soon, Jack.'

Jack was looking at the clock on the screen rapidly reversing. 'We've only been at it for thirty minutes and are back to nine o'clock already, so by my reckoning we should be getting close to the incident, assuming it's been captured by this camera.'

No sooner had Sanderson sat down at the back of the room when Jack called him back. 'Here you go Michael, check this out.' Jack stopped the video and waited for Sanderson to re-join him. He then cued up the video and played it at normal speed. It showed two men standing with their backs to the camera. They were talking to two young woman, one of whom had hidden something up her short skirt. *That old trick.* The women turned and walked away from their dealers, then the men moved away as well, walking closer to the camera. 'That's Amir and Jasar.' They were heading towards the only vehicle in camera shot. Simultaneously, two more men came into the scene, both with their backs to the CCTV camera.

The two new arrivals stepped forward, positioned themselves next to the vehicle, withdrew pistols from their jeans and aimed them at the men. Jack and Michael watched as the two drug dealers leant up against the wall with pistols pointed at them. All four men were now side-on to the camera, but neither Jack nor Sanderson could make out the features of the new arrivals clearly. Then after a brief scuffle the two drug dealers were shoved across to a dumpster where one of them was beaten repeatedly with a thick pole. Jack was surprised to see Amir and Jasar then lift themselves up onto the rim, swing their legs over and hesitantly lower themselves into the dumpster. He and Sanderson watched in stunned silence as one of the new arrivals reached into the dumpster and fired into it. He had obviously shot both men. The second man closed the lid and placed a padlock on the dumpster. The new arrivals then turned and calmly walked towards the camera. Jack discerned a smug expression on the taller gunmen's face. He also knew who he was looking at.

'Shit, Michael, this is definitely payback for Lucie Chan's attack,' Jack said resolutely. 'That's our man, Yong.'

'Oh, yeah, buddy, nothing surer.'

The detectives arranged for the hotel manager to download the footage onto a USB drive and then returned to AFP Headquarters.

31. AFP Headquarters

Saturday 23rd May

'Let's have a look in their belongings and see what we've got, Jack'. The two detectives were back on the tenth floor of AFP Headquarters planning their next move. Sanderson opened the first of two clear plastic bags. 'There's not much here that's useful and we can't access their mobiles without a warrant. I do have their driver's licences though. She's definitely Lucie Chan and his name is Wang Yong.'

'Now that we have that CCTV footage we might be successful in obtaining a warrant for their mobiles. Yong's at least.'

'Let's hope you're right. I'll write up an application and get it submitted by my COD, Jack.'

'Is there a set of car keys in there somewhere?'

Sanderson saw the stylised H on the remote. 'Yeah. A set for a Honda of some unknown model.'

'I'll bet that's Lucie Chan's Honda CRV. Can your guys at Day Street run a vehicle registration search for both Yong and Lucie Chan? Then we also should apply for a warrant for either or both vehicles, but particularly the Honda.'

'Okay, I'll get the guys onto that too.'

'Alright, Michael. Let's go see what these two have got

to say for themselves. I'll take Wang Yong if you're happy to interview Lucie Chan.'

'Lucie Chan, I am Detective Michael Sanderson and I have few questions for you. Just so you understand your basic rights, you have the right to silence, you can refuse to answer my questions or decline a record of interview. You can answer my questions by saying, "no comment," and your silence does not mean you are guilty. Do you understand, Miss Chan?'

Lucie Chan had lived and studied in Sydney for many years and consequently spoke English fluently. She would, however, play the dumb immigrant and revert to clipped speech. 'Yes, now you hurry up, I have many things to do,' she demanded.

'Miss Chan, can you tell me where you were on the evening of Friday 15th and the morning of Saturday 16th of this month?'

'How I remember this from long ago?'

'Come on, it's only a week ago.'

'I no remember.'

'Then let me refresh your memory.' Sanderson nudged an A4 sized photo across the table. He discerned a slight look of acknowledgement on her face. 'That is your vehicle turning into York Road in Queens Park at five fifteen on the fifteenth of this month. You can clearly see your face. Where were you going?' She didn't respond.

'Let me fill in the gaps for you then. You drove down York Road, turned left into Birrell Street and then right into Birrell Lane and stopped behind the house at 19 Ashton Street.'

'You tell boring story.'

'After that you were bashed by the local drug dealers and left to die. I guess they didn't take too kindly to you encroaching on their territory. I see you still have a slight bruise on your face.'

'I fall over.'

'Of course you did. Look, Lucie, we have a witness who can

place you at the scene at five thirty the following morning and we know the identity of your client.'

She smiled at the revenge that Yong had exacted in her honour on that arsehole Bourdain. 'He wery unrucky man.'

'And who attacked you as well. In fact, your assailants are in hospital after being attacked themselves. But, you knew that already.' Sanderson saw a self-satisfied smile wash across her face.

'They wery unrucky too.'

'Lucie, one of your customers has made a statement confirming you were selling them illicit drugs,' he said, tampering with the truth. 'You were dealing drugs in the area and when I interrogate your mobile phone I bet I will find more evidence to corroborate their statement. Then I will charge you with trafficking a commercial quantity of an illegal drug.' Sanderson paused. Chan remained impassive. 'You are a smarter woman than you are making out with your contrived, clipped vocabulary. You know it's not you I want, but your boss. Make a statement against Wie Ping Lie and we might be able to make your impending charges simply disappear.' It was a stretch, but he had to try it on. 'And what do you think Wie will do when he finds out you are sleeping with your minder?' He paused and gave her time to consider this. 'Do you wish to make a statement or not?'

She sniggered. 'You are wery funny man.'

'You won't be laughing when we charge your boyfriend for attempted murder. He will go to prison for a long time. Who will protect you from the Lebo's then? Your boyfriend escalated the situation when he shot Amir and Jasar, so it stands to reason they will respond in kind. They will come after you and bruises to your pretty face will be the least of your worries then. Next time they will kill you.' Her smug expression was fading fast, so he continued to take advantage of what he hoped was her softening attitude.

'You can end this drug war before it ramps up and gets out of control. It's up to you, Lucie.' Sanderson pleaded as he held his arms out like a preacher. He knew from one of the numerous detective training courses he had undertaken that this gesture portrayed a constructive attitude and projected sincerity and trustworthiness. He was counting on it now. 'Do you wish to make a statement or not?' he repeated. She sniggered again. Back to the hard-arse Lucie.

Sanderson needed something out of this interview and reverted to Plan B. 'Okay, how about this then? What if you provide a statement implicating Amir and Jasar in the attack on you and I will ignore the commercial trafficking charge?'

Chan smiled patronisingly. 'You don't have sufficient evidence to charge me with any crime, detective, and I am not providing you with a statement. So, if you don't have any further questions for me I wish to leave,' she replied articulately.

She was correct. 'Get out of here, Lucie. I hope the next time I see you it's not in the morgue.'

'Well at least we know why you were so eager to escape your apartment and leave your girlfriend behind this morning, Yong,' Jack said smugly. The Triad enforcer looked up from his handcuffed and chained hands at the sound of his name.

'Yes, we know who you are and what you've been up to.'

'Fuck you,' he said angrily.

'That's what your girlfriend said, however she's got a better chance than you, buddy,' Jack replied, grinning at him.

'Maybe you not laugh so much if I fuck your girlfriend too.' Yong gave Jack a telling smile.

Jack accepted the insult as false bravado aimed to unsettle him. 'You're such a tough guy. Some minder you are letting your woman get bashed and left to die like that.'

'You don't know anything.'

'Aah, but I do. You see, Yong, if you'd bothered to check the area in the laneway before you started popping unarmed men, you might have noticed the CCTV camera high up on the adjacent wall. How do you like that for starters, smart mouth?'

'I have no idea what you are talking about.'

'Yong, Yong,' Jack said feigning exasperation. 'The Gilded Nugget Hotel has a camera in Kiaora Lane positioned above the dumpsters behind the hotel. Is this ringing alarm bells for you yet?'

'I don't know what you are talking about.'

'You sound like a broken record.' Jack took out an A4 sheet of paper and slid it across the table. 'Now do you get it, smart guy?' Yong was looking at a grainy photo of himself walking away from the scene in Kiaora Lane.

'That not me.'

A wily defence lawyer could plant enough seeds of doubt about the authenticity or integrity of the original video and that might be enough to sway the mind of a judge or jury. Jack needed more corroborating evidence.

'Oh, but I think it is and when I obtain a warrant to search your vehicle what do you think I will find? I'll bet there will be a long object in there and I reckon my FSG guys will find some embedded fibres that will be a match to your victims clothing.' Yong was maintaining his disinterested expression. 'Still not convinced, hey? The second task for the FSG guys will be to fingerprint the dumpster. You see genius, when you reached in to shoot the two victims you gripped the lip of the dumpster for leverage. That was a rookie mistake.'

'That not me.'

'Well, we'll soon find out won't we. In the meantime we are going to detain you without charge for twenty four hours. If we need to we can obtain a Detention Order from a court for an extension of another twenty four hours. We will continue to do that until you provide the answers I want or until the test results come back. It's entirely up to you. Is that clear?' Yong remained silent. 'Enjoy your stay.'

32. Wie's Penthouse

Monday 25th May

Wie was staring vacantly out the window at the Chinese Garden of Friendship in Darling Harbour while contemplating the increasing scrutiny that his business was attracting from the authorities. The electronic door mechanism clicked and he looked around to see Danielle walk into the penthouse.

'How come you're not having dinner at the restaurant, Hǔ?'

He liked it when she addressed him using the Chinese word for tiger. It displayed the appropriate respect for a man of his standing. 'It is becoming too unsafe for me to go out in public now, so I will eat here for a while.' Wie said while picking at his now cold steamed vegetables.

'I understand you being cautious, but you can't stay here forever. Have you thought any more about us getting away from all of this and just lying on the beach somewhere until this blows over?'

'It is not possible at this time, there is much still to be done.'

'Alright,' she said reluctantly. 'What can I do to help you?'

'What you can do for me is to find out what that detective knows about my business. You haven't told me anything new lately. I am blind to his investigation.'

'He came to my place for dinner last week, but for the first time he didn't stay the night. That wasn't like him, so he must becoming suspicious if that's the case.'

'Yes, I agree. Any man would want to spend the night with you. I can't have him poking around in my business, so you will have to be more persuasive next time. Do you understand, Nǚrén?' he demanded. 'Very persuasive.'

Danielle knew exactly what he meant. 'Okay, I know what I have to do, though I'm not happy about it at all.'

'I don't care. This is an important task for you to undertake for me, and for us.'

'I think someone has been watching my apartment too.'

'La shi,' he blurted out angrily. 'How do you know this?'

'I spotted a man sitting in a car outside my apartment for three consecutive nights last week. He just sits there reading the newspaper for hours at a time. Who reads the paper anymore, and at night in a car, no less?'

'Did you get the car's registration number?'

'Yes, I wrote it down just in case.' She scrolled to the Notes app on her iPhone and read out the registration.

'I will find out who is watching you.' He rang a contact on his mobile phone. 'Nǐ néng bāng wǒ zhǎo gè qìchē dēngjì ma?'

'Nǐ jǐnkuài zuò'

'Who did you call and what did you say?'

'I have a contact who can tell me who is spying on you.'

'Really, you can do that,' she said, surprised.

Wie's mobile rang moments later. 'Nà hěn kuài. Nǐ fāxiànle shénme?'

'Xièxiè,' Wie said by way of thanks and disconnected the call.

'What is it, Hǔ?'

'The car is owned by MPS Security. That is the same company that was protecting the Granger woman when she was interfering in my business earlier this year.'

'Jack has told me before that he doesn't believe in coincidences and I realise why now. I am being watched. This is not good.'

'No, it is not. The Granger woman is having you watched at the same time that Wagner has arrested Yong and Lucie. They must be working together again. Maybe you are correct about leaving this city for a while.'

'What, Lucie and Yong have both been arrested. When were you going to tell me about that?'

His nostrils flared. 'You don't need to know everything about my business,' he snorted.

Danielle felt her cheeks flushing in anger. 'Are you damn well kidding? I have given up two months of my life playing his dutiful girlfriend just so you can keep tabs on him and then you have the nerve to speak to me like that.'

She was correct and he needed her more than ever now. He clasped her hands. 'I am sorry. With Lucie and Yong not being available I will need you to help me with some tasks. I am running out of people that I can trust.'

'You should have trusted Lucie anyway,' she said pointedly.

'Don't speak about her like that,' he replied, too defensively.

She had long wondered whether there was something more than an employer employee relationship between the two of them. Danielle knew Lucie was a loyal employee and was valued by him, but why was he extraordinarily protective of her? She didn't like what she was thinking. 'What do you propose to do about them? Can they be trusted to maintain their silence?' she asked.

'Yes. They were both well rewarded for their work and they knew the risks involved.'

'I hope you're correct, Hŭ. You think that they are both loyal to you, however, faced with a long stint in prison, you don't know how they will react. If they opt for survival then your own freedom will be at risk. Are you prepared for that?'

'They can both be trusted,' he insisted.

'Maybe you're right, but you should expedite moving the rest of your product and then we should leave here as soon as possible. While we still can.'

'Yes, we should, Nŭrén.'

Finally.

33. The Wild Rover

Monday 25th May

Jack was leaning on the bar sipping his namesake and Coke and wondering where JA was. They hadn't seen each other for over two months and had only spoken on the phone a few times in the interim. His detective mind was wondering why she was so eager to catch-up after all that time. Maybe it was simply due to the easing of the lockout restrictions. Now she was half an hour late.

Julie-Anne was taking her time getting ready for her catch-up with Jack. He would be disconsolate at what she would reveal tonight and she was dragging her feet as a result. Staring blankly into the bathroom mirror for the umpteenth time she wished it to be a bad dream that would somehow magically disappear. She was sad for him. You can't delay this forever, so you need to get moving girl, she told herself. She booked an Uber and took the stairs down to the street.

Fifteen long minutes later she strode into the bar and immediately spotted her ex ensconced at the bar itself. He rose from his stool to greet her. 'Interesting tee shirt, Jack,' she offered. He was wearing a tan leather jacket over a white, printed Nick Cave and the Bad Seeds tee shirt. Below the image of three guitars were the words FROM HER TO ETERNITY. *Talk about prophetic.* Of course it was the name of a studio album, but unfortunately it was also apt for what she was about to reveal.

'Yeah, I like it. How are you, JA?'

'I'm good thanks, especially now that dreadful lockdown has eased and life can get back to normal.' She greeted him with a peck on the cheek and sat on the adjoining stool. 'And you?'

'Likewise, it's great to be out and about again. What are you having?'

'Just my usual, thanks, Jack.'

'Still a Bellini?'

'You know me all too well.'

He shrugged, as if to say, well I should. 'So, what have you been up to?'

'Like the rest of Sydney, not a lot really. I had my first proper human interaction for two months a couple of weeks back when Sophie came to dinner.'

'Good for you. How is she?'

'Going a little stir crazy having been confined to mostly studying from home. At least she's still able to live the dream in Coogee and she's bodysurfing to her heart's content.'

'Good for her. What about you, JA? How have you been?'

'In a word, Jack, boring, but at least now I can get on with my job and start investigating again.'

'So, why the catch-up after so long?'

'Straight to the point, eh detective,' she replied.

'Well, we haven't seen each other for ages and then you call me out of the blue for a catch-up. I didn't get to be a detective for no reason and you know we are a suspicious breed by nature.'

'No, I guess you didn't, and yes you are,' she replied knowing him all too well. *Here we go, Julie-Anne, it's time.*

'Got me in one.' The barman slid the sparkling concoction across to her and that bought her a few precious seconds. 'Cheers, Jack.' Julie-Anne sipped her Bellini and then placed it on the bar before swivelling on her stool to face him. 'There *is* actually something I need to talk to you about.'

'Okay, that sounds ominous, go on.'

'You have to hear me out, so please don't interrupt me. Can you manage that?'

'I'll try.'

Julie-Anne paused for a moment and gathered her thoughts. She wanted to deliver the news as gently as she could, but even as well as she knew him, there was no easy way to break this to her ex. 'When we were having drinks on your balcony following that long lunch at The Boathouse, Sophie mentioned something to me. She thought that she recognised Danielle from somewhere, but couldn't place where.'

At the mention of Danielle's name Jack looked at her curiously, wondering where this conversation was heading.

'She said that on one of her escort dates with Li Qiang she went to lunch at the Golden Phoenix. As her and Li walked into the restaurant a young blond woman was leaving. Given the layout of the restaurant, Sophie figured that the woman had come from the direction of Wie Ping Lie's table.'

Jack's face reddened. 'I see where this is going now, JA. You're going to suggest to me that the woman was Danielle. Am I correct?'

'You promised to let me finish, Jack.'

'No, I didn't, I said I'll try,' he said, becoming agitated now.

'I'm going to continue. For obvious reasons I let it go when we were at your place and didn't think any more of it until Sophie came to dinner where the topic came up again.'

'And I wonder just who raised the topic,' he intimated cynically.

'You're not the only one who doesn't believe in coincidences, detective,' she responded tersely. 'I thought it was worth looking into, so I started my own investigation.'

Jack wheeled around on his barstool. 'You did what? You've been investigating my girlfriend. Christ, JA. Is this all about you and me? Are you jealous of me having a successful relationship with Danielle?' He was angry now.

Julie-Anne wasn't happy either given his obvious misguided insinuation about their past relationship. 'Don't be ridiculous, we had our fun, Jack, and then we both moved on.'

'Well, I have, but I'm not so sure about you, JA,' he said.

This wasn't going according to plan. She needed to push on and get through this. She took a deep breath and continued. 'I arranged for Danielle to be followed—'

Jack didn't allow her to finish. 'Geez, the hits just keep on coming.'

Keep calm, Julie-Anne. 'Look, I take no joy from sitting here and telling you this, Jack, but it has to be done. Neither am I seeking to make you unhappy, however, this is significant. I'm going to continue and if you interrupt me again, I'll just keep talking over you until you have heard the whole story,' she said stridently. 'Now, as I was about to say, I arranged for Danielle to be followed in an endeavour to ascertain whether there was any substance to Sophie's assertion. Like you, it's my job to investigate.'

Jack's mind went back to last Thursday night when he had spotted the stakeout outside Danielle's apartment and his subsequent conversation with Bedford. His ex-girlfriend had arranged for his current girlfriend to be watched. *Nice.*

'Anyway, it was confirmed to me that Danielle had lunch with Wie Ping Lie on Wednesday of last week and I have photos of her entering the Golden Phoenix restaurant confirming that.'

'She could have been having lunch with anyone,' he responded unconvincingly. 'And let me guess who was following her.'

'What do you mean by that?'

'I saw one of Bedford's guys parked outside her apartment last Thursday night. He was conspicuous by his amateurism.'

'Well, what did you expect? Of course I was going to engage Bedford as I trust him after he watched over me particularly well earlier in the year. I'm going to continue. The person who was tailing her on Wednesday went into the restaurant on the pretence of meeting someone for lunch. He sat at the bar for a plausible amount of time before leaving. He clearly saw Danielle seated at Wie's table.' Jack didn't bother to answer and Julie-Anne watched on as he stared forlornly into his drink.

'I'm sorry, Jack.'

He looked up from his bourbon. 'What else have you got?' he asked.

Julie-Anne didn't want to continue and had hoped that what she had told him was convincing enough. She really didn't want to elaborate further if she could avoid it. He was her friend after all. She reluctantly opened the Photos App on her mobile, clicked on a particular photo and handed the phone to Jack.

'Oh, shit.'

Julie-Anne watched helplessly as Jack's expression darkened and the colour drained from his face. She didn't speak. What could she say? The photo showed Wie Ping Lie and Danielle being all touchy feely as they entered the foyer of the Sussex Street Apartment Building.

'Do you know where this was taken, JA?'

'Unfortunately, I do.'

He felt sick in the stomach, but forced himself to speak. 'So do I. That's the building where we raided an apartment earlier in the year. You know the rest of the story.'

'You can scroll across for the rest of the photos if you really need to see them.'

He swiped right viewing numerous revealing and

confronting photos until he could look no more. 'What other joyous news do you have for me?'

Julie-Anne gently placed her hand on his arm. 'Haven't I caused you enough heartache for one night?' she asked gently.

'You may as well get it all out in the open. I'm sure I'll read about it somewhere very soon anyway.'

She let that cheap shot go through to the keeper. 'Well, there are a couple of things actually.' She paused for a moment, knowing her next revelation would be the deal breaker. 'Okay, while I was awaiting the results of the stakeout I undertook some research.' She paused and inhaled deeply. 'She doesn't have a brother, Jack. She is an only child.'

'Geez, the hits just keep on coming. Did I say that again?' he replied, sounding defeated.

'You do understand the implications of that, Jack. If that is correct then your DC, and maybe even the DPP, may want to revisit her involvement in the money laundering operation.'

'Yeah, that's the first thing I thought of. Christ. She only told me last week that the medication was working and her brother's heart function continues to improve. The whole thing's just one big lie.'

His hangdog facial expression was a window to his feelings, so she allowed him time to absorb her latest revelation. She turned to sip her second Bellini.

Out of nowhere, Jack spoke. 'I really liked her. She was a breath of fresh air, carefree and free spirited and just seemed happy to go with the flow without placing any demands on me.'

Julie-Anne picked up on the subtle inference. 'What, and I did?' she blurted out.

'Oh, JA, it's not about you, that wasn't what I meant at all; get over it,' he replied sharply.

She inhaled and exhaled slowly to calm herself. 'There's one more thing, Jack.' Given the way the evening had unfolded,

Julie-Anne may as well get everything out in the open. 'The apartment Danielle resides in is owned by Than Ping Lie.'

'Shit, I can just see the headlines now. "Detective seen walking into apartment owned by drug kingpins mother", or whatever she is. And I imagine Bedford's guy probably got photos of that too. Christ, JA, what have you done to me?'

Stay calm, Julie-Anne. 'I haven't done anything to you, Jack. I'm just doing my job,' she said quietly. She had hoped the evening wouldn't degenerate to this level, but it had always been a possibility, given her stark revelations and their previous history together. She sighed. 'Okay, I might leave you to your thoughts. I'm sure you've got a lot to think about. I'll check in on you tomorrow. I'm really sorry.' She went to kiss him on the cheek and understandably, he pulled away. Who could blame him? She had ruined his life as he knew it. 'Bye, Jack.' Julie-Anne rose from her stool and strode out of the bar.

34. Quay Restaurant

Monday 25th May

Ben Chandler had called Sophie on Saturday while he was walking along the shoreline of Brisbane Water in the heart of Woy Woy. She didn't want him to know that she had saved his number into her phone, so she had answered formally. "Sophie speaking".

Coincidentally, Sophie was walking along the boardwalk at Coogee Beach on her way up to the Bali Memorial. They chatted away merrily about nothing in particular and were enjoying the easy-going conversation. She wondered why he was walking alone and where his family was. As if on cue, he had opened up and explained that the wife was working in her business. He had added "as usual". And the boys were off bush-bashing on their trail bikes in the nearby national park.

State parliament wasn't in session during the coming week, but he had meetings booked, so he would be in town anyway. "Would you like to have dinner on Monday night?" He had asked. "I have managed to secure a booking at Quay down on the harbour?" Sophie was well aware that she shouldn't be having a non-agency booked appointment, yet she felt safe with, and trusted this man. Plus, she was attracted to him. "That sounds wonderful," she had replied, trying not to gush.

Ben had secured a table in the upstairs, circular dining room with its stunning views of the glittering harbour, the bridge, and of course, the opera house. The maître 'd escorted Sophie upstairs to a window table where Ben was waiting. 'Wow,' he blurted out, too loudly. He had made her feel momentarily self-conscious, but Sophie had dressed to impress tonight, so she would get over it. Wanting to appear sexy, yet stylish, she was wearing a body loving, one shoulder, black bodycon dress with a hip-high slit and lace insert. Her matching Jimmy Choo heels and black clutch completed the ensemble. She felt great. It was coolish outside, so she had brought her favourite lightweight black leather jacket that the maître 'd had kindly checked.

'Hello, Ben. It's nice to see you.'

'You too, Sophie. And you look stunning as always. I love the dress.'

The white jacketed maître 'd seated and napkinned her before handing them menus, and passing Ben the wine list. He poured them still water and left the table. 'Did I say that too loudly?' he asked.

She caught him glimpsing the split in her dress. *Well you picked the dress, girl.*

'No, you were fine and it's generous of you to say so. You look very stylish too. It's the first time I've seen you out of a suit.' He was wearing tailored navy trousers, a slim fit white shirt hung loosely and a light blue, linen weave, sports jacket.

They chatted away merrily for a few minutes before the waiter returned with the wine Ben had ordered. 'Have you decided on dinner, sir and madam?'

'Can you give us a few minutes please?'

'Certainly, sir.' The waiter poured the wine and silently removed himself.

'Here's to a wonderful evening.' Ben raised his glass and

clinked with Sophie. 'It's a Ten Minutes By Tractor chardonnay from the Mornington Peninsula. I hope you like it.'

'That's an interesting name. There just has to be a story behind it.'

'There is. Apparently the name was chosen after the owner's families met to discuss a name for their new winery. One of them described themselves as being about ten minutes by tractor away from the others, and the name duly stuck.'

'I love that.'

Ben explained to Sophie that the restaurant only had two dinner options. They were both degustation menus, one six course and the other eight.

'Gosh, I could never eat eight courses, so six will be fine thanks, Ben.'

He laughed generously. 'Wait until you see the size of the dishes and you might change your mind. The word morsel comes to mind.'

He was funny and she liked his company. A short time later the first course arrived. 'Okay, can you help me with a description for this?' she asked innocently while staring curiously at the stylishly presented dish.

'If I remember correctly the menu said it is Smoked Eel Cream with Seaweed and Ossetra. Do you know what Ossetra is, Sophie?'

She thought for a moment. 'I read somewhere it is the second most expensive caviar behind Beluga. How'd I do?' she asked sassily while giving him a cheeky pretend flutter of her eyelashes.

'That's my girl.' Her expression darkened slightly and he realised his faux pas. 'Sorry, that didn't come out right, it wasn't meant to sound possessive. My apologies.'

She smiled at him. 'Thank you for saying that. I'm not some card carrying women's liberationist that's hung-up on political correctness, but neither am I a wallflower.' He was attentively listening while looking longingly at her. 'Uh-oh, I'm on my soapbox again,' she said self-effacingly. 'Come down this minute, Sophie,' she said, pretending to scold herself.

'You are so funny.' He loved that this vivacious woman before him had strong moral values and opinions, and yet, could quickly turn to self-effacing humour.

'Okay, here we go,' she said as the next course was delivered. 'This is an easy one, so I'll let you have the honour, Ben.' She projected her mischievous smile again.

'You are just too magnanimous. Alright, it's Mud Crab.'

'Yay,' she said mockingly while clapping her hands. Other diners had heard the applause and heads were turning. 'Oops,' she said, placing her hand over her mouth.

'You're on a roll now. I think they liked your Flipper impersonation.' They laughed heartily together.

An hour later they had finished the dessert and were sipping their Botrytis Pinot Gris. 'Well, you made it, Sophie.'

'Made what, Ben?' she asked innocently.

'You managed to get through all six courses. Well done.'

'Haha, it wasn't hard. Julie-Anne's entrée was more filling than those six courses combined.'

'Who's Julie-Anne?'

'She's a good friend of mine and I had dinner at her place a couple of Fridays ago. Her entrée was a rockmelon bruschetta with goat's cheese and prosciutto and it was yum.'

'Sounds delicious. A mix of sweet and savoury.'

They finished their wine, he paid the check and they made their way down to street level. 'Let's go for a stroll around the harbour. What do you say, Sophie?'

'That's an excellent idea. Lead the way.' He held her leather jacket open while she wriggled into it. *A gentleman, no less.* Then they seamlessly linked hands and ambled along the forecourt of the Museum of Contemporary Art admiring the glittering sights of Sydney Harbour and the hustle and bustle of the ferries still shuffling in and out of their terminal. They continued along to the eastern end of the Circular Quay wharf and he paused. Having been there twice before she knew his hotel was only one hundred metres away up Phillip Street. She guessed that was why he had stopped. The moment of truth.

Ben gazed deeply into her eyes. 'I've had a wonderful evening, Sophie. You are a fascinating woman, and I have become fond of you. Would you like a nightcap?' he asked, somewhat apprehensively.

She knew full-well what he was suggesting and she had a quick decision to make. He was a married man and becoming involved with someone else's husband was something she abhorred and avoided. Ben had intimated that he and his wife led separate lives and she trusted him that that was the case. He had been a gentleman since they first met and surely he wouldn't be spending time with her if his homelife was bliss. *Decision time, girl.*

'That would be lovely, thanks, Ben.'

He beamed a smile and she thought about the kid in a candy store cliché. They held hands as they strolled up Phillip Street towards the International. As they passed the Justice and Police Museum a dishevelled, unkempt man stepped out from the shadows of a pitch-black alcove. 'You got a few dollars for the homeless, cobber?' the man asked.

Ben reached out with his arm and shepherded Sophie behind him. 'Of course. Take a step back if you would.'

'Why? Do I smell or somethin?'

'No, just step back.'

The man stepped back, Ben extracted his wallet and handed the man a twenty. 'There you go, now have a good night.'

As they continued arm in arm up Phillip Street Sophie asked, 'why were you insistent that he step back, Ben?'

'So he was out of reach of my wallet.'

Sophie laughed. 'A street smart politician. That's a first.'

Rounding the corner he paused at the hotel entrance and turned to face her. His piercing blue eyes were locked on hers and then he leaned forward and engaged her lips. She placed her hand gently on his cheek. After a moment he pulled away. 'Would you like that nightcap now, Flipper?'

Sophie tried to make the guttural clicking sound of a dolphin, but failed miserably.

'Ten points for effort. Come on, let's get you that nightcap,' he said as they linked arms and entered the foyer.

The man was seated at his desk and opening the app that was linked to the video camera. He clicked on the live play icon and checked that it was working as it should be. Now he waited. He had followed Chandler to that over the top, over-priced restaurant and waited across the forecourt by the harbour until Chandler's date had arrived. There she was again, the same woman. This was the third time they had been together and he hoped that he was correct about the third date rule. Now he needed to progress his plan. Once the woman had entered the restaurant he knew he had at least two hours to return home and get set-up for what would undoubtedly come to pass later that evening. It was now nine thirty, exactly two hours after the woman had entered the restaurant. The room was still silent, and empty. Where were they? *Nine forty five, ten o'clock, ten oh five.* Then he heard the electronic click and finally the heavy door of the man's hotel suite opened. 'Qiao.' Here they are at last.

Chandler held the door open as the woman walked into the room. He gestured to the sofa and she sat down. The man heard Chandler ask her what she wanted to drink and he was now pouring two glasses of champagne. He sat down next to the woman and they clinked glasses. They were chatting away, smiling and laughing constantly. Then the conversation subsided as Chandler gave the woman that primal look that desperate men do. Then he placed his glass on the coffee table, leant across, clasped the woman's chin and kissed her. Here we go, thought the man watching on his laptop. *Game time.* It was the only Americanism that he liked. The woman set down her own glass, shifted slightly on the sofa, placed her hand on his left leg and leaned into him. *'Come on, come on,'* the watching man implored. After their excessive smooching, the man was excited to see Chandler then slowly stand up, clasp the woman's hand and lead her across the suite and into the bedroom. The man hastily switched cameras in time to catch them fall onto the king size bed together. *Game time.*

35. Jack's Apartment Balmain

Tuesday 26th May

Jack was sitting in his dining nook, sipping his extra strong latte, wishing for some sunshine to soften the coolness of the morning. Normally he'd be out on the balcony, however today it was dark, dank and bucketing down. He had a well-deserved hangover after propping up the bar until the barman started packing up the stools around him; the message coming loud and clear. He would work from home today. The throbbing in his head wasn't helping him make sense of JA's revelations from the previous evening. How had he been so blindsided by Danielle's charm? It was the physical attraction that had him entranced initially, but it was her happy-go-lucky nature and carefree attitude that had kept him there. She never placed any demands on him and he could still lead his own life untethered. Now, he clearly realised why. She could lead her alternate life without scrutiny. He recalled her gleaming, naked body from the first time they had made love in the warm waters of that cute little bay near South Head. From that moment on he was hooked. Now, as he mentally walked back through the various occasions that they had spent together during their relationship, certain things became crystal clear to him. *A bit late now, Jack,* he admonished himself. He recalled that first night in the Bennelong Room when she flirted with him across the bar. Then she had invited him for a drink after work where she had looped her arms around his neck and pashed him on the dancefloor. All too easy. She had apparently made him for a detective early in the evening having astutely picked up on his supposedly innocent questioning about certain members of the Oceanic's Bennelong Room clientele. Then on another occasion they had lunch in Bondi when she began asking questions about what he was investigating. Observing the Oceanics' Security Manager, Jim Brennan's number pop-up on Jack's phone had obviously spooked her. Now he knew why. Later that afternoon at Icebergs, feigning playfulness, she had challenged him again about his investigation and had even mentioned Li Qiang and Tony Woodard. How had he not seen that for what it was? A clever interrogation seeking inside information. And then, although not appearing enthusiastic about attending The Boathouse lunch, she had turned up unannounced. What had changed her mind? Was she trying to find out more information about his or Julie-Anne's investigation from the assembled gathering? Later that night after she had suddenly left the afterparty, Jack had called her mobile and left a voicemail message. She texted back immediately. Why didn't she return his call instead? He was now wondering where she went for the remainder of that night. And what about her brother? Jack had bought Danielle's sob story about his supposed heart condition lock, stock and barrel. He was a detective and should have checked that out, irrespective of their relationship. And his DC would be furious at having been duped by that not so little untruth of hers. Then, more recently, there was the matter of that large bruise on her inner thigh. She had explained it at the time, but he had his doubts about the veracity of her explanation. As her boyfriend, if that's what he ever was, his first instinct was to confront her, however, that would now be counterproductive given his investigation into Wie Ping Lie's drug importation activities.

He was lost in his thoughts when the ringtone of his

mobile brought him back to reality. It was JA. Was he really up to talking to her now? Given she had brought all this unsavoury information to light he had little choice. He now felt a perverse obligation to her. 'Hi, JA.'

'Hello, Jack, how are you? she asked tentatively. 'Are you okay?'

'I'm sure you can well and truly imagine how I am feeling.'

'Yeah, I know and I'm very sorry. Do you want to talk?'

'Not really, but personally I should, and professionally I have to,' he replied matter-of-factly.

'Where would you like to start?'

'I have no idea, so maybe just walk me through your processes again since Sophie mentioned her suspicions to you. Some of it seems like a blur this morning.'

'I imagine it does.' Julie-Anne revealed what she knew about the whole sorry saga and the unfolding of the various revelations. 'As part of my investigation, I want to interview her, tell her what I have learned about her and see how she responds. Once I validate all my information I'll have enough to write a follow-up to my original story, and I have supporting photos for colour. It should be front page again.'

'You can't do that, JA.'

'Why not, it's my story and I sourced the information myself?' she replied incredulously.

'A few reasons. Firstly, she's not going to admit to anything that will incriminate her as she has nothing to gain from speaking to a reporter. Secondly, she will be afraid of repercussions from Wie Ping Lie if she does speak to you. And finally, I've told you before, you should be wary of Wie yourself. He won't be happy at all about you exposing his girlfriend, if that's what she is. And he will be even less joyous about you drawing unwanted attention to him and his illicit activities. Also, now that the lockdown has eased I have renewed my investigation into Wie's activities and

I have some leads I'm working on with the state police. If you publish he will undoubtedly go to ground.'

'Aah, there's the real reason. Your worried that your own investigation might be undermined. And by the way, I can take care of myself.'

'Just look where that cavalier attitude got you last time. You could have been killed by his guys.'

Julie-Anne momentarily recoiled at the memory, but brought herself back to the issue at hand. 'Jack, my loyalty is to my employer, not the AFP, nor the state police for that matter, and this story definitely falls into the public interest category.'

'I know that, JA, although at best, you will only have a postscript to your original story. You will potentially scuttle my investigation in the process and you may also miss out on a far bigger story yourself,' he said, doing some pleading of his own now.

'Unlike you, Jack, I'm open to suggestions,' she responded while absentmindedly holding her hands open in the 'give me something to work with' gesture. She realised he couldn't see her. *Durrr.*

'You want this to be a joint investigation, don't you?'

'Yes, there needs to be something tangible in it for me if I'm expected to sit on my story. You know how this works, Jack.'

Neither spoke and there was an uncomfortable silence on the call. It was obvious to both of them that they had reached a stalemate. Someone had to acquiesce.

Jack broke the silence. 'Alright. If you can hold your story for a few days I will give you an exclusive into the entire investigation when it is completed. And, JA, given your own investigation began with Sophie's suspicions, no one else should have the story anyway.'

'Okay, on one condition. I want to know what information you have already from your investigation into Wie, and no holding back, Jack,' she demanded.

He told her about the bashing of the woman found in the wheelie bin, the Honda CRV, traffic camera vision that placed Lucie Chan in the area at the time, her connection to Wie Ping Lie through the dial a dealer network, the retribution from Wie's men for Chan's bashing and their subsequent arrest of Wang Yong at the Sussex Street apartments.

'My god, that's the same building that Danielle was seen entering, Jack,' she replied excitedly.

'Yeah, thanks for reminding me.'

Julie-Anne knew Jack to be a good detective, and a proud one at that. As well as the sadness he was feeling he would be embarrassed at the professional situation he found himself in. 'Again, I'm sorry, Jack.'

'Thanks. We also have our suspicions about Than Ping Lie's involvement. Even more so after our chat last night.'

'Can you send me a photo of Lucie Chan and I'll have a snoop around, Jack? I promise I won't compromise your, oops, *our* investigation. And I'll be careful.'

'Yeah, alright and thanks for the chat, I appreciate it. JA, before you go,' he called out down the phone.

'I'm still here, what?'

'I'll set-up a group just for us on WhatsApp and send you an invite. It's encrypted so we can communicate securely on there.'

He must be concerned for her welfare if he was implementing that protocol. 'Okay, thanks, Jack.'

As he disconnected the call Jack recalled a comment Wang Yong made during his interview on Saturday. "Maybe you not laugh so much if I fuck your girlfriend too." *It all added up now.* Given Danielle was obviously Wie's girl, Yong wouldn't dare, but Jack still understood the meaning. That reminded Jack that his supposed girlfriend was coming to dinner tonight. *Shit.*

36. Bennelong Room

Tuesday 26th May

Julie-Anne disconnected the call, leaned back in her chair and thought about everything Jack had told her. Given all that was occurring in his investigation and the revelations her own scrutiny of Danielle's activities with Wie had uncovered, she wondered whether the woman was more deeply involved than either of them were aware. Was she really Jack's girlfriend and leading a double life with Wie, or vice versa. Maybe she really liked Jack, but Wie was offering her an introduction into another, more exciting and highly profitable world. She thought back to Danielle's involvement in the money laundering operation and how she had profited sizeably from that. If she really was with Wie, then Julie-Anne assumed there would need to be a monetary incentive involved. Or, could she just be a naïve young woman savouring the attention of two good-looking and dynamic men. *No, she's not naïve. She lied about her brother.* Julie-Anne had an idea and rang her friend and colleague Deb. Deborah Atkinson was the best known entertainment reporter in Sydney, was equally well connected, and if anyone could get Julie-Anne into the Bennelong room at the Oceanic Casino and Resort, then Deb surely could.

'Hi, Deb, how are you?'

'Yeah, I'm all good, better now this damn awful lockdown

has eased and people can get out and about again. Now I can get back to doing my job shining the light on the bold and the beautiful.'

'Good for you. I need some information on a story I'm researching and it involves the Bennelong Room at the casino.'

'Really, that sounds interesting. Anything in it for your favourite entertainment reporter?'

'No, not at all. Well, not yet anyway. Do you have any connections with the Bennelong Room by any chance?'

'You're onto something juicy again, aren't you?'

'Yes, I think so. It involves that woman your photographer snapped with Jack at that laneway bar in Pyrmont earlier this year.'

'The gorgeous young blonde?'

'You got it in one.'

'Okay, give me a few minutes, grab yourself a coffee and I'll call you back.'

'That was quick, Deb.' Julie-Anne hadn't even returned from the foyer cafe with her soy latte when her mobile rang.

'I know right. Your request is my command,' she said quoting the famous line from Aladdin. 'Alright, note this name and number down and make sure you tell them you are my friend. Don't mention that we are work colleagues and make sure you fly below the radar, if that's even possible with you,' she laughed.

'I'll do my best, Deb.'

'Sure you will. Anyway, how are you and Melissa going?' Deb had taken Julie-Anne to a cocktail party at the Chinese Consulate earlier in the year where she had met Melissa Wu.

'Things went off the rails one night when I had a few too many champagnes and started reminiscing about Jack. Melissa, understandably, decided a raincheck of our relationship was in order. I haven't seen her since and I miss her.'

'Oh, JA, that's so sad.'

'Thanks for your help and also your kind thoughts, Deb.'

Fly below the radar, really? Like everyone else in the country Julie-Anne had been in lockdown, so she wasn't going to miss this opportunity to glam up for the first time in two months. After all, she was going to the opulent Bennelong Room filled with so called high rollers. She rifled through her wardrobe until she found what she was after. *There you are.* She pulled out a silver sequined, sleeveless and strappy, mini evening dress. *Oh, yeah, girl.* She found her matching clutch and would complete the look with her favourite patent leather pumps.

That evening Julie-Anne rode the elevator up to the eighteenth floor of the casino and exited into a subtly lit, grand looking foyer of decorative marble, heavy burgundy velvet drapes and plush charcoal grey carpet. She strode confidently across the room to the reception area. 'Julie-Anne Granger, you should have my details,' she said while handing over her identification and offering her most engaging smile.

'Certainly, please come with me, Ms Granger. May I take your jacket?' She was ushered through the large mahogany doors and into the Bennelong Room proper. The stylishly dressed hostess gave her a tour of the facilities and explained the house rules of both room etiquette and gaming. 'If there's anything else I can do for you, Ms Granger, please let me know. I'll be at reception. In the meantime, enjoy your evening,' she gushed while offering her practiced smile.

Julie-Anne felt mildly uncomfortable walking through this predominantly male dominated domain of the wealthy. She was attracting unwanted glances from some of the portly Asian men at the gaming tables. *Should've kept your jacket on girl.* She steered away from the tables and made her way to the bar. Julie-Anne wasn't one of those women who wouldn't venture out unaccompanied, rather she was comfortable in her own skin and could handle herself in most situations. Having thought that, she was well aware what conclusions the men in the room would draw from a woman wearing a revealing mini dress sitting by herself at the bar of an opulent gaming room full of wealthy men. She was sipping her Bellini when she observed a tall, tanned, handsome man in a stylishly tailored business suit walking in her direction. She looked away while taking another sip. The man sat alongside her and ordered a drink.

Julie-Anne couldn't help herself. 'You do realise they have table service in here, right?' she said brazenly over her shoulder.

'Do they really? Well they kept that a well-guarded secret,' he replied, hamming it up.

'How can you be so obtuse?'

'Aah, I see you're a fan,' he replied.

Julie-Anne swivelled on her stool. 'How could you not be? It's a wonderful feelgood movie.'

'My favourite scene is when Red is walking along Zihuatanejo beach towards Andy Dufresne and their faces light up at the sight of each other.'

'That scene brings a tear to my eyes every time. Do you remember the last line in the film?' she asked.

'Now you're testing me. Let me think for a minute.' The man placed his thumb and index finger on his chin and stared at the ceiling, pretending to think. 'Okay, I think I've got it. "I hope the Pacific is as blue as it has been in my dreams". How'd I do Ms—?'

'Close, but no cigar. I hope the Pacific is as blue as it has been in my dreams, is correct. Then he adds "I hope". I'm Julie-Anne, pleased to meet you.'

'Very good, Julie-Anne. I'm Jordan Doherty and the pleasure's all mine.'

She was searching the room for the woman she wanted to

speak to. 'This really is the domain of the Asian high rollers. Until now it hadn't dawned on me just how important they are to the casino's business. You must be one of the few Caucasian men in the room.'

'I'm sure you're correct, however, if I may say so, you are definitely the most intriguing woman in this room.'

'You're funny. I'm one of only two or three women in the entire room so the odds are in my favour, Mr Doherty.'

'Would you like another Bellini, Julie-Anne?'

'Oh, that's awfully discerning of you. I'm guessing this is not your first Bellini rodeo.'

'Well, the peach colour is a definite giveaway.'

At that moment she spotted the woman she was looking for. A well-groomed, mid-forties woman conservatively dressed in a navy blue business suit was exiting an unmarked door in the back corner of the room. 'I have to go and speak with someone, Jordan. It was good to meet you.'

'Likewise, Madam Bellini.'

Julie-Anne smiled as she walked away.

'Hi, Michelle, how are you?'

'Good evening, ma'am. Do I know you?' the woman replied, guardedly.

'I'm Julie-Anne Granger, a friend of Jack Wagner's.' Michelle Ironside had been inadvertently caught up in the money laundering operation earlier in the year. She had even been kidnapped by those involved to prevent her from revealing what she had gleaned. The woman was understandably nervous at the mention of the investigating detective's name.

'Oh. How can I help you, Ms Granger?' the woman asked, maintaining her professional demeanour.

Julie-Anne could see the woman was being cautious. 'It's okay, Michelle, I was just hoping to bump into Danielle. I haven't seen her for ages,' she said feigning friendship for the deceitful young woman. 'I was in the vicinity, so I thought I would say hello to her.'

'Ms Granger, with respect, I doubt you just happened to be in the vicinity. This is an invitation only facility and you are definitely not a member,' Ironside replied curtly.

Julie-Anne felt her face flush with embarrassment. She had been too clever by halves and this woman had her measure.

'Anyway, Miss Mortimer no longer works here. She left the casino's employ back in March, if you must know.'

'I didn't realise. It's been so difficult to keep in touch with friends during these challenging times.'

'Yes it has. Ms Granger, you do actually add a touch of much needed glamour to the Bennelong Room, so feel free to enjoy the facilities for the remainder of the evening. I don't expect I will see you here again, though.' Michelle Ironside turned on her block heels and returned to her office.

37. Jack's Apartment Balmain

Tuesday 26th May

Given the torment swirling around in his mind Jack had completely forgotten that Danielle was coming to dinner this evening. He needed to develop a plan, but first he needed to lose the hangover and clear his head. It was a mild twenty degrees, so he dressed in a full tracksuit to work up a decent sweat while on his run. He would duck and weave around the winding streets that abutted the harbour until he reached Illoura Reserve on the foreshore itself. Then he would navigate heartbreak hill and run all the way up Darling Street through the heart of trendy Balmain to his apartment. That was a run of around six kilometres all-up and should be enough to restore his physical and mental equilibrium. And just long enough for him to do some planning as well. Now, twenty minutes later, calling into QE Foodstores he quickly gathered what he needed for dinner, loaded them into his backpack and then continued up the hill. Ten minutes and a torturous two kilometres later he arrived at his apartment building. His was sweating profusely and panting heavily, so he leaned against the facade, lifted his chin and breathed deeply. *That's what I needed.* After regaining his breath he swiped himself inside, took the stairs to his level and entered his apartment. Okay, time for Chef Jacques to go to work and for Detective Jack to do some thinking. He planned to cook a Chicken and Asian Veggie Stir-Fry to go with Danielle's favourite white wine, Pierro LTC. He normally bought the wine by the case, so at thirty five dollars a bottle he would save substantially on his alcohol purchases once she was out of his life. He was thinking about how hard he could push and prod Danielle for information without making her suspicious. Given how she handled herself on both sides of the money laundering operation, and then so easily played him for the past two months, she obviously wasn't someone to get too cute or clever with. He would have to adopt a subtle approach. And he needed to stay in control. Two hours later the building's exterior access system buzzed inside the apartment, breaking his train of thought. Jack walked across to his front door and depressed the door release button.

'You're kidding,' he blurted out as he opened his apartment door moments later. Danielle was wearing the same white sleeveless and backless short mini dress with a deep, scalloped neckline that she had worn on the night they met. He felt himself hardening already.

It was cool outside, but given what Danielle wanted to achieve tonight, she needed to get him off balance. The sight of her near naked body would do just that. She greeted him on the cheek and held up a shopping bag. 'I know you don't cook entrees, so I brought some sushi for us to start with.'

Jack went to the kitchen alcove and placed the sushi in the refrigerator. He turned around and Danielle was standing directly in front of him. Her leather jacket was laying on the floor and just like the previous occasion that they were together she had dropped her shoulder straps and was naked from the waist up.

She stepped forward, pushed him back against the refrigerator, leaned in and kissed him passionately. She slid her hand down between his legs. 'Mmmm, that's my Jack.'

The last time they caught up he hadn't stayed the night for the first time since they had been dating. That wasn't like him at all and she knew something else was at play. She was reminded about what Wie had told her, "be more persuasive", so she needed to ensure that whatever happened tonight it was all on her terms. Not giving him time to think, she undid his belt, lowered the zipper in his dress jeans and slid her hand inside his boxer shorts. Putting her other hand behind his head she pulled him back into another hungry kiss.

Confusing notions were swirling around in Jack's mind for the second time today and he was holding back. Well mentally anyway, his thoughts being contradicted by his body's involuntary reaction. This wasn't part of the plan, but her actions were causing him to fast lose control of his emotions as he fell further into the erotic abyss. *Bugger it,* he would roll with it for now. He opened his mouth and reciprocated.

She had him, *now to seal the deal.* Danielle released him, levered his jeans and boxers to the floor and whispered into his ear. 'I'll be back in a while.' Lowering herself onto her knees, she grasped him and guided him into her mouth. He leaned forward and clasped her full, firm breasts. She gripped his buttocks, pulled him in closer, flexed her mouth around him and began to pulse up and down.

'Ooh, aaagh,' she heard him moan and groan and she knew him to be close already. *That was easier than I thought.*

She increased the intensity of her pulsing and his grip on her breasts intensified. He was close. 'Are you ready, Jack?'

'Oh, yeah.' She tightened around him and her head gyrated in a feverish motion.

'Oh, yeah, oh, yeah, oh, god,' he moaned. He was there.

'Oh, wow, that was spectacular,' he drooled as he leant back against the refrigerator for support. 'Wow, Danielle, where did that come from?' he asked. 'Pun intended.'

'Too funny. Well you didn't spend the night last week, so I made up for lost time.'

'Well, you certainly did that. That was amazing, you have many talents.' *Even more than you think I'm aware of.*

'Just call it a little appetiser to go with my entrée,' she teased. She recalled an expression someone had once assigned to her. *Now you've got him by the balls.* Yes she did.

After regaining his composure Jack poured her a glass of wine. 'Your favourite as always. Cheers. Make yourself comfortable while I plate up the sushi.'

'So, how have you been detective?' She used his title hoping to get his mind into work mode.

He wanted her to be answering questions, not him. 'I'm really good. I've just been for a six kilometre run around Balmain this afternoon to blow out the cobwebs and am now feeling all invigorated.'

'And just when I thought it was me who had blown out the cobwebs,' she said facetiously while fluttering her eyelashes.

'Funny. Very funny.'

'Do you like the sushi, Jack? I went to Mori's in Glebe Point Road just for you. It's my favourite.'

'Oh, yeah, especially these King Crab Rolls, they're delicious.'

'So, what was so urgent that you couldn't stay over last Thursday?' she asked casually while taking a nibble.

'We had an early morning meeting to plan for a raid we were about to conduct.'

'Really, that sounds ominous. Who did you raid? Was it dangerous? Did you get your guys?'

'Whoa, slow down, one at a time please quizmaster.'

'Sorry, but it sounds exciting.' *Come on, tell me what I already know.*

'Do you remember I told you about the woman in the wheelie bin?'

'Yes, Lucie Chan wasn't it?'

'Good memory. Anyway, we raided her apartment last Saturday. We wanted to interview her about the assault that nearly killed her and ascertain who was behind it.'

'Was she the only person you arrested?'

There it was. She was posing a question she obviously already knew the answer to. He guessed she wanted to keep him moving forward. 'As it came to pass, her minder turned boyfriend was sleeping with her and we caught him with his pants down, literally.'

'Really?'

'Yes, he tried to escape through a hidden doorway into an adjoining apartment, but we had that covered too. It was a bonus really. Eventually we garnered sufficient evidence to charge him with the shooting of the guys who attacked Lucie Chan.'

'Wow, that's great. Where did this all happen?' she queried, faking surprise.

'Sussex Street Apartments. Do you know the building?'

'No, but I'm guessing it's in Sussex Street.'

Jack had a brief flashback of JA's photos showing Danielle with Wie outside the apartment building. He quickly refocussed. 'Too funny. Interestingly, it's also where the former lieutenants of my old nemesis, Wie Ping Lee, had an apartment. You remember the one we raided back in March.' As he stirred the main course Jack tilted his head towards Danielle looking for a tell, but her blank expression revealed nothing.

'Yeah, you mentioned that once before, I think.'

'Okay, sit tight and enjoy your LTC while I finish preparing dinner.'

'Do you need a helping hand?'

'Nope, here you go, my world famous Chicken and Asian Vegetable Stir-Fry. I hope you like it,' he replied while placing the steaming bowl on the table. 'It should match nicely with your wine.'

They sat down at the small dining table. 'After you,' he said, handing her the silver serving spoons. 'So, how's work, Danielle? Have you been walking into any more fridge doors lately?'

Well, she got that right. He definitely had his detective head on now and she needed to be careful. 'I've actually resigned, and given the coronavirus induced downturn in the casino's business, they finished me up straight away. They paid me out all of my entitlements plus a generous four week's pay.'

'That's great, but aren't you buying your apartment? How are you going to manage to pay your mortgage? Especially in these times of rising unemployment.'

She wondered whether it was a genuine question raised out of his concern for her or did he know something different entirely. 'I have some money saved which will get me through for a while,' she responded.

Jack was on a roll now and would keep probing. 'Do you still have access to the money you saved for your brother or have you spent that on his treatment?' Her face blushed slightly for the first time. *Maybe she does have a conscience.*

She didn't want to mention her non-existent brother by name. 'I still have the handling fee money I earned from Woodard's money laundering operation which I keep separately.'

'Good for you. Will you stay in the hospitality sector or look elsewhere?'

'Probably not. I need to find something where I can be challenged and use my brain.'

You're using it now.

She needed to get the topic of conversation away from herself. 'Enough about me. What's next for you on the work front, handsome?'

Danielle had flipped the Q and A straight back to him.

Time to throw out some bait and see where that would take the conversation. 'Now we've charged Wang Yong I'm going to go after his boss and try and bring down his drug empire.'

She was conflicted now. She didn't want to lose Wie, however, this might also play well into her agenda to finally convince him that they should leave the country. 'Good for you, Jack. Are you and Julie-Anne working together again? You both did an excellent job last time when you teamed up.'

'No,' he replied emphatically. 'She's still onto that old chestnut of hers, that being Chinese interference in Australia. As you pointed out our investigations do occasionally overlap.' He wanted to keep JA out of the conversation and not provide Wie with any excuse to target her again. 'I think she's keeping her distance from me since she was attacked by Wie's guys though.' Her face reddened once more. 'Are you okay, Danielle?'

'Yes, why?'

'Your face flushed when I mentioned Wie's name,' he replied, deliberately provoking her.

Shit, she had shown emotion at his assertion. 'I thought you told me his guys were out of the picture, so shouldn't Julie-Anne be okay then?'

Clever. Very clever. He would continue to probe her while scanning for a crack in the façade. He stared into her eyes. 'I'm sure she will be. Wie surely wouldn't be stupid enough to go after her again.' She could take that message back to her boyfriend.

Danielle was thinking about the guy who she'd seen propped at the Golden Phoenix's bar without ordering a meal. He had to be linked to one or both of their investigations. And that meddling Bedford had sent the guy who was watching her apartment? She needed to get out of this country. And soon.

'I think I might hit the road, Jack.'

'That was sudden, is everything okay?'

'I have an interview early in the morning, so I need my beauty sleep.'

That would be just another lie and he could have challenged her as to who it was with, but he'd had enough of mental jousting for one night. All they had done was play mind games and she would only add one lie to another. She was a clever woman, so he hadn't pushed her too hard for fear of alerting Wie to what was coming.

'Are we becoming distant, Danielle?' he asked as she rose from the table and he helped her with her jacket.

'Why would you ask that? We had a laugh, chatted all night, drank good wine and had a very tasty three course meal. Oh, well, I did anyway,' she said, chuckling.

'You're a comedian.' Jack accompanied her down to the waiting Uber. 'Thank you for coming over and thank you for the delicious sushi.' They embraced and then he opened and closed the car door for her.

She wound down the rear window. 'And thank you too for the delightful appetiser,' she said, cheekily winking at him.

Jack watched on as the car accelerated up Longview Street, navigated the corner at Bayville and disappeared into the night. He wondered if he would ever see her again.

38. Bennelong Room

Tuesday 26th May

After being firmly rebuked by Michelle Ironside, Julie-Anne figured that she may as well take advantage of her invitation. The surprisingly brusque woman had made it abundantly clear that Julie-Anne wouldn't be admitted to the room again, so she may as well make the most of the remainder of her evening. She walked back to the bar and ordered another Bellini. As she took a sip of her drink, over the top of her glass she observed a smartly dressed Asian couple walking towards the bar. 'Here we go,' she murmured to herself.

'Ms Granger, if I'm correct. It is good to see you again.' Wie Ping Lie said as he offered his hand. Julie-Anne had been introduced to Wie while having lunch with one of the targets of her previous investigation.

'Hello, Wie,' she said coolly, while accepting his hand out of politeness.

'This is Lucie Chan.'

Julie-Anne had already calculated that was exactly who the woman was, given her phone conversation with Jack earlier in the day and the follow-up photo he had sent. 'Hello, Lucie.'

'And hello to you too, Ms Granger,' she said with fake politeness. The woman was clearly aware of Julie-Anne's reputation via Wie, one that no doubt wouldn't have painted a flattering picture.

Lucie Chan was wearing a figure hugging, high necked, deep blue satin dress adorned with golden cherry blossoms. She looked stunning in the traditional Chinese outfit that Julie-Anne knew to be a Quipao dress. Chan was unusually tall, slim, stunningly attractive and reminded Julie-Anne of Melissa and Sophie. She wondered why the woman was out on the town with Wie when Jack had intimated that she was shacking up with her minder, Wang Yong.

'And what brings you here, Ms Granger?' Wie asked.

She despised this man who's thugs had tried to kill her earlier in the year when she was in the middle of her original Chinese influence investigation. For now she would play nice though and see what she could learn. *Stay calm, Julie-Anne.* 'I just came here on the off chance of seeing a friend, but apparently she doesn't work here any longer.'

'That wouldn't happen to be Danielle Mortimer, would it?'

'Now, why would you suggest that?' Julie-Anne asked while noticing the sudden downturn in Lucie Chan's expression.

'Well, she was involved in a dubious business venture with an acquaintance of mine that didn't end well for him. You once had lunch with him, if I'm not mistaken. I believe your western expression is putting two and two together.'

'Yes, Li Qiang, who I believe is now receiving free board and lodging at the government's expense.'

'That's funny, Ms Granger.'

'Yeah, I thought so,' she replied.

'And how is your boyfriend, or is it your girlfriend? I get confused between the two,' he asked smugly.

'They are both well thank you, especially the detective.' Julie-Anne could joust with the best of them and was starting to relish this little tête-à-tête. She glanced at Lucie Chan who seemed to recoil at her reference to Jack. And Julie-Anne knew precisely why.

'They were interesting articles you wrote about Chinese influence in Australia earlier this year.'

'My tens of thousands of readers obviously agree with you, judging by the volume of website traffic and print sales they generated,' she replied proudly.

'I wasn't too pleased with you mentioning me as a person of interest and also linking me with Li and the Consul General. I am just a simple businessman trying to make his way in this wonderful city.'

Julie-Anne's mood darkened at that phony declaration. 'No, you're not,' she said in a hushed tone, mindful of her environment. 'Don't give me that simple businessman bullshit; you're a drug dealer and you tried to have me killed on Raglan Street two months ago. How did that work out for your thugs, hey?'

Julie-Anne turned her attention to the Chan woman. 'You should tell your minder, or is he your lover, to be careful, Lucie. Oh, that's right, it's too late for that now. He's in jail and won't be coming out anytime soon.' Julie-Anne stared hard at the other woman who's mood had darkened even further.

'Julie-Anne, there you are.' She heard a man's voice calling out from behind her.

'Nice chatting,' she said sarcastically as she turned away from Wie and Lucie.

'You should look after yourself, Ms Granger,' Wie called out. 'It's a dangerous world out there.'

'Hello, Jordan. I think I'm ready for that Bellini now,' she answered while ushering him to the opposite end of the bar. 'Let me guess, you forgot about the table service again,' she said playfully, masking her internal anger.

'Guilty as charged. No not really. I was watching your

conversation and it seemed to be heating up, so I rode in on my trusty steed to rescue you. How does that sound?'

'Aah, like my knight in shining armour.'

'Seeing as you put it that way, yes. And that reminds me of a joke.'

'Okay, make it a good one.'

'Here we go,' he said. 'Three knights walk into a bar. The first knight asks the bartender for a cup of ale. The second knight asks the bartender for a mug of ale. The bartender turns to the third knight and says, don't tell me, you want a jug of ale? The third knight says, none for me, I'm two knight's designated driver.'

'That's just terrible. That's the worst joke I've heard *two knight*, Jordan.'

'Touché. That was almost funny. Let me get you that drink.'

He handed her the champagne flute. 'Cheers.'

'And to you too, Jordan.' She caught him glance at her cleavage. *Well, you've got the girls on show, Julie-Anne.* She thought of Jack who would have done the same thing. 'You do know that's seven years bad sex, don't you?'

'Sorry, you do have lovely skin though and a great tan for this time of year.'

'A timely recovery. I'll let you off the hook, this time,' she said.

'Do you feel like a late supper, Julie-Anne? There's a fabulous late night place in Surry Hills that started out as a pop-up taco joint.'

'El Loco.'

'You know it? Bugger. And I was trying to impress you too.'

'I'm sorry to take the wind out of your sails, but it's just around the corner from my office. I loved the spit-roasted pork with pineapple salsa soft taco before they changed the menu.'

'Is that a yes then?'

'That's a yes. Shall we go?'

'I see you like men again,' she heard Lucie Chan utter sarcastically as they walked past.

Julie-Anne lifted her head, straightened her posture and ignored the woman.

'These are delicious.' Julie-Anne said as she tucked into her mystery taco. 'I've asked the manager numerous times and he refuses to tell me what the ingredients are.' Jordan picked up her napkin and gently dabbed at the taco juice on her chin. 'Thank you. How good are these Jalapeno Margarita's?'

'Scrumptious. So, what were you and that couple arguing about, if I might ask?'

'It wasn't really an argument, more like a Mexican standoff.'

'That's funny. You do realise where you're sitting, don't you?'

'In a Mexican restaurant, durrr.' Julie-Anne liked this guy, so she would start by being open and honest with him. 'Anyway, to answer your question, I am an investigative journalist and I wrote a piece about Chinese interference in Australia earlier in the year. The direction of the investigation changed and it finished up being more about Chinese criminal enterprises than what I intended and that man runs one of the largest of them.'

'Wow, and I thought you were a model.'

'At my age, I don't think so. I did walk the occasional catwalk in my younger days though.'

'That's fascinating. Do tell me more about your investigation.'

'Maybe another time. I had enough of negative talk back at the casino. What about you, Jordan? Are you a model, too?' she asked while blatantly staring at his chest.'

'Touché on both counts. No, my family own and manage three aged care facilities. I primarily oversee the commercial and contractual affairs of the business and also occasionally dabble in a few other areas. One of those being as a sports agent where I provide similar services for a number of sportspeople.'

'Aren't you going to drop a few famous names?'

'Somehow I just don't think that would work with you, Julie-Anne.'

'Well spotted. I've had a fun night, however, I really must go. I've got an early start in the morning. It was nice to meet you, Jordan.'

'Can I see you again or at least ask for your phone number?'

She noticed the puppy dog eyes and felt for him. He was keen and she liked him too. 'How about we start with the phone number? Enter this into your phone.'

'At least allow me to escort you to your Uber.'

Julie-Anne was seated in the back of her Uber, thinking about Jordan. He appeared to be a genuine guy, well-mannered, obviously intelligent, funny and she liked that he could be self-effacing. She wondered whether he would call or if she really wanted him to, given she wasn't a great success at relationships.

39. Wie's Penthouse

Wednesday 27th May

'What have you learnt from Wagner?' Wie asked as Danielle walked into his penthouse early the following morning.

'And Nǐ hǎo to you too, Hǔ.'

'Yes, yes, okay, but it is more important that you tell me what the detective has told you, that is why I allow you to see him.'

'You allow me. Really!' she replied feistily. 'I'm the person who is demeaning themselves, not you, mister. I readily admit that I was aware of what I was getting myself into, but it was *my* decision to do this for us, not yours.'

Wie sighed impatiently. 'Yes, alright, tell me what you found out.'

Danielle told Wie the little that Jack had imparted last night. 'He did say that now they've charged Yong he's going to go after his boss and try and bring down his drug empire. I can't decide whether he was baiting me for a reaction or he meant what he said. I think it was both, Hǔ.'

'I agree, I think it was both too.'

'He also said you wouldn't be stupid enough to target the Granger woman again. I think he was sending you a warning through me. Hǔ, he obviously knows, or thinks he knows about us, and more importantly, about my double life. I can't see him anymore and you should be extra careful now.'

'I agree you shouldn't see him again.'

'Thank you, thank you,' she gushed. Danielle looped her arms around him and pulled him into an embrace. 'Thank you, Hŭ,' she whispered into his ear.

He pulled back from her. 'I saw the Granger woman in the Bennelong Room last night, too. She wasn't too pleased to see me.'

'La shi,' she blurted out mimicking him when he was angry. 'What were you thinking going there and who did you go with?' Her first thoughts were of that Lucie Chan woman.

'As if it is any of your concern, but I went to play a few hands of pai gow, that's all.'

'You should be very careful going out in public, especially given everything we have discussed. It is becoming dangerous for both of us. Did you speak to Granger?'

'Yes, we had an interesting little chat at the bar before she was escorted away by a man. When we walked into the room earlier—'

She interrupted him. 'You said we. Who is *we?*'

Wie frowned. 'What are you talking about?'

'You said "when *we* walked into the room".'

He had slipped up and needed to recover. 'The hostess who escorted me into the room. Anyway, the Granger woman was there talking to a woman in a business suit.'

'You're kidding,' she blurted out. The few women she had seen in the Bennelong Room from her time working there would never be seen dead in a business suit. 'Describe the woman.'

'She was maybe in her late forties, dark hair and wearing a navy blue business suit. She was probably a shift manager. Why?'

'That is my old treasury boss. I can guarantee you Granger being there wasn't by accident. She is still digging and now she will definitely know the truth about my employment circumstances. And if she knows, then so does the detective.'

'You are correct and they must also be working together again.'

'Hǔ, I don't want to lose you, so this might also be the appropriate time for us to leave the country,' she said, urging him for the umpteenth time.

'Yes, and we should move you from that apartment as soon as possible too.'

She picked up on his slip-up. 'You have no intention of going away with me do you?'

He feigned a puzzled expression. 'Why would you say that, Nǚrén?'

'If we were actually going away you wouldn't need to move me at the moment, would you? We could just pack a few things, disappear off into the sunshine and worry about relocating me when we come back in a few months.' Something else popped into her mind. This was her best opportunity to remove Lucie from his life permanently. 'Jack also talked about Yong and Lucie.'

'What did he say about her?' He silently cursed himself for the slip-up.

'*Them*, Wie, *them*. Jack said, "her minder turned boyfriend was sleeping with her and we caught him with his pants down".'

'Really?'

'Yes. He said when they raided the apartment Yong tried to escape through a hidden doorway into an adjoining apartment.' She would exaggerate now. 'He also said Lucie was obviously banging Yong.' She watched as his face reddened. He was clenching the jaw and pressing his teeth together.

'I will destroy them both—' he ranted before his voice trailed off. After their evening together in the Bennelong Room, Wie and Lucie had returned to his penthouse high above the city. She had stayed the night, pleased him as he was accustomed, and left earlier this morning.

'Well, at least she's not banging you then. Or is she?' He raised his hand as if to strike her. 'Don't you even think about it, mister,' she responded furiously. 'Don't even think about it.'

She calmed herself knowing she was on a good thing here for the time being. 'Look, we need to seriously consider getting out of this city for a while, at least until things cool down. And especially now Granger is snooping around too. Look, Hŭ, you have lost everyone of importance in your crew in the past few months, you have no one to protect you and the police are closing in. You have to get out of here.' She paused noticing his face colouring and jaw tightening again.

'Stop pushing me about that,' he replied angrily. 'I'm not going anywhere until I have finished my important business here. I still have more product to move.'

She placed a placatory hand on his arm. 'I know and I'm sorry. I fear for your safety, especially now that Yong is no longer around to protect you.'

'I will be okay. It would help me if you could do something for me on Friday.'

'Of course Hŭ, what do you need me to do?'

'I need you to collect a package for me on Friday afternoon. It will only take you an hour or so and you'll be back in time for us to have dinner.'

'I like the sound of that.'

'Now, why don't you go down to Far East Travel and see what destinations they recommend for this time of the year. Mention my name and they will take care of you. Are you happy now?'

'Yes, for now. Alright, I have to go. I'm having lunch in Bondi with a friend and I'm late.'

'Take my car then and you can save some time.' He handed her the keys. She kissed him on the cheek and left.

40. Sussex Street Apartments

Wednesday 27th May

The wheels of the judiciary moved at a snail's pace at times and it had taken Sanderson's guys two days to obtain a warrant to search Lucie Chan's vehicle. He rapped on her apartment door and this time she opened it in a timely manner. 'Miss Chan, this is a duly issued judicial warrant that allows me to search your vehicle. You will need to provide me with the vehicle's keys and then accompany me while I search your vehicle.'

'My car's not here, detective.'

'Lucie, do you think that I'm stupid? I checked the carpark first to ensure the vehicle is on the premises before I came up to your apartment. Shall we start again?'

Lucie Chan was holding the door open with one hand and the other resting on her hip in a display of obstinance. 'You must be mistaken.'

'Come on, Lucie, get the keys and let's go.' She drifted slowly back down the hallway and he watched her disappear into the living room. Sanderson thought that she had been back in the apartment for an inordinate amount of time. 'Lucie, come on, we haven't got all day,' he called out.

'What are you doing? Let me go you bastard.' Sanderson heard her yelling angrily and he turned towards the disturbance.

'You didn't learn much from your boyfriend's mistake the other day did you, Lucie.' She had tried to escape through the hidden door and the adjacent apartment just like Yong had two days earlier. Jack held her firmly by the arm as he walked her back to where Sanderson was waiting.

'Lucie, Lucie, really. Do I look that stupid? Did you really think I would come alone?' Sanderson savoured the crushed expression on her face. Moments later Sanderson exited the elevator followed by Lucie Chan still firmly in Jack's grip. As they navigated the alcove a grey metallic Audi A6 flashed past, speeding through the carpark. 'You're kidding.'

'About what, Michael?' Jack asked.

'Nothing, just that car was going too fast,' Sanderson replied, thinking quickly on his feet. He spotted a hint of recognition on Lucie Chan's face. As they walked on towards her vehicle she turned her head slightly and gave him a look of acknowledgement. She had seen what he had.

Approaching the Honda CRV she observed the two gloved-up men dressed in dark blue overalls standing by the car. She knew these were forensics guys and they would search her vehicle, and thoroughly.

'You don't look so smug now, Lucie,' Sanderson prodded. He handed the keys to the senior of the two Forensic Service Group technicians.

Jack spoke to the lead technician. 'Gavin, can you dust the steering wheel, console, glove box and dashboard for prints first, please? I want to firstly ensure we can directly connect Ms Chan here to the vehicle.'

The technicians opened the two front doors, leant inside the vehicle and softly began brushing a fine white powder across the black surfaces of the Honda. Fifteen minutes later they emerged from the vehicle with Gavin holding up a few little plastic evidence bags and waived them in Jack's direction.

'I wonder how many of those belong to you, Lucie,' Jack smarted.

The two technicians then began their search. As they did so Jack scrutinised the rear cargo compartment while Sanderson guarded Lucie. Jack then walked around to the driver's side, leant in an pulled the bonnet release. He shone his torch into the engine compartment and began to search. He could hear the FSG guys now pulling the inside door panels off and placing them on the concrete. Next they unscrewed the dash console and he heard that hit the concrete too.

'I've got nothing front or back boys,' Jack called out.

'We're almost done here too, Jack.'

One of the techs exited the vehicle and went to his equipment bag where he retrieved a barbell shaped device. Jack knew it to be a Crime-lite forensic light used to detect drugs and drug residues at crime scenes. It worked by illuminating substances with different wavelengths of light, causing them to fluoresce.

'Here you go, Jack, check this out?' The tech stepped back and passed Jack the hand-held device.

Lucie's head dropped as she saw the giveaway UV illuminating the interior of her CRV.

'Nice, Lucie. You should be more careful when you're bagging up your goodies.' The UV light was showing up fine white particles lodged between the passenger seat and the console, but not enough to get Jack excited.

A few minutes later the two techs stepped back from the vehicle. 'I think we're done here, Jack.'

Jack was deep in thought. Lucie and Yong wouldn't be stupid enough to keep their day-to-day supplies in the two apartments. They would need to have ready access to their product to keep up with short notice orders. 'Gavin,' he called out. 'Something's not right here. I've been watching her demeanour in between searching and she appears to me to be quite anxious. She's normally a cocky bitch. We've missed something.'

The tech went back into the front of the vehicle with his UV light and slowly began a grid search across the dashboard, console and seats. He saw a fine, almost negligible speck of powder in the small storage space behind the gear selector. 'Hand me a screwdriver,' he called out. After removing the cover he retrieved his mobile phone from his overalls pocket and snapped a number of photos.

'Here we go, Jack,' Gavin exclaimed, holding up a black box about the size of an electronic tablet, but thicker. 'It's a portable, lockable safe and it was hidden at the back of the storage recess behind the gear selector.'

'Good work, guys. Make certain we print that too,' Jack ordered.

'Okay, Michael, once they've dusted the safe let's tag and bag that too and take Lucie here for a little drive shall we? Can you grab that bamboo pole from the back and we'll take that as well? I think we know what that's been used for recently.' Jack started to turn away. 'No, on second thoughts, Gavin just impound the vehicle itself.'

'Roger that, Jack.'

Sanderson turned away to grab Lucie's arm. Her defiance and anger had been replaced by a look of defeat and resignation. 'Not so smug now, are you?'

It was too late in the afternoon to commence an interview with Lucie Chan. Sanderson knew her form and she would resist their questioning and the interview could drag on well into the night. Instead, the two detectives decided to place her in a holding cell and interview her in the morning. An hour later they were walking to their vehicles in the AFP's secure underground carpark. Sanderson stopped and put his hand on Jack's arm to pull him up.

'Jack, I didn't want to say anything in front of Lucie Chan, but did you see who was driving the Audi A6 that sped past us as we exited the elevator back at Sussex Street?'

'No, I was behind you, why?'

'This is going to sound bizarre. He paused and reconsidered what he was about to say. 'It's okay, don't worry about it.'

Jack could see the tortured confusion on Sanderson's face. 'Something obviously bugging you, so what is it, Michael? Let's have it.'

Sanderson looked directly at Jack then paused again.

'Michael, what is it?' Jack was concerned himself now. 'Is everything alright?'

'Jack.' Sanderson took a deep breath. 'I think Danielle Mortimer was driving the A6. You know her better than I, but what reason would she have to be in that building?'

Jack was rocked by the observation and his head was spinning to make sense of it. It shouldn't have been, particularly after JA's disclosures. 'Nah, you must have been mistaken Michael; she lives in Glebe and works in Pyrmont. She would have no reason to be here and she doesn't drive an Audi anyway,' Jack said, not believing a single word of it.

'Jack, you're a copper just like me, you don't believe in coincidences either, but maybe there's an innocent explanation.' Sanderson gripped Jack's shoulder. 'I certainly hope so buddy.'

After JA's startling revelations, Jack knew all too well what the explanation was, he just hadn't worked out how to deal with it yet.

41. AFP Headquarters

Thursday 28th May

Given the lateness in the day of the arrest of Lucie Chan yesterday, she was held in custody in the AFP's holding cells overnight. Now, for the second time in less than a week she was in IV1, this time with her arms handcuffed and chained to the desk.

'Good morning Lucie, how was your accommodation?' Michael Sanderson asked.

'Fuck you.'

'You wish. Given your boyfriend won't be seeing daylight for a long time, that might be your only option,' he said, deadpan.

Sanderson was about to conduct the interview solo. He hadn't been able to contact Jack this morning and he assumed that might be related to his revelations around Danielle's unexplained presence in the Sussex Street Apartment Building carpark the previous afternoon. The AFP's Deputy Commissioner, John Robertson, had made it clear to Sanderson that at this stage, the arrest of Lucie Chan was based on possession and possible trafficking of illicit substances. These were state based crimes, so unless the case developed into one of importation or cross-border trafficking, the AFP would have no further involvement. For now though, Sanderson would utilise their facilities.

'Okay, Lucie, let's get started shall we? And no more playing the illiterate immigrant and speaking in pidgin, okay? You are an intelligent and articulate woman, so start acting like one.'

'I not no what you mean,' she gibbered while offering him a mischievous smile.

'Okay, that's very funny. Now, for the record. I am Senior Detective Michael Sanderson from the New South Wales Police Force. You don't have to confirm anything as this whole interview is being recorded on a video surveillance camera. Firstly, I need to inform you that drug possession is an offence under Section 10 of the Drug Misuse and Trafficking Act. The maximum penalty is two years in prison and or a fine of two thousand two hundred dollars. We have you in possession of forty grams of cocaine, so that charge will comfortably be proven.'

'The blow isn't mine,' she blurted out.

'Well, we'll soon know when the results of the fingerprint tests are back.' As a matter of procedure Lucie Chan had been fingerprinted last Saturday when she was arrested with Wang Yong. 'The Honda is registered in your name and that's where we found the coke, so if the prints taken from your vehicle come back positive to you, that closes the loop and you are done, Lucie.' Sanderson let that hang for a moment. 'And that's just for starters.'

'I told you before, the blow isn't mine,' she denied emphatically.

Sanderson wasn't buying that for one second. 'More seriously though, Section 25 of the Act, the supply of prohibited drugs of not less than a commercial quantity is an offence under sub section 2, which carries a penalty of fifteen years imprisonment. Lucie, we already have a witness statement from one of your clients,' he lied. 'Once we interrogate your mobile phone I'm sure we will have corroborating evidence to prove that charge as well.'

'So you say.'

'Lucie you're going to prison; for how long is entirely up to you. It will only take your boss five minutes to replace you and then it will have been all for nothing. Come on give me something, so I may be able to help you.' He stopped talking to allow her some serious contemplation time. Sanderson leaned back in his chair and linked his hands behind his head.

'Since he's been fucking that woman his head has been all over the place.'

He would use her anger to his advantage. Given what he had witnessed in the apartment complex's carpark yesterday, he assumed he already knew the answer to his next question. 'Which woman?'

'That blonde bimbo.'

He was thinking about Jack now and one part of him didn't want to ask the obvious question. 'Is that Danielle?'

'Yeah, that's her. You obviously know her. Is she still screwing your partner as well?'

Sanderson ignored the taunt. 'So, you weren't number one anymore and that made you jealous, Lucie.'

'What are you my shrink now?'

'No, that's way above my pay grade. Now, let's go back to your earlier outburst. Who were you referring to when you said, "his head has been all over the place"?'

'You're the detective, you work it out.'

'Okay, I'll give it my best shot. Bruce Lee – how'd I do?' He was humouring her now and slowly trying to break her down.

She seemed to have recovered from her earlier flare-up. 'That's almost funny. Close, but no cigar. Isn't that what you westerners say?'

'Yes, we do. How about I try again? What about his brother, Wie Ping Lie?'

She laughed aloud. 'Do you have a match?' she asked while pretending to hold an imaginary cigar.

She appeared more relaxed after her outburst, so he would try and get an admission out of her. 'So you were spending your evenings driving the streets of the eastern suburbs doling out his product, obviously risking your life, while he was screwing his blonde girlfriend. That must have been infuriating, Lucie.' He watched her face redden sharply as he anticipated it would.

'She's not his girlfriend,' she responded adamantly. He waited while she calmed down. 'Anyway, she already has a boyfriend; your detective friend, I believe.'

Sanderson again ignored the taunt. 'What did you mean when you said earlier, "his head has been all over the place?" Is that because of his relationship with Danielle?' He was banking on her becoming angry again and that would keep her off balance.

Surprisingly, she sighed instead. 'We had a flourishing business in Chinatown, but he decided he wanted to get into the posh eastern suburbs with his new product. I told him it was someone else's territory, but he didn't care. And look what happened to me as a consequence?'

'The bruises are hardly noticeable now. You're almost back to your radiant self, Lucie,' he said, deliberately flattering her. 'What else did Wie say?'

'Last night he got angry at the casino when he saw that Granger woman, the reporter. I'm sure he wants to kill her.'

Lucie was opening up now, so he would keep prodding. 'What did he say to her?'

'He told her she should be careful and to look after herself.'

'So, he threatened her?'

'He was clever the way he worded it, but yes, I'm sure that was his intent.'

Whilst it was an interesting and entertaining chat with Lucie Chan she hadn't admitted to anything illegal nor made any definitive statements about Wie's activities. It was time to up the ante. 'The Lebos will want their pound of flesh for the brutal attack on Amir and Jasar and now that your boyfriend, Yong that is, is about to be incarcerated for some considerable time they will come after you instead, Lucie. And with a vengeance too, I imagine. And of course, Yong can't protect you and Wie is too busy with his girlfriend.' He let her consider that for a moment. 'The alternative, Lucie, is to give me something to work with and we may be able to reduce your pending charges, potentially even down to a suspended sentence or even a manageable fine.'

'And then what will I do? I can't go back to China because he has many contacts in the government and bureaucracy there and if I stay here Wie or the towel heads will find me anyway. Either way, I'm dead. I can't win.'

Sanderson saw the hint of moisture in her eye and decided now was the ideal juncture to take a break and give her some time to stew on her own thoughts.

'I'll be back in a while, Lucie.'

42. Jack's Apartment Balmain

Thursday 28th May

Jack had spent the previous night trying to separate his personal feelings for Danielle from his professional responsibilities. Personally, he had been struggling with the knowledge that his supposed girlfriend had been leading a double life. She was a vibrant, playful, eye-catching young woman and he was hooked from the start. She had enthusiastically engaged with him from the beginning and he thought they had really enjoyed their time together ever since. One of the things that he liked about Danielle was that she realised how important his job was to him. And as a result, she made no onerous demands on his time and in return she was free to live her own life. In hindsight, given what he now knew, that made complete sense. She had played him. As if JA's revelations from Monday evening weren't damning enough, then Sanderson's assertion that he had seen Danielle at the Sussex Street Apartments was the dagger in the wound. From a professional perspective, she had supposedly been inadvertently involved in a money laundering operation at the Oceanic Casino earlier in the year. It was becoming apparent to him that she had played a double game there too. She had facilitated the successful laundering of some of the profits from Wie's drug empire through the casino's Bennelong Room. Then, pretending to switch sides, she had assisted the police in a sting operation against some of the key players, but not Wie. And as a result, Jack's Deputy Commissioner and the DPP had seen fit to only issue her with a fine instead of charging her with a more serious offence. And no conviction was recorded. It had become clear to Jack that she must have been working in conjunction with Wie Ping Lie all along. Danielle had seen Jack in the Bennelong Room and made him for a detective straight away. She couldn't have him snooping around, so she had quickly developed a plan to ingratiate him. She invited him for a drink and his little brain had said yes. She played him perfectly and he fell for it hook, line and sinker. *Some detective you are.*

Jack called JA on WhatsApp.

'Hi, Jack, how are you?'

'Getting back to my old self,' he fibbed. 'And you?'

'That's good. I've been busy. Shall I go first?'

Jack wasn't looking forward to telling her about Sanderson's observation, but in the spirit of their new partnership he no choice. 'Of course.'

'Okay. I went to the Bennelong Room a couple of nights ago—'

He instantly cut her off. 'What the hell were you doing there and how did you gain access anyway?'

'Are you going to keep interrupting me?'

'Sorry, go on.'

'You know I have contacts, Jack, so it shouldn't be a surprise. Anyway, I bumped into Michelle Ironside—'

'What, you just happened to bump into her? You've never met even her, JA, so I doubt you just happened to *bump into her.*'

'May I continue?'

'Sure.'

There was no delicate way to tell Jack the next piece. However she said it, it would be another blow to his sagging confidence. 'We got chatting and after a while she mentioned that Danielle wasn't working at the casino anymore.'

'I know. She told me two nights ago that she had just resigned and was looking for something more challenging,' he replied.

Uh-oh. 'Jack, I don't know any other way to say this, so I'll come straight out with it. Danielle left the casino in March.' Julie-Anne paused briefly then broke the silence. 'I'm really sorry.'

So, if she hasn't worked at the casino for more than two months, where was she on the nights she wasn't with him? *I'm working tomorrow night, can we do the following night, Jack?* He knew the answer now and it was another kick in the teeth. He felt sick in the stomach. And he guessed where the bruise had actually originated, too. Given what Sanderson had already told him, this was the final straw. 'How could I have not been aware of any of this stuff? Some detective I am,' he lamented.

'Jack, just because you're a detective doesn't mean you're supposed to be suspicious of everyone you date. You'll never be able to have a fulfilling relationship if you're going to carry that baggage around with you. Sometimes you just have to go with the flow and make the most of it, which is what I gather you did. Don't go beating yourself up, she's obviously a very cunning young woman.'

'Well, JA, let me put the final nail in the coffin for you. Sanderson claimed he saw her driving an Audi A6 in the underground carpark at the Sussex Street Apartments two days ago. I doubted his word at the time, now I guess, given all of your revelations, I owe him an apology.'

'Oh, Jack. I'm really sorry. You do realise that I would never consciously set out to hurt you. I was just following my investigative instincts.'

'Yeah, I know.'

'While we're chatting, I also ran into Wie and Lucie Chan at the casino.'

'Gee, you did have an interesting evening.'

'Tell me about it. What a stunning woman that Lucie is. I'm sure she's a real piece of work under her designer outfit though. Wie made some implied threats, but I just ignored them and moved on.'

'I've told you before, you need to be careful around him. Just so you know, Sanderson has charged Wang Yong with the attempted murder of the two drug dealers. We also have Lucie Chan in custody after finding forty baggies of coke hidden in her vehicle. Michael should be interviewing her as we speak. Wie won't be a happy man with any of that and he'll be beside himself if we take action against our Ms Mortimer.'

'What are you planning to do about her?'

'I'm not certain just yet. The DC will be aghast, as will the DPP, when they learn of her original deception, so it will be up to them what action, if any, is taken.'

'That *will* make for an interesting conversation. Now, I'm about to commence writing my piece and hopefully I'll have enough to submit to Chris in time for Saturday's edition. I'll need some more specifics, so can I call you as required please, Jack?'

He wanted to say no, but that wasn't fair on her. 'You're revelations have ruined my life, but if it wasn't for you we wouldn't be in a position to progress this component of the investigation, so sure, call me,' he replied matter of factly.

Julie-Anne wanted to say something in her defence, but realising that he was speaking from a position of pain and disappointment, she let it go. 'Thanks, I'll call you when I need to fill in the gaps.'

'And, JA, you need to watch your step.'

'I will. Thanks, Jack.'

43. AFP Headquarters

Thursday 28th May

Sanderson took the elevator from the basement to the tenth floor. He was surprised to see Jack at his desk. 'You missed the Lucie Chan interview.'

'I had something personal to attend to,' he replied abruptly. 'How did you go with her?'

'It was more of a chat really. She's a street smart woman with a tough emotional exterior, so I was just trying to soften her up. The seriousness of her situation finally dawned on her and I think she might just turn.'

'Really?' Jack asked.

'Yes, really. She is acutely aware that she's going away for two years for possession and if we can prove a trafficking charge then her model looks will be well and truly gone by the time she gets out. So, I've left her down in holding to have a serious think about her future. She's an intelligent woman and I think she will want to deal her way out of this. Anyway, we'll find out in a while.'

'Yeah, I guess we will.'

Sanderson looked down at his partner's sullen demeanour. 'What's going on? You're not your usual positive self. What's up, buddy?'

Jack wasn't one to discuss his personal life with work

colleagues, however, there was a potential criminal element that required some serious deliberation, most notably by his DC. 'I've been thinking about your observations regarding Danielle. You're correct in what you said yesterday. We don't believe in coincidences, Michael,' he said soberly.

'Are you saying it definitely was her?'

'Probably. There's more, much more, Michael. Take a seat. JA has been doing some investigating of her own and it turns out that she's done a better job than I have. Danielle doesn't have a brother, doesn't work at the casino anymore and has been shacking up with Wie Ping Lie on her off nights from me. That last revelation would seem to confirm your thoughts on who was driving that car, especially given Wie lives in that very building.'

'I'm shocked. I don't know what to say other than, I'm sorry, Jack.' Sanderson had run the Audi's plates through the state police's database and confirmed that the vehicle was owned by Wie. He wouldn't tell Jack for fear of driving another nail into his emotional coffin.

'She played me, both personally and professionally. I can accept being blinded to her subterfuge by her looks, energy and vivacious personality, but as a detective I should have been much more alert to the numerous coincidences. It was all too convenient.'

Sanderson felt for his partner. 'You weren't to know. She must have been awfully convincing.'

Jack thought back to dinner with her only two nights ago and laughed self-consciously. 'Yeah, she was. All the warning signs were there. I just didn't see them for what they were. And now I have to go upstairs and explain the whole scenario to the DC and he will be equally unhappy at being hoodwinked by her. After all, he could have thrown the book at her for her involvement in the money laundering operation, but, as she provided us with full cooperation, he and the DPP agreed to let her off with a manageable fine. He will no doubt feel just as foolish as I do and will be seeking some sort of legal retribution. And god knows what he's going to say about me and my career given it's my ex-girlfriend we're discussing here.'

'I don't envy you having to have that conversation. I'll take Lucie Chan any day, Jack.'

'Alright, I had better go do this and get it over with.'

'Before you go, Jack. If you're talking to JA, you need to tell her to be careful. Apparently, according to Lucie, Wie delivered an implied threat to her at the casino the other night.'

'I have told her numerous times and I reminded her this morning during the call when she dropped her latest bombshell.'

'Okay, I'll go back downstairs and see if Lucie's had an epiphany.'

Jack took the stairs up to the twelfth floor, entered the executive domain and walked across to the DC's office. Through the glass wall he could see John Robertson was busy with paperwork, so he knocked firmly on the door and stood back. After a moment the DC glanced up, and with a wave of his hand, motioned Jack into his office.

'Just give me a minute to check and sign these documents and I'll be with you, Jack.' John Robertson was in full dress uniform today which signified that he was attending a formal occasion or meeting with government representatives, maybe even the minister himself.

'How's your joint task force going? This whole setup amounts to nothing for the AFP if we can't prove importation, which seems to me to be where this case is heading.' The DC asked while continuing to tick and flick the documents in front of him. 'Do you have any good news for me, Jack?'

'Unfortunately no, not at this stage. We haven't been able to uncover any new intel since we lost track of the shipment over a week ago. As far as Lucie Chan goes, Sanderson is continuing his interview with her as we speak. He is confident that the state can easily make the case against her for possession of a prohibited substance, and potentially even trafficking. He's also fairly confident that he can turn her, so if he does, then there may be something in it for us regarding the importation.'

'If it does come to that, the state police may not be too enthusiastic about dropping their charges in exchange for her assisting us with a federal investigation. Let me know how that pans out, as it will be my job to convince the State's Assistant Commissioner to consider the bigger picture in the national interest.'

'Okay, will do, boss.' Jack remained seated while the DC continued flipping pages.

'Is there something else?'

Jack was unsuccessfully trying to prevent his internal torture from manifesting in his facial expression. 'Yes, there is actually,' he replied quietly.

'I'm under the pump, so let's have it.'

'Well, I'm not sure where to start, boss.'

The DC stopped flicking papers and looked up. 'That sounds ominous.'

'Yes it is. It's related to Danielle Mortimer. Do you remember her?'

'Of course, how could anyone forget that woman; she's a looker for sure. Isn't she your girlfriend?'

Jack wriggled uncomfortably in his seat. 'Yes. Well she was until recently.'

'If this chat is about your personal life then you've got the wrong man. I'm just about to get divorced again.'

'I need to tell you a story which is going to be unpleasant for both of us.'

'Jack, what's going on?'

'Where to start?' Jack paused and took a deep breath.

'Danielle Mortimer isn't who either of us thinks she is. Apparently she has been leading something of a double life, and as it turns out she is close to Wie Ping Lie.'

Robertson looked over the top of his glasses. 'How close?'

Jack produced a number of photos from an envelope and slid them across the desk. One of the photos depicted her in an embrace with Wie outside the Sussex Street Apartment building. Robertson shuffled the photos. 'Julie-Anne Granger has been investigating her.'

'Jesus, that's definitely what I'd call close.'

Jack didn't really need to be reminded about Danielle's double dealing, but he would have to cop it on the chin. 'I know. I think that he originally planted her into the Bennelong Room to ensure Li Qiang didn't abscond with the proceeds of their drug business during the money laundering operation. Then she saw an opening and ended up conducting the transactions herself for a handy little fee.'

'Yes, she did at that.'

'Embarrassingly, she picked me for a detective straight away when I attended the Bennelong Room while investigating Li. She obviously saw an opportunity and proceeded to ingratiate me. And I fell for it,' he said meekly. 'Now, I have to assume she nurtured our relationship hoping that she could monitor my investigation into Wie's activities.'

'Christ, Jack, you're supposed to be my best detective. How long did you date this woman for, one month, two months?' Robertson bellowed. 'And you didn't smell a rat at any stage? What, were you thinking with; your old fella? And adding insult to injury, a bloody reporter had to give us the good news as well. Oh, of course, she's your ex-girlfriend too. They've both made a fool of you,' he scolded.

Jack had never seen him this angry and he knew why. The DC interviewed Danielle himself and had obviously also fallen for her charms. Then he had convinced the DPP to reduce the money laundering charges, so she would only receive a nominal fine. He was probably as embarrassed as Jack. 'Look, boss, I'm embarrassed and ashamed—'

The DC cut him short. 'You're embarrassed and ashamed, I'm the one who has to go cap in hand to the DPP and see if they can charge her all over again,' he said, continuing the tirade.

'Can we charge her again?'

Robertson appeared to have calmed a little. Jack certainly hoped so. 'I'm not certain. We would have to produce new and compelling evidence, which it doesn't appear we have. Then the new charges must relate to a serious offence, but we would need to confirm with the DPP whether money laundering fits the bill, and finally, it needs to be in the interests of justice. It will ultimately be up to the DPP though.'

'There's more, boss,' Jack said nervously.

'What do they say in the classics? The hits just keep on coming. What else, Wagner?'

Wagner. Jack paused. His next revelation would be the match to light the DC's fuse again. 'She doesn't have a brother with a heart condition. She doesn't even have a brother.'

'Did Granger give you that piece of news as well?' The DC didn't wait for a response. 'Maybe I should offer *her* a position within the AFP. She's sure producing more results than us,' he said sarcastically.

Now wasn't the time to be disagreeing. 'Yes, boss.'

'The primary reason that I reduced Ms Mortimer's charges was due to her brother's heart condition and now I find out she doesn't even bloody well have a brother. Have you spoken to her about any of this?'

'No, I wanted to speak with you first. Maybe there's a way that we can turn this to our advantage.'

'Well I damn well hope so, Wagner. What are you proposing?'

'I was thinking, irrespective of what the DPP decide, that we call her bluff and offer her a deal. Work with us to ensnare Wie and we make the upgraded charges go away.'

'Yeah, that worked out so well for us last time, didn't it?' the DC fumed.

Jack leaned forward in his chair and pressed on. 'Look, boss, Sanderson thinks he can convince Lucie Chan to give up Wie and we hopefully hold all the cards with Danielle. Why not give both of them the opportunity. Whoever accepts first gets the deal of a lifetime and the other goes to prison for a long time. It's a win-win, boss,' Jack pleaded.

'After the way Ms Mortimer has embarrassed us I'm inclined to wait for the outcome of Lucie Chan's interview. Let's wait and see what Sanderson produces first. Is there anything else?'

'No, I think that's enough for one day, boss.'

'Well, there's an understatement for you,' Robertson grumbled.

44. AFP Headquarters

Thursday 28th May

Sanderson nodded at the guard, entered IV1 and took his seat at the table. 'So, Lucie, you've had an ample opportunity to consider your future. What'll it be?'

'You not bring handsome detective with you?'

'He's having a haircut to make himself look good for you. Now, let's cut the crap, shall we?'

Chan leaned forward and rested her arms on the table. 'I don't know what to do, I'm torn. Wie has been good to me, I have been well rewarded for my work and I have had a good quality of life.'

Sanderson saw an opening. 'Let's stay with those thoughts for a minute, shall we? You say he's been good to you, well where was the protection when you were bashed and left for dead? My guess is Wie was probably having dinner with his girlfriend,' he said trying to make her livid and force her to come to terms with her precarious situation.

She smiled. 'Nice try, but I'm not biting. I have to think about me and not allow my dislike for her to influence my judgement.'

'Good for you; that's exactly what you need to do.' She had provided him with the opening, so he would go all in. 'You said you were well rewarded by Wie. Well, what if we were to go after your assets, whatever they are. I'm sure it won't be too difficult to prove that your lifestyle was funded by the proceeds of crime. If that turns out to be the case then we are entitled by law to seize all your assets, starting with your CRV. Then we'll move onto your bank account and everything else you own; jewellery, designer clothes, everything worth anything. And, Lucie, there goes your quality of life. Will I get a bite this time?' She tried to stare him down, but behind the steely façade she had to be thinking about her future, or lack of it. He nodded at her hand. 'By the way, that's an expensive ring you're wearing.' Now he would move onto Plan B. 'We are well aware of Ms Mortimer's activities over these past few months. She is a smart woman, so I imagine she will endeavour to deal herself out of doing any prison time.' They had nothing on Mortimer at this stage, but Lucie Chan wouldn't be aware of that. 'I'm sure she loves her boyfriend dearly, but—'

She interrupted him. 'I told you before I'm not biting, detective. Oh, sorry, maybe you were referring to her other boyfriend,' she said chuckling.

'You're quite the comedienne, Lucie.' He was trying to provide an exit for her and she was annoying him with her naivety and now her frivolity. 'Stop that rubbish, this is serious. I guarantee you that she won't hesitate to turn on Wie in order to avoid gaol time. The thought of going to gaol can be a serious motivator. Have you heard the expression *gay for the stay*? You're both attractive women, so either of you will be flavour of the month among the doughnut bumpers. Don't let that be you, Lucie.'

'You're very funny, detective.'

'It wasn't intended to be humorous.' Sanderson leaned forward. 'What you need to realise here, is that whoever does the deal first could potentially walk free or worst case, incur a fine. The other won't breathe fresh air for years. That doesn't have to be you,' he said, before pausing to allow that to sink in. 'And just to prove my point, my AFP partner is meeting with the Deputy Commissioner as we speak and I'm certain they will be discussing Ms Mortimer's future, which will include the possibility of an exchange of information for her freedom. All the while you're sitting here worrying about who's banging your boss,' he said provocatively. 'So, what's it going to be, you or her?'

Sanderson leant back in his chair and pretended to scroll through his mobile. After a couple of minutes he thought of something else that might be the clincher. 'And don't forget, if you cooperate and we can successfully prosecute your boss, then he will no longer be in a position to do you any harm.'

'That may be true, but if the towel heads can't get revenge from Wie or Yong they could still come after me,' she said.

'Maybe, just maybe, we could help you with that. I know who you're referring to and I could pay them a visit and simply remind them of the consequences of seeking any retribution for Yong using them for shooting practice. That's assuming of course that Amir and Jasar recover from their injuries and are back on the streets anytime soon.'

'Will you do that for me?'

'You're probably not an altogether bad person, you just keep bad company. Yes, I will do that for you. Anything to reduce the violence on our streets. And you will then have an opportunity to start a new life, unencumbered by fear.'

She crossed her arms and leaned back on her chair. 'Alright, what do you need from me?'

'Everything you know about Wie's importation process and China based connections, where he stores the coke and his distribution methods. And who is Than Ping Lie?'

'Really, is that all?' she asked mockingly.

Sanderson frowned. 'Have you been listening to anything that I've said?'

After a pronounced silence which Sanderson couldn't interpret she harumphed. 'Okay, I will tell you everything.'

'Lucie, I have to go back to my home station and speak to the Chief of Detectives and he will in turn have to get sign-off on any proposed deal from the State Director of Public Prosecutions. You might be here for a while. Don't let that deter you from what you need to do to protect yourself and safeguard your future. The guard will now take you down to the holding cells, but I will be back as soon as is practical. Okay?'

'Sure. Don't take too long please.'

45. Ministerial Offices – Martin Place

Thursday 28th May

This was Ben Chandler's last day in Sydney for the week. With parliament not sitting on Fridays he would finish early Thursday afternoon and catch the train home. His wife would be busy being busy and the boys would undoubtedly be off on their trail bikes all weekend, so he was looking forward to simply chilling out following a hectic week of politicking. Listening to Al Green's greatest hits and taking energising walks along the Brisbane Water were high on his agenda. He had been preoccupied with Sophie all week and realised that he had quickly fallen for her. Monday night had been one of the nights of his life. He had texted her daily from his personal mobile and felt like a child on Christmas morning when he received a response. He would miss her over the weekend. His executive assistant, Loretta Farrelly, knocked on his office door and entered without waiting for a response. 'Here's your mail, Ben. There's one marked strictly private and confidential in bold caps, so of course I didn't open it.'

'I can't believe in this day and age people still send so much snail mail, Loretta,' he said exasperatingly. 'Surely they have email.' He place the A4 envelope to one side of his desk.

After a hectic day completing the week's ministerial tasks he was about to head out into Martin Place and catch the city circle train to Central Station. As he turned to lock the office door he noticed the unopened envelope. He had been so busy that he had completely forgotten about it. He returned to his desk and collected it. He had an hour and a quarter on the train to Woy Woy, so he would read the contents then.

As he expected, the regional train was packed with commuters endeavouring to beat the peak hour rush, so, like nearly every other passenger, he amused himself by scrolling through his phone. By the time the train left Hornsby forty minutes later the previously crowded train had thinned out. There was now no one next to him, so Ben placed his briefcase on the spare seat and removed the envelope marked private and confidential. He hadn't realised just how thin it was and was now wondering what on earth could be so thin, and yet so darn important. *Well it's obviously not divorce papers,* he laughed to himself. He flipped the envelope over, tore off a corner and slid his finger along the inside of the flap. Under the seal he felt a single smooth document and he was still none the wiser as to the contents. As he extracted the document he recognised it as photo quality paper. He flipped it over.

'Oh, shit. Shit,' he said too loudly as his hand began quivering. 'Oh, no,' he muttered. Thank heavens he had managed to secure the window seat at the rear of the carriage and no one could see over his shoulders. He was equally glad that he hadn't opened the envelope in front of Loretta. He was aghast at what he was looking at and a gazillion confusing thoughts were running through his now jumbled mind. *How could this be?* Ben was staring at a photo of he and Sophie embracing on the hotel suite's living room sofa. It was obviously taken on Monday when Sophie had stayed the night. 'Shit.'

How could this possibly be? How would anyone be able to intrude on his privacy like this? This is Australia for heaven's sake, this doesn't happen in this country, he thought, naively.

Obviously, someone was sending him a message, but what did they want? What was he working on that was so darn sensitive or controversial that someone would stoop to this level to garner his attention. He had made numerous important decisions this year in the midst of the coronavirus pandemic. Not all of them were popular with the schools, academics, teachers, parents nor students, but he couldn't think of any previous related threats that would have escalated into this. And what about Sophie? Was she involved in this? No, she couldn't be. Surely not. She was a psychology student, not a tech head. He couldn't imagine her being technology savvy enough to pull off something as sophisticated as installing hidden cameras. Maybe she was working with or for someone. No, she wouldn't have done this. His accommodation was booked well in advance to coincide with the parliamentary schedule and he always stayed in the same suite. Many of the hotel staff would be familiar with his strict routine, and they had ample access to his suite to set up a hidden camera. But, what to do. He wouldn't go to the police yet. He couldn't. He recalled the story of a crossdressing footballer who had his photos widely shared on social media by members of the police force themselves. Ben and his family didn't deserve that, and nor did Sophie. He wondered if the photo had been sent to anyone else. No, whoever the perpetrators were wouldn't do that before submitting their demands, whatever they were. That much he was sure of.

He stared out the window at the scenery flashing past. *Come on Ben, you're a lawyer and politician, use your skills.* Both professions required the application of good judgement, the use of analytical and problem solving skills, being creative, and have the ability to think clearly using logic and reasoning. Time to put them into practice. Firstly, you need to calm down, he told himself. Hopefully, spending the weekend in the tranquil surroundings of Woy Woy would allow him to clear his mind and consider his options. His wife and the boys would be occupied all weekend as usual, so he would have an abundance of thinking time. He would need it. He wouldn't mention it to Sophie at this time, as whatever was at play here, she was surely an innocent bystander and potentially, an unwitting victim.

After a sleepless night, Ben was out walking along the Brisbane Water early on Friday morning. He was applying his analytical skills and one-by-one working his way through everyone he had meaningful contact with in the past few weeks and what possible motivation they might have to implement a stunt like this. There were plenty of people in the education sector who had differing opinions on his handling of the pandemic, but none that had shown any open hostility towards him. He considered his current stoush with the New South Wales Teachers Federation over the government's plan to bring all public school students back to class for one day a week. The Teachers Federation had been highly critical of the government's plan, saying it "beggars belief" and fails to comprehend the massive logistical challenges it would cause. Some high-profile principals and teachers had also been arguing on social media that sending students back at all would put teachers' safety at risk. It was of little concern to the teaching fraternity that hundreds of thousands of parents were struggling with the pressure of supervising lessons at home while working full-time. He didn't think that their ideological differences were sufficient reasons for them to resort to this level of intimidation though. *You need to keep digging Ben.*

46. Sydney Daily News

Thursday 28th May

'Hi, JA, how's your investigation going?"

'I'm well, thanks for asking Chris,' she responded light-heartedly.

'Alright, ease up. I've been busy trying to layout two editions and I hope you have some good news for me for Saturday's feature.'

Chris Russell was her editor and the person responsible for recruiting her from her regional television role in the Northern Rivers. He was supportive of her, but he still had his deadlines to adhere to.

'Yes, I think I have enough to go to print with.' Julie-Anne talked him through the timeline of her story and laid out the key facts. She would start with some background, recapping her earlier story about the money laundering scheme and particularly the role of Danielle Mortimer. 'As a reminder I'll drop a paragraph in about Mortimer ingratiating a high-profile detective, her brother's health issues that led to her involvement in the scheme, turning whistleblower, and finally the DC and DPP agreeing to reduce the charges against her.'

'That won't go down well with Jack,' Russell replied ominously.

'I know, however, it is crucial to the story, particularly given the whole thing started when she cosied up to him in the first place. The AFP's DC won't be pleased either as she duped him too.' Julie-Anne continued detailing the results of her updated investigation into the saga. The story would highlight the non-existent brother with the debilitating heart condition who Mortimer supposedly needed money for in order to cover his medical expenses. Then Julie-Anne intended to expose the deceit regarding Mortimer's employment and the reason behind it. Finally, she would reveal details of the double life the woman had been leading as the girlfriend of both the detective and the head of a notorious Chinatown based Triad. 'And finally, we have David Bedford's photos of Danielle and Wie together which will provide visual corroboration, even if we don't mention Wie's name.'

'Do you have any comments from the state police or AFP to add?'

'Not at this stage, but I have approached both Deputy Commissioners for comment.'

'Anything else for me, JA?'

'The state police have charged Wang Yong with the attempted murder of the two drug dealers and they also have Lucie Chan in custody after finding forty grams of coke hidden in her vehicle. She's the woman who was bashed and left to die in a wheelie bin in Queens Park. Both cases have direct links to Wie Ping Lie although neither has been proven in a court of law yet. What do you think, Chris?'

'Keep the stories separate for now otherwise you will dilute the impact of your original piece on Danielle Mortimer's deception. Put a few paragraphs together, then we might run it as an add-on to the primary story or a teaser for another feature next weekend.'

'Okay, that works for me, but there will be more to come on this story. Danielle Mortimer isn't done yet, of that I'm certain.'

'Okay, JA, as usual you've got until our standard deadline at four o'clock tomorrow to submit the completed articles for mine and legal's review and approval.'

47. Melissa's Townhouse Canada Bay

Thursday 28th May

Melissa Wu had invited Julie-Anne to her place for dinner. With the coronavirus lockdown restrictions in-place across the state they hadn't seen each other since Julie-Anne's emotional backflip on Jack's balcony back in March. She had called Melissa to clear the air and the conversation had gone well. They had both agreed that their relationship had progressed far too quickly without either woman giving due consideration to other factors in their respective lives. Julie-Anne had used the time to clear her head and was looking forward to seeing Melissa again. She had to admit she was feeling slightly nervous at the prospect though.

'Wow, don't you look fabulous,' Julie-Anne gushed. 'And you're wearing clothes this time.' The last time she had been here for dinner she had been greeted at the front door by Melissa wearing a skimpy bright red bikini. She had been grabbing the last rays of the setting sun on her deck.

'You're still funny, Julie-Anne. Come in, please.'

Melissa closed the door behind her and there was an unusual period of quiet.

'Are you checking out my new jeans?' Seeing how chic Sophie looked in her Citizens of Humanity jeans at dinner two weeks ago Julie-Anne had gone shopping and bought herself a pair.

'Of course, amongst your numerous other attributes.'

Julie-Anne turned around and was greeted by a warm, gentle kiss. She savoured the moment before pulling back. 'Where did that come from?'

'You do have a great arse, but I've missed *you*.'

Julie-Anne grasped Melissa hands, leant back, and regarded her. 'I've missed you too. You look fabulous, even if you're only wearing about twenty grams of fabric.' Julie-Anne wasn't sure what the atmosphere would be like after their relationship breakdown, so she had dressed modestly with jeans, jacket and a buttoned up blouse. Melissa, on the other hand was wearing a bright red (*of course*) mini with a side slit, open back and a severe drape neck which left little to the imagination. Of course, she was also wearing her fire engine Jimmy Choos which made the mini appear even shorter.

'I just love your hair, Julie-Anne. What a vibrant, rich colour. Now, come through and I'll introduce you to Paul,' she said as she ushered Julie-Anne towards the living area.

Paul? Julie-Anne assumed she was having dinner with just Melissa. What do they say about assume? *That ridiculous acronym*, she thought.

Julie-Anne was surprised and slightly taken aback. 'Who's Paul?'

'A good friend of mine, you'll like him.' Julie-Anne had never heard Melissa mention a Paul before, so if he was a good friend, he was a new good friend.

'Julie-Anne, this is Paul Gao.'

To Julie-Anne's eyes Paul Gao could have been created from the same mould as Melissa, just the male version. He was tall, athletically built, looked smart in tight fitting dress jeans, a slim fit cream linen shirt, untucked, and brown leather loafers. He had caramel coloured skin, dark almond shaped eyes, a big smile and what she guessed was a number three haircut that accentuated his strong facial features. He was a handsome man and she could see, at least physically, why Melissa was with him, if she were *with him*, of course.

'Hello, Paul. I'm pleased to meet you.' With her hand extended she walked across to him.

He accepted her hand and lightly caressed it. 'It's lovely to meet you too, Julie-Anne. Melissa has told me so much about you. That sounds like a cliché, but it's true, I swear.' He playfully placed his hand on his heart as he gazed intently into her eyes.

Julie-Anne felt her face flushing. Had this guy gone to the Melissa Wu school of flirting. If so, he must have received a distinction.

'Okay, let's have some bubbles and then you should try some delicious oysters with my very own special salsa creation,' said an excited Melissa.'

'Cheers to you, Julie-Anne, it's wonderful to see you after all this time,' Melissa said while raising her glass.

Paul's gaze was focused on Julie-Anne again as they clinked glasses. She felt his hand in the small of her back as he ushered her to the table.

'Alright, check out these babies.' Melissa arrived holding a platter of oysters that were resting on a bed of Himalayan sea salt. She handed Julie-Anne and Paul an oyster fork. 'Be sure to loosen the oyster first and then slurp them into your mouth.'

'That salsa is spectacular. What are the ingredients?' Julie-Anne asked while reaching for another oyster.

'Can I trust you with my secret recipe?' Melissa teased. 'Okay, there's six ingredients in there, all finely chopped. Lemongrass, garlic, ginger, coriander, chili, and freshly squeezed orange juice. I spoon the salsa onto the oysters and give them thirty seconds under the griller. It's a recipe from Near East, a favourite restaurant of mine in Melbourne which, unfortunately has now closed down. At least one of their signature dishes lives on, if only through me.'

Paul was topping up their champagne. 'Melissa, they are delicious. You should be proud that you can recreate such a culinary delight.'

'Julie-Anne, do you want to clear the table and I'll finish off preparing the main course?' Melissa asked.

'Of course.' Julie-Anne collected the platter and tiny forks and brought them across to the kitchen area.

Melissa turned to her friend. 'So, what do you think of Paul?'

Julie-Anne actually thought he was a tad too touchy feely, but she put it down to being a cultural thing. 'He seems like a really nice guy and you two appear well-matched,' Julie-Anne replied, not sure why Melissa was asking.

'Oh, it's not like that, really.'

'Then what's it like, *really*, and why are you asking me, of all people?'

'We have an arrangement of mutual convenience. We are both busy with work, so we just catch-up when both of us have a coinciding gap in our schedules.'

'Anyway, why the racy look? You are showing more skin than fabric. You seemed to have changed somewhat, Melissa. More carefree, if that's even possible.' Julie-Anne said with a laugh.

'No, I'm the same person you knew, Julie-Anne, I just realised that as an upwardly mobile young woman I should be enjoying this wonderful world we live in and making the most of my life before I drift into middle age and miss the boat. And I wanted to impress you.'

'Oh, you succeeded in that endeavour alright. You look hot. Damn hot.'

Paul topped up their champagnes again and the women stopped talking until he had walked away. 'I've been so busy chatting I almost forgot about main course. Go and take a seat and dinner will only be a few minutes.'

'So, Julie-Anne, Melissa told me about your investigation earlier in the year and the dangers you encountered. That must have been terrifying for you,' Paul stated with a concerned frown.

'Yes, parts of it were definitely scary, but overall it was a rewarding investigation and the story made the front page, which is always a pleasing outcome for a journalist.'

'Good for you, what have you been working on lately?' he asked as he leant forward onto his elbows and clasped his hands under his chin.

Julie-Anne was flattered by his interest. 'All media xenophobia aside, I definitely think there is something worth investigating surrounding potential Chinese interference in Australian daily life. China publicly states that it is committed to developing relations with other countries based on principles of mutual respect and non-interference in each other's internal affairs. We all know that's not the case.'

'That's very topical, however, I'm not sure everyone thinks that China interferes in other country's affairs,' he replied defensively.

'Well, Li Qiang and his cronies were trying to catapult Melissa into state parliament, and given her candidacy was to be funded by drug money laundered through the casino, I doubt their intentions were honourable.'

'I read about that. So, that was your feature. Well done, Julie-Anne,' he said while patting her hand in approval. 'So, where does the Chinese interference kick in?'

'Aah, that's an easy one. Li Qiang had links to the Consul General, but I could never prove that the CG was involved with the promotion of Melissa's candidacy,' she replied. Paul sat upright and Julie-Anne noticed his face reddening. He had an Asian surname, however, his appearance was Eurasian and he was Melissa's friend, so she hoped he wasn't offended by her comments. 'Sorry, that was a tad full-on.' She was just about to ask him about his own work when Melissa delivered their main course.

'Here we go, dinner's up, guys,' she said as she placed the terracotta tureen in the centre of the table. Hang on while I get the rice.'

'That smells delicious, what have we got here?' Julie-Anne asked.

'Red Duck Curry. I had it once at the Hanuman Restaurant in Darwin and loved it so much that I asked for the recipe. Enjoy guys.'

The three of them chatted about anything and everything, past, present and future with Julie-Anne carefully avoiding continuing on with the previous topic while Melissa was at the table.

'You've finished already, Paul,' Julie-Anne commented.

'He's a quick eater, Julie-Anne, although he assures me that he does actually like my food,' Melissa replied. 'Well, I sure hope so.'

'You know I do honey.' I'll be back shortly. He stood and left the room.

'You two act like a happily married couple,' Julie-Anne said, smiling warmly. 'Anyway, you work hard, so if he makes you happy and treats you with the respect and kindness you deserve, then that's wonderful. So, why am I really here, Melissa?'

'I have told Paul a lot about you, so he understandably wanted to meet you and I can see he already likes you. And of course, again, I wanted to see you.'

Julie-Anne felt herself getting ever so slightly lightheaded after her three champagnes and a glass of wine with dinner. She drank a glass of water and then breathed deeply. 'I should stop drinking if I'm going to drive home.'

'You don't have to drive; you can stay here.' Julie-Anne presumed Melissa would sleep with Paul and she would utilise the second bedroom.

Julie-Anne's disappointment must have been plastered all over her face. Melissa turned to Julie-Anne, placed her hand behind her head, and pulled her into another kiss. 'God I miss that,' she said, looking yearningly into Julie-Anne's eyes. 'It's okay you can sleep with me.'

Melissa pulled back just as Paul walked over and topped up their wines. Again. He momentarily stopped, leant in, and kissed Melissa on the mouth. *Was he reclaiming his woman?* She looked at Julie-Anne out of the corner of her eye.

What did that mean? Did she like Julie-Anne watching or was she making her jealous. No, that wasn't her style, she was stronger than that. *It was nothing, Julie-Anne,* she told herself. She was in the sweet spot after her champagnes and wine, so she decided that she would just enjoy the evening and not read too much into anything. Although, she realised that she was slightly aroused at the sight of someone else kissing Melissa. Was that a natural or understandable reaction. She really needed to talk to someone about some of the unusual physical sensations she experienced around Melissa.

48. AFP Headquarters

Thursday 28th May

'Hi, Michael, thanks for coming back,' Jack said as he offered his hand in greeting.

Sanderson was now back on the tenth floor of the AFP's headquarters for the third time today. 'I spend more time here working with you feds than I do at my own office.' He had returned from Day Street after speaking to his Chief of Detectives in relation to Lucie Chan's situation. The COD had reluctantly agreed with his recommendations and had taken the case up with the state's DPP.

'How did you go, Michael?'

'Well, it took some persuasion, but we're a go.'

'That's great news, well done, buddy.'

'Not so fast, Jack,' he replied guardedly. 'Both my COD and the DPP understandably have placed a condition on the whole operation. They acknowledge that there is probably an international drug importation component to this, however, it will be up to you to chase any leads down that point that way. Both of them are happy for us to assist you in any way we can with that operation, if it pans out, but at this time it remains a state based operation. Are you okay with that?'

'Yeah, sure, I'll take whatever I can if it gets me closer to Wie's importation operation and his sponsors in China.'

'Okay, that's good.'

'It's late in the evening, so do you want to drag Lucie out of her holding cell and interview her now or wait until the morning?'

Sanderson had an idea from left field. 'Why don't we bring her up here and order Uber Eats to show some good faith towards her. Given she needs to trust us, that might help put her mind at ease.'

'It contradicts every regulation I can think of, but I will bow to your better judgement and if it goes south then we'll have to cop it on the chin.' Jack called down to the holding cells and arranged for guards to bring Lucie Chan up to the detective unit.

'What has the DPP agreed to that we are allowed to offer her?'

'As you can imagine, there's a few conditions and I don't necessarily agree with all of them, Jack, but it's not my call.' Sanderson told Jack that she must remain in custody until the operation is successfully completed and that she needed to make a statement detailing her knowledge of the shooting of Amir and Jasar including implicating Yong. Chan was also required to detail her knowledge of Wie's operation including where he stores his drugs. 'Finally, she is also to divulge everything she can about Than Ping Lie and who she is.'

'I've got something of my own to add to that list. I want everything she knows about Danielle's involvement in Wie's operation, which shouldn't be a problem for her, given her open hostility towards her love rival. This is now a state investigation and it was you who turned Lucie, so you should take the lead, Michael. What is the DPP offering in return?'

'If we get what we need out of her they have agreed to a fine of no more than five thousand dollars and two years' probation with no reoffending during that time.'

'Detective Wagner?' Jack heard his name called and he looked across to see two uniformed guards walk into the unit with Lucie Chan firmly in their grasp. Even the standard police issue orange overalls couldn't detract from her model's appearance.

'Hi, Lucie, take a seat over here,' Sanderson instructed. 'How have you been since we last spoke?'

Jack's mobile phone buzzed. 'I'll be back in a minute.' He instructed the attendant guards to wait until he returned.

Lucie Chan scowled. 'Better if I hadn't been locked away in that stinking hellhole downstairs,' she responded, not disguising her hostility.

'Come on, you knew that was going to happen. Detective Wagner and I didn't have to interview you tonight, but we wanted to show some good faith, given your intended cooperation and not keep you in custody any longer than necessary. If you want to go back downstairs then tell me and we can start again tomorrow.' He leant back in his chair and spread his hands in an imploring gesture. 'It's up to you.'

'Aright, thank you,' she replied.

'While we're waiting for Jack I will tell you how this is going to work. Both my COD and the DPP have agreed to participate in a trade of information in exchange for a reduced penalty.'

'What do you mean a reduced penalty. Be more specific, please?'

'That depends on how cooperative you are and the veracity of the information you provide. We have a list of questions for you that require your complete cooperation through your response. Answer all our questions truthfully and you could walk away with probation and a fine.'

'And if I don't?'

'You're acutely aware of the alternative. Look, you have obviously been marginalised within Wie's business, so this shouldn't be that difficult for you, Lucie. Whatever you get charged with that avoids gaol time will be a bonus. And just so you know we are going to record our conversation again.'

'Okay, here we go, Taste of Shanghai delivered to your desk.' Jack placed two carry bags of containers of steaming food on the desk. 'I was going to order Grill'd burgers, but I thought we should cater to our guest's taste.'

'Thank you, detective,' she said, her eyes searching his. 'That's very considerate of you.'

'It's late already, so let's get started, shall we?' Sanderson began. 'Lucie, why don't you start by explaining your role in Wie's business?'

'I am a delivery driver for him.'

'How does your role work?"

'I collect the product and deliver it.'

'Jack, turn the recorder off,' Sanderson demanded. 'Lucie, we know you are a delivery driver and what your job is already. I don't intend to sit here all night while you state the obvious and provide abbreviated responses to our questions. You need to be more forthcoming than that and elaborate with your responses otherwise we're done here. I'm more than happy to settle for charging you with possession and supply of a commercial quantity of an illicit substance. I will simply put you back down in the holding cells, go home and have a good night's sleep. Then I'll return all refreshed in the morning and charge you accordingly. It's your call.'

'Okay,' she said softly, accepting defeat.

'Now let's start over. Explain your role in Wie's drug distribution business.' Sanderson was more specific this time.

Lucie talked the detectives through her routine from the communications methods, receipt of an order, product collection, delivery method and payment. 'What is Wie Ping Lie's involvement in the process?'

'Wie doesn't handle the merchandise, it's all done by his lieutenants and delivery drivers. That's when you guys haven't already killed or arrested them,' she said sassily.

Sanderson ignored the gibe. 'Where does he store the bulk merchandise?'

'He has a storage unit somewhere.'

'Where exactly, Lucie? We will find out eventually, so save us the trouble if you don't mind.'

'Rent A Space Self Storage in Padstow.'

'Do they have specific times or days when they collect their product?'

'Not really, but obviously they need blow for the weekend trade so today or tomorrow would be logical.'

'Are you guessing or do you actually know?'

'I have collected product myself on both days.'

Sanderson smiled. 'See how easy this is.'

It was Jack's turn to interrogate her regarding the federal issue. 'What do you know about the importation process?'

'Nothing really. Li Jun used to be away for a week to ten days at a time and I assumed he was taking delivery of the product. Of course, that was before your guys killed him too,' she said looking downcast.

Jack ignored the latest barb. 'How much product is imported in each shipment?'

'I'm not certain, but I endeavoured to calculate the value once based on the volume I was dealing in a given time. I think it's probably around one hundred kilos, give or take.'

'You're doing well, Lucie. Do you know the source of the coke?'

'No. Wie would never share that information, however, Li Jun mentioned the China Shipping Company once. He said all the shipments were received from their vessels.'

That was consistent with what the MBC and AMSA guys

had determined through their own investigations. Lucie was being truthful. 'Who replaced Li Jun?'

'Wang Yong was Wie's new lieutenant and minder.'

Sanderson jumped back in. 'Now, this is important, Lucie. Did Wang Yong shoot Amir and Jasar?'

She was still looking at Jack. 'Yes. He knew where their delivery rounds were, so he went hunting for them in their territory, and you know the rest, I'm sure.'

'Who was the other guy with Yong?'

'I don't know. There are a few younger guys around who are wannabe gang members, like groupies, so they just let them tag along sometimes. Maybe like an apprentice I guess. Wie calls them his Blue Lanterns.'

'Now tell me, who is Than Ping Lie?'

'I've never met her, but I think it's his mother. I really don't know anything about her. I saw him having lunch with an older woman at a restaurant one day. Wie doesn't have any interest in older women, so I assumed that's who she must be.'

'The Golden Phoenix?'

'Yes, he eats there all the time.'

'We know he has lunch there with Danielle. Has he ever taken you there, Lucie?' he asked. Sanderson wanted her to remember the reason she was here and hoped her getting antsy at Wie's favouritism for Danielle would keep her on track.

'Of course, all the time' she lied.

'Than owns numerous properties, but do you know where she actually lives?'

'No, I don't.'

Jack spoke again. 'What can you tell us about Danielle Mortimer's involvement in his operations?'

'You mean other than dating you.'

'Knock it off, Lucie,' Sanderson said being protective of Jack's feelings. 'What's her role?'

'She doesn't have a role. I have heard that she was involved in money laundering when she worked at the casino, but other than that, I have no idea.'

'Does she live at the Sussex Street Apartments?'

'No.'

'What can you tell us about Sam Bourdain?'

'Nothing really. He's just a lowlife who received his just desserts for what he precipitated through his greed.'

'Now that wasn't so hard, was it, Lucie?'

Jack rang down to the holding cells and called the guards back up. 'She is to have no contact with anyone. No phone calls, no visitors, no messages. Is that clear?' he instructed them.

'How long will I be held for now?' she asked.

'Only as long as is necessary. If the information you provided actually aids our investigation it shouldn't be too long.'

She gazed into Jack's eyes. 'Thank you, detective.'

49. Melissa's Townhouse Canada Bay

Thursday 28th May

After dinner Paul had disappeared upstairs, so the women continued to reminisce about the fun times they had while they were together. The funniest memory was their joke telling at the QV Wine Bar in Surry Hills following the Consul General's cocktail party. 'Tell me that panda joke again, Melissa.'

'Give me a moment. I will have to try and remember it. Okay I've got it.' As she said that, just as she had at the QV, she leaned forward, placed both her hands on Julie-Anne knees, and stared intently into her eyes. 'Okay, here we go.'

'A panda bear walks into a restaurant, sits himself down, and asks the waiter to bring him a plate of bamboo. After the panda finishes his meal, he takes out a gun and kills the waiter right then and there. The restaurant owner was horrified. He says to the panda bear: "Why did you do this?", to which the panda replies: "Look it up in the encyclopedia." The restaurant owner takes out his encyclopedia, and under the entry of panda bear, he finds: "Panda. Giant mammal indigenous to China, eats bamboo and shoots".'

The women burst into sustained, raucous laughter. 'That was still so funny the second time around,' Julie-Anne gushed.

Their bout of laughter was slowly fading and was now replaced with the familiar look of longing. Without saying a word Melissa leaned further inward placed her hand on her cheek and kissed her softly. Julie-Anne found her mouth opening as she closed her eyes and leaned in. Melissa's tongue slid gently into her mouth, exploring, teasing. 'Mmmm.' Julie-Anne groaned. She could feel her nipples hardening and something was stirring inside her, just like the first time.

'Are you okay, ladies?' Paul was standing next to the women, dressed only in his boardshorts, and holding three glasses of white wine. Julie-Anne hadn't heard him come down the stairs nor go to the fridge, so she guessed he might have been there for a while. Maybe he had enjoyed watching them. She surprisingly wasn't embarrassed at all. She loved her time with Melissa.

Paul placed the glasses on the nearby coffee table, turned back to the women, leant across Julie-Anne, and kissed Melissa intensely. *Maybe he's reclaiming his woman.* Melissa placed her hand on the nape of his neck and held him in-place. His body was alongside Julie-Anne. She could smell his subtle masculine fragrance; his ripped body was gleaming in the downlights and there was a bulge in his boardshorts. She tried hard to banish all three stimuli from her mind and breathed deeply to help rid herself of the sensory overload. She was unsuccessfully trying not to appear awkward, but after what seemed like an eternity, Paul pulled back and turned his head towards her. She was flushing, but kidded herself it was the alcohol.

'Sorry, Julie-Anne that was quite rude of me.'

To her surprise, he placed his hand gently under her chin, tilted it upwards, and kissed her tenderly. Even more astonishingly, she didn't withdraw.

'Okay, who's up for a swim,' he blurted out as he pulled back. He picked up the three glasses of wine and walked out onto the deck.

Julie-Anne was still flustered as Melissa led her through the glass doors. The women sat on the matching sun lounges and sipped their wine. 'What a beautiful evening, Julie-Anne, it's still twenty degrees.'

Melissa was obviously choosing to gloss over what just happened or maybe she was comfortable with the scenario that unfolded. Julie-Anne didn't know what she was supposed to say, but when in doubt, sure, let's talk about the weather. 'It's quite balmy for this time of the year and I love it out here. Do you remember the last time we were here?'

Melissa smiled affectionately. 'How could I forget. That was the wonderful night we consummated our friendship. Everything about the evening was just perfect.'

Paul had exited the pool at the far end and was fiddling with the filter mechanism. Apparently happy he had fixed whatever the issue was, he stood up, and Julie-Anne guessed for effect, he lifted his hands up and ran them through his hair. His wet caramel skin was glistening in the pool lights and his ripped upper body formed a textbook vee from his six pack to his broad shoulders. *And the boardshorts were gone.*

'I'm going for a swim, are you coming, Julie-Anne?'

'Not on your life, it's not warm enough for me. Call me when it gets to forty degrees,' she joked.

'Don't be silly, it's heated. I had it installed before the winter set in.'

Melissa rose, and just as she had once before, lifted her dress up over her head and laid it across the lounge. Julie-Anne watched Melissa walk to the pool edge while admiring her toned, toffee coloured body. Melissa shallow dived in and swam a couple of laps of the small pool. Julie-Anne was sipping her wine while Melissa and Paul duck-dived and frolicked like dolphins. Then Melissa swam over to Paul, looped her arms around his neck, and appeared to wrap her legs around his body. Was he just holding her, was she gripping him to prevent herself from slipping, were they just having a cuddle or was it the fourth option? If Julie-Anne were flushed before she couldn't begin to describe the sensations running through her body now. She picked up her wine and took a large gulp.

'Julie-Anne, it's beautiful in here, come on in. I promise it's lovely and warm.' Julie-Anne wasn't sure whether the cliché two's company, three's a crowd was applicable but, if it had been the fourth option, then she was staying right where she was. As if on cue, Melissa pulled away from Paul and called out to Julie-Anne again. *Impeccable timing.*

Oh, why not. 'Okay, give me a minute.' She placed her empty wine glass down on the table and took off her jacket and kicked off her heels. She undid the buttons of her new favourite jeans, peeled them off and placed them next to Melissa's dress. Slipping out of her blouse she folded it over her jeans. The wine must have emboldened her and she stood there in her ocean blue coloured, lacy underwear watching Paul and Melissa canoodling. She unclipped her bra and stepped out of her French knickers, lifted her arms up and fluffed her newly coloured locks. She was fully extended and had attracted Melissa and Paul's attention. She saw Melissa whisper something to Paul. Walking over to the pool she tested the temperature with her toe and then dived in. She swam laps and was loving the soothing feel of the warm water washing across her naked body. She couldn't recall the last time that she had savoured the liberating freedom of a skinny dip. Paul and Melissa were now leaning with their backs against the pool wall chatting away. Julie-Anne glided across to join them. 'This is just wonderful and I can't believe the water is so warm.'

Melissa floated around to Julie-Anne, righted herself and moved into her. Julie-Anne saw the hungry look she had seen in her friend's eyes previously and she knew, hoped, what was coming. Melissa leaned forward, her lips gently caressing Julie-Anne's.

Julie-Anne felt Melissa's hand move down between her legs and she parted them willingly. 'Aah, that touch.' She was moving her hips slowly in response and released a soft moan.

'Yours too. I've missed you. Do you remember the last time we did this?' Melissa whispered into her ear.

'Yes, how could I forget.' Melissa's hand was working its magic and she had found Julie-Anne's sweet spot, again. 'Oh, that's wonderful.' She was so invested in the moment that she completely forgot that there was another person there.

Out of the blue, but not totally unexpected given the obvious flirting earlier, Julie-Anne felt a soft peck to the back of her neck, then another, and another. A rock hard body leant into her and two strong hands firmly clasped her breasts, bringing her out of her trance. She had winced involuntarily and should have said something, but what? Julie-Anne was emotionally and physically invested in the moment with Melissa and she was aroused. Highly. Paul's sensitive kisses were taking her to another level. This was all new to her. He was now caressing her breasts and tickling her nipples. She examined Melissa's face seeking guidance.

Realising what Julie-Anne was wrestling with, Melissa placed her free hand under Julie-Anne's chin and pulled her into a fierce kiss, not giving her time to think. She probed deeply with her tongue.

Julie-Anne became more aroused as Melissa explored. Then she was reminded of the hands on her. *God, what is happening.* The hands slowly drifted south to her hips. She could feel his hardness pressing up against her. Melissa leant forward, grasped Julie-Anne's breasts and tenderly caressed them with her tongue, moving from one to the other.

'Oh, wow, that's wonderful, oh, yes.' Julie-Anne placed a hand on the back of Melissa's head.

At that moment she felt Paul move in between her legs.

She should have been startled, but she wasn't, such was the increasingly erotic nature of the encounter. He clasped Julie-Anne's head and turned it towards him. Julie-Anne's glazed eyes stared deeply into his. He was looking hungrily at her. He wanted her and her body wanted him too. Now. Leaning forward, he kissed her feverishly and she looped her arm around his neck, held him in place and responded with a feverishness of her own. He parted her with surprising tenderness and slowly entered her, her muscles momentarily tensing. She gasped as he thrust up into her. 'Aaagh.'

Julie-Anne was gyrating in time with his thrusting and Melissa was still teasing her breasts with her tongue. She gripped Paul's firm buttocks and held him tightly in place. She was in sensory overload. 'Oh, ooh, aaahh.'

Melissa whispered breathlessly into her ear. 'Are you ready yet?'

Julie-Anne groaned. 'Oh, yeah.'

Melissa gently massaged Julie-Anne in a circular motion. Then she tilted her head and began pecking Julie-Anne on the neck. Her other sweet spot.

Julie-Anne felt Paul's strong hands clasp her breasts again. 'You are truly a magnificent woman,' he whispered. Her nipples had never been this hard and the tingling was off the charts. He kissed the other side of her neck while pushing up into her and picking up his pace. 'Are you ready?' he whispered.

'Oh, yes, yes, go on, now.' She upped the pace of her gyrating and now longed for him to finish her off. He was thrusting hard and deep now and she was still tingling at Melissa's touch. Her body was being ravished by these two. This was sensory overload on steroids. She had given her body over to them, they had her in their clutches, she was completely at their mercy, and revelling in it.

She was close now and she grasped Melissa's back firmly

with one hand, reached around Paul with the other and pulled them in tight. 'Oh, yes, yes, yes, oh, yes,' she cried, and with his one final deep thrust, she was there, and her body began spasming and trembling as she cried out in ecstasy.

50. Melissa's Townhouse Canada Bay

Friday 29th May

The women were lying in bed, not speaking, with neither seemingly knowing what to say about the previous evening's events. The morning sun was sweeping through the sheer curtains and Julie-Anne was savouring its warmth, although her mind was muddled, and swimming with unanswered questions. Someone had to break the impasse and she decided it may as well be her. She rolled onto her side to face Melissa and propped on her elbow.

'So, how did that come about? Did you guys have that planned all along?' she asked pointedly.

'No, not at all. I wouldn't do that to you.'

Julie-Anne stared at her disbelievingly. 'So, when you invited me to dinner, that was just an innocent invitation?'

Melissa placed her hand gently on Julie-Anne's cheek. 'Yes, it was, I wanted to see you.'

'So, how did we end up having a threesome in your pool then? That's a quantum leap from a supposedly innocent dinner invitation.'

'I know, I didn't see it coming either. Sorry, no pun intended,' Melissa replied, stifling a laugh.

'Any other time I would have found that funny,' Julie-Anne responded blankly.

Her friend was entitled to an explanation, but Melissa didn't know if she could provide a credible one. 'There was considerable sexual tension in the air all night, from me checking out your arse in your stylish new jeans, Paul flirting with you and sensuously caressing your hand when you arrived and us flirting in the kitchen. Then when Paul leant across you I caught you looking at his body, and I thought, mmmm, what's happening here?'

'So, you're saying I instigated it?' Julie-Anne replied, incredulous.

'No, not at all, although I did think when Paul kissed you at the table and you didn't flinch, that things might not finish there.'

'I should have said something, but I thought he was just shamelessly flirting, and you didn't react either, so I just let it go. I also didn't want to create a potentially embarrassing situation for you, especially not knowing the status of your relationship, Melissa.'

'Back to your original question. To be honest, Julie-Anne, when you were standing on the deck naked, fully stretched and fluffing your hair, Paul and I were gobsmacked. You looked like a goddess. I said to him, "Isn't she magnificent?". "Yes, she is, that body, he said". Then he grabbed my hand and placed it on him. He was rock hard and obviously stimulated by you. I found that extremely erotic and became aroused too. I guess I thought, subconsciously, that if I couldn't find a way to have you to myself…'

'What? That the two of you would share me.'

'No, it wasn't like that. It just evolved organically.'

'Organically huh. Somehow I think your new friend might have had something to do with it. He was enthusiastically plying us with drinks all night after all and then he conveniently took advantage of our affection for each other.'

'Maybe. Anyway, didn't you enjoy yourself, Julie-Anne?'

'I like to think of myself as an intelligent, well-adjusted and socially aware woman. In the space of three months I've gone from being a life-long heterosexual to having a relationship with you, and now a threesome.'

Melissa tilted Julie-Anne's head towards her. 'You didn't answer the question.'

Julie-Anne wasn't embarrassed, but for some reason she was avoiding responding. Was it the betrayal, being seduced by a relative stranger, the loss of her power, Melissa's complicity or that she had revelled in it.

'What question?'

'Didn't you enjoy yourself, Julie-Anne?'

'Of course I did. It was a first for me. I found the whole encounter extraordinarily sensual, and I was flying in the end. It was the most erotic experience I've ever had. I'm obviously not some prude, but it might be nice to be suitably prepared for something as potentially confronting as a threesome though. Lord knows what the neighbours thought. I don't know whether to be embarrassed or laugh at that prospect. Anyway, back to your earlier comment, you could have had me to yourself, Melissa.'

'Yeah, I know and in some ways I wish I had,' she replied pensively. 'I must admit I was a little jealous towards the end when you and Paul were so invested in each other.'

'And what about you; what did you think?'

'Oh, yeah. Two months without you I guess I thought I'll take you any way I can, even if that meant sharing you. Although, that wasn't what I originally hoped. I was wishing you and I could just drift away by ourselves after dinner, but that all changed when we ventured into the pool. You should have seen yourself, Julie-Anne. The whole thing was so sensuous and erotic and you were magnificent the way you just rolled with it.'

'I think the amount of alcohol we consumed might have had something to do with it.'

'Well, whether it did or not it was a fabulous experience. I was more aroused than ever.' She leant forward and pulled Julie-Anne into a soft kiss.

After a moment Julie-Anne rolled over onto her back. 'Anyway, where's your boyfriend?'

'He's not my boyfriend,' Melissa replied emphatically.

'What, so I was screwed by a simple acquaintance last night? Well, I sincerely hope he's a discreet one then.'

The women were quiet for some time, both assuming that the other was revisiting the events of the previous night, and pondering the possible repercussions. 'So, where is the man of the moment?' Julie-Anne eventually asked to break the ice.

'He went to work early.'

'Oh, okay, where does he work, and what does he do for a career?'

'He's an emissary at the Chinese Consulate. We met at a consular cocktail party before the lockdown kicked in.'

Alarm bells were now ringing for Julie-Anne and the revelation disturbed her. Conspiracy theories were bouncing around in her head. 'Melissa, who's idea was it to invite me to dinner?'

'Mine of course. I wanted to see you.'

Julie-Anne persisted. 'Are you certain, this is important?' No answer. 'Melissa?' she demanded more forcefully.

'Okay, Paul suggested it over dinner one night. He said he had heard so much about you that I should invite you to dinner and he could meet this woman who swept me off my feet.'

'And you think that's just a coincidence? Shit, Melissa, I'm investigating Chinese interference in Australia at the moment, and what, you think he wasn't aware of that. And if he wasn't, he certainly is now after I told him so in no uncertain manner at the dinner table.'

'No, Julie-Anne you're wrong about him,' she replied. 'He has even nominated me to participate in a study tour to China later in the year.'

'Really, a study tour of China, and who pray tell is sponsoring that?' she asked.

'The United Front Work Department. It is a division of their government that promotes mutual cooperation with China around the globe.'

'You should research them first before making any commitment. Now, back to the interference discussion. You're a lawyer with a naturally challenging mind. I imagine a scenario where at some stage you were telling him, probably quite innocently, about how your political candidacy was undermined, Li Qiang's money laundering activities, Wie Ping Lie and my investigation potentially linking the consulate, his employer by the way, to all of the above. How am I doing, Melissa?' Julie-Anne asked fervidly.

No reply, so she continued. 'And now in hindsight, it's obvious why he was so enthusiastically topping up my drink all night. He was evidently hoping to get me talking at some stage, which he did. You need to be careful around him until I can thoroughly check him out. I have no idea what his angle is, but I certainly gave him some ammunition to use last night.'

Julie-Anne urgently needed to get to the office and finalise her feature. Then, if she had time she would follow-up on just who Paul Gao was. She quickly showered and headed for the door. Ducking her head back into the main bedroom she said, 'and please, until I find out more information, keep this conversation between us, Melissa. And remember, be careful around him.'

51. Sydney Daily News

Friday 29th May

I really don't need this today, she thought as she involuntarily yawned. Julie-Anne had gone to Melissa's for what was expected to be dinner just for the two of them. It was meant to be a relaxing evening of reminiscing before she would be confronted with her looming deadline in the morning. Now, she was mildly hungover, sleepy tired and exhausted from the other unanticipated activity of the evening. Somehow she needed to focus and pull her story together by four o'clock. She dropped two Beroccas into her glass of water and stirred furiously before gulping down the whole concoction. The digital clock on her desktop showed ten fifteen already. *Damn*. With her deadline rapidly approaching she couldn't afford to lose any more time. She wanted to speak with Jack again, but she would allow him to settle into his day before calling. Instead, she began writing a recap of the version of events from her published feature back in March as a preface to provide the link to her current story. She started with the relationship of Wie and Li Qiang and their connection to the Chinese Consul General. She provided some background on Li Qiang and his fondness for western excesses such as fine scotch whiskey, Cuban cigars, gambling and attractive escorts, a combination of which had led to his downfall. Then she moved on to the money laundering operation

Li Qiang was running to finance Melissa Wu's candidacy for state parliament. Julie-Anne emphasised that Ms Wu was not involved in, nor had any knowledge of the criminal activities. Julie-Anne highlighted the Oceanic Hotel and Casino's Vice President, Tony Woodard's role in laundering the money, his incarceration and the devastated family he left behind. Li Qiang was also now in prison, but no one seemed to be missing him. Julie-Anne then highlighted Danielle Mortimer's role in handling the cash and chips exchange before changing sides and assisting the joint agency taskforce to close down the operation and prosecute the bad actors. She reiterated that Mortimer's involvement was only due to her having to raise funds to provide the necessary medical support for her brother's congenital heart condition. And finally she reported on the DPP's decision to reduce the woman's penalty down to a manageable fine, given her whistleblower role and her brother's medical issues.

Once Julie-Anne was happy with the introduction to her current story she began to detail the sequence of recent events as they occurred. She would open her story with a tale about the lead detective from the money laundering case falling in love with Danielle Mortimer. She would allude to a fairy tale romance. Next she would highlight the anonymous tip that she received about rumours surrounding Danielle Mortimer and the Sydney Daily News subsequently engaging the services of a private security company to either substantiate or debunk them. She would confirm that Miss Mortimer was in fact in a relationship with two men; the detective and the head of a notorious Chinatown based Triad. She would need to insert photos at this juncture to provide validation of her assertion.

She went to the story's folder on the Daily News' server and double clicked on the photos icon. She scrolled across the thumbnails until she found what she wanted. She chose two photos, one showing Wie having lunch with Danielle and a second that showed them embracing outside the Sussex Street Apartments. The photos would provide proof that there was a tangible link between the Triad head and the casino's former treasury officer. The readers could see it with their own eyes and form their own judgement. With her fingers flying across the keyboard she disclosed how the Triad was endeavouring to penetrate the eastern suburbs drug market with the establishment of a 'dial a dealer' network.

> *The Triad is now operating in plain sight, using the encrypted messaging app Wickr to hide their crimes. The app uses end-to-end military grade encryption on all messages and files which ensures that third parties are unable to access the data as it transfers from one device to another. Wickr also allows users to set messages to "auto-destruct". Users are able to set a time for each conversation between one second and six days when the message is then automatically deleted from its system.*
>
> *The incumbent drug networks in the eastern suburbs weren't enamoured with the increase in competition, and in particular, the loss of business due to the higher purity cocaine the new arrivals were selling. So much so that Lucie Chan, one of the Triad's trusted distributors, was viciously bashed while on a delivery run and left to die in a council wheelie bin in a laneway off Birrell Street in Queens Park. Chan eventually recovered, but was later arrested in an apartment in the same building where Wie Ping Lie and Danielle Mortimer were photographed. Both the apartment where Lucie Chan was arrested and the apartment where Danielle Mortimer lives in Glebe are owned by Than Ping Lie, a relative of Wie Ping Lie.*

There was a gap in her story as she had been unable to confirm the relationship between the apartment's owner, Than Ping Lie and the Triad head, so she would just allude to it for now.

Then, she would provide the kicker to the story.

As a result of her turning whistleblower, the DPP had decided not to charge Danielle Mortimer with the more serious charge open to his office under the Proceeds of Crime Act 2002. Nor had the DPP seen fit to confiscate the proceeds of the crimes committed by her. This reporter has established that this decision was based on compassionate grounds given the proceeds were presumed to be used to support her brother's congenital heart condition. The Sydney Daily News can confirm that Danielle Mortimer does not have a brother, biological or otherwise. This now begs the question as to why Miss Mortimer's claims about her brother weren't thoroughly investigated by either the DPP or Australian Federal Police before her charges were downgraded. The Sydney Daily News has reached out to the DPP and the AFP's Deputy Commissioner for comment. We received no response to date.

It was only midday and Julie-Anne was comfortable with her first draft, so she pressed the send icon and away it went to her editor. It would take Chris Russell and the legal department a couple of hours to review her story, so she had some time to herself. Now, she desperately needed another strong latte. And maybe a quick nap.

52. AFP Headquarters

Friday 29th May

'Good morning, did you get some sleep, buddy?' Sanderson enquired as he walked in with a takeaway coffee in each hand. 'Latte with two, correct?'

'Thanks, I'll take anything this morning.'

Jack had arrived at his desk early to prepare an application for a judicial warrant to access the office records at Rent A Space in Padstow. 'When are you thinking we should conduct the raid, Michael?'

'I think we should put a team together and stake it out first. I'm betting Lucie knows precisely what she's talking about and we might get lucky and catch them picking up stock for the busy weekend trade. We also don't know if Wie has any contacts inside Rent A Space who might be predisposed to tipping him off in advance. I wouldn't mind taking the first shift if we get the warrant in time. You up for that, buddy?'

'Given I'm obviously single again, what else would I be doing on a Friday night? What time are you thinking?'

'Maybe from around three o'clock until midnight or so and if need be we can get the uniform guys to cover the graveyard shift.'

'Okay, that sounds like a plan. You will need to sign the warrant application given this is a state based operation, Michael.

I'll print it out in a minute, then once you've signed it, I'll scan it and submit it electronically.'

'Works for me, Jack. If you don't mind me asking, are you okay with the whole Danielle scenario. Lucie threw a couple of jabs at you yesterday. How are you doing?'

'Personally, I'm struggling with Danielle's betrayal, but I'm getting better by the day. If I'm honest, I do miss her though. She was a breath of fresh air. Professionally, I am embarrassed that I didn't pick up on any of the warning signs though, so now I want to put that cute arse of hers in prison.'

'How are you going to achieve that?'

'It's up to the DC and the DPP to now decide what action they take, and if they propose to re-arrest her, then I will be front and centre in that operation,' he stated with conviction.

Jack's mobile phone rang. 'I have to take this, Michael.'

The caller was JA, and as usual when he was in the middle of an investigation and she had a looming deadline, the competitive juices flowed freely. The tone of the call degenerated rapidly. After the verbal volleying had gone backwards and forwards for at least two minutes he disconnected the call while she was in midsentence.

'Check this out, Michael.' Jack was pointing to Google Maps on his screen. 'We've had a win there, buddy. The map shows a parking area inside Padstow Park that is directly across Davies Road from the Rent A Space storage facility. It looks like it has excellent line of sight too.'

'Okay, we'll set-up there,' Sanderson said.

'What's tickled you?'

'That's the same storage place where that dodgy copper Roger Rogerson killed that small time criminal and then botched the disposal of the body.'

'Yeah, I know. What a silly old bugger he was.'

Jack heard the ding sound emanate from his desktop

that indicated he had received an email. 'Jesus, that was quick. Someone obviously has a hot date tonight and wants to leave the office early.'

'What on earth are you on about?'

'The warrant. It's been signed and returned already. Go figure.'

Sanderson rubbed his hands together. 'Alright let's do this.'

53. Sydney Daily News

Friday 29th May

She glanced at the desktop's clock. *Jack's had enough time to get his day moving.* Julie-Anne took another gulp of her strong latte, picked up her mobile and hit speed dial.

'Hi, JA, how are you?'

'I'm worn-out and a tad run down if you must know, Jack.' Ex-boyfriend or not he would be horrified if he knew the reason why.

'Why, what have you been up to?'

Her mind rewound to the previous night. The debauchery, lust, eroticism, sensuality, the carnal desires, the memories and mental pictures came flooding back. *Focus, Julie-Anne.* 'Nothing out of the ordinary really, I'm just tired.'

'As long as you're okay.'

'Yes, I am, thanks. Do you have anything else for me? I've only got a few hours until my deadline and my first draft needs some more grunt in the story.' Julie-Anne knew there was definitely more to come, but if she waited another week every media outlet in the state will have the story and she will have missed her scoop.

'JA, we don't run investigations in accordance with your deadline.'

'Jack, our biggest readership is on Saturdays, so this story needs to be in tomorrow's edition. It won't be kept under wraps for another week, you know that. If it was just your investigation I could possibly hold it, but the state police leak like a sieve. You know that also.'

'It's up to you what you run with. You'll just have to publish what you've got. I have to go.'

'What's going on? I can tell by your voice something's happening. What is it, Jack?' She was pleading now.

'Look, JA, we're about to go on a stakeout, so I can't stay on this call forever listening to you tell me about your deadlines.'

'Give me something to work with and I'll leave you alone. Come on, Jack, pleeeease.'

Jack still felt some loyalty to her that emanated from their time in a relationship. He was endeavouring to distance himself from her professionally, however, he realised they still had a connection, albeit a personal one. And he had promised to share information with her. 'Okay, we're going to stakeout Wie's storage unit this afternoon and see if anything eventuates.'

'Where, Jack?' She was desperate now knowing something crucial was in play.

'JA, I have to go.'

'Wait, give me something, anything,' she said pleaded again.

This was important to her, but he needed to get her off the phone without being abrupt. He also understood that the cooperation of the media could be advantageous at times. 'Get your deadline extended and if anything goes down in the next few hours I will give you something to add to your story. I won't be giving you specifics, though. You need to understand that. Am I clear?'

'Yes, I'll take whatever you have, Jack. Thank you.'

She remembered something else. 'Did Lucie roll over? Jack, Jack—' He had already hung up.

She was excited now. This was the part of the job she loved.

The adrenaline rush she got from chasing the final pieces of her investigative puzzle while the deadline clock ticked down was what she lived for. She thought back to the episode in Melissa's pool. Was that what happened last night? Was she addicted to living her personal life on the edge as well? *She would receive her answer soon enough.* She barged through the fire door, into the stairwell and her long legs took the stairs two at a time to the top floor to her editors office. She could see through the glass partition that her boss was in. *Phew.* Julie-Anne knocked loudly and then burst through his door.

'Jesus, JA, you scared the shit out of me.'

'Sorry, but I need a favour Chris. A big one.'

'What is it this time, JA?'

'I am waiting on new information for my feature and need an extension to my deadline.'

'What new information?'

'Jack has located Wie Ping Lie's storage unit and they are going to conduct a stakeout shortly. If it pans out this could be a sensational conclusion to my story. It would close the loop, so to speak. Pleeeease?' she begged unabashedly for the second time in minutes.

He sighed. 'You can be so high maintenance sometimes. It's like I've got a second wife.'

Julie-Anne's eyebrows raced up her forehead. 'That's very politically incorrect and sexist of you.'

'Thank you for pointing that out. Okay, you've got until seven o'clock, not a second longer, and it had better be worth it, JA.'

'Thank you, thank you,' she gushed while racing out the door. *This is going to be touch and go,* she said to herself.

54. Rent A Space Padstow

Friday 29th May

Jack and Sanderson were seated in Jack's police issue, unmarked Holden Commodore. They were parked under a large eucalypt tree in the Padstow Park carpark across Davies Road from the Rent A Space storage facility. Even though it was a gloomy day, from their vantage point they were able to see all the comings and goings of the beige and orange coloured complex. Most importantly, they had clear line of sight to the entry driveway and the keypad which provided pin code access to the storage facility proper. Having studied a number of late afternoon arrivals already, Sanderson calculated that it took the imposing roller shutter approximately fifteen seconds to rise to its maximum height once the code was entered. This delay provided them with ample time to view and identify all persons entering the facility. To ensure he had a close-up of their faces he had brought along his high powered Nikon Aculon 16 X 50 binoculars.

'Given the lockdown has ended, I imagine the majority of people will be making the most of their new-found freedom and spending Friday night in their favourite pub or RSL club. I don't envision there will be many people wanting to waste their time depositing or retrieving household goods tonight, Jack.'

'You're correct, and that should make it all the more straightforward to identify our suspects, if they show up of course.' They were hoping that given the demise of Li Jun and his associate back in March, with Wang Yong and Lucie Chan in custody, and Johnny Chang long gone, Wie himself might be forced to retrieve his stock. They very much doubted that he would be that brazen though, nor would they be so fortunate. That being the case, and given they were dealing with a Chinatown based Triad, it was reasonable to assume that they were on the lookout for a person or persons of Chinese extraction. Jack was thinking about his disenchanted state colleagues down south in the state of Victoria. The government there had over time disempowered the police force and reduced it to that of a police service where such thoughts would be considered racial profiling and condemned by the PC brigade. To Jack it wasn't profiling at all, rather just plain common sense. He and Sanderson knew exactly who and what they were potentially dealing with on this stakeout. And as a consequence they were armed with their Glock 22 .40-calibre semi-automatic pistols. As planned, they had arrived at three o'clock and taken up their observation post. Throughout the first hour they had watched as Mums, Dads, families, couples, singles, tradies and businessmen and women had come and gone, but they had seen no one that aroused their suspicion. Behind them the sun was dipping lower in the sky and the late afternoon air was becoming cooler. Soon it would be dark, but the driveway was guarded by LED lights hanging from tall aluminium poles like drooping flowers. Rent A Space was a twenty four hour a day facility, so it was reasonable to assume there would still be some activity occurring into the night.

On the two hour mark Sanderson leaned forward in his seat. 'Does that car look familiar, Jack?'

'No, why?'

Sanderson had seen the car pull up to the entry keypad and observed the female driver try unsuccessfully to reach the keypad from the driver's seat. It was the same vehicle that he had checked the registration plates in the state police's database yesterday. He watched on as a tall, blond woman exited the vehicle and stood at the keypad. 'Well, if the car doesn't then I'm damned sure the woman does,' he said with disbelief as he handed the binoculars across.

Jack brought the glasses up to his eyes. 'Oh, shit,' he blurted out as he eyed Danielle standing at the keypad.

'It looks like your ex-girlfriend has graduated to the bigtime, buddy.'

Even though she was obviously in a relationship with Wie all along, Jack didn't want to believe that she would be actively involved in his drug business. But, the image in front of him didn't lie. He sent his mind into overdrive trying to think whether she had ever mentioned having any of her possessions in storage. If she was living in the Than Ping Lie owned apartment, then maybe she did have her own furniture and appliances locked away. *You won't move much in the A6 though.*

'It certainly appears that way, Michael. This is your component of the gig, so how do you want to handle this?'

'No, no, no. She's your ex-girlfriend, so what do you want to do?'

'I'm excluding myself from that decision for that very reason. It's up to you, buddy.'

Sanderson sighed. 'Well, we have a couple of options. We can let her carry on and follow her in the hope we can catch Wie with the drugs red-handed, when she hands them over. But, without back-up, we could easily lose her in peak hour traffic. A one car tail never works and you know what Friday nights are like on the road. Or we can grab her when she exits the storage facility and see what she has to say for herself. At least we'll have the coke off the streets, but we won't get Wie. Either way we need to decide soon, Jack.'

Jack watched on as the Audi finally entered the storage

facility proper and the roller shutter began its descent. 'We have a couple of minutes, so let's not rush this. I think she'll turn on him in a hurry when she realises that she'll be going to prison for an eternity. She's an intelligent and astutely devious woman. I'll think she'll quickly come to the realisation that the game's finally up.'

Sanderson nodded. 'Okay, let's go say hello and see what she has to say for herself.'

They turned left out of the carpark, then made a right through the break in the main road's median strip and entered Rent A Space's carpark. Jack exited the car and went into the administration office while Sanderson stood by the adjacent roller shutter.

Jack held up his badge to the just out of high school, blonde receptionist with purple bangs. 'All staff are to stay inside this building until advised to the contrary. And lock the front door after I leave, miss,' he demanded. As he exited the office he heard the screeching sound of the heavy metal roller shutter ascending. He walked across to where Sanderson was standing and stood beside him.

The shutter slowly continued its agonisingly slow ascent and Sanderson saw the vehicle's registration plate before the vehicle itself came into view. 'It's her, Jack,' he said as he drew his Glock from its holster. Jack followed suit and both men held their weapons in a two fisted grip down at a forty five degree angle.

As the shutter continued to ascend Danielle's face came into view. 'Turn off the engine. Now, Ms Mortimer,' Sanderson shouted.

The stunned look on her face made Jack feel momentarily sorry for her. He ducked inside the door and pressed the red emergency button to prevent the shutter from descending. Simultaneously, Sanderson moved around to the driver's side of the car. 'Put the vehicle in park, take your hands off the wheel and exit the vehicle slowly,' he ordered as he took a step backwards.

She was wearing white jeans, a white linen shirt with two buttons open and knee high, chestnut coloured boots which made her appear even taller. Sanderson could see why Jack had fallen for her.

'What's going on here? I was just retrieving my winter wardrobe. Jack! What's happening?'

Jack looked through the rear driver's side passenger window and saw a collection of clothes on hangers dangling from the coat hook. His heart momentarily sank. Had they got this all wrong? *Not another bloody coincidence.* He was just about to alert Sanderson when he spied a cobalt coloured, lambskin, leather jacket wedged in between the clothes. He opened the door and pulled it off the hook. A part of him was disappointed. And sad. It was the same jacket that Danielle had so enthusiastically discarded at dinner only three nights ago. He had to hand it to her, she was crafty. Jack dangled her favourite jacket in front of her face and wiggled it for effect. 'Nice try.'

Shit. 'I can explain,' she said, sounding desperate now. 'Jack, please?'

'Turn around and place your palms firmly on the roof of the vehicle,' Sanderson insisted, disregarding her pleas. 'Jack, do you want to do the honours?'

Jack was hesitant, but he needed to get his detective head on. 'Stand with your legs apart,' he demanded.

Her head twisted towards him. 'Where have I heard that before?'

He ignored her and ran his hands up and down the inside and outside of her long legs and patted down her shoulders, sides and back.

'Be careful, I bruise easily, detective.'

'Tell that to your boyfriend. Turn around.'

He loosened her belt and ran his fingers around the hips of her jeans then turned her pockets inside out. He eyed her shirt, but the material was see-through and he couldn't see anything hidden under it.

'She's clean, Michael.'

'Jack do you want to cover her while I search the car?'

Jack felt as if he was standing in front of a stranger. She could have been someone he had never met such was the disconnect he was feeling. It was only three days ago that they had been intimate when she had taken advantage of his lust for her, but it seemed like a lifetime ago now. How did he get it all so wrong? *Was it ever a relationship?*

'Bingo, Jack.'

Sanderson was holding up a bulky, brown paper packet about the shape and size of a packet of kitchen flour. Not wanting a clever defence lawyer to question the search and seizure, he had snapped photos of it from different angles with his mobile. He turned back to Danielle. 'What's the unit number?'

'Wouldn't you like to know,' she replied.

He extracted a folded piece of A4 paper from his jacket pocket. 'Ms Mortimer, this is a duly issued judicial search warrant for this facility. I can go into administration and troll through their files for hours on end while you stand out here in the cooling evening until I find what I am looking for. Or, alternatively you can provide me with the number and combination for the storage unit I need to search. It's your call,' he said stubbornly.

Danielle wanted to get this charade over and done with, so why prolong it. She sighed. 'Four seven two and two three two three.'

'Michael Jordan. Of course.'

'I'll keep her secure in the office while you retrieve the remainder of the stash, Michael.'

While they waited in reception Jack asked, 'how did you ever let yourself get caught up in this mess, Danielle?'

She made a cutesy face. 'If you're going to question me aren't you supposed to read me my rights first, detective?'

He turned side-on to face her. Gee she was beautiful. 'Don't be a smartarse, this isn't the time nor the place for flippancy. You're going to prison for a very long time. See if you can find something frivolous to say about that.'

Her expression darkened. 'He'll come after you.'

'Who's he? Your dragon tattooed, two-timing, drug dealing lover?' he said, deliberately goading her.

'My real lover,' she replied ardently.

'You appear very confident about that. I wonder if he'll manage to find the time in between shagging Lucie Chan, his real girlfriend,' he said.

She swung around to hit him, but forgot about the handcuffs she was wearing and only managed to unbalance herself and crash to the floor. 'You bastard,' she yelled while struggling to stand up.

How could this possibly be the same woman who had been such an integral part of his life these past few months? In Jack's mind they had shared so many wonderful moments together and now she was calling him a bastard. He was dumbfounded. He brought himself back to the present. 'On your knees again I see,' he taunted.

'Fuck you, Jack.'

The receptionist sat bolt upright and stared at them over the top of her glasses. 'It's all okay, miss,' Jack said, waving congenially to placate the young woman.

Moments later Jack heard the screeching sound of metal on metal and saw Sanderson duck under the ascending shutter. He had another seven packages stacked along his outstretched arm.

'Wait here and don't try anything stupid, Danielle.' Jack rose and walked out the door and across to Sanderson.

'There's more in there so I'll need to make several trips.'

'I have an idea, Michael.' The two men spoke briefly and then Sanderson re-entered the storage facility. Jack made a phone call before re-entering the admin building.

'Miss, can you bring up the records for unit four seven two please?' Jack asked as he showed her the warrant. He scanned the electronic document on the desktop, found what he was looking for and requested the receptionist take a screenshot and print it out. He then grasped Danielle by the arm and marched her out to their waiting vehicle just as Sanderson was exiting the adjoining storage facility.

'Okay, we're all good, let's go, Jack.'

An hour later the Commodore pulled up in one of the dedicated police parking bays in the cul-de-sac adjacent to the Day Street Police Station on the periphery of Chinatown. Jack grasped Danielle by the arm and escorted her through the automatic glass doors to the reception counter.

Sanderson walked up and stood alongside them. 'Sarge, can we have this woman booked in, printed and then placed into a holding cell please?' Sanderson marched her to the booking room where she sat on a bench and leant against the wall. He exited, locked the door behind him and returned to reception where he handed Mortimer's wallet and mobile phone to the duty sergeant for inventorying. He turned to Jack who handed him the original bag of coke. Sanderson placed it in an evidence bag, passed it across to the duty sergeant and waited for a receipt. 'Sarge, can we arrange for that to be printed first thing tomorrow please?'

The burly, balding officer glared up at him. 'You do realise tomorrow's a Saturday don't you?'

'Priority please, sergeant. Now, Jack, do you want to do this tonight or tomorrow?'

'I'm knackered, so I'm more than happy to have a good

night's sleep and interview her tomorrow, but it's your case, Michael.'

Sanderson turned back to the duty sergeant. 'Sarge, once you've booked in Miss Mortimer can you place her in holding for the night and we'll interview her in the morning?'

'Okay, will do. Is there anything else I can do for you two distinguished gentlemen on a Friday night?' he asked, heavy on the sarcasm. 'Maybe a haircut or massage?'

'No, I think we're all good. You up for a beer, Jack? After all, apparently it's a Friday night.' Sanderson winked at the duty sergeant.

'Not really, but what else am I going to do?'

55. Sydney Daily News

Friday 29th May

It was now six o'clock in the evening and Julie-Anne was waiting in her cubicle figuratively twiddling her thumbs. There was a fine line between calling Jack too early and interrupting his stakeout and waiting too long and missing whatever information he could potentially have for her. *Call him, Julie-Anne, it's time.*

'JA. I'm surprised that you haven't rung a dozen times by now.' She would have been on tenterhooks and wanting to call him every few minutes.

'Hi, Jack, do you have anything for me?'

He pushed open the door and walked out of the noisy bar. 'Straight to the point hey.'

'Sorry, but you of all people know how anxious I get with a deadline looming.'

'Only too well,' he replied.

'Well, how did your stakeout go?'

'It went well, however, I can't go into too much detail.'

'Alright, I'll settle for whatever you can give me, Jack.'

'That's terribly accommodating of you, JA.'

Julie-Anne chuckled internally at just how accommodating she had been recently. 'What do you have that I can use, Jack?'

'We have made an arrest and have someone in custody as we

speak.' He knew JA like the back of his hand and she wouldn't be satisfied with that snippet.

'Can you give me a location, a name, details of what you found, and who is we?'

He sighed. 'JA, we had reason to believe that a storage facility in the southwestern suburbs was being used for the purposes of storing a prohibited substance. As such, we undertook a surveillance operation on the facility and eventually we witnessed a person of interest arrive at the facility. That POI has been detained for further questioning.'

He had reverted to type. 'Did you read that verbatim from the AFP's media relations handbook?'

'Look, all I'm prepared to tell you is that we found fifteen kilos of cocaine in a storage locker that is linked to Wie Ping Lie. You can't mention his name nor make any reference to him or his Triad, though.'

'Thank you. Now who have you arrested?'

'We haven't interviewed the person yet, so it would be inappropriate to say any more.'

'You said "we", who is we?'

'Michael Sanderson and I.'

'Can I at least call it a joint taskforce then?'

He sighed. 'If you want.'

'Thanks, Jack, I have to go.'

With her deadline looming she started typing furiously, her fingers racing across the keyboard.

> *A source close to the Sydney Daily News has confirmed that a storage facility in southwestern Sydney was raided by members of a joint taskforce comprising officers of both the Australian Federal Police and the New South Wales Police forces yesterday afternoon. A significant quantity of high grade cocaine was discovered.*

It is believed that the storage facility in question is linked to people referred to in this article. A suspect arrested at the scene is scheduled to be interviewed by detectives today.

56. Rent A Space Padstow

Saturday 30th May

Wie, still in his silk bathrobe, was seated on the sofa sipping his Golden Leaf green tea while admiring the view across the Chinese Garden of Friendship to Darling Harbour. He always thought the garden was ridiculously misnamed given the open antagonism towards the mother country. There were other more important issues that occupied his mind at the moment though. He had not seen nor heard from Lucie since she left his penthouse early on Wednesday morning and now his other woman had disappeared too. That was just too coincidental for him. He had called Danielle's burner phone numerous times last night, all to no avail. He had also spoken to Huang from the restaurant and he had neither seen nor heard from either woman. Wie had directed his Blue Lanterns to check her apartment and the others he owned down on the fourteenth floor, but they had come up empty handed. The women didn't have many friends and he had no idea who else to contact. And where was his product? As uninitiated members of his triad, he couldn't send his Blue Lanterns to collect it. His dial a dealer distributors would be beside themselves at not being able to fulfil their weekend orders and their self-entitled clients would be equally anxious. Thankfully none of them were aware of his existence. He knew what he had to reluctantly undertake. After showering and dressing, he grabbed the spare set of car keys and rode the elevator down to the basement. He made his way across the carpark to Lucie's parking bay.

'Tā mā de,' he shouted. *Where was her Honda?* The vehicle wasn't in her designated parking bay and he was now seriously wondering whether something sinister was at play. His eyes searched the carpark, repeatedly pressing the fob button in case she had parked in another bay. Nothing. Given Danielle had borrowed his Audi to collect his product, and she too had disappeared, he was without a vehicle. He had no choice, but to pull out his burner phone and order an Uber from an account that wasn't linked to him or his regular credit cards.

An hour later as instructed, the driver drove slowly past Rent A Space in Padstow and Wie had him pull in at the petrol station fifty metres from his target. He exited the vehicle, did a sweep of the area, and seeing nothing suspicious, crossed Davies Road and entered the carpark that fronted the road. He walked along its tarmac until he was level with Rent A Space and leaned up against the waste high cyclone fence. He was concerned at seeing his Audi stationary in the visitors carpark and he worked various scenarios around in his mind. There was no logical reason for it to be there unless it had been abandoned. Why would she leave the car there? He trusted this woman, after all she had compromised her beliefs and submitted her body to that detective, all so she could monitor the investigation targeted at him. Her loyalty was beyond question.

He had been watching for over an hour and had spotted nothing suspicious. He now had a decision to make and one of his favourite proverbs popped into his head, *"he who rides the tiger can never dismount"*. He knew that to mean that once a dangerous or troublesome venture is begun, the safest course is to carry it through to the end. He wasn't so sure that applied to his current situation, especially given he had little information to work with. He thought of the English language expression, "*caution is the better part of valour*". But what about his dealers?

Wie waited for another hour in the hope that Danielle would eventually appear from the facility, get in his car and drive safely away. That was his heart talking, but his mind was telling him another story altogether. His torment was complicated by the six million dollars of product he owned that was stashed in a locker barely fifty metres across the road. He couldn't walk away from that. He wouldn't. Wie picked up his backpack, straddled the fence and made his way across the busy arterial road. He adjusted his jacket to ensure his weapon was concealed, strolled nonchalantly through the entry gate and up to the access keypad. He entered the code and stood back while the roller shutter shrieked its way upwards. He ducked under the ascending shutter and paused, waiting for his vision to adjust. He scrutinised the area, and once he confirmed that there was no one else in the vicinity, he strode down the aisle towards the section containing his locker. He turned a corner near the rear of the building and strode across the aisle to the locker. Clasping the upper padlock, he one by one turned the four dials until he was able to release the shackle. Taking a stepped back, he knelt down and repeated the process on the second padlock. Removing both, he opened the door and placed them on the lower shelf. He stood and gazed admiringly at the stacks of packages stowed on the two upper shelves. He thought about Danielle and her continued badgering of him to take a long holiday. He would find her and once he moved the remainder of this shipment they would leave the country together for a long holiday in the sun. Wie placed his backpack on the lower shelf and began inventorying the packages in the locker. 'La Shi,' he said out aloud. The count was one short which meant that Danielle must have been here. So where was she, and where was his missing coke? Her and the coke were missing, but his car was here. *What did that mean?*

He knew of only one conclusion. He retrieved his backpack and stowed two packages into it. He needed to get out of here, and fast. He picked up the two padlocks and closed the door. One at a time he looped the shackles of each padlock through the clasp, clicked them closed and spun the dials until he saw four different numbers displayed on each. He swung the backpack over his shoulder and turned to walk away.

'Armed police stay where you are, do not move,' he heard a man shout from further down the aisle. Wie swung around and saw a uniformed man holding a semi-automatic weapon in the horizontal position, aimed squarely at him.

'Stay where you are, do not move.'

Wie swivelled his head in the opposite direction to check for an escape route. At that precise moment the roller shutter on the unit directly across the aisle erupted upwards. A second uniformed man in black coveralls, ballistic vest and helmet was also pointing a semi-automatic at him. Wie flicked his jacket up and reached around for his Type 67 semi-automatic pistol.

'Don't do it,' another voice yelled from above him. 'Don't do it.'

Wie didn't look up and kept his hands perfectly still while he gathered his thoughts. His options were diminishing and he had to think quickly. He could easily take out the man in the aisle, but could he get to the other two men making up the triangle before they took him down. He didn't want to die. He was equally horrified at the thought of going to prison. Ever so slowly he adjusted his body position while letting his right arm gently drift backwards.

'Don't even think about it; keep your hands where they are,' a voice yelled from behind him.

He was surrounded now and he had missed his one opportunity.

'Get on the ground, now. Get down,' the men were yelling.

The three men on ground level were now rushing towards him, shouting continuously. He sighed in defeat, slowly raised his hands above his head and knelt down. He thought about Danielle and her repeated warnings. *He should have listened.*

'Stephenson, grab his weapon and backpack and then search him.' The SRG officer lifted Wie's jacket and retrieved the semi auto. 'Chinese crap.' He then removed the backpack and the other two officers grabbed his arms, lifted him up, and pushed him against the wall. The first of the officers kicked Wie's legs apart and ran his hands up and down Wie's clothing.

'He's clean, boss.'

Oliver Campbell, the head of the AFP's Special Response Group stepped forward. 'Stephenson, do you have the apparatus?' The young Soggie reached into the large canvas bag sitting on the floor of the storage unit opposite and withdrew a pair of industrial strength bolt cutters. He stepped across the aisle and one by one cut the shackles of the two locks.

'Check this out, boss,' he exclaimed while stepping back from the locker to allow Campbell access.

'You might have been better off if you had forced us to shoot you, Mr Wie. You're looking at a lengthy holiday at the government's expense for this lot. Okay gents, let's tag and bag this haul and get him out of here.'

57. Day Street Police Station

Saturday 30th May

'Sarge can you please put Ms Mortimer into an interview room and I'll be with her in a moment?'

'Sure, detective.'

Sanderson entered the detective bureau mid-morning and sat at his desk. He woke his desktop from its slumber and accessed the Share Drive. He navigated to the document template folder and found what he was after. Downloading a copy to his case file he duly typed the relevant details into the formatted text boxes. After clicking on the print icon he retrieved his document from the printer then he made his way back down the corridor to the interview room. Through the glass window he saw Danielle Mortimer leaning back against the wall with her arms folded across her chest. With sleep in her eyes, the make-up diminished, her mussed hair and wrinkled clothes, she looked anything but the glamour from the previous day.

'Ms Mortimer, how are you?' he asked cheerily as he sat down at the metal desk.

'Why couldn't we get this over and done with last night?' she demanded.

'Did you have something pressing to attend to?' She directed a deadly glare at him, but didn't reply. 'No, I didn't think so. I am Detective Michael Sanderson and I have a few questions for you. Just so you understand your basic rights, you have the right to silence, you can refuse to answer my questions or decline a record of interview. You can answer my questions by saying, no comment, and your silence does not mean you are guilty. Do you understand, Ms Mortimer?'

'Yes, now can we move this along?'

'Ms Mortimer, I'm not sure you really understand your predicament. You were found in possession of a kilogram of cocaine. And we found a further fourteen kilograms inside the storage unit. You're not going anywhere anytime soon.'

'Oh, but I think I might be somehow,' she replied cockily.

Sanderson leaned back in his chair. 'And why pray tell would you be thinking that?'

'Well, you see Detective Sanderson, I imagine you are only interviewing me because you don't have anything more productive to do, like interviewing my boyfriend.'

'Is that so? Which boyfriend would that be?' he replied, chuckling.

She would play with this detective just like she had with Jack. 'Yes it is. I'm only a small fish and you want the big catch which you obviously don't have, so that's why you're sitting here wasting your time with me. And what's more, you won't ever get your big fish; he's too smart for you,' she boasted.

Sanderson could play this game too. 'Okay then, do you have any ideas as to how we can remedy that situation then?'

'I might,' she teased. 'What's in it for me if I help you go fishing?'

'Let's go at that from another angle shall we. What's not in it for you is any cooperation from me if we don't get to land the big fish himself. In fact, what will happen is that I will charge you with being in possession of, and or trafficking of, a commercial quantity of an illegal substance and you will spend the next ten to twenty years in the Mary Wade Correctional

Centre. And with your looks you'll be popular with the bean flickers, Ms Mortimer. And I imagine the guards will be falling over each other to conduct daily strip searches too.'

The woman across from him didn't respond; she just sat there impassively, projecting the smug expression she had perfected. Sanderson would try another tack. 'Have you asked yourself why you were in Padstow picking up the coke rather than one of Wie's underlings? And how you now find yourself under arrest and parked here in these salubrious surroundings. You think that just happened by chance?' He watched on in silence as the smugness slowly faded from her face. 'Exactly, you were set up to take the fall, Danielle. With the loss of Li Jun, Wang Wei, Yong and his sidekick from his band of merry men, Wie had no one left that he could trust. He certainly didn't have the courage to put his own freedom at risk. And then my guess is he thought "oh, what about my loyal servant, Danielle". And voila, here you are.'

To reinforce his point Sanderson handed a mobile phone across the table to her. 'See anything unusual, Danielle?'

He watched as she scrolled up and down obviously searching for something. He allowed himself a knowing smile as her facial expression grew darker. 'You see there were seven missed calls between five and eight o'clock last night and then suddenly they stopped. What do you think was at play there?'

'Screw you.'

'I don't think so. You seem to be busy enough in that regard already.' He smiled facetiously at her. She sneered at him.

'Okay, then let me help with that little conundrum of yours then. I'm guessing that the reason he has stopped calling is that he has found someone to replace you already, and I wonder who that could be. Any ideas, Danielle? Sanderson leaned back in his chair again, folded his arms across his chest and put his feet up on the table.

After a long pause she spoke. 'That doesn't mean anything, he was probably busy,' she said unconvincingly.

'Oh, please. Do you really think so? He needed his product so his dealers can hit the streets for the busy weekend trade. I seriously doubt he was *busy* as you call it, more like he has found a replacement for you already. Did you know that he and Lucie Chan spent a romantic evening together at the casino earlier this week. Where were *you* that night, Ms Mortimer?'

Danielle knew exactly where she was that evening. At Jacks. *"You will have to be more persuasive"*, Wie had said the night previous. And dutifully, she had been. While he was fucking Lucie Chan. *Bastard.*

Sanderson noticed the sudden downturn in her demeanour, so he would use that. 'My guess is they will be shacked up together before you even get checked in at Mary Wade.' The reality was very different, with Jack interviewing Chan while he jousted with Mortimer. 'You're already yesterday's news, Ms Mortimer,' he said.

Jack had given him the screenshot from the Rent A Space receptionist's desktop that showed a Than Ping Lie as the renter of the storage unit. 'You give me Wie and Than Ping Lie, and against my better judgement, you walk; it's that simple. You already know the alternative.' He extracted the sheet of paper from his jacket pocket and handed it across the table to her.

'So what this?'

'Look at the title of the document.'

'Immunity from Prosecution. So, what good is this to me?' she questioned as her eyes scanned back and forth, up and down the document while she perused its contents. She threw the document back across the desk.

'That's right. It's useless unless you and I both sign it and I have it authorised by the state's DPP. It's completely your call as to whether this document is worth anything or not.'

'Noooo,' she screamed. 'Noooo.' Her face had turned ashen and she wore an agonised expression. 'Noooo,' she repeated as she bolted upright from her chair and stared intently out of the interview room's window, tears running down her cheek. Sanderson calmly turned to see what the cause of her anguish was. Oliver Campbell and Officer Stephenson were frogmarching Wie Ping Lie down the corridor to the holding cells.

Danielle reached across the table and snatched the document back. 'Do you have a pen please, detective?' she asked in an angelic voice.

'Aah, Miss Mortimer, so near yet so far. Feel free to keep that useless piece of paper, it will make a nice souvenir,' he goaded.

'Pleeeease.'

'Miss Mortimer, under the Drug Misuse and Trafficking Act of 1985, you will be charged with the supply and trafficking of a commercial quantity of a prohibited substance. That charge carries a maximum penalty of twenty five years in gaol.'

'Screw you. Screw you.'

'Goodbye, Miss Mortimer.'

58. AFP Headquarters

Saturday 30th May

It was mid-morning on Saturday as Jack walked into IV1 where Lucie Chan was waiting. He had a mild hangover from his night out with Sanderson, so he had allowed himself the luxury of a sleep in. To make up time he had called ahead and arranged to have Chan brought up from the holding cells.

'About time,' she sighed exasperatingly. 'Where have you been?'

'Lucie, settle down. Detective Sanderson and I have been busy and it takes time to get all your necessary paperwork in order.'

'Settle down? Really! I've been stuck in that stinking hellhole downstairs since Wednesday and if you haven't noticed it's now Saturday.'

'I know what day it is and the delay couldn't be avoided if you want your freedom or something close to it.' It wasn't in a detective's make-up to share information when interviewing suspects or witnesses, especially if you wanted to maintain the upper hand in an interview. Jack thought this case could be the exception to that time honoured tenet given the information previously provided by the woman. 'We raided the storage unit yesterday, but didn't catch Wie.'

'It's not my problem if you came up empty handed. You

obviously know then that the information I gave you was correct.' No reply. 'Well come on, what did you find?' Lucie demanded.

Jack knew that she was correct. 'We found the coke, and plenty of it too, but no Wie,' he replied, sounding disappointed. 'So you see it is your problem after all.'

'That wasn't the deal. You asked me "where does he store the bulk merchandise?" word for word, and I told you. You never asked me where to find Wie.'

'Lucie, did you really think that I was only interested in the coke. It was implied that I wanted Wie as well. And now I want Than Ping Lie too, so it's up to you.' He extracted an A4 sheet of paper from his jacket pocket and held it up in front of her face.

'What's that?'

Jack waved it for effect. 'You know darn well what this is. It's your passport to freedom. Now, whether you get to have it stamped is entirely up to you.'

Her gaze was fixed on the sheet of paper. She sighed. 'There is a penthouse on the twenty first floor of the Sussex Street Apartments. He lives there. I told the other detective before that I don't know where or who Than Ping Lie is. I think maybe she's Wie's mother, but I don't know for certain.'

'Lucie, the storage unit is rented in the name of Than Ping Lie and her address is listed on their records as Apartment 1419 in your building. That's your apartment, the one we raided earlier in the week, so please don't insult me by saying you don't know where or who she is,' he said staring her down.

'Detective, I can't explain why my address would be connected to her, but I can assure you she doesn't live there.' Lucie clasped her hands together and leaned forward. 'Let me pose a question to *you*. Did you find any evidence of her presence when you raided my apartment? Well did you?' she challenged, now giving him a stare of her own. 'No, I didn't think so.'

'Guard,' he called out. A uniformed man entered the

interview room. 'Can you take Miss Chan back to her accommodation please?'

She was incredulous. 'What? I told you what you wanted to know, so why am I still being held in custody?' she demanded.

'Lucie, as soon as I verify what you have told me, then you might be out of here. In the meantime I can just continue to obtain a Detention Order from a court to keep extending your custody arrangements for another twenty four hours until I'm satisfied with the information you have provided. So, I hope for your sake you've told me everything.'

Jack's mobile rang as he rose from the table. 'Hi, Michael, how's Matahari doing?'

The Michael mentioned had to be the detective, Sanderson, so Lucie leaned forward, trying to hear both sides of the conversation.

'That's good news. I'll see you soon.'

'What's happened, detective?'

'Aah, this might just be your lucky day, Lucie.'

'Tell me, what's happened, please?' she pleaded. 'What's happened? Come on tell me. Pleeeease,' she repeated, more desperately this time.

'Your boss and lover has been arrested.'

Lucie Chan leapt from her chair. 'Yeehaa, I'm outta here.'

Jack wasn't smiling. 'Not so fast, Lucie. He has still to be questioned and your freedom is wholly dependent on his answers. You're not going anywhere for the moment. Guard,' Jack called out.

An hour later Sanderson was ensconced in Jack's bullpen. 'A great day all round, good buddy,' he lauded. Based on a hunch, Jack had called the DC from Rent A Space the day before asking for Wie's storage locker to be staked out. While Sanderson was returning the coke to the locker Jack had provided an overview of their case to his boss and requested the support of the SRG.

Being a state based operation the DC had initially hesitated, but when Jack told him Wie was running out of lieutenants and may be tempted to collect his product himself, John Robertson finally relented and the operation was a go.

'Oh, yes it is, Michael, a great day for the good guys.'

'Jack, I know neither you nor the MBC got what you wanted out of the investigation, but we took six million dollars of coke and the head of a notorious triad off the streets. What's more, between you and I, we have ripped the heart out of the rest of his operation too. That's a big win in anyone's language.'

'Yeah, I get that, but it's a hollow victory for me and the AFP though.'

'Sometimes we just have to take the wins wherever we can and be satisfied with that. What are you going to do about Lucie Chan?'

'I'm not sure. She finally gave up Wie's address and we would have nabbed him eventually, albeit maybe without the coke in his possession. But, she did give us Rent A Space and we grabbed Wie and the coke, so I'm inclined to cut her loose, but it will be up to the DPP. Given he got burnt with Danielle I doubt he will be predisposed to doing Lucie any favours.'

'That's a shame. I don't think she's a bad person, Jack, rather she just saw dealing as an opportunity to get ahead in life.'

'I know. I'll see what I can do.'

59. Bank Hotel Newtown

Saturday 30th May

Paul Gao was walking along King Street in Newtown keenly watching on as the Granger woman entered Dolce Vita, a hair and beauty salon. Maybe she was being waxed. No she didn't need it. He had been thinking about the investigative reporter often since Thursday night at Melissa's. He had been introduced to Melissa Wu at a consular cocktail party. The Consul General had told him that Melissa had been close to the Granger woman who had been investigating potential Chinese influence in Australia earlier in the year. This was of great concern to the Consul General, so as a dutiful servant of both Xiao and the Party, Gao had decided to use his initiative and take matters into his own hands. He had worked diligently to firstly ingratiate Melissa, and then take their friendship to the next level. Once in a position of trust he was able to manipulate her into inviting the Granger woman to dinner. He had spent the evening keeping Melissa aroused, flirting with Granger and plying them both with champagne and wine. Whilst he hadn't learnt anything of value he had to admit that he had enjoyed the romp with them in the pool. And he was glad he had screwed the Granger woman. That was the least she deserved after she had impugned the good name of the Party and the mother country. Now he would find out what she had learned with her latest investigation and whether it had any implications for his beloved homeland. He had followed her from her nearby apartment, and he would *accidently* bump into her following her beauty appointment. He needed to buy a book as a prop, so he walked along King Street to Elizabeth's Bookshop. These western women were so self-absorbed he knew that he had ample time before Granger would finish being pampered. Gao was browsing through the shelves of old, dusty, tattered and yellowed books, not searching for anything in particular, when he saw it. 'O wǒ de shàngdì.' He couldn't believe it. How appropriate after the antics of two nights ago. He picked it up and was staring, almost disbelievingly, at the front cover of the Kama Sutra. It was first published in the eighteen hundreds and was obviously an extraordinary and controversial book for the times. In conservative China it still would be.

'Hello, Paul.'

He heard the sultry voice, but couldn't imagine who would know him in this weird part of town full of strange people. He turned his head and was looking straight at the Granger woman. What was she doing here? Wasn't she being spoilt and cossetted back up the street? *This was all wrong.* 'Hello, Julie-Anne, how are you?' he replied while trying to mask his surprised expression.

'I'm well thank you. Fancy seeing you here,' she teased. 'Are you an avid reader?'

'I love reading,' he responded while holding up the book to validate his words. He quickly realised his mistake, withdrew his hand and placed the book behind his back.

'Kama Sutra hey? I wouldn't have thought you would have needed that,' she said coquettishly. Surprisingly, she wasn't embarrassed. She knew Paul Gao would be a worthy adversary the further she ventured into her investigation of him, but for now she was having some fun at his expense. She had already decided to use this unexpected opportunity to her advantage.

Is she flirting with me now? he wondered. 'No, it's not just about that, Julie-Anne. It's about the art of living, emotional connection, the power equation in relationships and emotional fulfillment in life,' he responded, too eagerly, and unconvincingly.

Maybe this guy is one of a rare breed that has an emotional compass. She allowed herself to laugh inwardly. No chance. 'You keep believing that and you'll be fine, Paul.'

Even though his plan had been reversed on him he saw an opportunity. He needed to keep this woman engaged, so he would adapt. 'So, are you an avid reader too, Julie-Anne?'

'Yes, however, I'm not shopping for literature today. I just made a forward booking at a salon and was walking back past here when I spotted you through the window.'

'Do you live around here?'

'Yes, I do. This is a very eclectic area full of bookshops, hidden treasures, cafes and great bars, and I love it. I wouldn't live anywhere else. She was hamming it up now, but he was already aware of where she lived. She had easily detected him following her from her Alice Street apartment. His rookie mistake.

That generated an idea in his head. 'Would you like to have a drink? It's your area so you should choose.'

She already knew what her response would be, but she paused for effect. He didn't break the impasse. It was obvious that both of them were playing the cat and mouse game. 'Yeah, sure, why not.' Julie-Anne turned and began walking towards the exit. 'Don't forget your book,' she called out as she sauntered away, allowing herself a self-satisfied smile.

They made the short walk down the hill to The Bank Hotel. 'This is my local, so I hope you like it. It has a cosy outdoor courtyard area in the rear, so we should make the most of it while it still reasonably warm.'

They walked through the bustling hotel and found a small table out the back. 'Would you like a champagne, Julie-Anne?'

'Yes, please. Just a Bellini thanks.'

A short while later he was walking back with their drinks. He was wearing tight fitting jeans and a slim fit white linen shirt, both of which accentuated his athletic physique. He looked good in his smart casual attire.

'Cheers, Julie-Anne, here's to chance meetings.'

'Yes, here's to chance meetings, Paul,' she replied, eyeing him over the lip of her glass.

There was an elongated pause while they sipped their drinks and neither of them appeared to know where or how to begin. Maybe it was the cat and mouse thing again, so Julie-Anne thought she may as well launch straight in. 'So, Paul, Melissa tells me you are an emissary at the Chinese Consulate. I sincerely hope I didn't offend you at dinner the other night.'

'No, not at all,' he replied too quickly. 'But, I am a Special Emissary.'

She stayed with the topic. 'That must be a fascinating role in these challenging geopolitical times.'

'Yes it is and I enjoy it immensely. And your job would be no less interesting.' Julie-Anne picked up on the short response and the diversionary tactic. He was going to play that game.

'Yes it is and I enjoy it immensely,' she replied verbatim. She could play that game too.

They both clearly realised what the other was up to and there was another awkward silence. Julie-Anne wouldn't find out anything if this exchange went tit-for-tat all day. She doubted he would let anything slip, then again, if she didn't get him talking, she would forever be wondering. 'I am an investigative reporter for the Sydney Daily News, but you already knew that.'

'Yes, Melissa told me.'

'And I mentioned it over dinner, too. Don't you remember?' He wasn't very good at this.

'Oh, yes of course.'

'I'm fortunate that I have an exceptionally accommodating editor who mostly allows me free rein with my investigations, so I get to select what areas of criminal and illicit activities I delve into.'

'Have you worked on anything of note recently?' There it was. His first probing question. And she would answer it.

'Well, I know that you are aware how Melissa's political candidacy was undermined. The man who was supposedly going to fund her campaign was laundering money at the Oceanic Casino. That same man had some tenuous links to a drug dealer in Chinatown, so I authored an article about both of their activities and the link between them.' Having seen his facial reaction firsthand at dinner, she would leave out the part about the connection to the Consul General for now. She would see how Gao reacted to her first offering.

'That must have placed you in some considerable danger, Julie-Anne.'

'Yes, it did. I was shot at while driving to work one day, and luckily for me, they missed. I just suffered concussion and bruising from the resultant car accident.'

'That is terrible,' he replied, affecting disbelief. 'Did the police apprehend the offenders?'

'Yes, thankfully they did. The shooter himself was killed during an SRG raid and his accomplice was extradited to Queensland for a related killing. They were both linked to a Chinatown based Triad.'

'You should be able to go about your business without intimidation,' he said while still feigning shock at her pronouncement.

'What, like in China, Paul?' She could see that comment had hit its intended mark when the fine vein in the middle of his forehead started throbbing and his jaw clenched. Bugger him, this is the guy, who in more ways than one, took advantage of her friendship with Melissa to get close to her, both figuratively and literally. After what Julie-Anne would call a pregnant pause, he spoke.

'I don't know of such things. My family lives far out in the west of the country and they don't concern themselves with these issues. They are busy just living their humble lives.'

Julie-Anne witnessed a subtle change in his demeanour. He appeared to be reflecting and she would play to that. 'What about you, what do *you* think?' she asked.

'I think the media have an important role in delivering the news and informing the populace about issues that are important to the people and impact their daily lives. So, if you achieved that with your story, then well done.'

'A political and predictable answer.' She continued. 'So, what do you want for your country, Paul?'

'I would like to see my homeland realising the dream of the great rejuvenation of the proud Chinese nation and a return to its former glory. But, it is not for me to have an opinion about how they achieve that.'

A modesty based qualifier, she thought. Julie-Anne excused herself and headed for the ladies. She could feel his eyes boring into her. Was he repulsed by her continued probing or was he just checking her out in her new jeans. Either way she could care less as long as she achieved what she needed to today.

He was watching her as she walked away from the table and he allowed himself to think about her naked body from Thursday night. Even though she was being obviously provocative with her probing questions, he still felt himself hardening at the sight of her. He would have her again tonight. He smiled congenially as she resumed her seat. 'It's getting a bit chilly, Julie-Anne and I didn't bring a jacket. Do you also have a favourite restaurant where we can warm up and have dinner?'

Given the seesawing conversation Julie-Anne wouldn't

have considered dinner to be an option. She just knew there was more to this guy than what his politically correct answers were portraying. 'Sure, come on, it's only a short walk back up King Street. There's this cute little tapas style restaurant that serves shared plates, so we can graze through the menu.'

60. Camperdown – Inner Sydney

Saturday 30th May

They found a table away from the chill that followed them through the door. 'What would you like to drink, Julie-Anne?'

'Oh, that's an easy one. Can I have a French Martini please?' He ordered a pilsener made by a local craft brewery for himself from the attendant waitress.

'Julie-Anne, as this is your choice of restaurant, would you like to order dinner for us? I am sure you are more knowledgeable than I,' he suggested.

'Of course I can,' she replied agreeably. 'What if I just order some share plates and we can pick our way through them?'

'That sounds perfect as I'm not overly hungry anyway.'

While they waited for their dishes they just made small talk, discussing families, the fluctuating weather, and of course, the lockdown. Julie-Anne would avoid bringing up the source of the coronavirus that had led to the horribly disruptive lockdown in the first place. Eventually the dishes arrived and the conversation briefly moved to the delicious flavours. Julie-Anne wanted to do some more probing.

'So, Paul, your emissary role at the Consulate sounds interesting. What does it entail?'

There was that pause again. 'I am a Special Emissary and

why do you keep asking me all these questions? I thought we were just having a delightful meal.'

Here we go. 'I'm just making conversation. I told you about my job, my history in the media and you already know quite a bit about me from Melissa. I know nothing about you.'

'Tā mā de.'

'What does that mean?' She knew full-well what it meant from her time with Melissa, and he wasn't happy.

'Nothing, just an expression.' He paused again. 'I undertake varied tasks for and on behalf of the Consul General that he is too busy to embark on himself.'

He's finally opened the door. 'That must be challenging. What sort of tasks?'

He was becoming agitated at her persistence. 'Mostly meetings with junior level state politicians that the Consul General is too eminent to meet with himself.'

'Interesting. Were you involved in the negotiations with the state government before they banned the Confucius Institute Program from their schools?' No response. Julie-Anne decided to push on. 'That would have been a difficult time for you and the Consul General, and highly embarrassing for your country too,' she prodded, provocatively.

Why was she asking about this? Had she found out about his task for the Consul General? Had she been following *him*? He would have to be extra careful around this woman and he needed to find out what she knew.

Julie-Anne could see his vein and jaw doing their thing again, so she backed off. For now. He wasn't going to respond anyway.

They had finished their share plates and he observed that she had nearly finished the wine she had with dinner. After a moment he spoke. 'Would you like a nightcap, Julie-Anne? I have a bottle of French champagne chilling at home and I don't live far from here.'

'Damn,' she mumbled under her breath. She was blindsided by his invitation and her mind was spinning with a myriad of competing thoughts. Given the way the evening had unfolded, why was he inviting me to his place, and why am I even hesitating saying no? *Make a decision woman.* She had to think quickly. Maybe he might loosen up after a couple of glasses of champagne. After all, he had followed her from her apartment, so he was definitely up to something. Maybe she would get an opportunity to snoop around his apartment. Something popped into her head, however, it would come at a cost. *You better be up for this girl.* She offered her most appeasing smile. 'Sure, I could go a glass of bubbles.'

Their Uber pulled up out the front of a modern three story apartment building that she knew wasn't far from the Chinese Consulate. 'Nice place, Paul.'

'The apartment is modest, but I hope you will like it and be able to relax here.' She assumed that was a reference to her continued questioning earlier. They entered the sparsely furnished apartment and he went to the refrigerator and retrieved two frosted flutes from the freezer.

To Julie-Anne the place had the appearance of a bachelor pad, but she would be the polite guest. 'This is a lovely apartment, spacious, and I adore the floor to ceiling windows.'

'Thank you, I like it and it is close by the Consulate.'

She flinched at the sound of the popping cork.

'Here you are, Julie-Anne.' He handed her a glass and she watched the fine beading work its magic. 'Cheers, Julie-Anne.'

'And to you too, Paul. Thank you.'

They leaned against the balcony railing. Julie-Anne marvelled at the view of the city skyline. 'If I lived here I would spend my entire time out here admiring this view.'

'Yes, I sit out here quite often, especially in the

morning sunshine having my tea while reading the morning newspaper.'

'Would that be the Sydney Daily News?' she asked playfully.

'Of course and also the South China Morning Post, so I can keep up with affairs in the homeland.'

'I would have thought you would be more a Global Times kind of guy,' she taunted, deliberately referencing the Chinese Communist Party's People's Daily newspaper.

'I know what you are doing Julie-Anne, but I'm not taking your bite.'

She unsuccessfully tried to smother a smirk at his annunciation of the cliché.

He looked at her, perplexed. 'What?'

'I'm not taking the bait, like a fish not biting.'

He smiled uncomfortably. 'Okay then, I am not biting.'

Once again they talked about mundane topics that were far removed from what Julie-Anne wanted to discuss. She would try to encourage him to open up by raising his work again. 'I'm sure that you appreciate living so close to the Consulate. It must be very convenient for you and allow you to be more productive in your emissary role.'

'Yes it is and it does,' he replied abruptly without adding anything else.

'Did you replace Fan Chen in the role.' She was goading him now. Fan Chen was the Consulate's attaché who had kidnapped the Oceanic Casino's Treasury Manager to prevent her from revealing her knowledge of the money laundering operation. Diplomatic immunity from prosecution wasn't granted and the man was now a long term resident of Silverwater.

Gao's face reddened. 'No, he was only an attaché whereas I am a Special Emissary.'

Touchy. She pushed on. 'Were you aware that he tailed me one morning and also tried to intimidate me on another occasion?' His vein started doing its throbbing thing again. 'I assume the Consul General would be aware of such behaviour by one of his employees,' she prodded.

'He is an eminent, much respected man with many critical issues to deal with, so he would not involve himself in such matters,' he replied testily. He would make this woman pay for her impertinence. 'I am feeling a chill, so I might get changed. Are you okay?'

Damn. He was backing away from the topic again. This was going to go nowhere, and she was thinking she might abandon her plan and leave. 'Yes, I have my jacket, I'm fine, thanks.'

'Would you like a top-up, Julie-Anne?' Gao called out from the kitchen.

She turned around to respond in the negative and noticed he was wearing a red, satin bathrobe. *Red, of course.* I'll give it one more try. 'Okay, thanks.'

He topped up their glasses and they turned back to the view. 'That's better, I am much warmer now. Cheers, Julie-Anne.'

Julie-Anne was gazing at the view and lost in its wonder when she felt his hard body nudge up against her from behind. He put a hand inside her blouse and began kissing her on the neck. Two nights ago she had been artfully seduced by Melissa and propelled into a world of eroticism before Paul took her to the peak. Julie-Anne felt safe at the time in the knowledge that the scenario wouldn't have eventuated without Melissa. Her girlfriend wasn't here now, only Gao was, and Julie-Anne was torn between conflicting emotions. She was excited at the prospect of what she might uncover, but dreading what she might surrender to accomplish that.

Okay, here we go, be strong. She didn't like this guy and her mind was telling her she should withdraw from his embrace. She wondered whether something else was at play in the dark recesses of her mind. Was this some variant of Stockholm syndrome? She knew that SS was a psychological condition that occurs when a victim of abuse attaches or bonds, positively with their abuser. Julie-Anne wasn't technically a victim and Paul Gao wasn't an abuser as such, but she had unwittingly submitted to his power and magnetism when he had taken advantage of her affection for Melissa. Did she feel inferior or subordinate as a result? She recalled his power equation reference at the bookshop. Julie-Anne would take control of him, show him what real power was and move her plan forward.

'You like this, yes?' he asked smugly while his other hand drifted down her leg.

She didn't respond. Releasing his grip instead, she grasped him by the hand and led him back into the living room. He appeared baffled, but she had cleared her head now. Grabbing him by the arms she forcibly pushed him down onto the sofa. He lay there wearing a dumbfounded expression. His robe was laying open and she stood there for a moment allowing herself to admire his rock hard, athletic body. Her mind was clear, and she would enjoy this, if only physically. Julie-Anne undressed, placed one knee on the sofa next to his leg and then lifted the other over his body. Leaning forward, she placed both hands firmly on his chest for leverage and then lowered herself. She pushed down and began gyrating at her own pace. She loved the sensations that she was creating for herself. She was in charge. With her hands behind her head, she stretched upwards and rode him rhythmically. 'Oh, wow, aaagh,' he groaned deeply. Julie-Anne didn't acknowledge him; this was about her, she was controlling this, and he was just a body under her, albeit a chiselled, rock hard one. She continued to indulge herself at his expense and his facial expression displayed just how incensed he was at her dismissive attitude. If she pushed it too far her plan wouldn't work. Okay, it's time, girl. 'Come join me,' she whispered. He sat bolt upright, wrapped his arms around her and buried his face into her breasts. She held him by the back of his head, continued her rhythmic gyrating, slowly picking up her pace until she heard him groan. Okay, he's ready. She flexed her pelvic muscles, constricting around him, and rode him until he moaned loudly. *Who has the power now?* She suppressed her own groan of fulfilment and stopped herself from crying out.

Julie-Anne didn't speak, nor acknowledge him afterwards, rather she abruptly climbed off of him and went in search of her clothes while she waited for the inevitable. She was acutely aware that a male orgasm releases a rush of chemicals from the brain that made men drowsy afterwards. And the amount of alcohol consumed would accelerate that process. By the time she had dressed he had obligingly fallen asleep. She covered him with his robe, not wanting him to be awaken early by the cold. *Now, where to start, Julie-Anne.* She looked around the living room, but there was nothing obvious that stood out to her. No bookcase, no wall units or even an under coffee table drawer where he could store anything of interest to her. She tiptoed across to the kitchen area and one by one quietly checked the overhead and under bench cupboards. Nada again. Julie-Anne was walking towards what was obviously the master bedroom when she noticed a door ajar to an adjacent room. She could just make out an office desk in the back corner. This must be his study or home office. Before entering she went back to living area and checked on him. He was still out to it. Julie-Anne tiptoed across the polished floorboards to the study. She gently pushed open the door and moved across to the desk. The desktop was bare except for some business papers placed under an ornamental panda. She picked up the heavy paperweight and after a quick scan she carefully put the papers back in place. She turned on her phone light and began rifling through the desk drawers. The top drawer had the usual assortment of pens, highlighters, post-it-notes, a stapler, a box of staples and not much else. She went to the second drawer and pulled it open. There were a few manilla folders stacked on top of each other. She lifted out the first folder and flipped open the cover. She gasped. Julie-Anne was horrified at what she was looking at and had to stop herself from shrieking in horror as her hands began shaking. This can't possibly be true. Oh, no, surely not. Time wasn't her friend, so she calmed herself and hurriedly flicked through the remaining photos which were differing shots of the same subjects taken in varying positions. She switched her mobile to the camera app and snapped each photo in the folder. Rifling through the remaining folders, and finding nothing of interest, she replaced them in the same sequence she had found them. Okay, that's it, let's get out of here. Just as she was putting her phone back in her jeans pocket she heard it. She turned her head slightly to check out the faint noise she had detected. Too late. A strong arm wrapped around her neck and started choking her. Purely out of instinct she bucked her body, kicked backwards and lashed out with her arms, all to no avail. He was too strong, but she already knew that. She was trying to stomp on his feet with the heels of her boots, but he was leaning at an angle and she missed each time.

'What are you doing? Are you trying to fuck me again?'

She heard his sinister laugh over her heavy, anxious breathing. 'No chance,' she gagged defiantly. Her face was heating up, she was having trouble breathing and her neck was beginning to throb from his chokehold. And the pressure on the cartilage in her throat was agonising. She had to do something, and soon. Then she remembered. With her heart racing, she strained against his arm, tilting her head down until she could just make out the object through her blurring eyesight. And it was within reach. She extended her arm, straining every sinew, until she grasped it in her hand. Gripping it firmly, she swiftly swung her arm in an arc, and as viciously as she could manage, slammed it into his head. Instantly she felt the warmth of liquid on her hand. She had hurt him and he was bleeding. Good. She took advantage of his injury, pivoting her body around and launching a kick straight into his groin. She left him doubled over on the floor. All those gym sessions finally put to good use.

Julie-Anne's long legs bounded down the steps three at a time. Smashing her palm against the green door release button, she burst out through the foyer door and ran all the way down the road to the tee junction, not risking a look over her shoulder. She came upon a Seven Eleven on the corner, ran inside and down the aisle to the back wall near the drinks fridges. She crouched behind a bulky rack of potato chips. Opening the Uber App she booked a ride as quickly as her shaking hands would allow. As the tense seconds passed, she stole a couple of nervous glances around the racks. *Come on, come on.* Julie-Anne exhaled when the app finally told her the car was two minutes away. The two minutes felt like a lifetime, her anxiety levels were rising and she was starting to panic. *Come on, come on.* Her hands were still trembling and her heart pounding like a bass drum. Gao could come barging through the door at any minute and she would be trapped. Then the app told her the car had arrived. She raced past the bewildered store attendant, charged out the front door, and threw herself into the back seat. 'Lock the doors and drive.'

Julie-Anne sucked in long, deep breaths and leant back against the headrest. As she regained her composure a quirky thought popped into her head. *Thank God I dressed first before I started snooping around.* She allowed herself a nervous smile at the mental picture of her running down the street and into the Seven Eleven naked.

And now she had a Panda story of her own to tell.

61. Julie-Anne's Apartment

Sunday 31st May

Julie-Anne had allowed herself the luxury of a sleep-in following the physical and emotional trauma of the previous evening. Now, mid-morning, she was on her balcony in her bathrobe sipping a homemade double strength latte and puffing on a rare cigarette. She was reflecting on the events of yesterday and last night. After realising she was being followed by Paul Gao she had promptly decided to turn the tables on him. Given Melissa's revelation that he was an emissary for the Chinese Consulate, and her own comments to him over dinner about her investigation into Chinese interference in Australia, being tailed by him wasn't a coincidence, nor a surprise. She had turned that to her advantage and used the timely opportunity to get closer to him and potentially ascertain what illegal activities he was involved in. She hadn't originally intended to get *that* close, though. *What the hell were you thinking?* Well, in more ways than one she had got more than she bargained for. Although, in some remote part of her mind she felt that she had liberated herself by taking control of him. She was a mentally strong woman and could compartmentalise with the best of them. She would do that now, and deal with the emotional fallout later. She had unfinished business with Wie Ping Lie. However, given these latest developments and the incriminating photos that lay before her, that project would have to go on the back burner, for now at least. With the swelling and bruising on her neck being apparent, she would need to avoid the office for a couple of days. Unless of course she wanted to explain to Chris Russell what had happened, and she didn't, couldn't. He would go ballistic at her wandering off the reservation again, as he liked to call it. Her editor would want to provide her with personal protection again and she couldn't do her job properly while being smothered by over-protective security personnel. She would have to be vigilant though, as Gao clearly knew where she lived, and he would be beside himself with rage after she had got the better of him last night. Following the attempt on her life earlier in the year her boss had engaged MPS Security Services to provide around the clock security and surveillance for her. Fortunately for Julie-Anne, David Bedford had arranged for security cameras to be installed outside her apartment at the time, and these were still monitored twenty four seven. She felt safer as a result.

Julie-Anne had earlier emailed the photos she had taken last night to herself in three point five megabyte size and printed them out. The A4 sheets were laying on the outdoor table in front of her and she was still in a state of disbelief. Her friend Sophie was in all six shots and this wasn't your everyday magazine shoot by any means. The low-life, freelancing members of the paparazzi would call them the money shots. Sophie was in various stages of nakedness with a man who's face Julie-Anne recognised, but couldn't place. She was tempted to call Sophie straight away, but what was she going to say. She didn't have anything definitive to offer and it would only alarm her. Julie-Anne would do some digging first and then, depending on what she discovered, she might be in a position to have what would undoubtedly be an agonisingly difficult conversation with her friend. Sophie had had a torrid time in the past couple of years and just when her life was back on-track, up popped these horribly compromising photos. Julie-Anne felt deeply for her.

Think, Julie-Anne, think. Eventually after delving into the deep recesses of her memory it came to her. She had seen the man in photos and doorstops on the evening news bulletin at some stage, but when and why? She was racking her brain and finally something surfaced. She remembered the controversy surrounding the state government's cancellation of the Confucius Institute Program and this guy had been aggressively interrogated about it by the voracious media. Who was he? He obviously had to be a spokesperson for either the education department or broader the government itself. It was time for her online business partner to do some work. She opened Google in her laptop browser and searched for the Education Department's website. There was the Secretary of the Department listed, so she double clicked on his link and the photo was nothing like the guy in Gao's illicitly taken photos. She navigated across to the New South Wales Parliament website and came upon a link entitled "Ministers", so she double clicked and scrolled down. Bingo. He was Ben Chandler, the Minister for Education and Early Childhood Learning. Okay, Sophie was involved in some way with the Minister and Paul Gao had in his possession compromising photos of them together. Julie-Anne wondered if this was the politician Sophie had mentioned that she had an appointment with. She assumed that it must be. And how and why did Paul Gao obtain the photos? It didn't take long for a theory to begin developing in her mind, but she needed more information to validate it. Julie-Anne Googled Ben Chandler and in zero point five four seconds Google had identified over sixteen million results. *Bugger.*

She eventually found an online profile of him provided by his political party. He lived in Woy Woy on the Central Coast with his wife and two teenage boys. He had been a lifelong member of the party since his Young Liberal days. Subsequent to university he had embarked on a successful law career before entering politics at a relatively young age. In no time at all he advanced through the party and was eventually rewarded with the education portfolio. Julie-Anne wasn't one to rush to judgement, although what was a family man, successful lawyer and politician doing booking an escort? *Aah, men.* Seeking more information to support her earlier theory Julie-Anne then went back to Google and typed in "Chinese interference in Australia". One of the first articles under the news banner was posted on the News dot com website. It began:

> *Operatives from a secretive arm of the Chinese Communist Party are on a mission to infiltrate and influence almost every aspect of Australian life, from politics and business to the media.*
>
> *That's the conclusion of a shocking new report about the work of agents and their recruits, whose goals range from the commercial to the downright sinister. Analysis from the Australian Strategic Policy Institute (ASPI) examined the operation of the United Front, which Chinese President Xi Jinping once described as his "magic weapon", whose tentacles already spread through our universities, corporations and parliaments."*

Julie-Anne wondered whether that influence extended to the Confucius Institute, as had been widely rumoured. The state government cancelling the Confucius Institute across New South Wales government schools would have been a slap down for China, highly embarrassing, and with potential geopolitical repercussions. She was in no doubt that they would be strident in their endeavours to rectify that scenario. She continued searching and found another related article in The Guardian, one of particular interest to her new investigation.

Last year, the Brisbane campus of the University of Queensland became a flashpoint for the ongoing international backlash against the China state, its influence on Hong Kong, the proposed extradition law and its mass detention of its Muslim Uighur population. That protest was infiltrated by pro-Chinese students who had attacked the peaceful demonstrators in a violent retaliation. It was intimated that these pro-Chinese students were operating under the orders of Hanban, the international arm of China's Education Ministry, and by extension, the Chinese Communist Party. The fallout from the protests highlighted China's reach into foreign universities through cultural programs such as the Confucius Institute Program.

Julie-Anne noted that the patriotic behaviour of the violent counter protesters had been praised by the Chinese Consul General to Queensland and reported in the South China Morning Post. No surprise there. She reread the last line.

The fallout from the protests highlighted China's reach into foreign universities through cultural programs such as the Confucius Institute Program.

If this was the case, then China would be seriously displeased about having the program withdrawn from New South Wales schools. The links in Julie-Anne's mental Gant Chart were joining up. She continued on.

The Attendees, who believe they were identified by

videos of the protest, were subsequently targeted online in doxxing attacks; in one case a Hong Kong student had his driver's licence, marriage certificate, student ID and other identifying information published on Chinese social media site Weibo.

Julie-Anne thought about Li Qiang's reach into Sophie's family back in China and how that had impacted on their life and freedoms. She went back to the ASPI article and kept reading.

The United Front('s) work encompasses a broad spectrum of activity, from espionage to foreign interference, influence and engagement. The Chinese Communist Party's (CCP) attempts to interfere in diaspora communities, influence political systems and covertly access valuable and sensitive technology will only grow as tensions between China and countries around the world develop.

In a speech at a meeting of United Front Work Department leaders in Beijing in 2015, President Xi praised its work in "strengthening the Party's ruling position". He described it as "an important magic weapon for realising the China Dream of the Great Rejuvenation of the Chinese Nation.

She would need to enlighten Melissa on the less than noble activities of her study tour sponsor.

Realising the China Dream of the Great Rejuvenation of the Chinese Nation.

Where had she heard that before? Of course, Paul Gao

had pretty much quoted that word-for-word when she had challenged him at The Bank last night. The word indoctrinated popped into her head. She went back to the top of the article.

Operatives from a secretive arm of the Chinese Communist Party are on a mission to infiltrate and influence almost every aspect of Australian life.

Was Paul Gao one of those operatives. The title Special Emissary, could be construed as anything, and with its potentially vague remit, it would be a convenient cover for a CCP operative. And it probably came with diplomatic immunity. Julie-Anne returned to her online business partner and typed 'Chinese Consulate Sydney personnel list' into the browser. She wanted to see if Paul Gao was listed as an officially registered representative of the Consulate. Under the DFAT website heading she found – China Foreign Embassies and Consulates in Australia where there were links to each state's Consulate. She clicked on the NSW link. Scrolling down she could not find a Paul Gao listed. Therefore, not being listed by DFAT meant that he wasn't an officially registered representative of the Consulate and therefore, would not be entitled to claim diplomatic immunity. *Game on buddy.*

Her mobile rang. Again.

62. Julie-Anne's Apartment

Sunday 31st May

Julie-Anne looked down at her phone and the WhatsApp caller ID said it was Jack. She'd had three missed calls from him on her mobile this morning, but she wasn't in the right headspace for an argument. Knowing precisely why he was calling she couldn't fob him off forever. He wouldn't be happy.

'Hello, Jack,' she said evenly.

'Shit, JA, how could you do that to me? I thought we were partners in that investigation and you go off and write that crap.'

That got her hackles up. 'It's not crap, as you call it, Jack. It's a public interest story and I have an obligation to my readership to tell it.'

'And let's not forget our history together. Doesn't that count for something?' he bristled.

'Not in this instance, no. I expected to hear from you yesterday.'

'I waited until my anger subsided.'

'It sure doesn't sound like it. What did you think I was writing, a nursery rhyme?'

'Surely it wasn't necessary to go into so much detail about the whole thing,' he challenged, still seething.

She was becoming angry herself now. 'The Sydney Daily News isn't a tabloid that publishes salacious, unsubstantiated rubbish, Jack. My readers expect quality journalism that is based on factual, verifiable information and that's what I produced. Besides, you weren't mentioned by name, so what's the issue here?'

'It's an extremely small world out there now, especially with the twenty four hour news cycle and omnipresent social media, and it won't take long for someone to put two and two together. Then I'll be a laughing-stock around here,' he lamented.

'You told me on Friday that I would just have to go ahead and publish what I have, and I did exactly that. So stop acting like a disgruntled pelican,' she said, endeavouring to lower the temperature of the conversation.

'A what?' he asked, oblivious.

'It's a famous line from Schitt's Creek, Jack. You need to get out more.'

'Oh, okay. I only said half-heartedly you should publish what you had, thinking you didn't have enough to go to press with.'

'Well, you should have thought about that at the time. You know me well enough that I always adhere to my deadlines. I told you that I couldn't hold the story for another week and risk the state police leaking it to the tabloids or posting about it on social media. What was I supposed to do?'

She heard him sigh. 'Yeah, but it still doesn't sit right with me.'

'Jack, might I remind you that you wouldn't have become aware of Danielle's deceptive behaviour if it wasn't for me.'

'Yeah, yeah, I get that as well. Did you really have to mention the celebratory lunch we had at the Boathouse? That was a private occasion.'

'Of course I did. You told me that Danielle wasn't attending then out of the blue she turns up. With my hindsight goggles on, it's obvious that she wanted to know what I might have held back from my original story. And I'm guessing she hoped you might divulge some non-public information from your investigation after a few glasses of wine. Keep your friends close and your enemies closer comes to mind. As we now know all too well, she's a crafty customer.'

'Well, JA, by going to print early you missed getting the whole story.'

'Why, what's happened?'

'Oh, now you want to hear what I have to say,' he replied mockingly.

'Give it up. Sarcasm doesn't suit you, Jack. What haven't you told me?'

'The person we apprehended and have subsequently charged is none other than my double-dealing ex-girlfriend.'

'What? You could have told me that on Friday evening?'

'No, I couldn't. We hadn't interviewed her at that stage and you publishing that information would have compromised another facet of our investigation.' Jack was becoming pissed off again. 'Do you have any idea how I was feeling when I had to arrest her or do you only care about your bloody feature article?'

She had made him angry. 'I'm sorry, Jack. I really am.' She would back off and allow him to speak when he was ready.

Eventually he resumed talking. 'We arrested Wie yesterday as well.'

Julie-Anne resisted the temptation to continue her interrogation. She wasn't on a deadline now, so time wasn't an issue. 'Congratulations, that's wonderful news. You must be so pleased.'

'I am, but as I told Sanderson, it feels like a hollow victory. After all, I'm no closer to nailing the head of the importation syndicate. Unless, of course, I can get Wie to talk, and that's highly unlikely to happen.'

'I'm with you on that. I feel empty as well after what he did to me. That's one crime no one will ever be charged with, unless of course he confesses. Which he won't.'

Jack's family lived in the country, and now that he was obviously single again, he would have no one to turn to or confide in. 'Do you need someone to talk to? We could catch up for a drink if you want,' Julie-Anne suggested. It was the last thing she wanted given her recent nocturnal activities, but she still cared for him, so would make the effort.

'Thanks, but I really don't feel like celebrating.'

'Who said anything about celebrating? I thought you might just want someone to talk to, Jack.'

'Thanks. I'm all talked out after the past couple of days I've had. I might just go sit out on my balcony and get drunk,' he said glumly.

She needed to take his mind off his current state of woe and give him something to get enthused about. 'I've already started on another investigation.'

That snapped him out of his bout of despondency and back to the present. 'Gee, you don't let grass grow under your feet, do you, JA?'

'I didn't plan to dive back in so soon, but by accident, I came across some damning information which merited further examination.' *By accident, really!* She involuntarily touched the bruises on her neck.

That piqued his curiosity. 'Anything you care to share with your favourite detective?'

That's better. He's on his way back. 'Not at this stage, although it relates to my favourite subject, so I might need your assistance.'

'Aah, that old chestnut. Chinese interference.'

'You know me too well.'

'Well, I should, we were in a relationship for six months.'

'Is that what it was, a relationship?' She regretted the words as soon as they disappeared into the ether. 'Sorry, I shouldn't have said that.'

'No, you shouldn't have. Anyway, moving on. Tell me about this latest investigation of yours?'

'It's early days, so there's not much to tell at the moment. There should be something in it for the AFP if I'm correct about what I suspect is unfolding. If I need some information can I call you?'

'Depends what it is, but yeah sure.'

'And in return I'll provide you with whatever evidence I uncover and you can go after my suspect and do what you do, Jack. Once I have my story, of course.'

'Of course, I know all too well where your priorities lie and how you work, JA.'

Julie-Anne let the slight pass. 'Stay tuned, I think this will be intriguing for both of us, Jack.'

'As always, you be careful out there.'

'Thanks, I will.'

'Okay, I'm off to get drunk.'

'Bye, Jack.'

After disconnecting the call Julie-Anne noticed a little red three overlaid on her green call button. She tapped on the icon and saw that one of the missed calls was from Jordan Doherty. Following her overactive Saturday night the last thing she needed at the moment was interaction with a suitor. She had broken up with Jack earlier in the year, then had a brief relationship with Melissa and now she was carrying the Paul Gao chip on her shoulder. She had though, enjoyed a wonderful evening at El Loco and had found Jordan refreshing and funny. And of course he was athletic and handsome, which didn't hurt. She pressed the missed call tab, then tapped on his name and waited for the call to go through.

'Hi, Julie-Anne, how are you?' he answered cheerily.

'I'm well thanks, Jordan,' she lied. 'And you?'

'Yeah, I'm all good thanks. Just too occupied with work as always. So, I got to thinking, now who do I know who could tempt me away from that drudgery and then I had a eureka moment. I started thinking, what was the name of that intelligent, attractive and funny woman I had supper with earlier in the week.'

He was flirting with her and she liked his style. 'And I'm guessing you couldn't remember her name, so you rang me instead,' she laughed.

'Funny. Very funny, Julie-Anne.'

'If I hadn't become a journalist I'm sure I would have gone into comedy. Apparently all I have to do is look at someone and they start laughing.'

'You're on a roll now, don't let me stop you,' he replied.

'That's all I've got. Anyway, why are you so busy with work, Jordan? I would have thought that now both the AFL and NRL seasons are in full swing all the hard work would be done.'

'You would think so wouldn't you, but the hard work starts now trying to renegotiate or renew existing player contracts. What about you? The world of crime doesn't take a holiday either, so I'm guessing you're always on the go too.'

'I literally just finished one investigation and immediately afterwards some information landed in my lap and into the deep end I go again.'

'I went to the Murray Rose Pool today and jumped into the deep end myself,' he said deadpan.

'Now who's the funny one, Mister Doherty?'

'Just trying to keep up with the Julie-Annes of this world. Now, I was wondering if you would you like to go to El Loco again? Or maybe somewhere different if you like. It would be lovely to see you.'

She hesitated responding, why she didn't know. Yes she did. Last night's events had stolen a part of her soul and she wasn't in the right headspace for another romantic entanglement. 'I'm actually quite busy with work at the moment. Can we take a raincheck?'

'Yes, of course,' he replied hesitantly.

'Thank you for calling, Jordan.'

She had been beating herself up after the Paul Gao episode last night and she liked that this man had put a smile back on her face. She had needed that.

63. AFP Headquarters

Monday 1st June

Jack arrived at AFP headquarters mid-morning on Monday nursing a well-deserved hangover after sitting out on his balcony well into the night over imbibing in a bottle of his signature bourbon and ruminating over JA's article. With the fog coasting around his head this morning the last thing he needed to be doing was writing status reports for the Deputy Commissioner. His desk phone rang and he wished it to be anything that would get him out of the office. Unfortunately it was the opposite. The DC wanted to see him. Now, Jack, hoping to clear his head, jogged up the stairs to the executive floor and walked across to the DC's office. He was motioned in with a wave of a hand.

'That was an interesting article by your ex-girlfriend. Where did she get her information, Jack?'

'I have no idea, boss, probably the state guys.' Jack thought he might be in for a good old fashioned bollicking, so he took a seat.

'Are you implying that Sanderson leaked the intel?'

'No, not at all. He wouldn't do that.'

'Well someone darn well gave her a head's-up and she could have compromised your investigation. You and Sanderson were just lucky that Wie obviously doesn't read the Daily News on a Saturday. If he had, all you would have achieved out of this was the arrest of your girlfriend. A bit player at best.'

The DC was on a roll now and Jack knew to button it up when he was in this mood.

'Now, I know you and Granger have history, but you need to put that aside and focus on your investigations and zip it up, Jack. In fact it would probably assist your career if you kept everything zipped up.'

'Boss, the state guys leak anything that will enhance their popularity with the journos, particularly if it garners favour with a woman like Julie-Anne. They just can't help themselves, you know that,' he fibbed.

'That may be true, nevertheless, you need to have a stern word with Sanderson and tell him to get his guys at Day Street under control.'

'Okay, will do.'

'While I realise this is predominantly a state based investigation I haven't given up hope on getting some intel out of Wie Ping Lie that leads us to the syndicate's heads in China. Do you think he will talk, Jack?'

'I very much doubt it. The China Shipping Company is bringing in his coke and they have direct links to the Communist Party in China and Wie won't risk being ostracised by them. He is smart enough to know how that ends up.'

'Alright, I have spoken to the Chief of Detectives at Day Street and assured him that I want to avoid an interagency pissing match at all costs. But, I have asked him to allow you to interview Wie when they have finished with him. Are you up for that or do you feel too conflicted given his relationship with Miss Mortimer? And yours for that matter.'

'No, I'll be fine.'

'While we're on the subject of Miss Mortimer, it seems you

were well and truly screwed by both women, figuratively and literally. Did I mention keeping it zipped up, Jack?'

'Yes, you did, boss,' he replied meekly.

'Now, what about this Chan woman? Where are you up to with her?'

'She finally cooperated and gave up Wie's address and we would have nabbed him eventually as a result. And she did give us Rent A Space. She was just a bit player like Mortimer, but it's up to you as to what the next course of action is.'

'I got burnt once already with my benevolence towards Mortimer, so I'm not about to repeat that mistake. Having said that, Chan did cooperate with you, albeit tardily. I suggest you talk to the state's DPP and convince him to agree to a heavy fine and probation. You never know, she could be useful in the future.'

'Will do, boss.'

Jack sat at his desk and composed an email to the New South Wales Assistant Director of Public Prosecutions. While Lucie Chan was a willing participant in Wie's illicit drug business she had already suffered at the hands of the rival Lebanese gang, had lost her lover and employer forever and probably her apartment too. In short Jack felt something approaching sorrow for Lucie Chan. He outlined her cooperation with both the state and federal authorities and what appeared to be her genuine remorse in the end. The courts didn't want to be seen to be filling up the prisons with low level criminals that were unlikely to reoffend. They would take into consideration mitigating factors, any criminal record, character evidence, the prospects for rehabilitation and the likelihood of reoffending. He imagined that Lucie would be keen to write a letter of apology to the court as well. Anything to stay out of prison. She was an intelligent, street-smart young woman, so Jack figured she should have no trouble finding gainful employment, if she put her mind to the task. He recommended to the Assistant DPP that she be charged with the lesser offence of possession of what is classified as a small quantity which, if the case went to court, would attract fifty penalty units or two years in prison. He suggested to the ADPP that a fine in the vicinity of five thousand dollars be levied and her placed on two years' probation. Finally, he recommended that she be directed to report to the police on a monthly basis for the first six months of her probation. He hit the send icon. Jack should have insisted that she make a statement detailing her knowledge of the shooting of Amir and Jasar and implicate Yong, but that was up to Sanderson. Anyway, he had sufficient evidence to put Yong away for a long time, so he shouldn't need her statement.

A whole week had gone by since JA had delivered the devastating news about Danielle. With nothing urgent on his plate now he might take a long walk in the sunshine down to the Opera Bar, take in the stunning harbour views and while away the afternoon with a few schooners. He spent the next hour finalising his status reports, uploaded them onto the server and then logged off from his desktop.

Jack pushed through the door of the AFP's headquarters and exited into the afternoon sunshine. His mood was buoyed as he gazed upwards and admired the cloudless, azure sky. For the first time in a week he was feeling good. Even the hangover was dissipating. He made a commitment to himself to remember this moment. He walked up Commonwealth Street, across Liverpool Street and into Hyde Park. The area for the park was set aside by Governor Macquarie in 1810 and it was regarded as Australia's oldest park. Pausing at the Anzac Memorial he thought about all those tens of thousands of Australians who hadn't returned from the Great War over one hundred years ago. His own personal problems paled by comparison when he considered those brave young men who had so valiantly given their lives for their country. He wondered if he could ever do the same. Walking alongside the Pool of Reflection it occurred to him that he had been doing a lot of that lately, especially regarding his unsuccessful relationships with Danielle and JA. He had been naïve and blissfully unaware of Danielle's duplicity throughout the entirety of their relationship. He was committed to his job at the AFP and appreciated the fact that she had afforded him the time and space he needed to focus on that. He now knew why, of course. JA had wanted more of his time. She wasn't needy, just wanting to do what normal couples do in a relationship. Spend quality time together and enjoy each other's company. His lack of commitment to the relationship had eventually allowed her to fall into Melissa's arms. He still missed JA, but consoled himself that they remained friends. Across the lawn he saw a larger than life size bronze figure perched atop a granite pedestal. The statue commemorated Captain James Cook who explored, charted and claimed the east coast of Australia for the British Empire in 1770. The country has come a long way in two hundred and fifty years. Jack wondered what the next two hundred and fifty years would hold for his country. In just ten years social media trolling had become an art form, free speech was denigrated unless you were a so-called progressive, if you weren't woke you weren't awake, cancel culture abounded, people messaged or texted rather than talked, self-entitlement was rampant and the ubiquitous selfie had facilitated a look at me generation. This was to be a day of clearing his head, so he banished those depressing thoughts to the deep recesses of his mind. He sucked in a deep breath, admired the beauty of the park, gazed upwards at the azure sky again and smiled. Resuming his meandering, he crossed Park Street, exited the park and continued northwards through the parliamentary precinct before detouring through the Royal Botanic Gardens where he arrived at the Sydney Conservatorium of Music. The heritage-listed music school was the oldest and most prestigious music school in Australia. He stopped to read some of the wall plaques.

> *It is a rare surviving example of the work of noted ex-convict architect Francis Greenway in the Old Colonial Gothic style. Greenway was instrumental in Governor Macquarie accomplishing his aim to transform the fledgling colony into an orderly, well-mannered society and environment.*

Jack wondered whether modern Australia was any closer to achieving the erstwhile Governor's honourable ambition. Given the self-entitled, boorish and intolerant behaviour he had witnessed throughout the lockdown, he seriously doubted it. He ducked back down to Macquarie Street, past the fountain and onto the forecourt. There in full view was the magnificent Sydney Opera House with the Sydney Harbor Bridge across to the left. Voilà. He continued along the forecourt until he reached the Opera Bar.

'How are you today, sir?' the chirpy barman asked.

Jack felt recharged and his mind was re-energised subsequent to his awe-inspiring journey through Sydney's glorious past. He was in a good headspace. 'I couldn't be any better thanks.'

'What would you like?'

Jack recalled the story he had regaled to his now ex-girlfriend only ten days previous. 'A schooner of One Fifty Lashes please.'

64. Camperdown – Inner Sydney

Monday 1st June

It was late morning when Paul Gao was awakened by the throbbing in his head. That biǎo zi, Granger had gotten the better of him on Saturday night and left him lying on the floor in the foetal position holding his manhood and with blood dripping from the side of his head. He had probably needed stitches for the wound and should have gone straight to the Emergency Department, but there would be too many uncomfortable questions fired at him. Instead, he had disinfected and bandaged it as best he could yesterday and spent the remainder of the day convalescing. He would need to wear a hat for a few days to shield the wound from prying eyes. Avoiding the Consulate would also be a necessity as the Consul General would not be pleased with how his extracurricular activities might be interfering with his appointed task. He should have just knocked out the Granger woman rather than try to detain and interrogate her. He had to assume she had seen the photos, so he would need to move quickly. Upon reflection, her bumping into him at the bookshop was all too convenient. She had obviously played him, right from the time he started following her until they ended up on the sofa. He had thought that he was in control all afternoon and evening. *He* invited her for a drink, then *he* suggested having dinner together and *he* invited her back to his apartment. And finally, *he* initiated the physical contact on the balcony. She appeared to just be rolling with the flow, but in reality, she had played him like a mandolin. He had been careless and now as a result, the Granger woman would realise the purpose of the photos. If she was the clever investigative reporter her reputation suggested that is. She undoubtedly was and he wouldn't underestimate her again.

The minister should receive the next instalment depicting his infidelities today. Gao knew it was a two day delivery time for mail to reach Woy Woy. To be certain he had the Minister's attention he would turn up the heat and mail the third photo today. It would be received by its intended target on Wednesday. Two days after receiving the second photo would be ample time for Chandler to seriously reconsider his position on the Confucius Institute. If not, the third photo should be very persuasive. He would also send a little video to two more deserving recipients. That would make for interesting conversation and potentially even remove an impediment to his cause. Gao decided to walk the one kilometre down Australia Street to the Enmore Post Office. The irony of walking down Australia Street while he was blackmailing one of the country's state government ministers wasn't lost on him. He needed to update the Consul General, so he would use the walking time to do just that. He called Xiao on his burner phone.

'Paul, I haven't spoken to you for two weeks. I hope you have some promising news for me,' the CG stated expectantly.

Gao picked up on the undertone of his master's statement. 'Mr Consul General, this is an intricate operation and it has a very defined, incremental approach that needs to be strictly adhered to. As such, it requires a degree of subtlety.'

'China has a history of playing the long game, but time and subtlety are not something we have in abundance on this occasion, Paul.'

'Mr Consul General, may I respectfully remind you of a favoured proverb. Patience is power; with time and patience the mulberry leaf becomes a silk gown.'

'Well, thank you for reminding me young man,' he replied, heavy on sarcasm. 'The Chairman of the Confucius Institute Headquarters Council has contacted me again. Tan Chailun is displeased with our progress, and if he is displeased, then so am I. You have one more week to complete your task otherwise I will make other arrangements. Maybe you have a proverb for that, too,' he said.

Gao began protesting. He was talking to himself. 'Tā mā de.'

Given the CG's veiled threats he mailed the items via express post and then took a leisurely stroll back to his apartment. He didn't anticipate any progress on his appointed task until Wednesday at the earliest, so in the meantime he would develop a plan to deal with the Granger woman. He needed to retrieve the photos she had undoubtedly printed out as well as acquire her electronic devices. He called Sun Jie and made the necessary arrangements. Now, what does he do about Melissa? He doesn't need her anymore and given his injuries he would have to avoid her anyway. That decision was made easier the minute he dropped the packages into the yellow mailbox. She obviously still had feelings for the Granger woman judging by her enthusiasm during and after dinner last week, so they could have each other for all he cared. She had outlived her usefulness, but maybe there was one more thing she would inadvertently do for him. He wished he could be the fly on the wall when that unfolded.

65. Chandler House - Woy Woy

Monday 1st June

State parliament wasn't in session until tomorrow and Ben Chandler didn't have any meetings or appointments before two o'clock this afternoon. It was now eleven. He had shaved, showered, dressed, packed his briefcase and he was leaning on the dining room table reading the broadsheet and sipping his homemade latte. He had a few more minutes of leisure time until he needed to walk to the station for his weekly commute to his parliamentary office in the heart of Sydney.

'You're still here, Ben,' his wife said as she walked into the dining room.

'I thought you were at your office, Sonja.'

'I was, but I needed to grab a couple of documents that I forgot. It was fortunate that I did and that you're still here. She handed him a mustard coloured A4 envelope addressed to him via her office and prominently marked strictly private and confidential in bold caps. It was identical in every way to the one he received on Thursday. His hands started quivering for the second time in four days. *My God, they even know about my wife's business.*

'Thanks, Sonja,' he mumbled distractedly.

'It's strange that someone would address correspondence to you care of my office, don't you think, Ben? And a strictly private and confidential one at that. That makes no sense, especially when you have two offices in Sydney and one here in town.'

'It's probably just someone local who didn't know my office address, but knew you were my wife, so they sent it there,' he replied, not believing his rationale one bit. He hastily slid the envelope into the side pocket of his briefcase, rose from the table and headed for the front door. 'I'll see you on Thursday night,' he called out.

Once more he was grateful that he had managed to secure the window seat at the rear of the train carriage. He shakily eased the paper out of the envelope face down, turned it over and held it up in front of his face. The photo showed a naked Sophie sitting atop him on the bed, fortunately with her back to the camera. Unfortunately for him, his head was resting on her shoulder, and clearly visible. Thank heavens Sonja didn't open the letter, was all he could think. He lowered the photo to his lap and flipped it over. On the back was a white cigarette packet sized label with a simple sentence printed across it. "You will reinstate the Confucius Institute". Well, at least now he knew what this was all about. And he assumed the photo was delivered via his wife's office as a hint as to where the next photo might end up. With a different addressee. He recalled his brief meeting with the Chinese Consul General. He had been employing soft diplomacy in his efforts to have the Institute reinstated, but Ben had stood his ground and rebuffed his entreaties. Had Xiao traded his diplomacy for another more aggressive approach? Surely not. This intimidation was even too blatant for him to be involved in. Or was it? The China of 2020 was comfortable picking geopolitical fights with an increasing number of its South East Asian neighbours, including Australia. Maybe, Xiao was under increasing pressure from Beijing. Ben cleared his head and called his executive assistant. 'Loretta, good morning. I need to adjust my schedule for the remainder of the day. Firstly, can you cancel all my appointments? Then I want to see the Chinese Consul General in my office at three o'clock tomorrow afternoon. In the meantime I will be at the hotel working from there.'

Ben checked into the hotel and went directly to his suite. Once inside, he turned the dead lock and slipped the security chain through its slot. He didn't want to be interrupted by enthusiastic housekeepers. He took out the first photo, held it up and walked across the room to the sofa. The only place the photo could have been taken was from the direction of the television cabinet. He then moved to the cabinet and searched in vain for any cameras or technological devices. Ben followed the same process in the bedroom with the second photo. He calculated exactly where that photo must have been taken from as well, but once again there were no offending appliances or devices to be found. He wasn't a technological genius, but he wondered if the televisions themselves had been remotely hacked into and that the photos had been taken through that medium. *Surely not.* Coming up empty handed, he sat on the end of the king size bed and considered his options. Even though he now knew what the ambition of the blackmailer was, what action to take was another matter altogether. Did he ignore it? Did he go to the police? What about a private security company? *And, the real kicker, do I tell the Premier?* And what about poor Sophie? She doesn't deserve this. He had never spent more than one evening with an escort before and he most certainly hadn't led them into his bedroom. He realised the moment he laid eyes on her that this would be different. He reconnected with feelings that had long lay dormant, suppressed by the drudgery of suburban life, his wife's apparent lack of physical interest in him, and his political career. He loved the butterflies he felt in his stomach whenever he thought of Sophie. It was like being a teenager all over again. And once her cool, calm, professional escort demeanour had melted away on the third date he knew she felt the same. And then there's Sonja. Even though her interest in him had seemingly waned over time as she found other pursuits in and around Woy Woy she was still his wife and the mother of his two boys. That wasn't something to be discarded easily, and after all, partners were supposed to work at their relationship. Of course, that was if one of them hadn't fallen in love with another person. There were so many different components, both personal and professional, to his predicament, and unlike the theatre of politics, he didn't know how to handle it. The one thing he did know though was that he wasn't about to reinstate the Confucius Institute, so the situation would undoubtedly escalate. And then there was Sophie to consider. Would he leave Sonja and the boys for her? What would Sophie think about that? She would undoubtedly feel complicit in his transgressions and that may drive her from his arms anyway. He appreciated how this would inevitably play out. Given the insatiable media obsession with sniffing out a scandal, the whole episode would become public in no time and then everything would be on the table. His reputation, career, family and probably even Sophie. And if the media identified Sophie as his mistress she would break it off in a heartbeat. And who could blame her.

He needed help, *but from whom and from where?*

66. International Hotel

Monday 1st June

Julie-Anne arrived at the service entrance of the International Hotel at precisely two o'clock that afternoon. She had spent most of her Monday morning out on her balcony in a delightfully balmy twenty two degrees while trying to move her investigation into Paul Gao and the compromising photos forward. By midday she had made no progress, but then she hit on an idea. Having retrieved her magnifying glass from her office desk she had returned to the balcony and picked up the first of the photos. She chuckled to herself at the thought that anyone would see her examining six photos of a naked couple through a magnifying glass. Not spying anything of significance in the first photo, other than the obvious, Julie-Anne flicked to the second photo. "Hey presto," she had exclaimed when she spotted what she was looking for. The leather mini bar menu folder was propped behind a rack of assorted snacks neatly displayed on a mahogany buffet cabinet. It was immediately behind the sofa that held Ben Chandler and her friend Sophie. Using her magnifying glass she had been able to identify the distinctive oval shaped "I" logo, which she knew from a previous staycation with Jack, represented the International Hotel. She guessed it wouldn't be the Double Bay hotel given its distance from parliament and Ben Chandler's ministerial office. She had then contacted the CBD hotel's security manager. Julie-Anne wasn't prepared to discuss the subject at hand over the phone, so she had spent considerable mental energy, without revealing any names, endeavouring to convince him that it was in the hotel's best interests to meet with her. Eventually the man had relented, she guessed just to appease her and get her off the phone.

'I'm here to see Andy Frances, your head of security,' she told the attendant in the entry booth. Julie-Anne's name was already on the guard's list, so he signed her in, locked his booth, then escorted her down a long basement corridor to the security office. She wondered why security offices were always located down long hallways in grimy, dingy basements. She guessed there was a significant disparity in the value of aboveground real estate compared to where she now was.

'Mr Frances, good morning.'

'Andy, please, Ms Granger.' Julie-Anne considered that an encouraging opening. Frances was a strongly built man in his fifties with dark, round eyes, a salt and pepper goatee and a well-earned beer belly that his suit jacket was failing dismally to hide. She guessed he was an industry veteran. 'Now, what can I do for you?' he asked matter of factly.

'Well, where to start,' she sighed. 'This is a really sensitive subject that could quickly get out of hand if not handled discreetly. Can I rely on your discretion, Andy?'

'I'm not certain, Ms Granger, as my first responsibility is to my employer, not a reporter seeking a story, which I imagine is exactly what you are doing,' he replied steadfastly.

Julie-Anne raised her eyebrows. 'I also imagine the hotel won't want to be implicated in any scandal.'

'Okay, what have you got?'

Julie-Anne talked him through what she had found out without revealing how she came across the incriminating evidence, showing him the photos she carried in her satchel, nor mentioning the high profile guest's name at this point.

'Have I got your attention now?' she asked.

'Maybe, given what you have just disclosed to me, however, I need to see the photos.'

'I can't do that, Andy,' she replied firmly. 'They're not for public consumption.'

'Ms Granger, I'm not the public and you came to me, not the other way around, so if you want my cooperation I need some evidence to support what you are implying,' he said, equally resolutely.

Julie-Anne wasn't going to win this point, so she retrieved the folder of photos from her satchel. She held them up facing toward her while she searched for the least explicit photo. One of the photos showed Ben Chandler and Sophie seated on a sofa, embracing with Chandler facing the camera. 'Okay, this is the only one I am going to allow you to see. It will provide all the evidence you need to validate my story and my concerns.' She reached across his desk and handed him the photo.

'Oh, shit,' he blurted out. 'Sorry,' he said sounding genuinely apologetic. He paused while staring at the photo. 'How do you know this was taken at the International?'

'Look closely at the small folder behind them. It's the mini bar menu and has the hotel's logo on the cover. You might need a magnifying glass, but I can assure you it's your logo. And I assume by your reaction, that you know the identity of the man.'

'Yes, I do.'

Julie-Anne pushed on. 'Someone has illegally installed cameras in one of your suites, Andy. That must concern you greatly, particularly as the head of security here.'

'It may have nothing to do with the hotel, Ms Granger, some voyeur could have taken those with their iPhone,' he replied defiantly.

She was shocked at his ignorance and his obvious attempt at diversion. 'Do you really think the state's education minister allows himself to be photographed in a compromising position, especially with someone other than his wife? Come on, Andy. You need to see this for what it is, an extortion or blackmail attempt. What else could it possibly be?'

'How did you get the photos?'

'We're not going there and it's not relevant at this point,' Julie-Anne replied with conviction in her voice and determination in her eyes. 'All you need to know is that the hotel has an opportunity to get in front of this story rather than be at the centre of it, Andy.'

He was quiet for some time. 'There's something you're not telling me, Ms Granger. You could just write and publish your story with the information that you already have. It's certainly salacious enough. You don't need my assistance or corroboration.'

'Yes, I could certainly do just that, but I work for the Sydney Daily News, not the tabloid, so I like to thoroughly research my articles and obtain the entire story before I go to print. Our readers expect nothing less.'

He went quiet again and sat there impassively with a resolute expression. He wasn't backing down. She continued. 'Okay, in the spirit of mutual cooperation.' Julie-Anne paused and took a deep breath. 'The woman in the photos is a friend of mine. She works for a reputable escort agency.'

'That photo doesn't suggest anything reputable to me, quite the opposite in fact, Ms Granger,' Frances replied crustily.

Julie-Anne sighed again. 'Yes, I know, and I can't explain that at this time,' she admitted. 'The woman in the photos and I had dinner a couple of weeks ago and she mentioned she had an upcoming booking with a politician. I'm guessing you and I both now know who that probably was.'

'Yeah, I guess we do too, Julie-Anne.'

She picked up on the use of her Christian name for the first time. Maybe his attitude was softening. 'Look, Andy, she is a good person who has been through a difficult time over the past couple of years, but she now has her life back on track. She keeps fit, lives a clean life and is studying hard for a psychology degree at Sydney Uni. I want to keep her out of this if that's remotely possible. I can assure you that she is an innocent victim in this ghastly episode. There is just no way she would be complicit in anything like this.' Julie-Anne was almost pleading now.

'So, if your friend's not complicit how did a camera get installed into one of our rooms?' he asked while considering the possibilities.

She wasn't going to mention Paul Gao's name at this point, she wanted the whole story including who planted the camera and the link to Gao. 'It obviously has to be someone inside your organisation with swipe card access, I would respectfully suggest.'

'Why not go to the police?'

'I want the whole story, especially who or what is behind this, not just some maintenance patsy who simply installed a camera. And I'm sure you do too, Andy. You need to know how this whole affair unfolded and where the hotel's breaches in security are. Also, the reputational damage to the hotel would be immense if this isn't handled discreetly and the police aren't notable for their discretion.' Julie-Anne was being as convincing as she could manage with this man whose job description would be black and white. No shades of grey in his world.

'Yeah, I imagine my GM wouldn't want the police involved either, at least for now. I'll need to advise him of your revelations and it will be up to him what action he takes.'

'Sure, go talk to him, I'll wait here.'

'He's not here at the moment, but he'll be back later this afternoon.'

'You need to advise him then, very clearly, that if he rebuffs my allegations or leaves me out of your investigation, I will have to go to print with what I have. You then won't be in any position to have input into the story nor provide a mitigating response.'

'You wouldn't do that, Ms Granger.'

She handed across her business card. 'You don't want to test that theory, Mr Frances. I'll expect your phone call before the close of business today.' Julie-Anne rose from her chair. 'I'll see myself out.'

As she walked along Macquarie Street she dialled a private mobile number that an industry colleague had provided to her. After a brief conversation the man on the other end of the call had agreed to meet with her tomorrow afternoon.

67. International Hotel

Tuesday 2nd June

Julie-Anne was back at the International Hotel first thing the following morning. She was in a small conference room along with Andy Frances and Michael Ziegler, the GM. Ziegler hadn't bothered with the usual pleasantries which set the tone for the direction of the discussion. Julie-Anne was up for the challenge.

'That's quite a story you communicated to Mr Frances yesterday, Ms Granger,' Ziegler said with a hint of a Swiss German accent.

Julie-Anne wriggled uncomfortably in her seat. *Here it comes.*

'I can understand why you might arrive at the conclusions that you did. Nonetheless, I'm afraid I can't agree with those conclusions. In fact, they're quite fanciful really.'

'And why would you say that, Mr Ziegler?' she asked calmly, masking her already rising internal anger.

'Our personnel are robustly vetted before they are even considered for employment at the International, so to suggest that an employee is behind this episode is quite simply, well ludicrous.'

Stay calm, Julie-Anne. 'Mr Ziegler, I can fully understand why you would come to the conclusions that you have also,' she replied, returning serve with his own terminology. 'After all, you have the reputation of a highly regarded international hotel chain to protect.'

'It has nothing to do with our reputation. It is all about the practicalities of anyone being able to pull off a stunt like this. It simply isn't feasible.'

'Oh, really! We both know this is all about protecting your brand. Let's try this then shall we? If the dozens of staff members here that would have access to master swipe cards haven't been involved in spying then who put that camera into one of your suites? And how did they gain access?'

'Spying. Really, that's a bit rich,' he responded incredulously.

'Well then, Mr General Manager, what would you call the installation of a secret camera into the room of one of the state's most prominent politicians?'

Andy Frances spoke for the first time. 'I agree with Mr Ziegler regarding the improbability of one of our staff members being responsible. I'm more inclined to think that your friend might be behind this stunt.'

Frances was blatantly trying to save face, and possibly his job, in front of his GM. Julie-Anne was angry now. 'Firstly, it's not a stunt, this is espionage of the highest order which I'm assuming will lead to an extortion attempt against the Minister for Education if that hasn't happened already. Secondly, I can assure you the woman is most definitely not behind this *stunt* as you so dismissively call it. It's just not her. And just to throw in some common sense, how do you two think that she managed to manipulate the Minister into various compromising situations while trying to manouevre her camera or iPhone into the perfect position? And in two separate rooms no less. He certainly wasn't asleep and neither does he appear to have been drugged,' she said, exasperated by their naivety.

'What do you mean two separate rooms?' Frances asked, now fidgeting in his chair.

Julie-Anne sighed. 'You saw clearly for yourself the photo that was taken in the living area. Four of the remaining photos were shot in the bedroom. The woman couldn't have done it, Andy.'

'We only have your word for that, Ms Granger.'

She was hoping to avoid showing them anymore of the revealing photos. Painfully realising that she had no option, Julie-Anne rifled through the photos in her folder until she found the least explicit one again. 'Here you go. I hate doing this, but I understand that you can't simply accept my word for it.' She handed Ziegler a photo of Sophie and Ben Chandler together on the bed. Fortunately, her back was to the camera and Chandler's head was resting on her shoulder facing the camera. She watched as the two men glanced across at each other. Eventually Ziegler spoke.

'Okay, Ms Granger, maybe we rushed to judgement regarding your friend,' Ziegler said contritely.

She noticed a look of contrition wash across Andy Frances' face as well. 'You've already checked the living room for cameras and found nothing, haven't you?' she inferred.

'Yes, but we didn't check the bedroom.'

'I imagine Mr Chandler has already left for his office this morning, so why don't we go and take another look and include the bedroom this time?'

'Ms Granger, I can't have you wandering around the hotel suite of one of our most important guests.' Ziegler replied.

'Oh, come off it, Mr Ziegler. If it wasn't for me you wouldn't even be aware of any of this. We're talking spying, probable extortion, breaches of your security, invasion of privacy, shall I go on?' she said, frustrated again. 'I deserve the opportunity to accompany you.'

Fifteen minutes later, upon receiving confirmation that Ben Chandler had left the hotel, the GM along with his head of security and Julie-Anne entered Suite 2501. The room had a soft feeling to it with its deep tan carpet and soft beige and cream tones. Julie-Anne adored the love seats along the windows with their views over Sydney Harbour. She moved across to the living room sofa where Chandler and Sophie were first photographed. She lined up the sofa with the buffet cabinet and stood back. 'Okay, the first photo must have been shot from this angle,' she said while standing with her back to the television cabinet. She turned around, stooped down and ran her fingers along the rear of the cabinet behind the DVD player. 'Check this out, Andy.' She held up her finger and the tip was covered in fine sawdust powder.

Frances removed a torch from his belt and shone it into the rear of the cabinet. 'Look at this, Michael,' he said directing his GM to the rear partition of the cabinet. He could see where a section of the partition about the size of a playing card had been cut out. 'This has been cut out and then glued back into position. It's sloppy work. No one would have found this for years given its location.'

'Shall we go and inspect the bedroom now?' Julie-Anne suggested in an I told you so tone.

They walked into the bedroom where Frances undertook the same process as Julie-Anne had in the living room. Firstly, he went straight across to the television cabinet and stood with his back to it, facing the large king size bed. Then he turned and ran his finger along the rear of the cabinet. He held it up to show Ziegler the fine powder clinging to his finger. Finally, he shone his torch into the rear of the cabinet. He saw the same outlines of where a small piece of the rear partition had been cut out and then replaced.

Ten minutes later they were back in the conference room. 'Ms Granger, this is an internal matter, so we won't need any further assistance from you. Thank you for bringing this to our attention.' The GM rose from his chair, extended his arm, and waited to usher Julie-Anne to the door.

'Whoa, I'm not going anywhere, Mr Ziegler. You wouldn't even be aware of the disaster your lax security measures have allowed to occur if it wasn't for me. And I assure you this is anything but an internal matter.' She manufactured a childlike, pouty, about to have a tantrum face and remained seated with her arms crossed over her chest.

'So, if you feel that something bigger is in play here, then would you care to share your information with us? I'm certain we are entitled to know,' he insisted.

'I'm sorry, but I can't go into specific details at this time, however, be assured this has potentially significant national and international implications.'

Ziegler shifted uncomfortably in his stance. It was obvious to Julie-Anne that he was alarmed at her latest revelation and was becoming nervous. She guessed he understood the likely ramifications for the international hotel brand and probably his career within the organisation.

'What sort of implications?'

'Alright, all I will tell you is that these photos were found in the possession of a representative of an international concern.' That sounded weak, but at this juncture she couldn't divulge the name or even type of organisation involved, so she had to be deliberately vague. 'And as you can see they don't play nice. I imagine Mr Chandler has probably already received the first of the photos.'

'That's just too imprecise for me, Ms Granger.'

He was annoying her now. 'Okay, I undertook some research overnight and I believe your hotel group owns, manages or franchises in excess of four hundred hotels in China. So, if this situation isn't handled judiciously the reputational damage to your wider hotel group could be disastrous. Is that less imprecise for you, Mr Ziegler?' She saw his face flush with colour. Was it anger, embarrassment or was he seeing his career diminish by the minute?

'So, you're saying that China is behind this?'

'I'm not saying anything of the sort, but if you work cooperatively with me, I promise to share with you, who or what I believe to be behind this scenario as the whole picture becomes clearer. Now, I think it would be appropriate if we focussed on who planted those cameras and why. May I suggest we pay your Human Resources Manager a visit and ask him or her a few pertinent questions.' She made the open hands gesture to support her suggestion. 'Shall we?'

'Andy, it goes without saying, that for numerous extremely important reasons, discretion is paramount here, so this stays strictly between the three of us,' Ziegler demanded.

68. International Hotel

Tuesday 2nd June

Julie-Anne accompanied Andy Frances along the executive corridor to the Human Resources Department. 'The HR Manager can be a bit pompous and protective of her domain, so let me do the talking please?' Frances knocked on the door out of courtesy and entered the modest sized office. 'Jennifer Muirhead, this is Julie-Anne Granger.'

The woman slowly lifted her head from her desktop monitor. 'Hello, Julie-Anne, what can I do for you?'

Andy Frances jumped in and Julie-Anne was pleased to see that he was indeed going to take the initiative. 'Jennifer, I am investigating an incident that has occurred within the hotel and I need some information from you.'

Indignation suddenly materialised on the woman's face. 'What sort of incident, Andy? I haven't seen any reports or been advised of anything untoward.'

'I can't go into that at this time. I need a list of all staff that commenced their employment with the hotel from the first of May this year until—,' he paused and turned to Julie-Anne.

She had found the photos at Paul Gao's apartment last Saturday evening. 'The thirtieth.'

'This might take some time, Andy,' Muirhead replied, ignoring Julie-Anne.

'We don't have time, Jennifer, so we'll wait,' he said forcefully. He saw her facial expression morph to indignancy while she sat upright, clasped her hands together and placed them on the desk. She obviously didn't take kindly to being challenged.

Julie-Anne interrupted the pair. 'Can we step outside for a moment, Andy?'

'What's up, Julie-Anne?'

'Why don't we start with the most recent departures and work backwards? I'm guessing the photos were taken between seven and ten days ago.'

'I know where you're going with his. You're thinking when the perpetrator had to have returned to the suite to remove the camera and repair his own handywork.'

'Bingo, Andy. Therefore, he or she would have left the hotel's employ fairly recently.'

They returned to the HR Manager's office where Jennifer Muirhead was on a call. Her face was reddening and Andy guessed she had tried to ring the GM, but had been fobbed off.

'Jennifer, can you provide the listing commencing on the thirtieth and working in reverse order back to the first of the month. Also, can you include their level of clearance and what access swipe cards were issued to each of them?'

'That could take ages, Mr Frances.'

'Ms Muirhead, we don't have ages, simply enter a date range, then apply a filter for the criteria I just mentioned. What are we talking about here, maybe ten or twenty people at the most? It will take you ten minutes.' The woman made a hmmph sound and turned to her desktop.

Andy and Julie-Anne waited outside in the corridor discussing the mechanics of how this scenario could have unfolded. 'So, if we find an obvious suspect on the list, what's your next step?' she asked.

'I will discuss the situation with the GM and obviously

be guided by him as to what action we take next. If your assumptions are correct then this won't bode well for the hotel and its reputation.'

'Mr Frances, I have your list for you,' the HR woman said gruffly as she opened her office door.'

'Thank you, Ms Muirhead, that wasn't so difficult, now was it?' She made the hmmph noise again, turned on her heels and stormed back into her office.

Andy and Julie-Anne walked back down the corridor to the conference room and sat at the table with the sheet containing the list of names in front of them. 'There's more names here than I thought. The hotel must have a high staff turnover.' Frances was running his finger slowly down the page of thirty plus names, pausing by each one in turn.

Julie-Anne on the other hand, was scanning for any Chinese names on the list. That was essentially racial profiling, but given a Special Emissary of the Chinese Consulate had the illicitly obtained photos in the first place, it wasn't a stretch to assume the installation of a secret camera would be by one of his associates.

'There he is,' she said too loudly. 'Got you buddy.' Frances apparently didn't hear her and was still scanning down the list.

'I've got two possibles, Julie-Anne.' Frances read out two names complete with their positions and employment commencement and end dates. 'And they both had all access swipe cards,' he said confidently.

'You missed one, Andy. Take a look at Sun Jie.'

'Shit, Julie-Anne,' he blurted out. You mentioned the Chinese connection earlier too.'

'No I didn't, I only alluded to the potential fallout for the hotel group in China.'

'You couldn't have gone through that list any quicker than me. You knew exactly what you were looking for, didn't you?'

He leaned back from the table. 'You need to tell me what's going on, Julie-Anne, otherwise the cooperation ceases. Now that you've pinpointed the name, I don't need you anymore anyway.'

'And what exactly are you going to do with the name, Andy? Run it through a security industry database somewhere, go to the police, confront the potential culprit, or heaven forbid, have your snooty HR Manager check him out,' she said sarcastically. She was on a roll now. 'You're smarter than that. This will leak from any number of sources and be all over the media in five minutes flat and you and your GM won't be able to control the fallout. The reputational damage to the hotel and the wider chain, especially in China, will be considerable. And what about the Minister? Where does that leave him, his family and his reputation?'

Frances was be pondering Julie-Anne's outburst and post a long pause, he finally spoke. 'Alright, so what are you suggesting then?'

That's better. 'I have a friend who is with the AFP and I trust him implicitly, so I will ask him to research Sun Jie first and then we'll see where that leads.'

'Why the Australian Federal Police? After all Ben Chandler is a state politician and surely they fall under the jurisdiction of the New South Wales police,' he contended. 'There's still something you're not telling me, isn't there? You're holding back again.'

'I tell you what, Andy, how about we first let the AFP detective check this guy out. I won't divulge to him anything other than the name for now. Then, if he provides the links that I think he will, I will give you everything I know and you and your Mr Ziegler can run with it. We're only talking forty eight hours tops. Deal?'

Frances stroked his goatee while he mulled it over. 'Okay.

I will tell my GM that we're still researching the staff database and we should have something for him by this time Thursday.'

'That works for me.' Julie-Anne shook his hand in agreement and then made her way to the security exit. It was a comfortable five minute walk along Macquarie Street to her next appointment, so she had time to make another call.

'Jack, it's Julie-Anne, how are you?'

'Certainly better than I was a few days ago. What's up?'

'I need a favour. That other investigation and I told you about on Sunday is moving along steadily, but I need your help. As I mentioned, if it goes in the direction I think it will then the AFP will need to be involved. I think there are potential national and international implications.

'Okay, I know there's no point asking you for details, so what can I do for you?'

'Can you see what you can find out about a Sun Jie for me please?' She spelt the name and gave him Jie's address and date of birth from the sheet provided by the International's HR Manager. 'Of course I need it yesterday. This will move quickly, Jack.'

'It's already mid-afternoon, but let me see what I can do and I'll get back to you.'

69. Ministerial Offices – Martin Place

Tuesday 2nd June

Ben Chandler walked into his office foyer at two forty five in the afternoon with the proverbial fire in his belly. He had no evidence that the Consul General was behind the blackmail attempt, but he wanted to fire a shot across his metaphorical bow regardless. There were the omnipresent sensitivities surrounding any dealings with the Chinese that he needed to be cognisant of and today would be no different. He entered his office and sat at his desk, his hands clasped firmly together in his lap.

'Minister, the Consul General is here as requested,' Loretta said through the desk phone's intercom five minutes later.

'Send him straight in.'

'Mr Consul General, how are you? Please take a seat.' Chandler didn't rise nor offer the sofa this time. He wanted the desk between him and Xiao to represent the ideological gulf that existed between them over the Confucius Institute.

'I am well, thank you. What can I do for you, Minister?'

Chandler needed to project a calm demeanour, not wanting Xiao to realise the extent to which this situation was affecting him personally. 'Xiao, I find myself in an unusual position. Can I be frank with you?'

'Of course, please feel free to speak at will,' Xiao replied, having no idea where this was heading.

'I have received correspondence requesting that I reinstate the Confucius Institute into our high schools and colleges. The concerning issue for me is that it was sent anonymously, and without any threat. I seriously doubt it will remain that way though.'

Xiao didn't know anything about any correspondence, but he assumed Gao must have implemented his plan, whatever it was. 'What are you asking me, Minister?'

'I am asking for your assurances that you have accepted my decision on the Institute. I thought we had laid that matter to rest at our previous meeting.'

'Minister, I have no choice but to accept your decision for I am simply a guest in your wonderful country,' he replied, faking congeniality. 'It does not mean I agree with it, of course.'

'If somehow you or your consular staff were found to be behind this there would be serious international ramifications for you and your country, Xiao.' Chandler said, staring him down.

'Minister, I am not behind anything, however, if you make unsubstantiated claims of this nature then you should be aware of the consequences for yourself. My country will not be pleased. We are your largest trading partner by some means and it would be unfortunate if your accusations were to put that at risk. This is especially true within your own education portfolio. Australia is becoming increasingly unsafe for Chinese students with your government's baseless accusations about the source of the Coronavirus. That has led to increasing racist based attacks on innocent students who simply want to study in your country.'

'Xiao, I haven't made any claims at all. I am simply saying that if any foreign government were to interfere in our internal affairs then there would have to be commensurate consequences. China would do the same.'

'That's not what you said. If I may be so bold, Minister, if you were to proceed with these baseless allegations, there could also be significant ramifications for you and your government too.'

'How so?'

'I just told you. China is the largest importer of Australian resources, goods and services. And as you know all too well as Education Minister there are over one hundred thousand Chinese students studying in your state. That provides a significant boost to your economy. So, it stands to reason that you would not want to jeopardise that status.'

'Aaahh, the Chinese, masters of the not-so-veiled threat.' Chandler was becoming angry now. 'Don't you get tired of being the schoolyard bully in Asia, Xiao?'

'Minister, I will ignore that. I do not know who is behind the correspondence you received, but there is obviously a straightforward solution to be proposed. Simply reinstate the Confucius Institute.'

Chandler sighed. 'I will show you out as I have to go now. Question Time is about to start.'

'That would seem to be an opportune time to consider your response then, Minister.' Xiao replied cryptically.

Ben was correct in confronting Xiao, although he wished he had more evidence to proffer to substantiate his theory. He certainly couldn't show Xiao the photos or even allude to them for that matter. He had tried to be subtle with his vapid assertions, but at the very least Xiao now knew he was on notice.

70. Day Street Police Station

Tuesday 2nd June

'Hi, Jack. Are you here to interview Wie?' Sanderson asked.

'Yes, did you get anything out of him?'

'No, he's not talking, but maybe you can be more persuasive.'

'I'll do my best and we'll talk afterwards.'

Jack walked down the corridor to the interview room where Wie was waiting. He was wearing handcuffs that were chained to a square, metal table which in turn was bolted to the concrete floor. As he entered the room Wie looked up from the table and greeted him with a superior smile. 'Aah, Detective Wagner. We finally meet. Apparently we have something in common.'

Jack wasn't taking the bait. He felt like a new man after his head clearing stroll across the city and a few beers at the Opera Bar yesterday afternoon. He was uncomfortable with the fact that the man across the table had shared a bed with Danielle, but he would bury his emotions and keep his detective head on. No doubt JA would say he was adept at that.

'Wie, you were found in possession of fifteen kilos of coke and the state police will charge you with being in possession of, and trafficking a commercial quantity of an illegal substance, and you will spend the remaining good years of your life behind bars. How's that for something we don't have in common?' Jack let that hang in the air. Wie sat there stone-faced and assumed a defensive posture with his arms folded across his chest. 'You will be well past middle age when you're released.'

'I have nothing to say to you,' he replied without emotion.

'That's fine by me, but I will ask you some questions regardless and let's see if we can find something else in common.'

Wie's lips widened and his cheeks puffed slightly as he tried to avoid smiling. 'You are a funny man, detective. Now you are single again, oops sorry, you always were, maybe I'll give you Lucie Chan. You will like her very much I think,' he taunted.

Keep it together, Jack. 'Tell me about Than Ping Lie?' He was probably wasting his time, but he would go through the motions and see if anything would drop. Wie's face darkened at the mention of that name.

Here we go. 'I see you don't like me mentioning your mother's name.'

'Do not speak of my mother. You are nothing compared to her,' he blurted out angrily.

Bingo. Jack had confirmed the mother's identity. 'Aah, you see I am actually because I hold the keys to her son's future in my hands. Your mother is about to lose her son, a son who she will be visiting in prison until she dies. I imagine that will break her heart. What a terrible way for a mother to spend her final years. Sad and all alone. But, it doesn't have to be like that. You do have some options open to you if you are smart enough to avail yourself of them.' Wie eyed Jack dispassionately and did not reply.

'Let me tell you a story then, just so you clearly understand your current set of circumstances. We know you have been bringing cocaine in from China using vessels flagged to the China Shipping Company, in particular the Chinese Horizon and Chinese Panorama. You know we captured and impounded the Midnight Express back in March, then your lieutenants, Li Jun and Wang Wei killed the Chinese Horizon's captain. Li was then killed in a raid by the AFP's SRG guys and Wang Wei is in Queensland charged with the captain's murder. That was then. This time you brought your coke to Australia on the Chinese Panorama and transferred it ashore via the drone your mother bought from Vulcan in the UK. The coke was transferred to Sydney by Wang Yong and Johnny Chang. Yong is in custody and about to go to prison for a long time and young Johnny had enough common sense to disappear. Now of course, your other girlfriend, Lucie Chan, is also in custody. With her looks she will be popular at Mary Wade. That's a maximum security women's prison by the way. Then there is Ms Mortimer who was caught with a kilo of coke in her possession. She was about to make a deal to flip you, but alas, her timing was terrible, so she is off to join Lucie for a few years. And now back to your mother. All those apartments you have bought in her name with your drug money will be confiscated by the DPP under the Proceeds of Crime Act. I will personally write and submit the application to the DPP and she will be thrown out onto the street. I imagine that she is well passed middle age, so a homeless woman of her advancing years won't fare well.'

Wie's nostrils flared, blood was rushing to his facial veins, severely reddening his complexion, and his expression contorted at the thought of his mother being homeless. He finally spoke. 'They can't do that.'

'Yes, they can, and they will. I will make certain of it.'

'Nǐ zhè ge húndàn.'

Jack smiled. 'I can only imagine what that means.'

'You bastard.'

'I thought as much. And that brings me to you, Wie. Being caught with a commercial and trafficable quantity of coke in your own possession will see you spend at least the next twenty years in prison. So, you see, I know a lot about your little drug importation and distribution business and I know one more thing. It is finished, wánliǎo, kaputsky, terminada. You are done.'

Jack folded his own arms across his chest and leant back in his chair. He locked his eyes unwaveringly onto Wie's and held them there. There was silence and Jack was in no hurry to break the impasse. This was the moment of truth for Wie, but he maintained his angry silence.

Eventually Jack spoke. 'If you have any information that you would like to share with me then maybe, just maybe, the federal DPP might talk to his state counterpart and there could be a deal on the table. It's up to you, Wie.'

'I want a deal,' he replied.

'Oh, you want a deal do you? Well, I want the head of your syndicate. Give me him or her and maybe, just maybe, your mother doesn't have to lose her apartment.'

'They will have me killed.'

'Your mother has obviously either knowingly or inadvertently supported your business by allowing you to buy at least four properties in her name. Heavens, she even allowed you to buy the Vulcan UAV using her name and that's how you repay her loyalty. Yes, you might be killed in prison, but at least your mother won't be homeless and end up dying alone on the streets. What a sad way to go out that would be. And that would be the end of the Lie family in Australia.'

Jack could see Wie's mind working away while he was talking. 'I want a deal,' he said more forcefully this time.

'I'm sure you do. Give me the syndicate head,' Jack repeated. Wie remained silent. 'Okay, I've got another scenario for you. If I try hard enough maybe I will be able to prove that your mother is actually the syndicate head.'

He could see the anger building further on Wie's face.

'She is not,' he blurted out.

Jack sensed an opportunity to break through Wie's defences.

'After all, she has unexplained wealth and I can prove she purchased the drone from Vulcan. And low and behold, where did you store the coke? In a storage unit rented in your mother's name,' Jack exclaimed incredulously, laying it on thick. 'Sure, it might all be rather circumstantial, although at a minimum we can charge her with being an accessory. That will keep her lawyers busy for a long time and I'm certain at her advanced age her physical and mental health would suffer enormously. Do you realise that mental health is a major issue these days, especially for older people, Wie?'

Wie's head was bowed and his eyes squeezed shut in apparent torment. He was thinking about his mother and considering her future. If he didn't provide the detective with the information he wanted his mother could be homeless. She had no family support in Australia other than him and her health would deteriorate rapidly. If he did provide the detective the information he wanted that might provide her with freedom, but for how long? His master in China would be less than pleased and he would seek retribution, and swiftly. 'Okay.'

Jack eyes widened in astonishment as Wie spoke and he tried to get his poker face back on.

'I can't give you what you want. It seems that whatever I tell you my mother won't live a long life anyway. If I provide you with the information that you are seeking there are people who won't take kindly to that and she will suffer payback for my sins. If I don't tell you then you will leave her homeless. I think you would call that a checkmate.'

Jack had mixed thoughts and wondered about his own mother and what he would do in the same circumstances. Wie was in a no-win situation. Jack was racking his brain searching for some middle ground that would give him what he wanted and allow Wie some wriggle room. 'Okay, if you can't give me a name, what can you give me?'

'You have heard of the China Shipping Company.'

'Of course; I've told you that. They transport your coke to Australia.'

'And you know of the Confucius Institute.'

'Not in any detail. Your nemesis, Ms Granger has written about it. What of it, Wie?'

'The United Front Work Department?'

'No.' Jack would need to ask JA about that.

'I know you are aware of the Consul General.'

'I am. Ms Granger tried her darndest to link him with Li Qiang in your money laundering operation.'

'Aah, of course, my old friend, Li Qiang. Were you able to interrogate his phones, Mr Detective?' Wie observed Jack's blank expression. 'No, I didn't think so.'

Wie was fidgeting now. He took a deep breath to calm himself. 'The person you are looking for has links to all of the above. That is all I am willing to tell you. As you westerners like to say, join the dots, detective. Now, what about my mother?'

'Is he based here or in China?'

'Really, Wagner. What do you think?'

'China.'

Wie didn't confirm or deny Jack's response. 'Now, what about my mother?'

'What about her?'

Wie snarled. 'Will you leave her alone now?'

Jack gave him a wide-eyed look and splayed his hand across his chest for effect. 'Oh, Wie. Do you really think I'm the type of guy who would leave an elderly woman homeless? What sort of man do you think I am?'

'You bastard,' Wie replied angrily as he tried to launch himself at Jack.

'You were right. We do have something in common. Goodbye, Wie.'

'Jack,' Sanderson called out.

'Sorry, Michael, I was miles away.'

'We received the fingerprint results back from Forensics. They matched two separate sets of prints on the packets of coke to Danielle and Yong.'

'That's good news and ties that up into a cosy little package. Have they been charged?'

'Yep, we had Yong for attempted murder anyway, so his latest charge will just further complicate things for him. Both of them were predictably denied bail and are being held in the respective remand centres at Silverwater. Also the results came back from the testing lab. That is some seriously good stuff Wie was bringing in. It's forty five percent pure. No wonder he was getting four hundred bucks a gram for it. Did you get anything out of him?'

'Nothing definitive. He wouldn't give up a name, but he alluded to the syndicate head being linked by the CSC, Confucius Institute, Li Qiang and the Chinese Consulate. Have you ever heard of the United Front Work Department?'

'Can't say that I have.'

'Okay, I'll check it out. It's up to me to establish what the links are and identify the kingpin. That won't be a walk in the park, Michael.'

'No, it won't, however, it does provide an endorsement of sorts as to what we thought at the time, Jack.'

'Yeah, now I just have to put the puzzle pieces together.'

'Good luck, buddy.'

71. Ministerial Offices – Martin Place

Tuesday 2nd June

Julie-Anne was waiting in the foyer of her appointment's office eighteen floors above the bustling peak hour streets and sidewalks of Sydney when her mobile rang. 'Jack.'

'You're in luck. My contact at Home Affairs, Sam Bourne, was still at his office in Canberra working to get those Australians back home who have been stranded overseas as a result of this coronavirus mess. He needed a break from the challenges of that, so was only too pleased to help.'

'What have you got, Jack?'

'I presume you're on your old hobby horse of Chinese influence in Australia, so you're going to like this intel.'

At any moment she could be called into her appointment's office, so Julie-Anne needed Jack's information forthwith. 'I'm in a hurry, come on, Jack.'

'Alright, hold up. Sun Jie entered Australia through Sydney Airport three years ago in March. His incoming passenger card confirmed his birth date, proposed residential address, and listed his vocation as an ICT technician. In March 2018 he then applied for a Temporary Work Visa. This was the renamed controversial 457 visa. The interesting part is that he was sponsored by the Chinese Shipping Company. Do you remember the CSC? That was the company Captain Liu worked for before he was killed and the same one that carries Wie Ping Lie's coke into the country. And we know that they have close ties to the Chinese Communist Party.'

'Ms Granger,' she heard a voice call out. 'I'm being called, I have to go, Jack. Thanks heaps.' Julie-Anne stopped pacing and turned towards the voice.

'Hello, I'm Loretta Farrelly, the Minister's executive assistant. Come through please.' The EA ushered Julie-Anne across the foyer and into an expansive office with plush maroon coloured carpet, two work desks and separate lounge and dining areas. 'Minister, this is Julie-Anne Granger. Ms Granger, Minister Chandler.' The gushy woman then left the room.

'Ms Granger, let's sit over here.'

Ben Chandler was a fit looking, handsome man with a strong jawline, a smooth and moderately tanned complexion and piercing blue eyes. He looked better in the flesh and she could see why Sophie was attracted to the man. Chandler ushered her across to the sofas where they sat across from each other, separated by a coffee table covered with the day's newspapers. Julie-Anne was pleased to see the Sydney Daily News prominently positioned.

'I see you are a fan of Philip Adams as well, Minister.' Chandler had a large print on his wall depicting pink and grey galahs flapping around in a eucalyptus forest.

'Being surrounded by the concrete jungle of the CBD the print reminds that there is another world outside of the political goldfish bowl that I reside in most of the time. And of course, also some of the galahs I deal with in politics.'

Julie-Anne smiled in agreement. 'That's an analogy I can relate to, Minister.'

'Now, those were some interesting assertions you made over the phone, Ms Granger.'

'Well, I would respectfully suggest to you that I wouldn't

be sitting here if they hadn't piqued your interest, Minister,' she replied forthrightly.

'Not necessarily, but please call me Ben regardless. How did you get my private number anyway?'

She ignored his question. 'Before we commence, I assume these offices are regularly swept for devices.'

'Yes, they are, especially in this day and age of industrial, political and cyber espionage.'

'Okay, that's good. You need to know I am here to help you, not to cause you more anxiety than what you must already be experiencing.'

Chandler frowned at her offering. 'You will understand that I become apprehensive when a reporter tells me they're here to help me, Ms Granger,' he replied cynically. 'I am a politician after all and you guys see us as fair game.'

'Yes, we do, and the majority of the time you are. Now allow me to alleviate your scepticism. Sophie Zhao is a friend of mine and I don't throw my friends under the bus.' She held his gaze until he looked away in embarrassment. His calm, stoic ministerial persona had evaporated at the mention of her name. Julie-Anne detected a show of concern; was it for himself or Sophie? To her trained eye he had clasped his hands together to prevent them from shaking. Following a long pause he spoke.

'How do you know Sophie?'

'We met earlier in the year through an investigation of mine and have become good friends since.'

'I assume you know what she does for a career.'

'Of course I do. She is an intelligent, articulate, grounded woman and those qualities are ideally suited to her interim profession, which you obviously agree with. The primary reason she works as an escort is to put herself through university and support her family back in China. She is a good person,' Julie-Anne said protectively.

'Yes, she is, and she explained her temporary career choice to me over dinner last week.' He went quiet again and was reflecting about his brief time with Sophie. 'So, back to the issue at hand. What do you think you know?' he asked.

'It's not what I think I know, it's what I actually know, so please don't insult me, Minister.'

'You, or even Sophie could be behind this, or at least components of it.'

'Really Minister. Are you serious?' Julie-Anne needed to calm herself after that ridiculous assertion. Chandler was obviously feeling more pressure than he was showing. 'Let's try this then, Minister. You are obviously well acquainted with Sophie, so you can make your own determination as to her involvement. Maybe consider backing your own judgement on that. As for me, I am a well-respected journalist working for an equally well-regarded broadsheet,' she said, nodding at the newspaper on the coffee table, 'so it wouldn't be in anyone's interest for me to stoop to the level of the corrupt behaviour you are suggesting. Your call, Minister,' she said, standing her ground.

'Alright, calm down, what exactly do you think is happening here, Ms Granger?'

'No, it doesn't work that way—'

He cut her short. 'You actually contacted me, so maybe you'll do me the courtesy of explaining yourself.' He was being forceful now, so she had a decision to make. Neither spoke for an extended period.

She sighed. 'I have been researching and investigating potential Chinese interference in Australia for most of the past six months. Back in March that morphed into a criminal investigation surrounding drug importation and money laundering, but now, months later I'm back on track. It's clear that arms of the Chinese Communist Party are on a mission to infiltrate and influence almost every aspect of Australian life, from politics and business to education and the media. And one of the most influential arms of their government is linked to the Confucius Institute. Ben, you removed the Institute from state schools late last year.'

Julie-Anne could see her latest pronouncement had struck a chord with Chandler, so she continued. 'I came into possession of some compromising photos taken at the International, and after some research, they led me to you, Ben. And once I found out that you were the Education Minister, that wrapped it up nicely for me. My guess is that you are now being extorted to reinstate the Institute. How am I doing?'

'That's an extraordinary assertion, Ms Granger.'

'Yes, it is. Now back to my question.'

This journalist was obviously all over the unfolding situation and he quickly realised it would be futile to deny it. 'You're on the money. How many photos are there?'

'Six in all. How many have you received?'

'Two so far, so this scenario obviously has some way to play out yet. Do you have the remaining photos with you?'

'Yes.'

He thought about asking to see them, but having received the second photo taken in the bedroom, he assumed the remainder would be even more explicit and compromising.

Julie-Anne anticipated what he must be thinking. 'You don't need to see them, Ben,' she said.

'I know. I do need to now consider how best to handle this whole disgusting situation though.

'I can help you with that.'

He was bemused. 'A reporter helping a politician, I'd like to see that,' he laughed. 'Did I say that before?'

Julie-Anne took it as the throwaway line it was intended and pushed on. 'In the meantime, Ben, I think you should disregard the implied threats. They, whoever they are, won't push it too far without making contact first. They need to achieve their goal and by releasing all the photos they will lose any leverage they have. So, we have some time.'

That riled him and he sat bolt upright on the sofa. '*We*, Ms Granger, really! There's no *we* here, it's me, my family and our lives that are being threatened here, not yours, so there's no *we*,' he replied indignantly.

Julie-Anne didn't rise to the challenge. 'Ben, your plan, whatever it is, doesn't appear to working very well now, does it? Whereas, I am pretty certain I know who planted the camera and who they're linked to. I can close this out in the next forty eight hours, if you're prepared to trust me. You don't have a lot of options unless of course you want to go to the police, in which case this story will leak like a sieve and your world will come crashing down around you.' She could see Ben Chandler was at least considering her proposal.

She marched on. 'I have a trustworthy contact at the AFP who, once I have all the pieces in place, I can take the story to. I'm sure you realise that this also has national and international implications, so the AFP are best placed to handle it anyway. And they are better known for their discretion than the state police.'

'I haven't spoken to Sophie about this as yet and I am supposed to have dinner with her tonight,' he said dolefully while staring at the ceiling. 'I won't be able to look her in the eyes.'

'For the sake of forty eight hours you should postpone dinner and you definitely shouldn't reveal anything to her until we have the whole story. She is an innocent victim in this. Just for the record, I haven't spoken to her either and I don't intend to yet. Are we in agreeance, Ben?'

He rapidly came to the realisation that this journalist was correct. He didn't have many options. 'Okay, I'll give you the forty eight hours, Ms Granger.'

'Julie-Anne's fine, and don't sound so grateful; what else are you going to do? And by the way, you need to go back to the International and change suites. And while you're at it ensure that you have Andy Frances, the hotel's head of security, sweep it for bugs.'

Five minutes later Julie-Anne was walking down Martin Place to the George Street Light Rail when her phone rang. It was Melissa, but she was too busy for a social chat at the moment, so she ignored the call and continued with her own round of calls.

'Jack, it's me again.'

'What's up, JA?'

'I need a couple of things so I can tie up this latest investigation,' she asked, now puffing from exertion as she raced to catch the light rail.

'You're pushing it again.'

'I know, I know, but it will be worth it for both of us, I promise.' She was pleading now.

'Okay, what do you want?'

'What was the address listed on Sun Jie's incoming passenger card?'

'Hang on a minute while I check my notes. Here we go. Unit 9, 27 Clayton Lane, Camperdown, why?'

Predictably, this was a different address to the one Sun Jie had provided on his employment application with the International. 'Bingo, Jack. Now do you have a forensic guy spare to take some prints?'

'Christ, JA, that's pushing it.'

'I wouldn't make a request like that if it wasn't important, you know that, Jack.'

'Okay, where and when?'

'Tonight, I'll let you know time and location soon.' She disconnected the call. Her phone rang. *Melissa Calling*. 'Sheesh, not now.'

As she fast walked along Eddy Avenue from the light rail to Central Station she called Andy Frances. 'Hi, Andy, we're getting close.'

'You only left a couple of hours ago, Julie-Anne. You don't let grass grow under your feet, do you?'

'Someone else told me that recently. I promised you forty eight hours, so no, I don't. I need to move fast. Speaking of which, can I have access to Chandler's suite tonight? I want to search for fingerprints.'

'No you can't,' he replied definitively. 'We can't have you anywhere near that suite again.'

'Alright, I get that, I do. Then can I make arrangements for a guy from the AFP's Forensic Services Group to meet you at your office at eight o'clock and you can accompanying him yourself.'

'What about Mr Chandler, won't he be in his suite?'

'No, he's going to be changing suites.'

Frances knew she was onto something if she was involving forensic guys already and she must have also spoken directly to Mr Chandler. 'Okay, that will work. Give him or her my mobile number and have them call me.'

'Thanks, Andy, I appreciate it.'

Next, she called Jack again. 'Jack I have arranged for your FSG guy to gain access to Suite 2501 of the International Hotel at eight o'clock tonight. Write this number down.' Julie-Anne recited Andy Frances' mobile number. 'Have your guy call Frances, he's the head of the hotel's security, and the necessary arrangements will be made. He will direct your guy to the appropriate areas we need printed. Can you arrange for the analysis of the results to be expedited, like early tomorrow please?'

'Christ, JA, what's going on here?'

'I'll tell you tomorrow, I promise.' She realised that she had made a heap of promises during the past couple of hours. *You better be right, girl.*

Julie-Anne was on the T3 Liverpool Train for the three stop journey to Newtown. She was thinking back to Saturday night. It felt like a lifetime ago given everything that had happened since. She had turned the tables on the manipulative Paul Gao and shamelessly used her body to get the better of him. As a result she had found the incriminating photos which started her latest investigation and led her to Ben Chandler. And if she hadn't gone to Gao's apartment in the first place she wouldn't have known that he resided at Unit 9, 27 Clayton Lane, Camperdown.

72. Julie-Anne's Apartment

Tuesday 2nd June

Julie-Anne was striding out on the short walk from the station to her Alice Street apartment in her treasured suburb of Newtown. Google Maps said it was a twelve minute walk, but her long legs would get her home in less than that. The waxing moon was doing it darndest to break through the light haze as she turned right off of King Street. Walking the last few metres down to her apartment she noticed a figure standing under the street light outside of her building. As she drew nearer she recognised the person. It was Melissa and she immediately regretted the calls she had ignored. Unless she happened to be in the area her friend wouldn't turn up unannounced.

'Hi, Melissa. What a lovely surprise,' she said tentatively.

'Let's go inside,' she replied bluntly, giving Julie-Anne daggers.

No air kiss, no embrace. Melissa was always excited to see her, however, this time she was unusually silent, wearing a dark and brooding expression. Neither woman spoke as Julie-Anne collected her mail and they took the stairs up to her apartment. As she slid her key into the door lock she spied two things that alarmed her. She took a deep breath, outwardly maintained her composure, and switched on the lights immediately. She placed her handbag, keys, mail and jacket on the kitchen benchtop. 'I'll be back in a minute, Melissa.'

Julie-Anne had no idea what had come over Melissa, but she needed to break the ice. 'Okay, would you like a glass of bubbles?' she asked, walking back into the living area.

'We have nothing to celebrate, but why not?' Melissa replied in an acerbic tone.

This was a very different woman to the one who had dressed so provocatively and tantalised Julie-Anne to the point of arousal last Thursday. Now, less than a week later, she was obviously seething and Julie-Anne had no idea why. *She should have.*

Julie-Anne would maintain her composure and wait until her friend was ready to open up about whatever was bothering her. 'Cheers, Melissa.'

The women were leaning against the benchtop sipping their champagnes in uncomfortable silence. Melissa looked across to Julie-Anne. 'Do you want to watch a video?'

Julie-Anne thought that a strange question. No one watched DVDs anymore let alone videos. Wasn't the world addicted to Netflix, Amazon Prime, Stan and the like. 'I don't have any,' she replied innocently, not sure where this conversation was heading.

'Oh, but I do,' Melissa responded.'

'I don't have any electronics that play DVDs or videos, Melissa.'

'That's okay, we can watch this one on my mobile. It's not really suitable for the big screen anyway.'

'Oh, okay,' Julie-Anne replied evenly, oblivious to whatever was going down here.

Melissa opened the video app on her mobile, found the file she wanted and pressed the play icon. 'Shall we?'

Julie-Anne looked over Melissa's shoulder at the screen of her Galaxy. 'Turn it off,' she shouted. 'Turn it off.'

'Not yet, it gets even better. You need to watch the climax. It's the best part,' she said facetiously.

'Fucking turn it off, Melissa. Now,' she demanded.

'You haven't finished.'

'That's not even funny. Turn it off. Pleeeease?' she asked in a softer tone. 'I can explain.'

'What? Are you a movie reviewer now?' Melissa asked, the question dripping with its intended sarcasm.

'Come on, stop it. Let's go sit down and I will explain.'

'This will be good.'

The women walked across to the living room sofa. As they sat Julie-Anne moved to place a placatory hand on Melissa's knee, but her friend shifted sideways. 'Melissa, you know me well enough that I would never do anything to hurt you or affect our friendship.'

'Well, you failed on both counts.'

'Let me explain, please?'

'You don't have to. Paul has already told me what happened and the video itself is self-explanatory, don't you think?'

'Oh, really! So what did he say happened exactly? This should be quite enlightening,' Julie-Anne mocked.

'It's not funny. Paul said you stalked him around the Broadway Shopping Centre, then when he spotted you, you invited him for a drink at your favourite pub, proceeded to get him drunk and finally took advantage of him. And of course after Thursday night we know how much you enjoy being screwed by him, don't we?' Melissa glared at Julie-Anne. 'Well?'

'That's obviously me in the video, so rather than me spending the whole night trying to explain my actions and defend myself against the indefensible, let me begin at the end.'

Melissa laughed disbelievingly. 'I've seen the ending too. Go on, this should be interesting.'

'Knock it off.' Julie-Anne needed to make her point, and quickly, then she would happily spend the remainder of the night answering her questions, once Melissa had calmed down. 'I found photos of Sophie and the Minister for Education that depicted them together in highly compromising positions. The photos were taken with a secret camera hidden in the Minister's suite at the International. They were in a folder in the second draw of a desk in Paul's study.'

Melissa's head was spinning now. 'Our Sophie? Oh, no, that poor girl.'

'Exactly, and fortunately she is not aware of the existence of the photos yet. She will be mortified to say the least.'

'I have a gazillion questions. My head is spinning. I don't know where to start.'

'Melissa, I told you on Friday morning that I was going to check Paul out, but I didn't even get the opportunity. On Saturday when I was walking up to King Street to book an appointment at Dolce Vita I detected him following me. He'd obviously been waiting near my apartment block.'

'You're kidding. What happened then?'

'My investigative instincts kicked in and I devised a plan to turn the tables on him. You already know that I had my suspicions about him, but I needed to find out precisely why he was tailing me. So, I followed him into a bookstore and pretended it was an accidental encounter. One thing led to another and we went to The Bank for a drink where I endeavoured to prise some information out of him. Unsuccessfully, I might add.'

'Then what happened?'

'He said he was hungry, so we went to dinner. I'm guessing he concluded that if he had more time he could find out about my current investigation. We jabbed and parried like a couple of prize fighters with neither revealing anything useful to the other. I tried to provoke him, but alas, that didn't work either.'

'That's still a long way from playing the bull riding cowgirl, Julie-Anne.'

Julie-Anne looked deadpan at her girlfriend. 'I'll ignore that. Then he surprised the hell out of me and invited me to his place for a nightcap. I hesitated for obvious reasons, but then I thought I would give it one more try and see if he loosened up in his own environment.'

Julie-Anne could see by Melissa's facial expression that she still wasn't convinced. 'Well, he certainly loosened up didn't he?'

'Let me finish, I'm almost there. God, that sounds terrible. Sorry.'

Melissa trying to hold back a faint smile. 'Forget it. Carry on.'

'There's no way of telling you the next piece without upsetting you. He went and changed and when I turned around he was standing in the kitchen area topping up the champagnes. He was now wearing a red bathrobe and the front was wide open. He was naked beneath the robe.'

'Why did he go and get changed?'

'He said he was cold, although in retrospect, I'm certain that we both know why. I had a decision to make, and quickly.'

Melissa guessed where this was heading, but didn't respond. She couldn't; the impending betrayal by both of her friends becoming clearer by the second.

'I promise Melissa, with hand on heart, I didn't initiate the next bit. Are you certain you want me to continue? Isn't that enough?'

She sighed. 'Go on, get it over with and hopefully I might be able to process it better if I know the entire sorry tale.'

Now Julie-Anne breathed a deep sigh. 'He initiated physical contact. I had no time to think and an idea sprung into my mind.'

'You thought if you screwed him he might fall asleep afterwards and then you could go snooping around. Sophie told me about a man's post coital chemical reaction and how that works.'

'Normally it would have been unforgiveable of me, except without having done so, I would never had found the incriminating photos. It was a means to an end.' She regretted her choice of words as soon as they left her mouth.

'Are you now saying that you planned the whole thing? What sort of woman are you, Julie-Anne?'

'One who needs to seriously re-evaluate her priorities obviously,' she replied meekly. What else could she say and no amount of explaining was going to mitigate the hurt she had caused her friend.

'How cold and calculating are you, Julie-Anne? At this moment I feel like I hardly know you.'

'Melissa, I completely understand why you would feel that way, but I knew Paul was up to no good. Anyway, this isn't all on me, after all he was actually following me, not the other way around. And it was he who prompted you to invite me to dinner last week. Have you asked yourself why? Surely it's obvious now.'

'Why would he send me the video?'

'My guess is simply to support the outrageous fairy tale he told you.'

Melissa stared daggers at her friend. 'Given your behaviour in the pool last week it doesn't seem that outrageous to me.'

Julie-Anne sat bolt upright. 'Really, my behaviour? You're still in denial. You two were frolicking naked and fondling each other long before I even entered the pool,' she responded indignantly as she pulled down the collar of her polo neck. 'While we're discussing behaviour, have a look at this,' she demanded feistily.

Melissa was staring disbelievingly at the ugly, bluish purple bruising across Julie-Anne's neck and throat. She had been holding back her emotions, but couldn't any longer. She burst into tears and sobbed uncontrollably.

Julie-Anne leant forward and drew her into an embrace. 'I'm so, so sorry, Melissa.'

73. Julie-Anne's Apartment

Wednesday 3rd June

The following morning the women were standing at the kitchen benchtop drinking their homemade soy lattes. Melissa had overcome her bout of despondency brought on by Julie-Anne's near implausible revelations the previous evening. 'Were you really hiding in the back of a Seven Eleven? I can't believe that,' she asked, incredulous.

'Yes, I was and I was terrified Gao would come barging through the door and find me. I was shaking like a leaf. Thank God the Uber turned up when it did.'

'That sounds like something you would see in one of those American crime dramas. Unbelievable. And did you really kick him in the groin?'

'Yes. It was fortunate that I momentarily caught him off guard while he was dazed from my whack with the Panda.'

'Wow, his manhood had one helluva workout that night,' Melissa said irreverently while bursting into laughter.

'Oh, stop that, it's not funny.'

'Yes, it is. And now you've got a Panda story of your own to tell.'

Her friend was using comedy to mask her own disenchantment with Paul that she clearly now needed to deal with. 'What are you going to do?'

Melissa was blankly staring out of the living room window into the dawning morning. 'He wasn't a boyfriend as such, but whatever he was is obviously over now.' She swivelled back to face Julie-Anne. 'I can't believe he used me to get to you. If I had been more aware this might never have happened in the first place. Clearly I won't contact him again and I'll just ignore him if he tries to make contact. It's apparent that he's not the man I understood him to be.'

'No, he most definitely isn't.

'And how are *you*, Julie-Anne? I don't want to put too fine a point on it, but you did sell your soul, all for the want of a story. Can you ever come back from that?'

'I don't know. I'm not proud of what I did, but I had no time to think, so I just made an on the spot judgement call. I think part of it was also to do with Thursday night when he conveniently took advantage of our affection for each other. Afterwards I felt like I had lost some control and I think in the deep recesses of my subconscious I wanted my power back. And I damn well got it. They say that the past prepares you for the future, but I'm not sure that's the case in this instance. I'm good at compartmentalising, but I'll have to make that my speciality now. I also obviously need to re-evaluate my priorities, however, I love my job and it means everything to me. It's who I am.'

Melissa nodded in acknowledgement. 'We all need to reassess our priorities at various stages in our life. After seeing my potential political career disappear before my eyes I decided to refocus all my energies on my legal practice.'

'Good for you. With a multitude of companies being outed by the day for underpaying their staff the world could do with more committed social justice lawyers. Now, back to your comment about selling my soul. From a professional perspective, I did find the incriminating photos though. I'm not trying to justify my actions, I promise,' Julie-Anne said with her hands in the defensive position, 'but if there is an upside to my bout of spontaneous madness, hopefully it will eventually lead to a successful conclusion to my investigation. And nothing less than the prosecution of Paul Gao will suffice. The bigger picture is that a successful prosecution would send a message to China that they can't interfere with political life in this country,' Julie-Anne said as she started opening her mail from the previous day.

'Where does your investigation go now?'

'I have already spoken to the Minister and he eventually acknowledged my suspicions that he is being blackmailed to reinstate the Confucius Institute into the state schools program. He has already received two of the photos I found in Gao's desk and the next won't be far away. I think I know how the whole thing went down and I'm waiting on Jack to call me with the results of tests he's running on my behalf. If the results prove my theory I'll be one step closer to snaring Gao and then I will hand him over to Jack.'

'How is he, Julie-Anne? Jack, I mean.'

Julie-Anne was distracted by the contents of one particular envelope. 'Well, at least I won't have to feel excluded,' she replied, while extracting a USB key from an envelope. 'We can assume what this contains. And it has an accompanying type written note.' She handed it to Melissa.

If you even think of interfering with my cause I will release this little video to your rival, the tabloid. I'm sure they would relish the opportunity to embarrass an opposition reporter. Do you know what a presstitute is?

'Well that little escapade might have backfired on me,' she lamented. 'That would put a full stop to my career and I would never be able to work in this town again.'

'He wouldn't dare, surely.'

'You know him better than me, Melissa. Would he?'

'Obviously, I'm now the last person you should ask, given how blind I was to his ulterior motives. Anyway, what exactly is a presstitute?'

Julie-Annes shuddered at the use of the word again. 'It's a term that references journalists and talking heads in mainstream media who give biased and predetermined views misleadingly tailored to fit a particular partisan, financial or business agenda, thus neglecting the fundamental duty to report news impartially. That's Wikipedia's definition. Paul's use of the word is more closely aligned with another definition which is used to describe journalists who are perceived to be selling their morals for money or political gain.'

'Oh.'

If ever there was a time to change the subject it was now. 'I think you might have dodged a bullet with your study trip, too, Melissa. I read that the United Front's remit encompasses a broad spectrum of activity, from espionage to foreign interference and influence. Early in the COVID-19 pandemic they mobilised Australian companies sympathetic to China and tasked them with collecting medical supplies and PPE and sending them to China, all at the expense of the Australian population. So, sponsoring study tours would be a cover for something less worthy. Of that I'm certain.'

'You did warn me, but I would have done my research first.'

'Anyway, back to Jack for now. I haven't told you,' she gasped. 'I can't believe that. To cut a long story short he caught Danielle red handed with a kilo of coke belonging to Wie.'

'Wait, none of that makes any sense. What's her involvement with Wie for heaven's sake? I'm totally confused.'

'Involvement is an apt word. Seemingly she has been in a relationship with Wie since before the money laundering scandal.'

Melissa's mouth was agape. 'You're kidding. And what, Jack didn't know?'

'No, and as you can imagine, he's highly embarrassed.'

Melissa smiled self-consciously. 'Jack and I should have a drink together as we obviously have a lot in common. We're both obviously such wonderful judges of character and human behaviour,' she said. 'You have to tell me all about it one day.'

Julie-Anne's mobile rang. 'Speak of the devil.'

'Jack, how are you?' she asked as she nudged her bedroom door closed.

'Better by the day, JA. Now, my FSG guy has called me with the results of his printing of Chandler's suite last night.'

'That's extraordinarily efficient.'

'Yes, it is. He headed straight back to the lab and went to work. It seems you're onto something. The prints he took from the television cabinets your guy Frances directed him to belong to Sun Jie. They were easily matched to prints taken following a previous misdemeanour. And I know that like me, you don't believe in coincidences.'

'No, I don't, Jack,' she replied as she nudged the bedroom door closed. 'Someone's been in my apartment,' she whispered, so as not to alarm Melissa.'

'What makes you think that?'

'Two reasons. Firstly, it appears that someone has sprayed a filmy substance on the camera lenses outside my apartment. And secondly, do you remember that little trick I do with a strand of my hair and the doorframe?'

'Are you sure you didn't forget?'

'Oh, no, I'm fastidious about that, Jack.'

'What are you going to do?'

'Nothing for now. Melissa is here, so I had a quick look around last night, but didn't discern anything else out of place. I'll get the locks changed today.'

'Do you want me to have the place printed?'

'Thank you, but I wouldn't bother. You can be guaranteed they were wearing gloves, whoever they were. Can you have the place swept for bugs though? That would be helpful.'

'Yeah. Can you arrange for Melissa to be there later on and I'll set it up?'

'Will do. I do think it's time we had a chat, Jack. Can I come in this morning?'

Jack was thinking back to when his relationship with JA was breaking down and he had wanted to discuss it. As usual she was too focused on her work. 'Oh, now you want to have a chat,' he replied light-heartedly.

'You're a comedian. I'll call you later.'

'Good news, Melissa. Jack's forensic guy matched a set of fingerprints to one of my suspects. Now all I have to do is link that person to your ex whatever he was.'

'He wasn't a boyfriend, but you're right, he's definitely an ex something. Now though, like you said, I will have to be careful.'

'Yes you will, especially given we now know he has a propensity for violence. Melissa, if you're worried about Gao paying you a visit you are most welcome to stay here.'

'Thank you, I might take you up on that, but I'll need to return home and collect some clothes.'

'We're pretty much the same size, so help yourself to my wardrobe. They'll look better on you anyway.'

Melissa beamed seductively. 'And you look better without them altogether.'

'You're incorrigible. I have to go, so make yourself comfortable and I'll see you later.' Julie-Anne turned towards the door and Melissa grasped her arm.

'I'm sorry about the things I said last night,' she said, filled with remorse.

'I probably deserved them, so think nothing of it. I'll call you later. I need you to do something for me.'

74. AFP Deputy Commissioner's Office

Wednesday 3rd June

Julie-Anne strode across Goulburn Street, weaved through the security bollards and strode up to the entry of the AFP's headquarters. Being an investigative reporter who had on occasions incurred the wrath of the federal law enforcement agency she never thought she would be invited into the holy grail. The building was purpose built for the AFP in 1990 and Jack had once told her it was bullet and bomb proof and included witness protection areas, a gun range and rooftop squash court.

'Julie-Anne.' She turned her head to see Jack walking towards her with a laminated security pass in his hand.

'Didn't you see me waiting?'

'No, I was checking out the security features,' she said while rapping her knuckles against the building's impossibly thick glass. 'Impressive.'

He handed her a day pass, swiped them into the building and they walked across to the bank of elevators.

'You pressed twelve. I thought you said your office was on ten.'

'It is, however, the executive offices are on twelve and the DC wants to meet you,' he said proudly.

Her face darkened. 'Is he going to give me a dressing down for my latest article, Jack?'

'I don't think so. You are one of Sydney's leading investigative reporters and there are times when the media can be useful to law enforcement, and vice versa, so developing a relationship can't hurt either of you. At the very least, it's a good opportunity for you both to put a face to the name.'

'Ms Granger, I'm pleased to meet you,' John Robertson said while extending his hand in greeting. 'I've heard a lot about you.'

'Me too, Deputy Commissioner, on both counts,' she said, gripping his hand firmly. He was tall and thick set, with a rugged complexion, close cropped hair with grey tinges and he was wearing the AFP's dress uniform.

'Jack told me you were coming in today, so I wanted to take the opportunity to say hello. Congratulations on your latest article. It was an interesting read,' he said evenly.

'Thank you.'

'Although—'

Here it comes.

'You do know of course that you could have compromised a federal investigation.'

'How is that?' she asked, genuinely perplexed.

'Well, if Wie Ping Lie happened to be a reader of yours he would have seen your article on Saturday morning. That article would have alerted him to the fact that his operation was compromised and we may never have been in a position to arrest him.' Robertson stared her down. 'That's how it is, Ms Granger.'

'Oh, come now, Deputy Commissioner, you don't think for one minute that he didn't realise his operation was already compromised when Danielle Mortimer was a no-show with his coke on Friday night? With the killing of Li Jun in March, and the AFP's arrest of Wang Yong and Lucie Chan, Wie had run out of lieutenants he could trust, so he was always going to be forced to retrieve the coke himself.'

'If you had waited a couple of days you could have covered the story in its entirety.'

'That's okay. I will write a postscript to the original story for this Saturday's edition anyway and we can milk it for another week.'

'And can the AFP and I be expecting another embarrassing mention?'

There it was. The real reason she was invited into the office of the AFP's Deputy Commissioner. 'With all the negative publicity over the past year surrounding the AFP's raids on media organisations and reporters, I can well and truly understand why you would be sensitive to any mention of the agency's activities, positive or otherwise, Deputy Commissioner.' She used his title to emphasise her point.

'Ms Granger, as the Deputy Commissioner, managing the AFP's public image isn't part of my remit, but ensuring investigations don't get compromised is. And that's exactly what your article could have resulted in. All I ask is that you consider this fact when making future deliberations about the timing of your articles.'

'Oh, but I do, however, I also weigh them up against what is in the public interest. That's what my readers expect of me.'

'Would that be your declining readership? Ms Granger, your readership also need to have faith and trust in their law enforcement agencies and your article potentially diminished both in relation to the AFP. I'm sure there was readership mileage in it for you to criticise our investigation into Miss Mortimer's activities, but it does nothing to engender the trust and faith in the AFP that I mentioned previously,' he said.

'Firstly, our readership's not declining,' she snapped. 'It's just morphing across into the broader electronic and digital media. You should try it sometime.' Julie-Anne deliberately glanced at the morning papers spread out on the coffee table.

'Our online readership is increasing exponentially, particularly as people become more accustomed to the paywall. In fact, we have a cross-platform readership in excess of six million and the Saturday edition is approaching half a million,' she said proudly. 'Secondly, unlike the tabloids, the Daily News readership have an expectation that we will maintain our commitment to quality investigative journalism, and we intend to do just that. And finally, it's not incumbent on me or my paper to promote faith and trust in the AFP and its activities; it's up to you and your people to earn it,' she said.

'Okay, if you say so. We might have to agree to disagree on this occasion.'

'Yes, I do.'

'Ms Granger, after the attempt on your life earlier in the year, I'm certain that I don't need to tell you that you need to be careful around these people.' *Did she glimpse a look of genuine concern on his face?* 'If you ever have any concerns over your personal safety don't hesitate to contact the detective here. I believe you are both well acquainted.'

She bit her tongue. 'Thank you, that's very kind of you, Deputy Commissioner.'

75. AFP Headquarters

Wednesday 3rd June

'I just knew he wouldn't be able to help himself, Jack,' she said as they took the stairs down to the detective's office.

'I thought you handled yourself well, JA. You stood up for what you believe in and so for that matter did he. Anyway, that might just be the first step in a beautiful relationship,' he said.

'Yeah, sure. I was referring to his little dig at our past relationship. And you could have at least told him that I gave you the lead on Danielle's deceit in the first place. That would have shown him that I do actually cooperate with law enforcement authorities.'

'He's well aware of that. Now, JA, what's got you so excited that you so urgently needed one of our FSG guys to print a room at the International?'

'Even more cooperation for the AFP. That's what.'

They sat side by side at Jack's desk. 'Okay, let's see what you have.'

'Well, I've finally made some progress on my old hobby horse of Chinese interference in Australia, and more particularly, our political system.' This was going to be tricky. She had to find a way to tell Jack what she had discovered without referencing her soul destroying activities from Saturday night. She told him of her suspicions surrounding Paul Gao that began with

Melissa's pronouncement that he worked as an emissary at the Chinese Consulate. 'I just knew it couldn't be coincidental that I was invited to dinner in the company of someone from the Consulate, and as it turned out I was correct. Then I caught him following me from my apartment to King Street in Newtown. That sealed the deal for me.'

'You should have called me straight away, JA.'

'At that stage I had nothing definitive to tell you, so what could you have done?'

'I could have warned him off or maybe I would have been even more persuasive.'

'Thank you, but then I wouldn't know what I now do and my investigation would have stalled. Some photos came into my possession and from there everything escalated.'

'What photos and why did they change everything?'

'There is a collection of explicit photos that depict Sophie in compromising positions with a prominent person. I have no doubt Paul Gao is behind it.'

Jack was confused. 'Hang on, JA, you're going too fast. How did Sophie get mixed up in this?'

'She told me a few weeks ago that she had an upcoming date with a politician. Well, as it turns out that politician was Ben Chandler, the state's Education Minister.'

'What, and you're telling me the photos are of the two of them?'

'Yes, unfortunately.'

'What do they reveal and how do you know this Paul Gao is behind them?'

'The photos were secretly taken by a hidden camera placed in Chandler's hotel suite with the majority being shot in his bedroom. You can draw your own conclusions as to the content.'

'Hence why you wanted the suite printed.'

'Exactly. I had my suspicions that Sun Jie was behind

the technological component. He had an unusually brief employment history with the International. That and the fact that his incoming passenger card listed him as an ICT technician made him an obvious suspect and then you confirmed the link to Paul Gao through his Camperdown address. That is Gao's apartment.'

'How do you know that?'

She had to think quickly. 'Melissa must have told me,' she replied nonchalantly.

'I'm guessing I know the reasons for the photos.'

Julie-Anne reminded Jack about the state government shutting down the Confucius Institute last year and the article the Consul General wrote condemning the decision. 'Ben Chandler is being blackmailed to reinstate the Institute and Gao has to be the perpetrator. Given Gao is employed by the Chinese Consulate that isn't a bridge too far to speculate. And that would mean the Consul General has to be behind this.'

'I read about Chinese interference in Australian life all the time, but I've never actually seen an example of it.'

'Well, now you have, Jack. What's more, Sun Jie's visa application was sponsored by the Chinese Shipping Company who in-turn have close ties to the Chinese Communist Party. The Consul General must be a member and he is Gao's employer. That closes the interference loop for me. This goes all the way back to Beijing, Jack.'

'How did you come into possession of the photos?'

Shit. She hated lying to her ex, but she couldn't tell him the truth either. He would be horrified at her behaviour. 'I can't tell you that.' She could feel her face flushing.

Jack eyed her with suspicion. 'JA, if they were illegally obtained then they can't be used as evidence. You know that.'

Illegally obtained. What an understatement.

She changed the subject. 'By the way, I've also checked the

DFAT website and Gao is not listed as a registered representative of the Consulate, so therefore he isn't entitled to diplomatic immunity. You can safely go after him.'

'Hold up. I haven't decided to go after anyone just yet. That decision will be made by the DC and given your recent history with him he may not be predisposed to supporting your theories and instigate any enquiry. There will also be political sensitivities surrounding any proposed investigation that the AFP will need to consider.'

'I have to meet with the Minister this afternoon, so where do we go from here, Jack?'

'You're doing that *we* thing again.'

'Of course I am. This is consecutive investigations I have brought to you in the past few weeks. You guys wouldn't have nabbed Wie and Danielle without me, so of course it's *we*.'

'Touché. Alright, I'll talk to the DC and give you a call later today. Now, I need something from you.' Jack opened the Notes app on his phone. 'What do you know about the United Front Work Department? Wie mentioned it during the interview.'

'I've done some research on it for my feature. In a nutshell, it's an arm of the Chinese Communist Party that, amongst other less savoury activities, uses its power to influence other countries' policy toward the CCP. It's one of Xi Jinping's so-called magic weapons designed to seize and maintain total political power. The United Front Work Department is responsible for coordinating domestic and foreign influence operations, primarily targeting susceptible individuals and corporations. A man called Tan Chailun is the head of the department and as a result he is a powerful figure within the Communist Party and he's close to Xi. Why do you ask?'

'Wie provided me with a puzzle that involves the China Shipping Company, the Confucius Institute, Li Qiang, the Chinese Consulate and the United Front Work Department.

He intimated that they are all linked. And that finding the link is key to solving my drug importation case.'

'Well, if that's the case, then Tan Chailun would definitely be at the top of that org chart. Apparently, according to what I've read, he's a heavy hitter. I think both investigations have links all the way to Beijing, Jack.'

'Okay, thanks.' Jack was quiet for a moment. 'I just thought of something else regarding the Chandler case. 'Can you ask the Minister if he will provide us with the original photos and envelopes he has received so far and I'll see if my forensic guys can extract DNA from them? We will also need a sample of his own DNA so we can exclude him. Then we just need to somehow obtain Gao's DNA and see if we have a match.'

Julie-Anne felt her face rapidly flushing. On two occasions in the past week she would have been smothered in it.

'Are you okay, JA?'

'Yes, I'm fine. I have to go.'

76. Goulburn Street Sydney

Wednesday 3rd June

Jack escorted Julie-Anne down to street level and out of the building.

'Don't forget to call me, Jack,' she called out over her shoulder.

'I won't.' Heading back inside he stood inside the buildings' front window admiring JA as she strutted across the forecourt and snaked through the security bollards. She was wearing tight fitting black jeans that hugged her shapely legs, a black knitted turtleneck, her favourite black leather jacket and black ankle length boots with killer heels. *It must be winter.* They had dated for six months and he had never tired of appreciating her leggy, athletic body, just as he was doing now. He was lost in his thoughts and didn't see the black Subaru Impreza WRX pull away from the curb further down Goulburn Street. Then suddenly out of the corner of his eye he spied the vehicle as it sharply accelerated up the rise. *Shit.* JA had stepped off the curb. The car was heading straight for her. 'JA, watch out, JA, JA,' he yelled. The warning cries went unheeded as they bounced off the bulletproof glass. As he raced back to the building's front door, he was startled to see the Impreza's front passenger door opening while it was still moving. At the last second Julie-Anne looked to her right. '—.' Jack could see her mouth open and release what he knew would be a bloodcurdling scream. Without taking his eyes off of her he smashed his hand against the green exit button and barged through the heavy glass door. 'JA, look out,' he screamed again. 'Look out.' He watched as her head turned back towards him and he could see the horrified expression on her face. She took a long stride back towards the curb, but wasn't quick enough to prevent the car door slamming into her trailing leg. The Impreza screeched to a halt at the same time it made contact with her. Jack watched, mortified, as JA's body was spun around sideways and then cartwheeled sidelong onto the sidewalk. She landed with a thud. He was astonished to see that a man of Asian appearance was already out of the car and collecting her laptop bag from the middle of the road. Jack saw a flash of recognition in the man's eyes. The man smiled wryly, then calmly took a couple of steps backwards and flopped into the passenger seat. The car's tires screeched as it accelerated away up the hill, sped through the red light and fishtailed around the shallow bend into Wentworth Avenue and out of sight. Jack allowed himself a brief glimpse at the disappearing vehicle.

'JA,' Jack yelled again as he sprinted towards her sprawled, motionless body. Stunned pedestrians were already gathering around, some with their mobiles out. He pushed past them and bent over her, immediately searching for signs of life. He sighed with relief when he noticed her chest slowly rising and falling. 'Thank God,' he said to no-one. Blood was now trickling down the side of her face from a head wound that he couldn't see. He removed a handkerchief from his pocket and dabbed at the blood.

'I've called an ambulance,' a woman said. 'It should be here soon.'

Jack didn't even hear her such was his focus on JA. After a moment he remembered there were other people around him. 'I'm sorry, what did you say?'

'The ambulance should be here soon.'

'Oh, sure, thank you.'

JA had landed on her side which was fortunate as he wouldn't have to move her to ensure her airway remained open. He needed to keep her warm, so he removed his jacket and laid it across the upper part of her body. His first aid training had told him that she should be able to hear him even while she was unconscious. 'JA, it's me, Jack. You're going to be okay.' *I hope.* He gently moved his hand across her head and found a large bump developing on the side where she had connected with the sidewalk. At a minimum she would have concussion. Again. Given she was wearing jeans he couldn't properly check for any damage to the leg that was struck. Nothing was protruding through the fabric which had to be a good sign. He heard the high-low wail of an approaching emergency vehicle. He knew the vehicle was close when he heard the yelp sound it made when crossing an intersection. Out of the corner of his eye he glimpsed the red and white liveried vehicle pull up to the curb. Two paramedics exited with their PRK kits in hand and approached the increasingly sizeable gathering.

'I'm Pam, do you know this woman?' the female paramedic asked.

'Yes, she is a friend,' Jack replied.

'Did you see what happened to her?'

'She was hit by a car, but I think the vehicle only made contact with her left leg.'

'Does she have any pre-existing medical conditions?'

'No, she is fit and healthy.'

'Okay, that's good to know.'

Jack stood up to allow the paramedic access. 'Is she going to be okay?'

'Sir, I don't know yet. Stand back and let us do what we do please,' Pam replied firmly.

Jack watched as she checked JA's airwaves before setting up an IV and connecting it to her arm. Next she placed a transparent mask over her nasal area and turned the nozzle on an oxygen pack. She then carefully fitted a cervical collar to stabilise JA's neck. The female paramedic gently moved JA's head looking for wounds. Finding the source of the bleeding, she cleaned the wound and applied a gauze pad. Finally, she wrapped another gauze bandage around her head, to hold the pad in place. Then the paramedic ran her hands down both of JA's legs feeling for broken bones. 'Johnno can you grab the LTS please?' she called out to her partner.

'I can't feel any breaks, but I want to stabilise the leg anyway, just in case.' Pam slowly lifted the leg and Johnno placed the splint beneath it before securing the velcro straps. 'Alright, let's grab the gurney and get her to hospital.'

'Jack, is that you?'

The female paramedic turned her attention to the man leaning over her. 'She's regained consciousness, sir. Are you Jack?'

Jack felt his eyes watering at the sound of JA's voice. He blinked away the tears. 'Yes.'

'I think she's asking for you?'

Jack wiped his eyes with the back of his hand. He realised he still had feelings for her. How could he not given their professional and personal history together. 'Welcome back, JA,' he said, smiling with relief.

'My bag?' she said weakly.

'What did you say?'

'My bag, Jack?'

He didn't want to alarm her unnecessarily, but the truth wasn't an option now. 'Don't worry, I'll find it.'

'Welcome back miss,' said Johnno. The young paramedic placed the gurney next to her while his partner straightened Julie-Anne's body and moved her arms to the side. Johnno slipped his arms under his patient's back and waist while Pam did the same under the hip and knees. 'Okay, Johnno, one, two and three,' she recited. Jack was watching as they carefully lifted JA and placed her on the stretcher.

'Where are you taking her and can I ride along please?' Jack asked.

'St Vincent's Emergency Department. It's not far, but I would prefer it if you drove yourself, sir.'

'Okay.' Jack raced across the forecourt, swiped himself into the building and rode the elevator back up to his office. 'Michael, it's Jack. I need a couple of favours,' he blurted into his mobile.

'Sure, but what's so urgent? You sound stressed.'

'JA's just been deliberately run down in Goulburn Street. I need you to run a plate for me. It'll be quicker if you do it.'

'Jesus, Jack, what happened?'

He gave Sanderson the short story. 'Also, can you arrange for a uniform to be placed outside her hospital room at St Vinnies for a couple of days?'

'Of course.'

'I'm going to the hospital now. Let me know about the plate as soon as you can.'

'Okay, consider it done.'

77. Camperdown Inner Sydney

Wednesday 3rd June

The rear of the Impreza began to drift as it made the shallow turn into Wentworth Avenue at speed. Jie knew not to overcorrect, rather he backed off the speed momentarily without touching the brakes until the car became balanced again. Once he regained control of the vehicle he made consecutive left hand turns that led to Pitt Street and then continued onto Broadway. 'That must have been that detective, Wagner, who came to her rescue,' he said to Paul Gao.

'You were fortunate that he cares more for her than chasing you, otherwise you wouldn't be sitting here,' Gao replied.

Jie nodded. 'I know. I saw the look of confusion on his face when you went for her bag. He was obviously conflicted. What have you found in the bag? Are the photos in there?'

Gao opened the laptop bag and slid out a manilla folder containing a collection of photos. 'Tiān nǎ, she's gorgeous and just look at that body,' Jie said, while watching Gao flick through them slowly.

Having spent time with Melissa Wu, Gao knew that the woman in the photos wasn't an exception. He mused about his time with Melissa. They had shared a bed where he had enjoyed her energy and enthusiasm. That would remain a distant memory now. 'Alright, Jie, that's enough, we have much to do,' Gao said sharply as they arrived back at the Camperdown apartment fifteen minutes later. There is also a mobile phone and a laptop. Can you hack into them?'

'Of course.'

'Okay, we have to leave this apartment. By now the Granger woman must have told the detective where I live. Although, he will probably be by her side at the hospital, I still want to be cautious. See what you can find out while I pack my things. Then we need to lose the car, Jie.'

Gao returned from his bedroom with a backpack looped over his shoulder. 'What did you find on her phone and laptop?'

'She rang the detective last night and he called her back early this morning. They're using WhatsApp, obviously for security reasons. She has also been talking to someone from the International. I recognised the number from when I worked there.'

That was not what Gao wanted to hear. 'The Granger woman knows more than I thought. She obviously knows about the Minister too.' *And she must know about you as well.* 'What else did you find?'

'I also found the photos on her mobile and her laptop.'

'That's good. We should have them all now and she won't be able to publish them.'

'Gao, she is a reporter, so she would certainly have backed-up her files to the newspaper's server or the cloud.'

'Give me her phone. What about the laptop?'

'I went through her search history. Yes, she must know about the Minister as she has been searching him. She has also been searching Chinese interference in Australia and the Confucius Institute in New South Wales. She is a clever woman I think.'

'Yes, she is,' Gao replied, thinking back to how Granger got the better of him on Saturday night.

'Jie, here is where you need to meet me if we get separated in traffic.' He handed his technical assistant a post-it note with a location listed. We will stay off the M4 and Parramatta Road to avoid the many traffic cameras installed there. By now the police will have issued an alert for the car. The journey will take longer, but it will be safer. And don't keep me waiting.'

'Of course not.'

'Okay, let's get out of here.' Gao had deliberately maintained a sparsely furnished apartment, exactly for a time like this. He didn't bother cleaning or sanitising the apartment as the Granger woman knew where he lived anyway, and by now, so would the detective. He wouldn't be returning. 'Let's go, Jie.'

Paul Gao was driving along George's River Road looking for the Boulevard turnoff when the Granger woman's mobile photo vibrated. He became excited. He might learn more about the woman who had become a thorn in his side. He saw the red number 1 overlaid on the WhatsApp icon. He pressed the green symbol and read the message. 'I'm coming for you, Gao.' The message said it was from Jack who Gao assumed must be the man he had locked eyes with in Goulburn Street. Somehow he had been able to quickly identify him. How much did this man know about his activities? It was one thing to neutralise a reporter, but Gao wasn't about to engage with a man with the resources of an entire police department behind him. After nearly an hour navigating through the backstreets of Sydney's inner west he arrived at Clyde. He had no choice but to cross Parramatta Road, a major thoroughfare, to get to James Ruse Drive which would take him closer to his destination. He didn't see any traffic cameras, but he wasn't unduly worried now as this task would be completed in fifteen minutes. He turned off of JRD, drove to the end of Grand Avenue and pulled over near the Hymix concrete plant in Camellia. Jie arrived in his own car a few minutes later, parked some distance away and walked across to Gao.

'Jie, pull the spare tyre out and place it on the back seat. Gao retrieved his bath robe from his backpack, soaked it in petrol and placed it across the two front seats. He smiled to himself as he recalled the last time he had worn it. Physically, the woman knew how to use her magnificent body and he was highly aroused by her, but she was amoral, anti-China and he despised her. He brought himself back to the present and wound down the two rear windows to create a chimney effect. Finally, he proceeded to pour petrol over the four wheels to soak the tyres.

'Jie, is everything out of the trunk?' Gao asked while walking behind him to the rear of the Impreza.

'I will check.' Jie popped the trunk again and bent over to confirm it was empty. Gao moved swiftly, launching a fierce knife hand strike to the back of Jie's neck. Jie's knees fell from under him and Gao used the momentum to roll his collapsed torso into the trunk. He retrieved the keys to Jie's vehicle from his jeans pocket and then folded his legs in. Gao slammed the lid shut and walked around to the side of the Impreza. He stepped back, retrieved a lighter from his pocket and ran his fingers firmly across spark wheel. Then he cautiously scanned the industrial wasteland, and not seeing anyone, he tossed the lighter through the open window. He followed it with the Granger woman's mobile phone.

As he was driving west back along Grand Avenue in the rear vision mirror he could see a toxic black cloud rising upwards. He felt relieved. Jie had proven useful to the cause, but he would have become a liability. If the Granger woman was talking to people at the International it would only be a matter of time before she found Jie and then made the link to he himself, if she hadn't already. Now, even if she had made that connection, it would no longer be of any use to her. He was driving steadily along Parramatta Road towards Sydney when his mobile phone rang. He saw it was the Consul General calling from his burner phone. He didn't really want to accept the call, but to ignore it wasn't an option.

'Mr Consul General, how are you?' he asked buoyantly.

'Because your progress is slow like the ox I now find myself having to check upon your activities more frequently. My consular duties are too important for me to play school principal, however, you leave me no option, Gao.' Xiao wouldn't tell him that he had met with the Minister yesterday, nor would he tell him that the Minister was obviously beginning to feel the pressure of his emissary's activities, whatever they were. He needed Gao to stay sharp and focused.

'I have made much progress since we spoke only two days ago. I hope to have a resolution by the end of the week.' He thought about the latest message he had sent which would be received today. 'Things should move quickly after today, Mr Consul General.'

'I hope you are correct with both of your assertions, Gao.'

'I must request the use of another safe house though.'

'Why? What has occurred that you need to relocate? Have you been compromised?'

Gao couldn't very well tell the Consul General the truth. 'No, not at all. It is just a precaution.'

'This is an important and noble task that I have assigned to you and failure to succeed is not an option. That would not be beneficial to your career.'

'I know—'

The Consul General spoke over the top of him. 'I sincerely hope I haven't made a mistake in appointing you as my Special Emissary.'

'No, you have not—' Gao said before realising he was talking to himself again.

78. St Vincent's Hospital

Wednesday 3rd June

For the second time in less than two weeks Jack found a park on Victoria Street in Darlinghurst and made his way into the Emergency Department of St Vincent's Hospital. He walked past the security guard, into the ED's reception area, and across to the nurse's station where he produced his credentials. The nurse was once more unmoved by his attendance. *De ja vu all over again.* He smiled at his anecdote. Eventually she acknowledged his presence. 'Yes, detective?' she asked with an exaggerated sigh.

'Mr Wagner.' Jack heard his name called, turned his head towards the source and waved in response. He had been parked on the uncomfortable plastic chair in the crowded waiting room for more than two hours. The desk nurse had been less than impressed as he regularly sought information, any information, on JA's condition. A woman with jet black hair, matching eyes and wearing blue nurses scrubs and white plastic clogs strode across to him. Her name badge read Aishwarya Parvati. 'Hello, nurse, how is she?'

'Hello, Mr Wagner. Ms Granger was extremely fortunate that she wasn't badly injured. She has a hematoma, but luckily it's only superficial and not cranial. She also has bruising to her Iliac and clavicle caused from hitting the sidewalk and also on the femoral shaft where I'm guessing the vehicle collided with her body. She has concussion, will be stiff and sore and have significant bruising and a headache for some time. In a while we will transfer her to a general ward where she will remain under observation for another forty eight hours or until we are comfortable releasing her.'

'Thank you, nurse. That's good news, I think.'

'Be assured, Mr Wagner, it could have been a whole lot worse. She's a lucky girl. You can go and see her now.'

Jack made his way down the sterile corridor, replete with its competing odours of antiseptic and floor polish, until he found JA's cubicle. Her eyes were closed and her head had been rebandaged. The oxygen was gone, but the IV drip was still in place. He tiptoed into the room and sat on a chair next to the bed. Surprisingly, given they had dated for six months, he didn't know anything about her family, or even if she had anyone who he should contact. He stood up, moved to the end of the bed, extracted the clipboard from its basket and began reading. He heard the sheets rustling.

'Hey, Jack, you're here,' she said croakily.

'Of course, I wouldn't be anywhere else. How are you feeling?' he asked as he kissed her on the undamaged cheek.

'I'm so sore. I have pain in all kinds of places.' She winced while trying to sit up.

'Then you should avoid going to those places,' he said as he helped her sit upright while adjusting her pillows.

'Stop it. It hurts when I laugh.'

'Where are you hurting?'

'Everywhere. My head is banging, my cheek is sore as is my hip and leg,' she replied while adjusting her body.'

'You look stunning as always although I'm not sure about your accessorising. The bandana really needs rethinking.'

'What did I do to my cheek?' she asked while patting the large dressing on the right side of her face.

'You landed heavily on the pavement, so you've got a big lump and a nasty bruise under that bandage. Which reminds me of another joke.'

'Go on. I know you're just dying to tell it.'

'When I was a child I always felt safer around women with bandages. I guess you could say I was a bit of a mummy's boy.'

'That's just terrible, Jack.'

'Yes, it was, but it's the only bandage joke I know. Say, before I forget, do you have family that you would like me to call?' In all the time they had dated he had never asked about her family. *Some boyfriend you were.*

'My parents live up near Lismore and I have a younger sister out in Orange, but I don't want to worry them. Can you call Melissa for me though?'

'Of course, I'll call her now.'

'Jack, did you find out about my bag?' He had avoided the issue until now, although he couldn't for much longer.

He hesitated. 'No, I didn't.' He wouldn't tell her just yet that her bag was the obvious reason for the hit.

She burst into tears. 'Oh, no, Jack. Everything I need for work was in there. And the photos too. Damn.'

'Don't get yourself all worked up. You need to make your health and welfare your only priority now. Not your job,' he said firmly. 'Was everything on your devices backed up?'

'Of course, but it's the inconvenience.'

'It doesn't really matter now, you're not going anywhere soon. You need to rest.'

'Did you see who was driving the car, Jack?'

Given the appearance of the man who had retrieved the laptop bag, Jack had no doubt it must have been Paul Gao's accomplice, Sun Jie. Who else could it possibly be, but he didn't want JA to be thinking about that now. He would be economical with the truth. 'No, it all happened too fast.'

'If it was Gao he must have had me followed from my apartment again. He had no way of knowing I would be at AFP headquarters this morning. Bugger. I should have checked my surroundings before I left. That's a rookie mistake, Jack, and I know better.'

'Are you okay?' Melissa asked as she rushed into the room half an hour later.

'Hey,' Julie-Anne replied. 'I've been better.'

Over the phone Jack had voiced his suspicions to Melissa on what he thought had gone down and suggested she avoid the subject for now. She would be feeling guilty enough given she had introduced Gao to JA in the first place. Melissa reached the bed, grasped Julie-Anne's hand and kissed her gently.

Jack's mobile vibrated in his pocket. He pulled it out and saw it was Sanderson calling. 'I have to take this, ladies. I'll be back in a minute,' he said, walking out into the corridor. 'How did you go, Michael? Any luck?'

'Sort of. The vehicle is registered to a Fan Chen. Wasn't he the guy who kidnapped the casino's Treasury Manager earlier in the year?'

'That's him. The one and the same. He's in prison though, Michael.'

'Well, it's definitely registered to him.'

JA had caught Fan Chen tailing her in the Impreza one morning back in March and she had reported on a potential link between him, the money laundering and the Chinese Consulate in her feature article. 'It would appear that someone has taken his place and their infatuation with JA continues.'

'I'll put out a KALOF for the car. What the hell has she got herself involved in this time, Jack?'

'I'll tell you when I see you. Can you do me another favour?'

'Sure, I'm intrigued now.'

'I'm more invested than intrigued, but I know what you meant. Okay, write this address down.' Jack pulled out his notebook and read out an address. 'Call me back when you have something to tell me please.'

'Will do.'

'Did you girls miss me?' Jack asked, bouncing back into the room.

'Of course. Who wouldn't?' Melissa responded sassily.

JA's eyes had closed again, so Jack seized the opportunity to quietly usher Melissa out into the corridor. 'You should continue staying at JA's until I sort this out. Whatever is happening here, clearly it has escalated.'

'Has Julie-Anne told you the whole story?'

'Yes, I think so. I know what is transpiring here. They've gone too far this time and will pay for what they have done to her,' he said.

'Did you see who hit her?'

'Yes, a man of Asian appearance jumped out of the car to grab JA's laptop bag from the road.'

Melissa scrolled through her phone until she found the photo she wanted. 'Is this him?' she asked bluntly.

Jack looked up from the phone and noticed tears forming in the corner of her eyes. The realisation of what she had innocently facilitated had hit home. He pulled her into an embrace.

'I'm so, so sorry,' she cried.

'I'll get him, I promise.' She wrapped her arms around him and held him tightly. Jack felt slightly uncomfortable the longer they held each other. He released his hold and stepped back. 'I'll get him, Melissa.'

She stared back at him with hopeful eyes. 'I believe you will too, Jack.'

'Now, just so you know, I'm sending a technician to JA's apartment to sweep it for bugs, so don't be alarmed if the entry buzzer goes off.' Jack couldn't tell Melissa that someone had been in the apartment yesterday for fear of further distressing her. 'It's just a precaution.'

'Thank you,' she said softly as she moved forward and hugged him again.

Jack was driving down Oxford Street towards his office and he called JA's editor, Chris Russell. He provided Russell with a brief account of the morning's event and advised him that she had not suffered any serious injuries.

'Well, I'm glad she's okay, Jack. That's a huge relief, particularly after what happened earlier in the year. I haven't spoken to her for a few days, so I guess she must have been making significant progress in her investigation if someone's gone to that extent to silence her.'

'Yeah, I know, Chris, but she needs to seriously consider the nature of the investigations she takes on. This can't keep happening and she might not be so lucky third time around. When she recovers I'm going to have a talk to her on a personal level. On a professional basis I think you should do the same.'

'I will, Jack, but you know as well as I do, she's like a dog with a bone once she gets the scent of anything improper.'

'All too well, Chris. Can you arrange another mobile for her and a tablet would be good too? JA will definitely want to keep her investigation moving forward when she's well enough.'

'Yes, I'll do it now and then go to the hospital and see her.'

'Cheers, Chris.'

79. Ministerial Offices – Martin Place

Wednesday 3rd June

It was early afternoon and Ben Chandler was thinking about grabbing a sandwich before making the short stroll to Parliament House for the Government Business session that he was required to attend. Normally this was a boring part of being a member of the government, but today he was glad to be attending and then continuing on to question time at two fifteen. Julie-Anne Granger had asked for forty eight hours to resolve his extortion case and both these tedious parliamentary activities would take his mind off his predicament for a few hours. He was eagerly looking forward to meeting with her later this afternoon though. His personal mobile rang. It was unusual for his wife to call him during business hours. She was usually too busy doing whatever it was she did to talk to him. He began to feel anxious.

'Hi, Sonja.'

'I'll give you fucking hi, Sonja. How could you do that to me, you bastard?' she yelled down the phone.

He hoped this day would never come, but it was always a possibility as the extortionist ramped up his threats. 'What are you talking about, Sonja?' he asked dispassionately.

'Don't act all innocent. You know damn well what I'm saying. You fucking some Asian hooker.'

He could do the deny, deny, deny thing, but what was the

point? His wife had obviously received a photo of him and Sophie in a compromising position. 'She's not a hooker,' he responded, too defensively.

'Oh, well, I suppose that just makes it all okay then, you bastard,' she ranted.

He could hear her crying now. *Why was she crying?* She hadn't shown any interest in him, either emotionally or physically for a long time. It had been ages since they had shared a bed and they were just as emotionally disconnected. She was probably more concerned about her reputation among her precious girl's breakfast club. If they found out her reputation would be in tatters and she would be a pariah around Woy Woy.

'Who is she then?' she demanded through her tears.

Out of respect for Sophie he wouldn't say she was a nobody, although neither could he confess that he was in love with her. Not now anyway. Like many politicians when faced with a challenging decision he opted for a vague response. 'Just someone I met one day.'

'What, do you sleep with and screw everyone you meet?' she argued in between sobs.

He was about to say he would be home tomorrow night and they could discuss it then, when he remembered his dinner date with Sophie. Plus, after what had transpired in the past week, he had a responsibility to tell her what she had inadvertently become involved in. She would be horrified. 'I'll be home on Friday and we can talk about it then, Sonja.'

Loretta, his executive assistant peaked in through the door. 'Is everything okay, Mr Chandler?'

'Yes, I'm fine,' he replied curtly.

'Who was that?'

'Just Loretta, my EA.'

'Jesus, Ben, you haven't even tried to apologise.'

He was silent while he considered his response. 'No, I haven't.'

'What's happened to you?'

Now he was becoming agitated. 'What's happened to me? Where have you been for the past six months, Sonja? You've been too busy doing whatever it is you do. We never see each other, when we do you're always busy on the phone chatting to whomever and we don't even get to spend quality time together. When was the last time we even shared a bed?'

'What?' she blurted out in anger. 'Now you're blaming me. This is nothing but duplicity on your part.'

He sighed. 'I'm not blaming you for anything. We've grown apart.'

'Oh, so that's the best excuse you can come up with; we've grown apart. Do you know how pathetic that sounds? Normal couples having difficulty in their relationships make a commitment to work at it together or at least give counselling a try. We've done none of that,' she said through a sniffle.

'Really, Sonja? When were we even going to talk about it? You're always so darn busy.'

'And you're always in Sydney playing the consummate politician. That's worked out well for you,' she said sarcastically. 'Anyway, who would send me such a disgusting photo, and why?'

'I'm being blackmailed.' They wouldn't resolve anything over the phone. 'Let's not do this now. I'll see you on Friday, Sonja,' he replied exasperatedly then disconnected the call.

Ben Chandler knew it was a standard forty eight hour delivery time from Sydney to Woy Woy, so the offending photo must have been sent on Monday. That was the same day the second envelope arrived at Sonja's office. Whoever was really behind this had obviously upped the ante to keep him focused on their demands. He wished Julie-Anne had made her discoveries a little earlier.

'Mr Chandler, there's a call for you on line two,' said Loretta Farrelly on the desk phone intercom. 'It's a Detective Wagner.'

Ben Chandler wondered if this could be the detective that Julie-Anne had mentioned could be trusted. Why was he calling him now and why hadn't Ms Granger alerted him first?

'Ben Chandler.'

'Mr Chandler, my name is Jack Wagner and I am with the Australian Federal Police.'

'Hello, Detective. What can I do for you?'

'I believe you were due to meet with Julie-Anne Granger this afternoon.'

'Yes, I was. You said *were*. Has something happened to her?'

'Yes, she was run down by a vehicle in Goulburn Street this morning and is now in St Vincent's.'

'Oh, my god. Is she okay?'

'She has concussion and numerous bumps, abrasions and bruises, but she will be okay.'

'Thank heavens.'

'I would like to come and speak with you, Minister? Now, if you don't mind,' Jack demanded.

Chandler was quiet, so Jack allowed him time to consider his position. After an awkward pause, the minister spoke. 'Okay, bring some evidence that Ms Granger is actually working with you, so I know that she has confided in you.'

'I'll be there in fifteen.'

Chandler called for Loretta. 'Can you make an apology for me regarding my attendance at the Government Business session, please?'

80. Ministerial Offices – Martin Place

Wednesday 3rd June

Loretta knocked on the door, and without pausing, continued into the office. 'Detective Wagner is here to see you and I have cancelled your remaining appointments for the day.' She took a deep breath. 'Is everything alright, Minister?'

'Yes,' he replied too harshly. 'Show him in please.'

Ben Chandler moved around to the front of his desk. 'Good afternoon, Detective. Let's sit over here,' Chandler said while ushering Jack across to the pair of sofas.

Jack dived in straight away. 'Mr Chandler, do you know why Ms Granger was meeting with you this afternoon?'

'Yes, but why don't you tell me, so I know that you and Ms Granger are actually working on this issue together.'

Jack sighed out of exasperation. 'It was my technician who printed your suite, Mr Chandler and I was the one who confirmed the name of the perpetrator who planted the video camera. And, in case you need a kicker, Sophie Zhao is also a friend of mine, so you could say I have a vested interest in this *issue*, as you so eloquently call it.'

'Alright, I'm sorry for my arrogance. It's been a tough day already, even before you told me about Ms Granger's accident. I had just got off the phone from my wife who now has an incriminating photo herself.'

'I'm sorry to hear that. And by the way, Ms Granger being run over wasn't an accident.'

Chandler's eyes widened. 'What? Oh, no. She was deliberately targeted because of me, wasn't she?' he asked, now feeling distraught.

'You can't think that way. She is a fearless journalist who sometimes pushes things to the limit, but she is well aware of the risks. This is the second time in three months that she has been attacked and ended up in hospital. She could have died twice, so with Julie-Anne working your case, you have a fierce, unflinching ally. She will give it everything she has until it is resolved. As will I.'

'I gained that same impression when I met her too. As you can imagine, as a politician I was initially sceptical. Politicians and reporters are like oil and water at times, although we both realise that we need each other, albeit for vastly differing reasons. This situation is no different. Given my very public persona I don't let people into my life without good reason. Her research was impeccable, she was tenacious and how quickly she analysed what was occurring was impressive to say the least.'

'Yes it was. I am going to become more involved in her investigation now. From a personal perspective Ms Granger obviously can't continue at the moment, so I'm going to take up the case on her behalf and also that of the AFP. Professionally, we can't have an elected public official being blackmailed by operatives closely linked to an overseas government.'

'Whoa, detective. What do you mean by that? That's a stretch.' Chandler became nervous at the mention of a foreign government.

'Not at all, Minister. Between Ms Granger and I we have established the identity of the man who inserted the camera into your hotel suite. His name is Sun Jie, he was a short term employee of the International and his visa application was sponsored by the Chinese Shipping Company. The CSC has close ties to the Chinese Communist Party. Sun Jie shares the same address as that of a Paul Gao, who was apparently in possession of the photos. As it turns out, Gao is a Special Emissary for the Chinese Consulate here in Sydney. By logical extension that would appear to implicate the Consul General. And as Ms Granger would say, this probably goes all the way to Beijing. Does that seem like a stretch to you now, Minister?' Jack asked boldly.

'Okay, you made your point, detective. Thank you. Now that you have outlined that little scenario, it is probably appropriate that I should tell you that the Consul General first paid me a visit a couple of weeks ago.'

Jack was caught between anger and curiosity now. 'What, and you didn't think to tell Ms Granger about this little snippet of information?' He breathed deeply. 'Go on,' he said while leaning forward.

'To put it plainly for you, Xiao asked me to reinstate the Confucius Institute program into New South Wales state schools. It is a program that—'

Jack cut him off. 'I know what it is Minister and I know a little about Chinese interference in Australia, too. Ms Granger brought me up to speed on both subjects. And to put it plainly for you, she suggested to me that you were being blackmailed for that very same reason.'

'Yes, I am.' Chandler opened his briefcase and extracted a mustard coloured A4 envelope, turned it over and handed it to Jack.

Jack read the message on the label of the second photo. "You will reinstate the Confucius Institute." 'Minister, when did you receive the first photo? Better still, give me a timeline between the Consul General's visit, you and Sophie at the International and the arrival of the first photo.'

Ben Chandler pulled his diary from his briefcase and flicked through the pages until he found what he was looking for. 'Xiao came to see me on the nineteenth of May and the first photo must have arrived on Thursday the twenty eighth.'

'Okay, so nine days after the Consul General's visit you received the first photo. That would have provided them with ample time to enact their plan. What night did Sophie stay with you at the hotel?'

'It was a Monday night, so it had to be the twenty fifth.'

'Is your commute schedule always the same, as in, same days of the week and do you always stay in the same suite?'

'Yes, to both. I arrive at the office on Mondays around midday and usually leave on Thursday afternoon.'

'So, somewhere between the twentieth and twenty fourth of May they have installed their camera into your suite. My guess was it would have been over the weekend when there would have been a lower occupancy and less staff on duty. That would be four or five days after the Consul General's meeting with you.'

'Your timeline makes sense, detective.'

'Who else other than Ms Granger and me, is aware of this situation?'

'Well, obviously my wife now, and myself.'

'You haven't told Sophie or your executive assistant?'

'No. I am having a discreet dinner with Sophie tomorrow night and I plan to tell her then.'

'Good, she deserves to be forewarned and she can be trusted to maintain the necessary discretion. What about the Premier?'

'Not yet, but I can't withhold it from her for much longer. The last thing the government needs now is a scandal of this proportion while they're dealing with the pandemic. And then there is also the state and federal government's relationships with China to be considered. If this leaks it will provide the China conspiracy theorists with plenty of ammunition.'

'Do you have both photos and the envelopes that they arrived in? I would like to send them to the lab and see if we can extract DNA samples from them. If we're lucky that may lead us directly to Gao.'

'Will they be discreet?'

'Yes. They're technical guys who get excited by their scientific findings, not explicit photos.' Jack pulled a cotton bud out of an evidence bag and passed it to the Minister. 'We need a sample of your own DNA, just so we can exclude you.' Chandler swabbed the inside of his mouth and handed it back to Jack along with the envelopes.

'Thank you, Minister.' Jack placed the swab in an evidence bag and rose from the sofa. 'Minister, I have work to do, but please call me if there are any further developments, and I will reciprocate.' It was crucial that Jack had the Minister's confidence. 'I give you my word.'

'Thank you again and please pass on my best wishes to Ms Granger.'

'You might want to do that yourself, Minister.'

81. St Vincent's Hospital

Wednesday 3rd June

It was mid-afternoon when Chris Russell quietly padded into Julie-Anne's hospital room. Her head and face were littered with bandages, pads and bruises and her eyes were closed. He was shocked at her appearance, but would maintain a stoic demeanour for her benefit. He was placing her replacement laptop and mobile phone on the bedside cabinet when he heard the rustle of the bedsheets. 'Hi, JA, how are you feeling?'

'I've been better, boss,' she replied feebly.

'Judging by your appearance that would be the understatement of the year.'

'Can you help me sit up please?'

He placed his hand behind her back for support, gently eased her forward and adjusted the pillows for her. 'Is that better?'

'Yes, I'm good now. Thanks.'

'Aah, JA, what are we going to do with you?' he asked, sighing.

'I'll be fine, I just need a day or two of rest, that's all.'

'A day or two, really? How about a week or two?'

'No,' she cried. 'I have an ongoing investigation and I'm getting close to bringing it to a conclusion. We should be able to run it this Saturday. Back to back investigative features on consecutive Saturdays. How good would that be, Chris?' she said excitedly.

'It would be a spectacular result, but not at the expense of your health and well-being, nor your safety for that matter, JA.'

'I'll be fine.'

Russell was truly exasperated now. 'JA, you need to back off before you get yourself killed. You are pushing too hard in your investigations without taking the necessary precautions. I hadn't heard from you for a few days, so I mistakenly thought you weren't making much progress. Obviously, I was wrong. If I had known you were in danger I would have had David Bedford's guys keep an eye on you.'

'Chris, I had no idea it would come to this.' After pushing the envelope too far with Paul Gao she knew he wouldn't take it lightly. At this stage she didn't definitively know that he was behind this, but who else could it realistically be?

'Alright, let's agree to disagree for now. Will you at least focus on your recovery and I will check-in again tomorrow and then we'll see how you're doing,' he said to placate her. 'Tomorrow's only Thursday, so we have some time. Agreed?'

'Okay.'

'I brought your replacement laptop and mobile phone,' he said while gesturing at the cabinet. 'I almost wish I hadn't though. The tech guys have set them up and they're ready to go.'

Julie-Anne reached for his hand. 'Thanks, Chris, I appreciate it. I'll be fine.'

Julie-Anne logged into both of her new devices. Firstly, she checked the voice messages on her mobile. They were mostly mundane tips and complaints from people wanting her to look into their own personal problems. She saw the final message was from Jordan Doherty earlier this morning. *'I've checked the weather forecast like you asked.'* He had cleverly turned her raincheck comment on its head for comedic effect, and it worked.

She smiled to herself. *"There is no rain forecast over the next four days, so we can comfortably have that Jalapeno Margarita at El Loco without getting drowned. What do you say?"* She liked this man and now realised she did actually want to see him again, but definitely not while looking like this. She was feeling a tad better, so she would call him.

'Julie-Anne, nice to hear from you.'

'You too, Jordan. Thanks for your message. It was very funny, Rainman. How are you?'

'I'm all good thanks, although I'm missing my favourite comedienne. Do you know where she is?'

'No, but if I see her I'll be sure to have her call you.'

'Aah, I see you're still doing your Fanny Brice routine.'

'What?' she asked innocently.

'Fanny Brice was the title character in the film Funny Girl and she was played beautifully by Barbara Streisand.'

'Oh, okay, I get it now. I really do need to get out more.' She regretted her choice of words as soon as they left her mouth and she knew he wouldn't miss the opportunity.

As if on cue he said, 'I can help you with that, hence the reason for my call. How about we do El Loco again and have that Jalapeno Margarita you were longing for on Sunday?'

'That's sweet, but I don't know if I can. There's a few things going on in my life at the moment, so I'm juggling somewhat, Jordan,' she replied.

'If by juggling you mean men then that's fine, I'll just—'

Damn, she had given him the wrong impression. She cut him off. 'No, no, not at all, it's not like that, really,' she responded too eagerly.

'No, it's okay if you are. I don't want to complicate your life, so I'll leave you to your juggling.'

She didn't know this man very well, but given what she had experienced so far, she liked him. He was charming and funny, and persistent. She didn't want to lose him before she even had the opportunity to get to know him better. Between her recovery, the incomplete investigation and her deadline to publish she had no time for socialising, well at least until Saturday anyway. 'What about later in the week; let's say Saturday?' she suggested.

She heard him sigh in relief and thought that was cute. 'That sounds good to me. I'll call you on Friday if that's okay, Julie-Anne.'

'That works for me,' she replied. *Geez, I hope these bandages are gone and the bruises have subsided by then.* She imagined turning up at El Loco looking like a female version of the elephant man.

She had only just disconnected the call when Jack walked in. *What timing.*

'Hi,' he said cheerily. 'I see you're back in business and have your phone and laptop already. There'll be no stopping you now.'

'Hello, Jack. This must be three times in one day. Who'd have guessed?' She laughed at her own reference to a comment she had once made when they were in a relationship.

'Now, where have I heard that before? You're a funny girl.'

Julie-Anne flinched at his use of the term funny girl and wondered whether he had overheard her phone call with Jordan. 'I don't feel all that hilarious at the moment, Jack.'

'You'll be much better before you know it. Now, back to business. Are you okay to talk?'

'Yeah, sure. What have you been up to?'

'You were due to meet with the Minister this afternoon, so I went in your place. Another photo has been received.'

'Was there another message?'

'No, there didn't need to be. It was delivered to his wife this time, and she's not a happy girl, as you can well imagine.'

'Damn. Gao's ramping up his campaign of intimidation. We need to find him, Jack, and soon. We won't be able to keep this under wraps for long.'

'Sanderson's on the case now, so we'll see what he digs up. I'll call him shortly for an update. Now that you have your new mobile and laptop I can tell you a couple of things. Firstly, you weren't the target.'

'Really, so how come I am stuck in here all banged up?' she asked, disbelievingly.

'Let me finish. They were after your laptop bag and obviously your electronic devices. You were collected by the car door and flipped back onto the sidewalk. If you were really the target they would have simply driven straight at you—' He stopped himself mid-sentence. 'Sorry.'

She felt a shiver shooting down her spine at the thought of that. 'I suppose you're right. What's the other thing?'

'I identified Gao as the guy who jumped out of the car and grabbed your bag.'

'How, Jack?'

'Melissa showed me a photo of him. It was definitely Gao.'

What goes around comes around. She had brought this upon herself and knew she had to seriously rethink about how she went about her job. 'Oh, well, I suppose that at least confirms that our investigation is heading in the right direction,' she replied matter of factly.

He thought she might be more excited about his revelation. Something came into his head and he gave her a quizzical look. 'You never did tell me how you managed to have the photos in your possession, JA.'

Christ, it was like he was reading her mind. She would have to come clean with him at some stage, but she had no idea how she could satisfactorily explain her ignoble behaviour. She fixed him with a determined gaze. 'No, I didn't.'

Jack knew her well enough to know when to move on. No doubt she would tell him in her own time. 'I sent Gao a message through our WhatsApp group.'

'What did you say?'

'I'm coming for you, Gao.'

'Hello, you two.' Ben Chandler said cheerily as he entered the room carrying a large bunch of colourful flowers wresting across his arm. His expression changed to one of shock. 'My God, what have they done to you, Ms Granger?'

'I have calls to make, so I'll leave you two to chat,' said Jack. 'I'll call you later, JA.'

'Okay, thanks, Jack.'

'It looks worse than it is, Ben,' she responded. 'Thank you for coming and for the lovely flowers too. Orange gerberas and purple Irises. I love them,' she cooed.

'Somehow I didn't think you were a pastel kind of girl, so I brought strong colours to match your strength of character, Ms Granger.'

'Julie-Anne, please. That's awfully perceptive of you. How are you doing, Ben?'

'Did Detective Wagner tell you about my wife?'

'Yes, and I'm very sorry.'

'Well, subsequent to the phone call from my wife I cancelled all of my appointments for the remainder of the day. I then found myself with some free time and voila, here I am.'

'I don't know what to say.' He had brought everything upon himself with his affair with Sophie and normally she wouldn't have any sympathy for his predicament. Her attitude was softened somewhat given her good friend was involved. 'What are you going to do, Ben?'

'It's not about me this afternoon, it's all about you. What have they done to you, Ms Granger? Oops, Julie-Anne.'

'Apparently, I must be getting close to the truth if they're resorting to something so brazen as a daylight hit and run, and right outside the AFP headquarters no less. Jack suggested that I wasn't the target, rather they were after my electronic devices for their contents. I have everything backed up anyway, but unfortunately they will now be aware of what I have uncovered. Ben, they will now escalate their activities as a result, so you should be prepared for that.'

'Sorry, I need to take this,' he said upon hearing a unique ringtone on his mobile.

Moments later Ben Chandler re-entered her room. 'Julie-Anne, I'm awfully sorry, but I have to go. That was the Premier and she wants to see me. Now. She was quite sharp in her tone and didn't sound very happy at all. Get well soon.'

'That sounds ominous.'

'Doesn't it just?'

'Thanks for coming, Ben, I appreciate it.'

82. NSW Premier's Office – 52 Martin Place

Wednesday 3rd June

Ben Chandler had his driver drop him outside of Parliament House and he walked the final few hundred metres down the hill to the Premier's office. He used the time to clear his head and prepare for whatever was troubling the Premier. A minute number of people were aware of the extortion, so it surely couldn't be that. *So why the urgency?* Upon arriving at Fifty Two Martin Place he rode the elevator up to the twelfth floor and presented himself at two desks occupied by the Premier's executive assistants.

'Good evening, Minister. Go straight in; they're waiting for you,' one of them gushed in her professional voice.

They're waiting for you. Such a simple phrase had turned this situation on its head. *What was this all about?* Ben breathed deeply, slowly exhaled, then knocked on the door to the Premier's suite and calmy entered the hallowed domain.

He was surprised to see the Secretary to the Department of Premier and Cabinet in attendance. Tony Riordan stood and offered his elbow in greeting.

'Hello, Ben,' said the Premier. 'You know Philip Thompson.'

'Yes, of course. Hello Philip.' Thompson was the government's legal counsel and if he was in attendance then the Premier obviously had a serious issue to deal with. Ben now understood all too clearly what that must be.

'It's late, Ben, so let's get on with this,' said the Premier. She was seated behind her large mahogany desk and her uncompromising expression told him she was all business. 'Something highly concerning has been brought to my attention and we need to discuss how we're going to handle it. More specifically how we mitigate any exposure for the government.'

That didn't take them long. True to form, they were already displaying their concerns for the government, not him.

'How can I help, Premier?' he asked feigning naivety.

She sat forward and leant on the desk. 'Let me come straight to the point, Ben. I have been informed that there is currently an investigation being run into an alleged extortion attempt that you are at the centre of.' She held his gaze, but he maintained his composure and did not respond. 'I assume this is ringing bells for you,' she stated grimly while staring him down. 'Well?'

'It's all under control. I've been dealing with it, Premier,' he responded, projecting self-assurance.

'Dealing with it, really? How did you allow yourself to be placed in a position in the first place whereby you could be compromised? What's going on here, Ben?'

'What's occurring here is that we withdrew the Confucius Institute from the state high school's curriculum last year and China isn't taking no for an answer,' he replied with conviction.

'Yes, I get that and we knew that would be the case. What concerns me though is what incriminating information do the perpetrators have on you that would allow you to be compromised.'

'What have you been told?'

'No, it doesn't work that way, I'm asking the questions here, Ben,' the Premier responded sharply.

He looked across to Riordan and Thompson and back to

the Premier. 'Do we have to have this conversation with an audience? Does this really need to be for public consumption?'

The premier breathed a sigh. 'Tony, Phil give us the room, please.' Chandler watched as the two senior bureaucrats begrudgingly rose from their chairs and left the room. 'Okay, let's have it, Ben.'

He drew in a deep breath and exhaled slowly. 'I have been caught in somewhat of a compromising position—'

The Premier interrupted him. 'I know that much already.'

'No, I've been caught in a compromising position, literally. Someone installed a hidden camera in my hotel suite and now as a result they have incriminating photos of me in their possession.'

'How bad are they?'

'Apparently there's six of them all together, but I've only seen two and they're incriminating enough,' he replied with head bowed.

'And I'm guessing it's not Sonja.'

'No, it's another woman who I allowed myself to become close to.'

'Jesus, Ben, you've done an outstanding job navigating the school system through the coronavirus pandemic. How could you allow yourself to be distracted like this, and compromised for that matter?'

'I certainly didn't plan on it. As you are acutely aware political life can be all-consuming and I sometimes need a release while working in this goldfish bowl. So, I occasionally avail myself of the services of an escort just for a discreet dinner and some company, nothing else.'

'And then you went back for more with this woman.'

'Yes. There's not much happening on the home-front these days between my career, Sonja busy being busy and the boys growing up.'

'So you found comfort from someone else.'

'No, not really. It just evolved and now I've become enchanted with her.'

'Just great, and as a result you're now being blackmailed to reinstate the Confucius Institute.'

He sighed. 'That pretty much sums it up, but it has become more complicated than that. There is a very resourceful investigative journalist from the Daily News who found out about it and she has pursued it like a dog with a bone. Ms Granger was the one who involved the AFP once it became obvious that the situation was escalating and she needed their support.'

'Julie-Anne Granger?'

'Yes, do you know her?'

'No, only by her reputation. She's well respected.'

'As a result of her investigation she was run down in Goulburn Street this morning and all her devices were stolen. Fortunately, she is okay apart from numerous aches, pains, bruises and a mild concussion.'

'My God, Ben, what a mess. Where is the investigation up to? The state police haven't given me much.'

'The state police aren't involved, that's why. Ms Granger and the AFP detective are certain they know who is behind it, although the AFP are yet to make their case or apprehend the culprit.'

'What's the link between this and the Confucius Institute?'

'The alleged perpetrator is apparently a special emissary with the Chinese Consulate and I just know in my heart that the Consul General, and through him Beijing, are behind this.'

'Christ, Ben, this has the capacity to develop into an international incident. You know what that could do to our reputation, particularly as a preferred education destination for a hundred thousand Chinese students.'

'I know, however, in the current geopolitical climate I don't think having a disagreement with China is such a negative thing. They're becoming international bully boys and this is a prime example, Premier.'

She sighed. 'Yes, they are, but we have to handle this delicately.'

Chandler could feel his face flushing and he felt like exploding. 'Jesus, Susan. They're using extortion to realise their goals and Ms Granger could have been killed this morning. What's next, a bombing, a shooting, an assassination attempt?'

'Calm down, they won't get away with it. All I'm saying is that we have to deal with this sensitively.'

'Well, it may not be your choice. The AFP are involved and they might not be so accommodating.'

'Now, what are we going to do with you, Ben?'

'I'm going to continue to do my job and hope that the AFP can wrap this up quickly and quietly.'

'You're just fortunate that we don't have an election for another three years. This could have seriously damaged the reputation of the government and hindered our chances of re-election. What about the woman. Can she be relied on to maintain her discretion?'

'Yes, I am having dinner with her tonight and I intend to lay it all out for her.'

'What? You're going back for more. You need to end this, and swiftly, Ben.'

'That's not going to happen, Premier,' he replied defiantly.

'Well, it's your career that's at stake, but I won't allow this government's excellent work throughout the pandemic to be tarnished. I hope for your sake the AFP can conclude this in a timely manner. And can Granger be relied on to be discreet i.e. leave your name out of this?'

'I sincerely hope so.'

'With the voracious twenty four hour media cycle driving

agendas no-one survives public scandals these days. The alternative won't be good for you or your career, Ben.'

'If there's nothing else I'll see myself out.'

'Keep me in the loop, Ben.'

83. St Vincent's Hospital

Thursday 4th June

Julie-Anne was leaning across to the bedside cabinet rearranging the flowers and smiling warmly when Jack walked into her private room early the following morning

'Look at you gushing over the flowers,' Jack said, pleased to see she was on the improve.

'I love receiving flowers, Jack.'

'Did I ever send you flowers?'

'No, Jack, gift giving wasn't one of your strong points.'

'Mmmm, okay,' he said as grabbed the drawstring to open the blinds. 'It's quite dark in here.'

'No, don't open them, please.'

'How come?'

'The doctor warned me that people with a concussion, even a mild one, can be sensitive to bright light which can lead to a range of symptoms including headache and nausea. And I have enough going on with my head and body already.'

'Okay, that makes sense. Now, I have some more news for you. I have just spoken to Michael and he's been a busy boy overnight. He and his offsider from Day Street went to Gao's Camperdown apartment last evening. On the pretence of hearing a disturbance, he kicked the door in and they had a snoop around.'

Julie-Anne was becoming anxious now and racking her brain for anything she might have left behind in her rush to safety on Saturday night. 'Did they find anything?' she asked as nonchalantly as she could manage.

'Not a lot. The joint was sparsely furnished and devoid of the usual trimmings and homely comforts. Sanderson said it appeared very much like a bachelor pad. There wasn't even any food or drink in the apartment. I think Gao probably kept it that way so he could disappear at a moment's notice if required. He's either in the wind or has moved house.'

She was relieved. 'That's a shame. It will be more difficult to locate him if you think he's dropped out of sight.'

'All is not completely lost. Michael found a pair of unwashed champagne glasses on the coffee table, so he took them to the lab first thing this morning for printing. Gao has obviously had a visitor or accomplice at his apartment in the past few days, so we'll hopefully find out who that was and see if there's a connection to the Chandler case.'

Julie-Anne thought she might throw up, her heart began to pound and she felt the blood draining from her face. Unless Gao had had another visitor since Saturday night her prints would be all over one of those glasses.

Jack detected the sudden change in her demeanour. 'Are you okay?'

She had to think, and quickly. 'Sure, I'm just a tad tired. I think it's all catching up with me. The state police were here until late last night taking my statement.'

'Do you want me to come back later?'

'No, continue, please.'

'Okay, secondly, and more importantly, Gao's car has been located.'

'That's great news, Jack. They should be able to extract his

DNA from the Impreza and the witnesses and traffic cameras should place the car at the scene of my incident—'

'Hold up, JA,' he interrupted. 'The Impreza was found burnt out in an industrial area at the back of Silverwater.'

'Bugger, there goes that opportunity then.'

'It gets worse. The charred remains of a male person were found in the trunk of the vehicle.'

'Really? I would like that to be Gao, but I seriously doubt it. He's too smart to let someone get the better of him like that. My guess is he's cleaning house and has disposed of Sun Jie. Melissa will be horrified that her ex whatever he was could be so ruthless and kill with no conscience at all.'

'He would only do something that extreme if he was feeling the pressure. The question we have to ask ourselves is who has turned up the heat on him, other than you of course.'

'I have no proof, Jack, but I'll guarantee you it is the Consul General. He wrote that article last year condemning the decision to close the Institute. Beijing will still be appalled and embarrassed by that and will be pushing Xiao hard to have it reinstated. They have lost face in their eyes and won't be disposed to backing off. That's why the Consul General met with Ben Chandler and when that proved ineffective he resorted to more traditional methods of intimidation. Gao works for him as his Special Emissary, however, he doesn't have the political smarts for a role of that importance. He's Xiao's heavy hitter, that's all.'

'I agree; it has to be Xiao. After all he is the Chinese government's representative in New South Wales, so the onus would be on him to do their bidding.'

'Unless of course there's another Li Qiang floating around out there somewhere, which I'm sure there could be.'

Jack sat on the end of the bed. 'Back to Gao. Sanderson made a good point this morning. Whoever is responsible for incinerating the Impreza would had to have access to a second vehicle for their getaway. Calling an Uber or taxi would have attracted unwanted attention to his location and provided witnesses, so it's not unreasonable to assume that the second vehicle would be Sun Jie's. Sanderson has tracked down the vehicle's registration and has issued a KALOF for it as well as for Gao.'

Julie-Anne was sceptical. 'If the state cops intercept it and arrest him, do they have enough to charge him?'

'Not for the extortion, but certainly for deliberately running you down. They could charge him with intention to kill, reckless driving causing injury, leaving the scene of an accident, etc, etc.'

'Jack, can we get the KALOF changed to follow rather than intercept? He could lead us to his latest accommodation, then you could obtain a warrant to search it and who knows what would turn up.'

'At the moment I think I would rather have him in custody, particularly so we can obtain a sample of his DNA. We may get something positive back from the DNA tests on the photos and envelopes and then we would have him on the extortion charge as well. It also eliminates the risk of him going to ground if he gets suspicious or spooked.'

'Okay, you're the detective, handsome,' she said.

'Now I'm handsome, huh,' he replied.

She laughed. 'You were always attractive to the eye, just not attentive, Jack,' she said, glancing at the flowers.

'Okay, look while I'm here I may as well tell you about our friend Wie. I finally got to interview him on Tuesday, and while he wouldn't reveal who the head of the syndicate was, he did provide me with a puzzle to solve.'

'What sort of puzzle?'

'He provided me with some clues that may lead to me finally solving the importation case.' He told her about Wie's assertion that there was a common denominator linking the

China Shipping Company, Li Qiang, the Confucius Institute, something called the United Front Work Department and the Consul General. 'Obviously, that has to be a person, so all I have to do is join the dots. Easier said than done though,' he admitted.

'I still have to write the second part of my feature on Wie's drug operation. Can I use any of that information?'

'Sure, you can make reference to it, although it's not much to go on from an investigative perspective. For either of us.'

'Okay, what if I just allude to a figurehead rumoured to have links to various Chinese related government and business institutions? It sounds a bit tabloid, but I think I'll get away with it.'

'I can't stop you, so knock yourself out.'

'I've done that once this week already.'

Jack laughed along with her. 'That you have. I have to go. Here's Melissa anyway, so you'll still have some company.'

'Hi, guys,' Melissa said as she bounced into the room. She gave Jack a firm hug and then headed for Julie-Anne. 'How are you feeling?'

'A little better today, although I'm still pretty sore.' Julie-Anne winced as she tried to sit upright. 'Ouch.'

'I'm sorry I couldn't come back yesterday, but a couple of Jack's tech guys turned up at your apartment and were waving these weird looking wands around. What's that all about?'

'They're radiofrequency detectors. I didn't want to unnecessarily alarm you, but someone was in my apartment sometime on Tuesday, so I asked Jack to have the place swept for electronic bugs.'

Melissa's hand went to her mouth. 'Am I safe staying there?'

'Did the locksmith turn up and change the locks?'

'Yes. It was then that I became more than just a little concerned.'

'You'll be fine, Melissa. There's nothing there that's of any use to them, whoever they are, although I'm pretty sure we both know who "they are",' she said making air quotes.

'Okay, you're the expert,' Melissa replied.

'I sure don't feel like it laying here all banged up.' Julie-Anne paused. 'There is something else I should tell you.'

'The Impreza that Gao was driving when he struck me has been found burnt out. Someone has incinerated the vehicle and the charred remains of a body were found in the trunk.'

Melissa's eyes widened with alarm and the colour drain from her face. 'Oh, no, was it Paul?'

'The remains haven't been identified, but I don't think it's him. It's more likely to be his offsider, Sun Jie. Melissa, I think that Paul killed his accomplice to remove the only person who can provide conclusive evidence against him. He is a dangerous man.'

Melissa was still ashen faced. 'I can't believe this is the same man that I considered to be my friend. He was always so kind and charming. He even shared my bed for heaven's sake. What sort of a judge of human nature am I?'

Julie-Anne noticed the sheen in her friend's eyes. 'Don't go beating yourself up. I'm sure he was genuinely fond of you. Things changed and he saw an opportunity once he realised you were my friend. He then used your relationship to his considerable advantage.'

'If only I hadn't introduced him to you in the first place none of this would have happened. Just look at you, Julie-Anne,' Melissa said, despairing.

'You can't think that way. The upside is that if you hadn't we wouldn't be any wiser to his activities, and if I'm correct, those of the Chinese Consul General. The Minister's career would be over and poor Sophie would be out there all alone in this mess. Now that we have Jack on the case we have an opportunity to make things right, for everyone concerned.'

'Thank you for saying that.' Melissa perked up. 'Okay, now you need to focus on your recovery so that you can publish your article and tell the whole world about it.'

'That's my girl.'

84. Day Street Police Station

Thursday 4th June

It was mid-afternoon and Detective Michael Sanderson had just about had enough of Thursday, especially after his nocturnal activities at Paul Gao's apartment the previous evening. It was a sparsely furnished apartment and the only items of interest he had come across were two unwashed champagne glasses. Commonsense said that one glass should contain Gao's fingerprints, but who was the second person who had been with him? Could it be an accomplice? Sanderson certainly hoped so. Rather than risk a courier, first thing this morning he had driven the evidence bag containing the champagne glasses to the Forensic Evidence and Technical Services lab out in Parramatta himself. Now, hours later he was emotionally drained, tired and his eyes were sore from staring at his desktop for hours on end while he updated his files on the open cases he was working. He was finally about to log off when a dialogue box popped up in the bottom corner of his screen. 'What now?' It was an email from the FETS lab. He was tempted to ignore it, but given the sensitivities surrounding the Minister's case that wasn't an option. He double clicked on the email and started to read the contents. 'Oh, shit,' he blurted out too loudly. Heads turned in the adjacent cubicles.

'Everything okay, Michael?'

'No, they're bloody well not.' He wouldn't be going home anytime soon, but that wasn't what triggered his anger. The FETS technician had emailed through the results of the prints taken at Gao's apartment. They had identified two separate sets of prints from the champagne flutes they had removed for testing. Unsurprisingly, the first prints were matched to Paul Gao from the samples held on file. It was the second result that had brought on his bout of angst. The prints taken from the second champagne flute were identified as belonging to a Julie-Anne Granger. He checked the address listed under this Julie-Anne Granger's name and sure enough, it was listed as an apartment in Newtown. Sanderson had never been there, but Jack had referenced the inner city suburb a few times back when he and Julie-Anne were dating. He had a myriad of thoughts racing through his mind, not the least asking himself, what the hell was she doing in Gao's apartment. He couldn't imagine any scenario that could lead to that conclusion, but fingerprints don't lie. Maybe there was another explanation, so he called Stuart Donaldson at Fingerprint Operations.

'Stuart, it's Michael Sanderson from Day Street. I have just received your email regarding the prints your guys identified from the champagne glasses last night.'

'Yeah, what about them?'

'Is it possible there could there be a mistake? Did your boys mix up the samples by any chance?' Sanderson knew that it was a long shot.

'No chance. I always double check the chain of custody myself before any results are distributed. It's as it should be with the paper trail confirming the collection, transfer, receipt, analysis and storage of the sample. The results are what they are.'

'Bugger, thanks, Stuart.'

'Is everything okay?'

'No, it's not,' he replied without the profanity this time.

Well that removed any element of doubt that was running through his mind about possible technical errors, so what to do now? He asked himself the question again. *What possible reason could Julie-Anne have to be in Gao's apartment?* The man was the prime suspect in an extortion investigation, so could there even be a plausible explanation. He knew exactly what he needed to do next, but he wasn't looking forward to making that particular phone call.

'Jack, it's Michael, how are you?'

'Good thanks. Did we get anything from the KALOF?'

'Not really. Jie's Corolla was spotted yesterday on Parramatta Road heading eastward towards town and then it disappeared near Stanmore. That's not far from Camperdown. Surely Gao wouldn't be stupid enough to go back to his own apartment. We were there until late last night and he didn't show. He's either moved or is on the run. The apartment's not far from the Consulate and we have eyes on both for a couple of days just in case.'

'Good. Now, the Minister provided me with the envelopes and photos he received and I've overnighted them to the AFP's new Digital Forensics Laboratory in Canberra. If Gao's DNA is on any of them they have the state of the art technology to identify and analyse it. We should have the results by tomorrow morning.'

'That's good news.' Sanderson hesitated before resuming. What he would say next wasn't going to go down well with Jack. He had previously been in a relationship with Julie-Anne and they were still close. 'There might be another way,' he said cautiously.

'Okay, that sounds interesting; let's hear it, buddy.'

'You might want to talk to Julie-Anne.'

'I have. I was at the hospital this morning.'

'Well, you might want to have another talk then, Jack.' Sanderson said before pausing for a second time.

'What's up, Michael?'

There was no subtle way to say what he had to, so Sanderson would come straight out with it. 'Her fingerprints were found on one of the champagne glasses in Gao's apartment.'

'Noooooo, that's not possible. There must be a mistake.'

'There's no mistake, Jack. I have spoken to Fingerprint Operations myself and they strictly adhered to the appropriate protocols that led to the positive identification. She was definitely in his apartment.'

Jack thought back to this morning when he visited JA at the hospital. Her demeanour had suddenly changed when he mentioned the search of Gao's apartment. *What was that about?* Now he knew. 'Alright, I'll head back to the hospital and have a chat to her. She is an investigative reporter after all and they're constantly pushing the boundaries, so I guess nothing's out of the question. I'll let you know what she says.'

'Jack, I'm knackered, so I'm heading home, but I'm intrigued to hear what she has to say for herself though.'

'Cheers, Michael, and thanks. I think.'

85. St Vincent's Hospital

Thursday 4th June

That same afternoon Julie-Anne was putting the finishing touches to her follow-up feature on the cocaine importation and distribution ring fronted by Wie Ping Lie. She was amazed at how rapidly her body was recovering from the physical trauma inflicted only thirty hours ago. Thank heavens for all those gym sessions. She still ached in half a dozen places, but mentally she felt okay, so she immersed herself into completing the second and final instalment of her feature. She commenced by providing a recap on her earlier story about Danielle Mortimer's deception and double life, the Chinatown based Triad openly operating, seemingly with impunity, and the arrest of Yong and Lucie Chan.

> *This reporter can now reveal that Danielle Mortimer was arrested at a storage facility in south-west Sydney in possession of a kilogram of cocaine. The arrest was the result of a targeted stakeout by members of a joint taskforce compromising the New South Wales state police and the Australian Federal Police.*

Does she remind her readers that Danielle had been in a

relationship with a high profile detective? Yes, she had to; it was a key component of the story.

> *The evidence would suggest that Miss Mortimer has morphed from a valued casino employee and the dutiful, loving girlfriend of a high profile detective into the drug courier of choice for the same Triad. This reporter has met Miss Mortimer in a social setting and found her to be a vibrant, vivacious young woman and is equally surprised at her rapid degeneration into the world of crime. She has now been charged under the Drug Misuse and Trafficking Act of 1985, with the supply and trafficking of a commercial quantity of a prohibited substance. That charge carries a maximum penalty of twenty five years in gaol.*
>
> *Her employer, the head of the same Chinatown based Triad, Wie Ping Lie has also been arrested and charged under the Act with the same offence. He is the fourth member of the notorious gang to be arrested and charged in the past week. This reporter understands that police are now seeking to identify senior Triad figures who may have their origins offshore. Requests for comment from the state and federal police were ignored.*

She was furiously typing on her laptop when she was interrupted by a familiar voice. 'JA,' Jack said as he barged in her private room.

'Hello, Jack.'

'We need to talk.'

Julie-Anne closed her laptop and levered herself upright. 'This sounds serious. What's happened since you were here earlier?'

'Your demeanour changed this morning when I mentioned

the champagne glasses that Sanderson found at Gao's apartment. Is that ringing a bell?'

After Jack told her about the glasses this morning it was only a matter of time before he found out the truth. As a result she had carefully deliberated over her response. 'Yes, it does. Why?'

'You know damn well why, JA,' he responded.

'Alright, I can explain.'

'This will be good,' he said cynically.

'Shut up,' she said angrily. 'I was only doing my job and maybe I pushed it too far.'

'How far, JA?'

He stared her down and she knew exactly what he would be thinking. And he would be correct of course, but no way was she ever going to admit that. *Ever.* It had been nearly a week since the night at Gao's, she was coming to terms with what she had done and the shame and guilt she felt was dissipating by the day. Her ex-boyfriend had become a trusted and valued friend and by not being honest and transparent with him she was putting that at risk. 'Not that far, Jack,' she fibbed. She needed to go on the front foot. 'Is this about you and me or the investigation? I'm confused.'

'Of course this is only about the investigation into Gao and his activities against the Minister,' he replied. 'Don't change the subject. How did your fingerprints end up on a champagne glass in Gao's apartment?'

'Okay, I'll tell you; it was nothing really,' she said. She hated lying to Jack, but the truth most definitely wasn't an option this time. She reminded him about noticing Gao following her from her apartment to King Street and how she had turned the tables on him. 'Then he surprised me by asking if I wanted to have a drink and I thought maybe I could find out what he was up to. We went to The Bank and that led to dinner and eventually a glass of bubbles on his balcony. There you go, Jack; now you know.'

'What a wonderful oversimplification, JA. What on earth were you doing drinking champagne on his balcony?'

'Is this still about the investigation?'

'Of course.'

'Okay, just checking. It just seemed like a fitting end to an interesting afternoon.'

'That's bullshit, and you know it. And then, only a few days later, he decides to run you down in broad daylight in the heart of the city. Apparently he didn't quite enjoy the balcony drinks as much as you did,' he said.

'Apparently not,' she replied glibly.

'JA, I'm a detective and as such, I have an enquiring and suspicious mind. You better than most are aware of that. There are two unexplained occurrences that I'm certain are linked. You have never told me how you came upon the photos, and secondly, why would Gao want to steal your laptop bag. He could have easily killed you, so we know you weren't the target. He wanted your laptop bag because he knew it probably contained the incriminating photos of the Minister. How am I doing, JA?' He fixed her with a stare. 'Well?'

She sighed. 'He fell asleep on the sofa, so I snooped around his apartment and eventually I found the photos. I took shots with my mobile and then left. Somehow he must have worked out what I had done. Maybe he had a little security trick of his own. There you go, Jack.' She felt better for getting that out at least, although it was only part of the sordid tale.

'So, let me get this straight. A guy who has illegally obtained, incriminating photos in his apartment just happens to fall asleep on the sofa. This allows the reporter who he started his day by following simply wander around his apartment unhindered looking for whatever,' he summarised. 'Have I got that correct, JA?'

'Pretty much.'

'Bullshit.'

'Think what you like, Jack.'

'I will. I'm sure there's more to the story than that, but at least I now know definitively that he is behind the extortion attempt.

Julie-Anne was relieved that the conversation was now moving in a different direction. 'Only if you can link him to Sun Jie and he won't be talking if his was the charred body in the Impreza.'

'We confirmed that the prints in Chandler's hotel suite belonged to Sun Jie, however, that is pretty much irrelevant now unless we can definitively link him to your friend Gao.'

'Yeah, I guess.'

'You should have called me, JA.'

'I had no time; it all transpired so quickly in one afternoon.'

'And evening by the sounds of it.' Jack's palm slapped his forehead as he had a light bulb moment. 'And that's how you knew about Jie's address. You'd actually been there.'

'Let it go, Jack,' she pleaded as she opened her laptop and resumed typing her story. She glanced up and watched him leave her room. The exchange hadn't gone well, but at least her indiscretions were out in the open now. *Well most of them.*

An hour later she had completed the first draft of the second instalment of her feature, prompted Chris Russell's name in the recipient box and clicked on the send icon.

86. Suite 2601 International Hotel

Thursday 4th June

Sophie sashayed across the bustling, light-filled atrium lobby of the restored sandstone, former Treasury Building that formed the heart of the International Hotel. She was in a buoyant mood as she passed the marble staircase and lion statues and made her way to the elevator. It had been ten long days since she had spent time with Ben and they had taken their friendship to the next level. He had been extremely busy, he had said, dealing with the impact of the pandemic on the schoolchildren of New South Wales. And of course, the weekend was off limits due to his time in Woy Woy. She was looking forward to seeing him again. This was to be a casual evening, so she was wearing her favourite Citizens of Humanity black jeans and a white long sleeve blouse with a lace hollow out. Her outfit was completed by a waist length, silver, sequinned jacket and matching pumps. She checked her appearance in the elevator's mirror and decided that maybe she should undo one more button of her blouse. *Mmmm, is that too much?* She flicked her shoulder length, silky black hair, turned on her heels and exited the elevator.

'Hello, Sophie, please come in.'

Ben closed the door behind him, grasped her hand, gently twirled her around and pulled her into a firm embrace.

'Nice move mister,' she said as she stepped back and curtsied for effect.

He held her by both hands, leant back and admired her. 'I've missed you.' He looked longingly into her dark, intelligent eyes. 'I'm not staring. I promise, I'm just appreciating everything about you. You are a magnificent woman.'

'Wow, what a reception, Ben. I've missed you too,' she said as she grasped his hands, leaned back and playfully mimicked him.

'Touché, Sophie. Now, make yourself comfortable while I pour us some bubbles. I thought we should have something special, so I arranged for a bottle of Bolly.'

'You've changed suites. I think I like this one better. Even softer tones.'

He felt self-conscious with every word that she uttered. He didn't want to articulate just yet exactly why he had to change suites. He intended to tell her about the whole sordid tale over dinner. He had planned something unique and hoped it would have the desired effect of minimising the fallout that would surely eventualise. 'The hotel kindly upgraded me,' he replied while facing away from her.

'Don't you go home to Woy Woy on Thursdays, Ben?'

'Normally I do, but I haven't seen you for ten days and I just couldn't wait another week. Cheers, Sophie, thank you for coming; I've missed you. Have I said that already?'

'Haha, yes. It's lovely to hear it again though. Cheers.'

They were interrupted by the chime of the suite's doorbell. 'Aha! With any luck this is my little surprise,' he said while rubbing his hands together in excitement.

'What's going on here, Ben? You're acting like the proverbial kid in the candy store again.'

He opened the door. 'Come on in please.' A waistcoated waiter with his starched white shirt, black trousers and black bow-tie walked into the suite pushing his room service cart.

'If you could just sign here please, sir.'

Sophie wondered just what the immaculately polished plate covers that filled the cart were hiding. 'What have we here? I thought we were going out for dinner,' she asked as the waiter exited the suite.

'I intended to, but then I had a little brainwave. As we haven't seen each other for some time I thought a quiet, intimate evening together would be more appropriate.' He would tell her the real reason behind their in-room dining later. 'Are you disappointed?'

'No, not at all. So, what have we here then?'

'Given the restrictions in place during the pandemic, Quay Restaurant are providing a delivery service through Uber Eats. So, I thought, rather than go to Quay, they can come to us.'

He began lifting the stainless steel dish covers one by one with the flourish of a magician. 'Okay, here we have beer-battered Barramundi fillets, grilled king prawns, crab claws, calamari, sea scallops and of course chunky chips. Check this out, Sophie.'

'What a wonderful idea. This is great,' she said while reaching for a scallop and dipping it into the tartare sauce.

'I'm sorry I couldn't get the Smoked Eel Cream with Seaweed and Ossetra for you.'

'Aah, you remembered.'

'Of course, I remember everything you've ever said to me. Unfortunately, the caviar's not on Quay's delivery menu.'

They were quiet for a few moments while they tucked into their seafood. Ben knew he had been delaying the inevitable. 'There's something we need to discuss, Sophie.'

His eyebrows were now raised and a broad frown had infiltrated his face. She reached out and held his hand. 'That sounds ominous. What's wrong, Ben?' she asked tenderly.

'I know it sounds like a cliché, but I'm really unsure where to start.'

Having no inclination as to what was occurring here Sophie became concerned. 'Well, while we're doing cliches, why not start at the beginning,' she responded in kind.

'I think I'll just give you the crux of what is happening and then I will answer all of your questions.'

'I don't even know what the topic is, so how do you know I will have lots of questions?' she asked, somewhat confounded.

She watched as his facial expression darkened further. 'I'm being blackmailed, Sophie.'

'Oh, no, I'm so sorry. Who, how, why, what's going on, Ben?'

'It gets worse.'

Now she found herself frowning. 'What's happening here? You're scaring me now.'

'Someone has managed to obtain photos of us from our last time together.' He paused and looked down at his tightly clenched hands. 'They're photos that depict you and I in compromising positions.' He leaned forward and clasped her hands. 'I'm so sorry, Sophie.'

She pulled a tissue from her jacket and dabbed at her moist eyes. 'How can this happen?'

'It seems that someone injected an associate of a Chinese Consulate operative into the staff roster here at the International. Then that person proceeded to plant a hidden camera into my old suite.'

'Why?'

'Do you remember we talked about the Confucius Institute once before and how my government withdrew the program from state high schools and colleges last year?'

'Yes. So, you're saying they're blackmailing you to have it reinstated.'

'Exactly. I've received two photos so far and one was sent to my wife yesterday.'

'Oh, no, this gets murkier by the minute,' Sophie replied. 'What did your wife say?'

'I don't really want to talk about her at the moment,' he replied coolly. 'This is about you and me, Sophie.'

'Somehow I don't think it's going to remain that way. You're a high profile government minister and the insatiable media will be all over you if this leaks out. Not even if, but when. And I don't want to be around when that happens. The other woman never comes out of those situations smelling like roses nor with her reputation intact,' she replied.

'I will handle this, I promise.'

'Oh, really, Ben?' Sophie was becoming annoyed at his naivety. 'And exactly how are you "going to handle this", as you say?' she asked while sighing with exasperation.

'The AFP has become involved, and thanks to information provided by a determined investigative journalist, they know who the culprit is and now they're searching for him.' It struck Ben what he had inadvertently revealed, however, it was too late to retract it. He felt his face flushing again.

Sophie's ears had pricked up. 'Who is the journalist, Ben?' she demanded, her eyebrows raised in anticipation of his response.

'I'm really sorry, let me explain, please?' he implored.

'It's Julie-Anne Granger, isn't it?'

He sighed in acknowledgement. 'Yes. She wanted to tell you herself, but I insisted that it was my place to tell you. I'm sorry—'

'I don't know what's worse,' she said interjecting, 'being involved in a scandal or being betrayed by my friend. I came here tonight looking forward to a romantic evening and now it's abruptly degenerated. How did I ever let myself become involved in something like this? I'm usually smarter than that,' she said. She was sniffling now and he handed her a tissue. 'Well, at least now I know the real reason why we're dining in your suite. You didn't want to be seen in public with me.'

'No, it's not like that at all.'

'Oh, really?' she blurted out.

'I don't know what to say; I didn't see this coming either.' He leaned forward to clasp her hands again.

She pulled away. 'How bad are the photos? Better still, do you have them with you?'

'You don't need to see them, Sophie,' he contended.

'If I'm going to be outed and shamed as the other woman, or even worse, the home wrecker, I damn well want to see what for,' she demanded feistily.

This was the first time that Ben had witnessed her be anything other than charming, so he knew she was serious. He relented, retrieved the envelope from his briefcase and handed it across.

'My god,' she exclaimed as she slid the photos out of the envelope. She flicked back and forth between the two photos then placed them back in the envelope and handed it back to him. She sniffled. 'Well, I guess neither of us can claim anonymity.'

They were both quiet and Sophie eventually broke the painful silence. 'I'm going to go,' she said softly.

'No, please don't. I need you to be with me, especially tonight,' he pleaded.

'Ben, after a couple of disastrous years I felt like I finally had my life back on track. I'm loving the challenge of studying, living in Coogee, spending quality time with friends, and of course my bodysurfing. I have been in a wonderful headspace and as a result, I allowed you into my life. You made me feel special and I loved our time together. I was even comfortable enough to dress sensually for the first time in ages. But, this is a bridge too far for me. I'm sorry, but I'm bailing before the inevitable media storm descends on me and I lose everything that I cherish. I'm not going to be paparazzi fodder for anyone.' She rose from her chair and gently kissed him on the cheek. 'Goodbye, Ben.'

'Sophie.'

'Sophie.'

87. St Vincent's Hospital

Friday 5th June

Julie-Anne woke early and rolled over onto her back. She was surprised at the ease with which she was finally able to achieve such a simple task. 'You should be going home dis mornin, Missie Granger,' she heard Nurse Chol say as she lumbered into her room.

'Good morning, Amal. That's good news.'

'De head nurse cum and see you 'dis mornin.'

'I have only heard the name Amal once before. Does it have a special meaning in your country?'

''Tis Arab name, but I am from Kenya. It mean to hab hope, Missie Granger and I hab many hope.'

'That's lovely. What do you hope for?'

'I hope to meet a good man, he marry me and we make many chidren,' the hefty nurse said while howling deeply with laughter.

Julie-Anne laughed along with the young nurse. 'Then I wish you good luck, Amal.'

'I cum back and see you fore you go, Missie.'

Julie-Anne would use the intervening time to make some phone calls. She was overdue to return Andy Frances' missed calls, so she would start with him. 'Hi, Andy, I'm sorry for being so tardy returning your calls.'

'You were supposed to call me with a response yesterday. My GM's going nuts and is worried sick this will leak to the media. What's going on, Julie-Anne?' he demanded.

'The investigation is progressing, but there was a slight hiccup on Wednesday.'

'Go on.'

She told him about Sun Jie, his link to Paul Gao and Gao being the perpetrator of the extortion attempt on the Minister. 'Sun Jie was an accomplice, although that's irrelevant now as his charred body was found in a burnt out car two days ago.' Frances' silence signified his concern at her revelations, so she continued. 'Gao is employed as a Special Emissary at the Chinese Consulate.'

'Shit, you were right about the international implications.'

'Yes, I was,' she said staunchly. 'There's more, Andy.' She hesitated. It was bad enough remembering the horrific events of Wednesday without having to recap them out aloud. He was entitled to be made aware of the seriousness of the situation though. 'I was run down by a car in Goulburn Street two days ago. They weren't after me, but rather they wanted the photos and my electronic devices to retrieve the evidence of their crime. Andy, the car was driven by Sun Jie and Gao was with him.'

'Jesus, are you okay? I'm sorry about busting your balls before.'

Julie-Anne laughed then grimaced at the sudden burst of pain in her cheek. 'Maybe save that particular reference for your mates. Anyway, I'm fine now and I'm about to be released from St Vinnie's soon.'

'That makes me feel somewhat better.'

'We're getting closer to Gao if you want to pass that onto your GM. And you might also tell him that according to the AFP detective, Ben Chandler is holding up well. That's assuming that he's even a consideration for your Mr Ziegler,' she stated derisively. 'And of course, keep this between the three of us; it's important, Andy.'

Just as she disconnected the call her phone rang. She saw it was Jordan calling. With everything that had happened, Julie-Anne had forgotten all about him and felt uneasy for doing so.

'If it's not Rainman himself,' she answered cheekily.

'Hi, Julie-Anne, how are you, funny girl?'

The head nurse and Amal walked into her room. 'Someone's just arrived to speak with me, so I have to go. Sorry, Jordan.'

'Before you hang up, would you like to have that Jalapeno Margarita tomorrow night? I know you've been dying for one.'

Given she still had bumps, bruises and bandages everywhere, being seen out in public definitely wasn't her preferred option, but she couldn't put this guy off any longer. Maybe by then she could give herself a passable makeover. 'Okay, make it eight o'clock. I'll see you there.'

No sooner had she disconnected that call and placed her mobile back on her bedside locker when she heard the ringtone again. Her heart skipped a beat when she saw that it was Sophie calling and she damned well knew why. Julie-Anne hit the message prompt and then tapped on "Can I call you later?" That was one call she couldn't avoid.

The head nurse removed her bandages, cleaned the wounds and applied smaller, less obvious dressings. 'There you go, Ms Granger, your friend might be able to recognise you now.'

'Thank you, nurse, that's great.'

'Now, Ms Granger, it's only been two days since your accident and there may be some residual effects, especially from your head knock. You still have mild concussion symptoms, so you need to take things easy for a few days.'

'Missie, do you hab a man to take you home?'

'No, but I'll be fine thanks, Amal.'

'You are good lookin' woman, but you must eat more. You should hab man in your life to look afta you too.'

'I wish. Thank you for everything, Amal. You are indeed a kind woman.'

Julie-Anne had one more call that she hated having to make. 'Chris, it's Julie-Anne, how are you?'

'I'm all good, JA, more to the point, how are you?'

'Heading home, hence the reason for my call. Can we have David Bedford's guys watch my apartment for a couple of days?'

'You've finally come to your senses. Maybe that bump on your head knocked some sense into you.' No response. 'Sorry, I shouldn't have said that.'

'No, it's okay, you're probably correct. So, you'll arrange it then?'

'Of course, consider it done.'

Half an hour later Julie-Anne exited the Uber and rode the elevator up to her apartment. She had forgotten that Melissa was staying there. *That's twice your memory has failed you this morning.*

'Julie-Anne,' Melissa blurted out. 'What are you doing here?'

'I live here,' she replied as Melissa embraced her with a gentle hug.

'I know you do, you comedienne, but shouldn't you still be in hospital? It's only been two days for goddsakes.'

'I'm fine, Melissa, really,'

'Okay, come sit down, tell me how you're feeling and I'll make you a coffee.'

'Why does everyone think I'm funny lately?'

'Who else thinks you're a comedienne?'

She hadn't mentioned Jordan to Melissa. After having been apart for a couple of months Melissa's feelings for her obviously hadn't waned judging by her enthusiasm before, during and after dinner the previous week. She would test the water and see what reaction she received. 'Just a guy I met a while back,' she replied casually, not wanting to hurt her friend's feelings.

'This is news to me. Which guy? Do tell.'

'It's nothing really. I met Jordan in the Bennelong Room when I was investigating Danielle.'

'Oh, Jordan is it? Melissa teased.

'We went to El Loco for supper, that's all.'

'And I'm guessing he wants to see you again.'

Julie-Anne felt her face blushing. 'Okay, so we're going back to El Loco for a Margarita tomorrow night.'

Melissa was shooting questions in rapid fire, but was left disappointed when there wasn't anything salacious to reveal.

'I'm not sure I'm up to a night out, so I might cancel anyway.'

'You have to go. I'll work some Melissa magic on you and you'll look gorgeous as always.'

Melissa's enthusiasm for her having a date surprised Julie-Anne. 'That's kind of you, but I don't know. I'll see.'

88. Chinese Consulate

Friday 5th June

'Yes, Mei Lin.'

'Mr Zhang, there are two detectives here to see you. Detectives Wagner and Sanderson.'

'What do they want, Mei?'

'They won't say, but they are being very insistent.'

'Wait five minutes and then send them in.'

Xiao rang Gao on his burner phone. 'What is going on, Gao? I have two detectives here at the Consulate waiting to speak with me. What have you done?' he demanded.

'Nothing, Consul General. Who are they?'

'Wagner and Sanderson. Why does that matter?' Xiao was becoming suspicious now. Why would Gao want to know who they were?

Gao knew who Wagner was, and if he was meeting with the Consul General, then he had obviously made the link between them. 'It doesn't, I was just wondering,' he lied. 'I don't know why they would be wanting to meet with you.'

'If this has anything to do with your appointed task there will be serious consequences. Do you understand, Gao?'

'Yes, of course, Consul General.'

Xiao opened his office door and beckoned the detectives in.

'Gentlemen, please take a seat,' he said, gesturing to the two desk chairs. 'Now, what can I do for you?'

'Consul General, I am Jack Wagner from the Australian Federal Police and this is Michael Sanderson from Day Street Police Station. We are here to ask you some questions about one of your staff members.'

Xiao maintained a neutral expression. 'Has one of my people fallen foul of the law?'

'Why would you ask that?'

'Well, why else would two detectives be in my office?'

Jack ignored the rebuff. 'The employee we wish to discuss is Paul Gao who I believe is your Special Emissary.'

The Consul General assumed the thinking position, rested his tented hands under his chin and glanced up at the ceiling. 'I don't think I know that name.'

Sanderson jumped in. 'Really, Xiao, do you really expect us to believe that? Would you like me to show you his mobile phone records?' He was bluffing, but the Consul General wouldn't be cognisant of that. Jack watched on as Xiao's face coloured ever so slightly.

Xiao was correct to be concerned about Gao. He should never have appointed him to the required task, but he would deal with that later. 'Oh, of course, Paul Gao. What would you like to know, gentlemen?'

'Where is he, Xiao?' Sanderson demanded abruptly.

'I have no idea. He works on special projects remotely from the Consulate.'

'So, would one of those projects include the deliberate running down of a reporter in Goulburn Street two days ago?' Jack asked.

'Oh, no, you are mistaken. He would do no such thing,' Xiao replied vehemently.

'Yes he would and he did. I was a witness to the incident

and personally identified him. Are you doubting my word, Mr Consul General?'

Now Xiao realised why Gao was requiring the use of another safe house. He was on the run from the authorities. 'I wasn't there, detective, so I can neither agree nor disagree with your allegation.'

'Apparently you yourself appointed him to the Special Emissary role, so I imagine he would therefore report directly to you. After all, this is only a state Consulate, not a full-blown national embassy, so how many staff can you possibly have here?' Jack asked, deliberately insulting him.

'I will have you know detective that the position of Consul General is well respected in international diplomatic circles and I am highly regarded within my country.'

'This isn't about your ego, Xiao,' interrupted Sanderson. 'We just want to interview Gao. Where is he?'

'I am sorry gentlemen, but I don't know of his current whereabouts and he is not responding to my telephone calls.'

Sanderson grinned mockingly. 'But, I thought you were well respected and highly regarded, Consul General. It appears that Gao doesn't share your lofty opinion of yourself.'

'He is probably busy with his appointed tasks.'

'And what are those tasks other than trying to kill a newspaper reporter?'

'Detectives, is there anything else I can do for you? My time is valuable.'

'Oh, we're not finished, Consul General, in fact we're just getting started,' Jack replied.

'Tell me about Sun Jie.'

'Who?'

'Sun Jie was an ICT specialist who worked for Gao and shared his apartment in Camperdown.'

'I don't know that name.'

'Well, let me enlighten you then. Sun Jie's charred body was found in the trunk of a burnt out Subaru Impreza that is registered to Fan Chen.' Jack revelled in the dark look that washed over Xiao's face. 'Exactly. I thought that name might be familiar to you especially as he was formerly employed by you and is now serving time in Silverwater for the kidnapping of the casino's Treasury Manager back in March.'

Sanderson jumped in. 'Is that ringing alarm bells for you now, Xiao? Well it should. Fancy someone being that stupid that they hadn't transferred the Impreza's registration into an anonymous name. That's a rookie mistake, especially for such a highly respected and well-regarded diplomat, don't you think?'

Xiao calmed himself. He had experienced challenging encounters with men far cleverer than these two. 'Gentlemen, if you insist on discussing motor vehicles I will introduce you to my Administration Manager who is much more acquainted with such menial tasks than I.'

Jack pressed on. 'Mr Consul General these are not the sort of activities Australia would expect from a representative of a foreign country. Rest assured we will find Gao and when we do we will charge him with the murder of Sun Jie and the attempted murder of the reporter amongst a host of other offences. I wonder if your Special Emissary will have anything to say about you,' Jack insinuated.

Sanderson handed Xiao his business card. 'Maybe you will see fit to call us if he ever answers your own call,' he said sarcastically. 'We will see ourselves out.'

The detectives had confirmed Xiao's worst fears that Gao had lost control of his appointed task. He picked up the handset of his desk phone and called a contact in China. He wasn't concerned at the call being monitored by Australian authorities as all his calls were secured by end to end encryption. 'I am in need of your services.' Xiao listened to the man on the other end of the call. 'Tomorrow.' Xiao continued to listen then said, 'check your secure email.' He replaced the handset and stared blankly up at the ceiling.

89. AFP Headquarters

Friday 5th June

Following their meeting with the Consul General and after dropping Sanderson off at Day Street, Jack headed back to Goulburn Street. He was eagerly awaiting the results of the DNA test. He had overnighted the envelopes, photos and Chandler's swab to the AFP's Digital Forensics Laboratory in Canberra on Wednesday. Sanderson was also having DNA extracted from the champagne glasses by the Forensic Evidence and Technical Services team in Parramatta. Jack hoped to be able to match Gao to both. He should have the results in his inbox today. More importantly, he also needed to find out how JA managed to be in the possession of the photos. It could be key to the investigation. He also wanted his suspicions either confirmed or undeniably refuted. He would give it another try.

'Hi, Jack,' she said hesitantly.

'How are you feeling today, JA?'

'Much better, and I'm home.'

'Great. How about we catch up for a drink and a chat then. Would tomorrow night work?'

That surprised her, but they had dated for six months and as a result, she knew him well. He would have an ulterior motive and she understood precisely what is was. 'I would like to, however, unfortunately I have a prior engagement. Maybe one night next week.' She was being truthful this time.

'Oh, okay then.' He paused.

'Jack, what's up?'

'I don't want to unduly alarm you, but it's obvious Gao followed you from your apartment to Goulburn Street. You should arrange for some protection.'

'Thanks, Jack and I have done just that. David Bedford's guys are watching my apartment for a couple of days just in case. It's just a precaution though, because if you're correct, then Gao was only after my devices and not me personally.'

'Let's hope so. Okay, take care of yourself.'

'Cheers, and thanks for the call, Jack.'

Parking his innate suspicions for now, he disconnected the call, logged in to his desktop and went straight to his email inbox. 'Hey presto,' he hailed to himself. There was an email from one of the techs at the Digital Forensics Lab. He read it purposefully. The laboratory had identified numerous DNA samples on the envelopes. Jack expected this given the number of hands they would have passed through between the original mailing and their final delivery to Chandler. He ignored the remainder of the explanation. The second samples were taken from the photos themselves and this is where he hoped to achieve a result. The testing identified two positive results and Jack already knew one had to be from Ben Chandler. He double clicked on the two attachments. Sure enough one had Ben Chandler's name at the top and then detailed twenty separate criteria which were all listed in an alpha numeric format that Jack would never comprehend. The results from the second document would be the ones that he could attribute to Paul Gao if he could match them with Sanderson's results from the champagne glasses. He clicked on the forward icon, deleted the three irrelevant documents and then typed a brief explanation. He addressed the email to

Sanderson and clicked on the send icon. Given it was a Friday he wasn't anticipating a response until Monday at the earliest. Jack also needed to be able to link Sun Jie to Gao, but they had been unable to take DNA samples from his handywork at the International. He would have to be happy with the fingerprints they had identified in Chandler's hotel suite and source another direct link to Gao. The highly circumstantial link of sharing an apartment together wouldn't do the trick.

90. Julie-Anne's Apartment

Friday 5th June

Melissa looked up from her laptop as Julie-Anne returned from the balcony. 'That was brief.'

'Yeah, I know. It was Jack.'

'Oh. Let me guess what he wanted?'

'He wanted to catch up for a drink, but I'm sure we both know precisely why he was calling. He's not going to give up trying to find out how I really obtained those damned photos. Sometimes I wish I had never gone to Paul's apartment,' she lamented.

'I don't agree with your methods, but if you hadn't both your and Jack's investigations would have stalled and neither of you might have been any wiser to his actions. Me either for that matter.'

Julie-Anne sighed. 'Yeah, I guess you're right.'

Melissa was working from Julie-Anne's apartment today, so Julie-Anne carried her coffee out onto the balcony and returned Sophie's call. She hadn't spoken to her friend since their dinner here a few weeks ago and she had been dreading the inevitable. Given Ben Chandler had said he was having dinner with her before he left for Woy Woy for the weekend she assumed the sensitive conversation happened last night.

'Hi, girlfriend,' Julie-Anne said cheerily, belying the nervousness she felt.

'You're my friend, Julie-Anne, why wouldn't you tell me?' Sophie demanded, launching straight in.

Julie-Anne detected her friend's sniffles. 'Oh, Sophie, I soooo wanted to tell you, honey,' she said, feeling sad for her friend. 'Ben felt it was his place to, especially given you were in that situation because of your association with him. That's why.'

That explanation didn't calm Sophie one bit. 'It's one hell of a coincidence that in a city of over five million people a close friend of mine just happens to be the person that comes into possession of a batch of scandalous photos that depict her friend in compromising positions. What are the chances of that occurring?' she insinuated, the question laden with suspicion.

'I completely understand why you would think that, but it was no coincidence, Soph. I went to dinner at Melissa's and that was when I was introduced to Paul Gao. I was suspicious of the motives behind him encouraging her to invite me to dinner, so I began to research him and eventually that led me to the photos.'

'How did you obtain the photos?'

Aaahh, that old chestnut. 'That's a complicated story and maybe I'll tell you over a glass of bubbles one day.'

'I would certainly hope so. Ben told me the Chinese Consulate was behind the extortion. Is that correct?'

'A man named Sun Jie, an ICT technician with links to Gao planted the cameras in Ben's hotel suite and Gao is employed as a Special Emissary at the consulate. We can prove Sun Jie's involvement, but the evidence against Gao is circumstantial at the moment, and it is the same for the Consul General.'

'I assume there's a feature coming soon and I would sincerely hope you're leaving me out of it.'

'Yes, in name only.'

'What do you mean, in name only?'

'I'm a journalist and I utilise my investigative skills to collect the specifics of a story and then I report the facts to the public.

I won't mention your name or Ben's, but both of your roles and respective lifestyles are essential ingredients that will help the readership understand the full story.'

'Don't do that, Julie-Anne. It won't take the voracious tabloids and online trolls long to put the pieces together and then our lives will be destroyed,' Sophie pleaded.

Even though Sophie was a close friend Julie-Anne had her journalist head on now. 'It doesn't work that way. I can't just write waffle and expect the public to swallow it. Anyway, I work for a respected broadsheet and our readers demand, and frankly deserve, quality, timely and accurate reporting. This is a particularly important issue that that involves Chinese interference in our democracy and as such, it has national and international implications.' She paused momentarily. 'Okay, I'll come down off of my podium now,' she said, laughing nervously.

'Whatever. I've ended it with Ben,' Sophie said, sounding resigned.

Julie-Anne could hear the sadness in her voice. She felt for her friend particularly after what she had experienced in her recent past. 'I'm sorry, but that was inevitable, Soph. The impediments to you guys having a successful relationship were enormous, if not insurmountable. A man isn't going to surrender his family, a high profile government role, a multi six figure salary and his entire lifestyle for his girlfriend. He would be shunned by everyone who knows him and end up completely alienated. He would be an outcast. Would you really want to be with that man?'

'You're correct of course and that's one reason why I broke it off before it went any further. He was a charming, kind and interesting man and I enjoyed spending time with him, especially given what I've been through in the past two years.'

'I've met him and found him to be just as you described, especially for a politician. I'm really sorry, Soph.'

'Thanks. Now let's have a drink soon. It might be the last time I'll ever be able to venture out in public,' she replied.

Sophie had enough to deal with, so Julie-Anne avoided telling her about her near death experience in Goulburn Street. 'Let me finish my investigation and then we can have a long catch-up over numerous glasses of bubbles.'

She disconnected the call and the mobile immediately started ringing. 'Ben, how are you?'

'I'm fine, Julie-Anne, but more to the point, how are you?'

'Much better already and I'm actually back home at my apartment.'

'That's wonderful. You must have some amazing recuperative powers.'

'If I do then a big thanks to my parents for their genes,' she replied. 'Were your ears burning? I've literally just hung up from talking to Sophie.'

'I thought she would probably call you. She was quite upset last night when I told her you were the reporter involved. How is she doing today?'

'After a few tense moments she eventually softened a little. She will still be disappointed in me for a while and she's sad to lose you, Ben.'

'Likewise, Julie-Anne, but ultimately it was her decision and I will respect that. For now. It doesn't mean I won't try to change her mind, however, I think it's better if I let the investigation play out first. Then if we have some clean air I might be able to convince her to change her mind.'

She chuckled in response. 'Good luck with that. She's a strong, determined woman that one.'

'I got carpeted by the Premier a couple of days ago, so I trust the investigation will reach a conclusion soon.'

'It should. How is the temperature back in Woy Woy?'

'Sonja was at work when I arrived back this morning,

but she is coming home shortly, so I'm steeling myself for the inevitable confrontation.'

'I wouldn't want to be a fly on the wall in your house, Ben.'

'That's okay, eventually this marriage will dissolve of its own accord. We've grown apart and if that wasn't the case then I wouldn't have so energetically pursued Sophie.'

'Good luck with everything.'

'Before you go. How do you intend to portray Sophie and I in your story, Julie-Anne? Discreetly I trust.'

There it was, the real reason behind the call. *Once a politician, always a politician.* 'Not by name or position if that allays your concerns. You're a politician, Ben, so you're fair game, but Sophie's my friend and I will go to great lengths to protect her. If I mention you by name or title eventually the tabloids will make the link to Sophie and then her life will become intolerable. I simply won't do that to her.'

'Okay, I suppose that's fair and reasonable given this is a problem of my making, not hers. Thanks, Julie-Anne.'

Julie-Anne walked back into the living area and sat down at the kitchen bench next to Melissa.

'I overheard you talking to Sophie. How's she doing?'

'She ended it with Ben last night and she's not too happy with me either. Understandably, she wants to know how I obtained the photos, but I couldn't tell her over the phone. I might tell her one day, although I seriously doubt it.' She paused and once more reflected on her actions that led to obtaining them. 'Jack found out I was in Gao's apartment.'

'Oh, no, how embarrassing for you, especially as he's your ex too. How did he find out?'

'The state police raided Paul's apartment and found two champagne glasses on the coffee table. They had them printed and unsurprisingly one came back positive to me. Jack, of course was furious and demanded to know everything. No way was I revealing exactly what happened, so I just gave him the basics. That didn't satisfy his detective's instinct, but want could he say?'

'You know him better than I, Julie-Anne, although I can't imagine him leaving it at that.'

'Nor can I.'

91. El Loco Surry Hills

Saturday 6th June

'I think I'm going to cancel.' It was late Saturday afternoon and Julie-Anne was studying her face in the bathroom mirror. She still had two bruises along her jawbone area and a small dressing on her right cheek. And she was certain that the egg on her head was visible for all to see. 'I look like elephant woman, Melissa.'

'No, you don't, princess. Anyway, you have to go. With what you've been through you deserve to have some fun. I'll work some magic on you and you'll be good to go. Turn around.'

Half an hour later Julie-Anne was again in front of the mirror, this time admiring Melissa's handywork. 'Thank you. I feel like a new woman.'

'I kinda liked the old one myself. Now, go and knock him dead.'

They were both still fond of each other and Julie-Anne wondered whether they would eventually rekindle their relationship. It had been less than two weeks since they were shamelessly flirting with each other at Melissa's dinner party for three. It was like they had never been apart. Until things kicked up a notch they may as well have been the only people there. Now, she was going on a date and Melissa was being magnanimous with her support. 'Thank you; you're a star.'

Julie-Anne entered the vibrantly coloured, Mexican cantina style, former bandroom, and spotted Jordan seated at one of the benchtop tables, facing the entry. He was wearing a white Mandarin collar linen shirt, slim fitting jeans and blue suede shoes which just had to be Ted Baker. He immediately stood and waved her over. Two Jalapeno Margaritas arrived just as she reached his table. 'Impeccable timing, Jordan.'

'Hello, Julie-Anne; it's lovely to see you and thank you for making the effort.'

'It was no effort. It's a pleasure to be here.'

'Really?' He frowned as he held her hands.

'Yes, really. Why?'

'Well, I'm guessing that the dressing on your cheek is not the result of walking into a door. Where else are you hurt?' he asked perceptively.

She was surprised at his powers of observation, so she wouldn't insult him by denying what happened. 'You noticed, huh?'

'You normally have a long, elegant, model's stride, but you were moving more gingerly than I remember. You also winced when we hugged in greeting, so I put two and two together—'

He was projecting a look of genuine concern and she was warmed by that. 'And you came up with four.'

'Are you comfortable telling me what happened? Or not,' he said, smiling.

Julie-Anne was all talked out about her misfortune, but she would get this over with so she could enjoy the rest of the evening. 'No, it's okay, Jordan. The target of my current investigation didn't take too kindly to me digging into his activities, so he decided to do something about it. I was deliberately run down in Goulburn Street on Wednesday.'

He stood there, mouth agape. 'What this Wednesday just passed?'

'Mm-hmm.'

'Wow. That must have been just horrible for you and scary as hell.'

'Yes it was, but I'm mostly okay now, thanks.'

'Mostly okay? Where are you hurting?'

'My hip and shoulder are still sore from where I hit the sidewalk, I have a mild concussion and my cheek sends me the occasional reminder, but other than that it's mostly cosmetic.'

Jordan was impressed that this woman had made the effort to keep her dinner commitment with him. Without getting ahead of himself that provided him with a glimpse of encouragement for the future. 'Cosmetic hey? You look just gorgeous to me.'

With all of her bruises Julie-Anne wasn't about to wear anything revealing, so she had opted for a colourful scarf print, long sleeve linen shirt, a pair of charcoal grey leather pants and her favourite leather jacket. 'Even though I put the girls to bed early?' she teased.

'Touché. I've learnt my lesson and only need to be told once,' he replied while exaggeratedly holding his gaze on her eyes.

Feeling slightly uncomfortable at the attention, she asked, 'So what's been happening in your world?'

'Before I bore you to death with my tales, are you hungry? I was thinking we could share some tacos.' He handed her a gaily coloured menu.

'Yum, can I have the Baja Fish Taco please?'

'That sounds good. I might have the Cochinita Pibil and what about a vego taco? The Coliflor Frita sounds good.

'Buena elección señor. Now, tell me what you've been up to since we last caught up.'

'You crack me up, Julie-Anne. I never know what little gem is going to pass your lips next.'

'Just keeping you on your toes, now come on, it's your turn to do the talking, mister.'

'Okay, okay,' he responded with his hands in the surrender position. 'Nothing as exciting or hazardous as you have experienced I'm afraid.'

'I thought you would be frantic with your aged care business given the risks posed to the elderly by the coronavirus pandemic.'

'The daily case numbers are declining dramatically and things seem to have settled down recently in our facilities, so I have devoted more time to my sports management business which I have neglected of late.'

'Are you going to name drop for me this time?' she kidded.

'Okay, just for you, Ms Granger. I have just arranged a deal for the Waratahs to resign one of my clients to a long term contract. Levani Bainivalu is a wonderful feelgood story as he originally heralded from the small village of Bukuya in the Fijian highlands which is a long way, both figuratively and geographically, from the Waratah's base in the leafy eastern suburbs of Sydney. His parents worked hard and made significant sacrifices so he could pursue his dream of playing senior level rugby. Through his own hard work and dedication he is now in the fortunate position of being able to provide financial assistance for the people of his village, including his parents.'

'That's a wonderful feelgood story. I'm amazed though that a team of big, strong rugby players is named after a flowering shrub though. What's next, the Shrinking Violets?'

'There you go again, funny girl. That sounds more like the name of a female punk rock band. And it's most certainly not something that could be ascribed to you.'

'I think that's a compliment, so I'll gladly accept it.'

'Now, you must tell me about your investigation.'

'Here's our tacos. Comiendo Feliz señor,' she said, grateful for the diversion.

'Okay, now back to you while I devour this delicious treat.'

'Are you referring to my latest case?'

'Yes, the one that precipitated the hit and run.'

Sheesh. 'I turned the tables on a man I suspected of having ulterior motives in his relationship with a good friend of mine.'

'How did you do that and what happened?'

She explained her misgivings about the motive behind her invite to dinner at Melissa's and how they were quickly confirmed by her. 'So, I started to investigate this guy and then suddenly I caught him following me from my apartment one day. That was a serious escalation, but at least it confirmed my suspicions.'

'Weren't you afraid? Being stalked I mean.'

'I was in my local neighbourhood, so I never felt unsafe.'

'When you said before that you turned the tables on him, what exactly did you do?'

'I started digging around and eventually ascertained that he was extorting a prominent public figure.'

'And he didn't take kindly to that I assume.'

'Apparently not.'

'Is this your turn to drop a name now?

Julie-Anne knew that it was intended as an innocent question. 'No. Out of respect for those involved I won't.'

'Well, I look forward to reading all about it in the near future. Well done, Julie-Anne.'

'Thank you.'

Those tacos were delicious as were the Margaritas. Would you like a nightcap?'

'Is that an alternative way of asking if I would like to go back to your place?' she asked non-accusingly. Having engaged in an erotic threesome and then blatantly using sex to progress her investigation now wasn't the time to be considering any potential relationship. That wouldn't be fair to this charming man until she had cleared the baggage from her emotional deck. She also had Melissa to think about and the status of their friendship. And her body could do with a rest after the physical exertion and trauma it had experienced recently.

'No, not necessarily,' he said sheepishly. He had hesitated in his reply and his face was awash with shades of red.

'Nice colour, Jordan. You're matching the festive surroundings.'

'Haha. I've always wanted to fit in and now I guess I do.'

'And a good comeback too. I'm going to take a raincheck and order an Uber.'

'Alright I'll keep an eye on the weather forecast then.'

'Goodnight, funny man,' she said, rising from the table.

'No, no, no,' he replied. 'With everything you've been through recently you're not walking out by yourself. I'll see you safely to your car.'

She allowed him to grasp her by the hand as he escorted her out onto Foveaux Street and her waiting Uber.

'I've had a lovely evening, Julie-Anne. Thank you for making the effort. I appreciate it.' He clasped both hands and leaned forward.

She offered him her good cheek. 'Goodnight, Jordan.'

Julie-Anne was seated in the back of the Uber and as was her habit following a date she was ruminating over the evening's events. Jordan appeared to be a very considerate man, intelligent and funny with an endearing self-effacing demeanour. Even if she had she been in a better space, both physically and emotionally, she wouldn't be accepting an offer of a nightcap anytime soon.

92. Julie-Anne's Apartment

Sunday 7th June

'So, how was it?' Melissa asked excitedly as she handed Julie-Anne a cup of coffee. 'Come on, give me all the goss,' she urged.

'There's not a lot to tell actually. We went to El Loco, had some delicious food and Jalapeno Margaritas, which are to die for.'

'What, and that's it?' Melissa asked, feigning exasperation. 'Really!'

'What do you want me to say? We chatted, laughed, swapped stories, etc. It was a fun night.'

'I didn't hear you come home. Let's get to the heart of it shall we? Last night or this morning?'

'I arrived home just before eleven thirty last night, *Mum*. I didn't want to wake you, so I slept on the sofa.'

'Haha. It was your second date, so he must have at least kissed you,' she pressed.

'Yes, on the cheek. Melissa, emotionally and physically I'm in no place to be getting involved at the moment. It was just a fun night out.'

'Shit.' Julie-Anne's mobile rang and she knew exactly who it would be. She stepped back from Melissa. 'I should probably take this.'

'Hi, Jack.'

'Shit, JA, how could you do that to me?'

'This is de ja vu,' she laughed. 'The Disgruntled Pelican comes to mind again.'

'It's not funny.'

'Yes it is, Jack. Look all I did was write one measly paragraph that linked my two articles. It just provided background into Danielle's life and reiterated the detective's involvement with her as she degenerated into a life of crime. And without mentioning him by name,' she added.

'Everyone will know it was me you were alluding to.'

'No they won't,' she decried. 'Only a handful of people close to the case will recognise you as the detective I mentioned, but they know already, surely.'

'Yeah, well, I don't like it.'

'Toughen up, Jack. During the six months we were dating you loved having a coffee on your balcony and reading my features. You would even compliment me on the depth of my research and you never once criticised me for mentioning names. Now that you're part of the story, you aren't so impressed all of a sudden. And at the risk of repeating myself, your name's not even mentioned.'

'Okay, okay. And you're still not going to tell me how you actually came across the photos are you?'

'I knew that's why you were really calling.' Maybe the cliché was true. *Sunlight is the best disinfectant.* But, she wasn't ready to shine a light on her poor behaviour just yet. 'I've already told you, Jack.'

'That wasn't the real reason for the call at all. Michael and I paid a visit to the Consul General with the aim of exerting some pressure. Behind his façade of denial I detected some nervous tension. Let's see if the plan worked and that causes him to make a mistake that we can pounce upon.'

'How will you know if he makes a mistake?'

'Michael's guys are sitting on both the apartment and the Consulate, so let's see what drops.'

'Okay, good luck.'

'How did that go?'

'He is persistent with the elephant in the room, that's for sure. I'm certain he thinks he knows the truth and of course, he would be correct, much to my everlasting humiliation.'

'Julie-Anne, Jack's a detective and they hate having unanswered questions. Not knowing will bug him until you tell him the truth.'

'That's never going to happen,' she replied steadfastly.

'Well, what *is* going to happen is that I'm heading home. I need to get myself together for a hectic week at the office. Will you be okay by yourself?'

'Yes, and thanks for keeping an eye on me. It was a delight to have you here.' She walked her bestie to the door.

Melissa stopped as she reached the entry, turned and kissed Julie-Anne. 'Thank you for allowing me to impose on you and for keeping me safe. It was just like old times.'

Julie-Anne closed the door, flopped back against it, looked up at the ceiling and sighed. This was becoming complicated. *Again.*

93. Camperdown – Inner Sydney

Sunday 7th June

Paul Gao swiped himself into his apartment building and rode the elevator to the third floor. He had no idea why Xiao wanted to meet with him nor why he had chosen this particular place. Maybe the Consul General wanted to avoid potentially exposing the safe house to unwanted, prying eyes. He inserted his key into the lock and hesitantly entered his old apartment. He assumed Xiao would buzz him upon his arrival, so he waited out on the balcony in the fading sunlight and admired the city skyline view for the final time. He heard a door open and thought it was unusual that Xiao had let himself into the apartment. He turned on his heels and was shocked to see a man dressed head to toe in black walk out of his study. A feeling of dread passed through his body. 'Who are you and what are you doing here?' he blubbered.

'Nǐ de chónggāo rènwù shībàile, Gao.'

'Bù wǒ méiyǒu. Nǐ bù míngbái.'

'Oh, but I do understand.'

'Guì xià, jiàng shǒu fàng zài bèihòu.'

Gao was shaking uncontrollably, but did as instructed. He knelt on the floor and placed his hands behind his back.

'You have been a disappointment to the mother country. You were given a simple task and you failed in your duty. Goodbye, Gao.'

Before Gao could protest the man aimed the silenced Sig Sauer P226 pistol at Gao's forehead and pulled the trigger. The man knelt on the carpet, positioned the pistol in Gao's right hand, placed his index finger inside the trigger guard and then wrapped the remaining fingers around the pistol's grip. The man stood and checked the area immediately around the body. Satisfied with the scene he had created, the man calmly walked across to the entry and left the apartment.

94. Camperdown – Inner Sydney

Sunday 7th June

Jack was reclinig on his sofa with a bourbon and Coke in hand while watching 60 Minutes. The program's Liz Hayes was speaking to Australians who are sick of being told what to do by the government and health authorities during the coronavirus pandemic. *"But what do these conspiracy theorists know that we don't, and why do so many people listen to them?"* she asks. Jack watches with interest as Hayes interviews the controversial chef, Pete Evans. Evans tells her he fears for his safety and thinks he could be targeted because he's so outspoken. Ominously he warns, *"If I disappear or I have a fricking weird accident, it wasn't an accident, okay?"* Jack thinks he's just another lunatic conspiracy theorist who seriously needs a reality check that he would be only too happy to provide. His thoughts were interrupted by the ringtone of his mobile.

'Jack, it's Melissa,' she said in a faltering voice. 'I'm sorry to call you this late.'

'What's wrong?'

'I just received a strange text message from an unknown number.'

'What did it say?'

'Your boyfriend wants to see you again. I'm at my apartment.'

'What do you think, Melissa?'

'I assume it's Paul, but I broke off all contact and haven't seen him for probably ten days. Given what he did to Julie-Anne, why would he want to see me? He realises she and I are friends and that I must surely know about his activities by now. Something's off here, Jack.'

'I agree. Do you have a key to his apartment?'

'Yes, why?'

'I'll meet you in the carpark of McDonald's in Stanmore in thirty minutes. Do you know where that is?'

'Yes, it's not far from here.'

Jack rang Sanderson as he went to the wardrobe safe and extracted his Glock 22. 'Michael, Melissa Wu has just received a text message from an anonymous number inviting her over to Gao's apartment. It purports to be from him, however, I'm doubtful about that. Do you want to meet me there just in case?'

'Of course, what's the address?'

'The same one you raided the other day. You said you had eyes on it.'

'We did, but after a couple of days of inactivity we called it off. Bugger.'

'Never mind that now. I'm picking up Melissa on the way as she has a key.'

'Okay, see you there.'

Forty five minutes later Jack pulled up in the laneway opposite Gao's apartment building in Camperdown. He immediately spotted Sanderson who was already walking towards the building's entry. Jack leaned across Melissa and retrieved his Glock and a magazine from the glove compartment.

'Is that really necessary, Jack?' Melissa asked, recoiling at the sight of the weapon.

He saw the fearful look on Melissa's face as he inserted the magazine and racked the slide. 'Yes, and Michael will be armed too. It's standard procedure, but ideally they won't be necessary. Can I have the key please?'

She handed over her keyring. 'You need to use the fob to access the building.'

'Alright, now you stay here and keep the doors locked, just in case. And keep your mobile handy.'

Melissa watched on with trepidation as Jack approached the other detective.

'How do you want to handle this, Jack?'

'I don't want to alert him if he's in there, so we'll let ourselves into the building and quietly make our way up the stairs to his apartment. Without cause we can't legally enter it, so we'll have to knock first, and if there's no response, then we'll announce ourselves and open the door. Let's go.'

The two detectives cautiously made their way up the concrete stairs to the third floor. Jack opened the fire escape door and they quietly padded along the short corridor to unit nine. Jack positioned himself to the left of the door and Sanderson moved to the right. Both held their weapons in a double fisted grip and pointed at the floor. Jack knocked with three precise, loud raps on the door. There was no answer, so he repeated the process. No response. 'Okay, let's do this,' he said quietly. Sanderson stood in the centre of the doorway while Jack inserted the key into the lock. 'You ready?'

Sanderson was now holding his Glock in the horizontal position in front of him. 'Yep.' Jack turned the key and upon hearing the lock click, Sanderson launched a brutal kick at the door and charged into the entryway. 'Armed police, I repeat, armed police,' he yelled while moving his weapon in an arc across the living area. Jack was now directly behind him, remaining silent to avoid any confusion in Sanderson's instructions. 'Check this out, Jack.'

Jack flicked the light switch and the two detectives stood in silence as they stared at the prone body of Paul Gao. Sanderson walked across to the body while Jack cleared the rest of the apartment. 'All clear,' Jack said as he joined Sanderson. The men placed their weapons back in their holsters. Gao's body was lying on its side, blood still seeping from a wound to the forehead. The pistol was in his right hand. Both men realised that there was no point in checking for signs of life. 'Do you think it's suicide, Jack? The scene would seem to suggest that.'

Jack cautiously moved around the body before focusing his attention on the head wound. I can't be sure, but given his recent history, I seriously doubt it.'

Sanderson nodded in agreement. 'There's a slight angle to the wound. It looks to me like the shot was fired from a position about forty five degrees above him. That's not easy to do yourself. His grip would be at an unnatural angle and he would need to keep his hand very steady and prevent any recoil. Anyway, the majority of firearm suicide victims simply put the weapon in their mouth and pull the trigger.'

'My sentiments exactly.' Jack knelt down and checked Gao's gun hand. 'I can't see any GSR, but the forensic guys will need to confirm that. I think this is a professional hit.'

'Are you thinking what I'm thinking?'

'Yep. Two days after our conversation with the Consul General his so-called special emissary is found deceased in mysterious circumstances.'

'Well, I guess we don't have to concern ourselves with trying to match his DNA anymore.'

Sanderson heard footsteps in the hallway and turned just in time to see two uniformed officers, with their service pistols drawn, cautiously enter the apartment. 'Put your hands in the air,' the taller officer demanded.

'We're detectives, he's with the AFP and I'm from Day Street,' Sanderson replied steadily while raising his arms slowly, not wanting to further alarm these young men who were simply doing their job. 'We have ID in our pockets.'

'Show me, slowly if you don't mind, detective.'

Sanderson turned his back on the officers so they could clearly see him extracting his wallet from the rear pocket of his jeans. He kept one hand in the air and used the other to throw the wallet back to the taller officer.

The young constable flipped open the wallet and checked the laminated ID card. 'Okay, thank you,' he said as he replaced his weapon in its holster.

'You guys got here awfully fast.'

'Apparently one of the neighbours heard a loud bang and called triple zero.'

'Good for them, it saved us calling it in. This man is obviously deceased, and although it appears on the surface to be a suicide, I think it's a murder. You should call it in to your watch commander as soon as possible. Sanderson handed across his business card. Have the detectives assigned to the case give me a call and I will provide them with some background. 'Let's go, Jack.'

The two detectives stood in the building's foyer sharing their theories on what they had just discovered. 'I'm convinced that was a professional hit, Jack.'

'I agree, and someone is cleaning house again. First, someone eliminates Sun Jie, probably Gao, and then he gets whacked himself. This is going back up the chain and I'll bet London to a brick on it leads to Xiao.'

'Jack.' He heard an anxious voice call out and he turned to see Melissa walking hurriedly towards them. 'Let's get outside, Michael. She can't come into this building.'

'What are you doing here? I told you to stay in the car,' he chided.

'I saw you standing in the foyer talking and I wondered what was happening.'

Sanderson turned to leave. 'I'll call you as soon as I hear anything from the case detectives.'

'Thanks, Michael. Let's get out of here, Melissa.'

'What detectives? You're a detective; what's going on, Jack?' she asked frantically.

This wasn't the time nor place to be having this conversation, but he couldn't delay it. She would understandably keep asking what they had uncovered until she had a response. He grasped her hands and took a deep breath. 'Paul is deceased, Melissa.'

Her mouth narrowed. 'Really?'

'Yes. I'm sorry.' He watched as her eyes began to water and then she started sobbing. Jack pulled her into him and held her tightly. She wrapped her arms around him and rested her head on his shoulder.

'What happened, Jack?' she whispered.

'Let's not have this chat here.' He grasped her hand again and led her across the road to his car.

Half an hour later they were settled on Jack's sofa, he with his usual and Melissa with a glass of red wine. She hadn't wanted to be by herself nor drive alone back to her townhouse just yet. 'Now will you please tell me what happened, Jack?' They had travelled in silence back to his apartment in Balmain.

'We knocked on his door twice, and when there was no response, we entered the apartment. We found him lying on the floor of the living area. He was obviously deceased. We don't know for certain what happened.' Jack was hoping she wouldn't ask for more information, so he could shield her from the gory details. But, Melissa was a lawyer with an understandably enquiring mind.

'How did he die, Jack?'

'It doesn't matter. That's not important.'

'Tell me, please,' she pleaded softly.

For a multitude of reasons he couldn't very well say that they suspected that Gao had been assassinated. 'Melissa, it appears that he took his own life.'

'Oh, no, why would he do that?' she asked haltingly as she began to sob. Jack grasped her hand and she slid across the sofa and nestled into his shoulder.

'I don't know. I didn't know him at all other than what you and JA have told me.'

Melissa spoke quietly again. 'I knew him reasonably well and he never struck me as the sort of man who would do something like that. He enjoyed his life too much and was proud of his new position with the Consulate.'

She was probably correct, but that would be up to the coroner to determine. 'Do we ever really know anyone properly? I see this situation all the time through my work with the force and friends and relatives of victims always say the same thing. Personally, I have always thought that it might be brought on by a momentary chemical imbalance within the brain, but I'm no neurologist.'

She lifted her head and spoke softly. 'I know you are holding something back from me, but I'm sure you have your reasons. I realise you're being protective of me too. That's thoughtful of you.' She leaned up and pecked him on the cheek.

He felt her warm tears against his skin. Jack hadn't been in this situation for years and he was doing his best to be a strong, empathetic and caring friend. He had a reaction when she had kissed his cheek and that confused him. He had always had a thing for her, who wouldn't? She was intelligent, funny and striking to the eye, but he had been in a relationship with Danielle during the entire time he had known her. He needed to banish those thoughts from his mind. He held her gently and left her to her own thoughts. After a while he broke the silence. 'What are you thinking?'

'Why would he or whomever, text me of all people? It

makes no sense. As I said earlier tonight, I've had zero contact with him lately.'

'Who knows why people do what they do when they're in that frame of mind.' He knew why they had contacted her. They wanted the body found quickly and publicly to create the impression that the extortion of Ben Chandler was at an end. Who better than the ex-girlfriend and the friend of the reporter investigating the case? 'I think it's highly likely he twigged that we were getting close to catching him, that his time was up, and he couldn't entertain the notion of going to prison.'

'Maybe, I don't know,' she replied through a sniffle.

'The Coroner will determine the cause of death, Melissa.'

'I don't want to be alone tonight.'

'Aren't you staying at JA's?'

'I was until today when I went back home to my townhouse.'

He tilted his head and looked down at her. 'You don't have to be alone. You're welcome to stay here; there's a spare bedroom and it's all made up.'

'Thank you.'

95. Jack's Apartment Balmain

Monday 8th June

'Good morning,' Melissa said as she bounced into the kitchen.

Jack turned away from the coffee machine towards the voice that eight hours ago he would never have imagined would be talking to him at seven o'clock the following morning. She was wearing one of his long sleeve shirts. 'Good morning to you too. How do you like your coffee?'

'With you,' she responded with a mischievous glint.

'You comedienne. I don't think you have much choice.'

'I'm really sorry if I put you in an awkward position last night, but I couldn't face being by myself after what happened. Are we okay?'

'We're fine. I'm about to have coffee with the most desirable woman at 13 Longview Street in Balmain. Who wouldn't be fine?'

She playfully punched him in the arm. 'I'm the only woman here.'

'That's not the point.'

'Do you know what the acronym FINE stands for, Jack?'

He turned to face her and held her hands. He briefly recalled having the same conversation with Danielle. 'No, go on,' he fibbed. 'I can see that you're just dying to tell me.'

'Fucked Up, Insecure, Neurotic, and Emotional. That pretty

much sums up how I felt last night,' she said ruefully. 'Women hate it when men say, 'I'm *fine,*' she added.

Melissa went quiet and Jack saw small droplets slowly rolling down her cheeks. He knew she must be feeling the intense sadness that someone experiences when they lose a person close to them. She had been masking her feelings through her playfulness. He pulled her into a firm embrace.

'Now for your coffee,' he said, releasing her. 'Here you go.'

'I need this, especially after those three glasses of red wine last night.'

'Would you like some breakfast?'

'No thanks. I have to go, Jack,' she said as she placed her coffee cup in the dishwasher. 'Thank you for everything. My life has been turned upside down this year and Paul's death just topped it off. I don't know what I would have done without your support last night.'

'You would have been *fine,*' he responded.

'Funny man. I doubt that very much. I feel much better this morning thanks to your consideration and kindness. 'Thanks again.'

'Wait,' he called out. How are you getting to back to your car?'

'I've booked an Uber, thanks, Jack.'

Melissa was sitting in the back of the Uber for the short five kilometre journey to collect her car in Stanmore. Her head was propped on the headrest as she recalled the past twelve hours of her life. So many thoughts were running through her head. Jack had been so strong for her and showed such unbelievable compassion and empathy that she had seamlessly drifted into his arms. As far as the demise of Paul Gao went, she had mixed feelings. He had been a good friend, which she valued at the time, but at some stage that changed. She knew exactly when.

The day she told him about her reporter friend who was focused on investigating Chinese influence in Australia. From that day on he had regularly asked about Julie-Anne, suggested Melissa invite her to dinner, then shamelessly flirted with her and finally had his way with her. She should have been alert to what he was up to. 'You're smarter than that, Melissa,' she said chastising herself.

'Are you okay, miss?' the Uber driver asked.

Allowing herself a momentary smile, she said, 'I'm *fine* thanks.'

She needed to get her life back in order and the best way of achieving that was to focus on her legal practice. That's what she would do. There were a number of new clients who were seeking to take action against Agnes Waters Lodge in her home suburb of Burwood over the loss of their loved ones in one of Australia's deadliest coronavirus outbreaks. They were claiming that Agnes Waters wasn't suitably equipped to adequately respond to the outbreak of the virus at the lodge. Moreover, they want an explanation as to why an infected staff member was allowed to continue working at the lodge and why at risk residents weren't moved to a safer environment. That would be her focus for the immediate future.

Back in Balmain Jack was reminiscing about the highly unexpected events of the past twelve hours when his thoughts were interrupted by the ringtone of his mobile. He saw it was Sanderson. 'Good morning, Michael' he said cheerily.

'Good morning yourself. What's got you so merry for this time of the day?'

'Oh, nothing really.'

'Yeah, sure, as if,' Sanderson replied. 'I saw you two embracing as I walked to my car last night.'

'Yeah, yeah, what's up, buddy?'

'The Forensic Evidence and Technical Services guys were able to lift some DNA from the champagne glasses and they emailed me the results earlier this morning. It won't bring you any joy to know that it was a match to the DNA genome sequence from the photos,' he stated soberly.

'That's some consolation I suppose. It's a small, hollow victory for our investigation, but it sure doesn't feel like it.'

'No, it doesn't. Do you want to have a long, lazy lunch and get pissed, Jack?'

'Nah, it's bucketing down outside, so I might just gravitate to the couch and binge watch Netflix. Thanks anyway.' He considered ringing Melissa and asking her if she would like to come back. He wasn't certain he was ready for where that could potentially lead.

'Okay, take it easy, Jack.'

96. Julie-Anne's Apartment

Monday 8th June

Even though she didn't feel she needed them, Chris Russell had kindly given her a few more days of sick leave and told her to work from home if need be. Julie-Anne was leaning up against the headboard with her laptop resting on her knees and updating the draft of her feature on Chinese interference. She was surprised by the sound of her apartment's entry buzzer. No one should be calling in on a Monday morning and she wasn't expecting a delivery. *What the hell.* She rolled out of bed and padded out into the living area.

There was a man's face visible on the entry monitor. She pressed the speaker button. 'Hello.'

'Ms Granger?'

'Yes, who is it?'

'It's Detective Taggart from Inner West Police Area Command at Marrickville. I would like to come up and talk to you, please.'

What the heck did a detective unknown to her want on a Monday morning? 'Hold up your ID card, please.' She watched on the little monitor and observed the ID card with the name of Thomas Taggart and the New South Wales Police logo clearly visible. 'Are you alone?' There were a hundred different ways an ID card could be reproduced these days and she wasn't about to allow a lone, unfamiliar man into her apartment.

'Detective Amanda Brown is with me.'

Julie-Anne was still unsure. 'You know the drill, Detective Brown.' The female detective stood in front of the camera and held up her own ID card. 'Okay, come up.' She pressed the door release button and waited, completely oblivious as to the nature of the visit. *She shouldn't have been.*

Suddenly aware that she wasn't dressed, Julie-Anne scurried to the bedroom, grabbed her robe and threw it on while walking back to the living area. There was a firm knock on the door and she eyed the peephole to ensure it was the same two people. Just to be certain she called out, asking them to repeat their full names and rank again. Once they had satisfied her as to their identity she partially opened the door, but didn't release the chain from its track. 'What can I do for you, detectives?'

'May we come in, Ms Granger?'

'What's this about first?'

'Can we talk inside, please?' Taggart asked more firmly this time. 'It's not for public consumption.'

'No, not until I know what this is all about,' she replied, equally decisively.

The male detective lowered his voice. 'It's in relation to a Mr Paul Gao. I assume that name rings a bell for you.'

Stay calm, Julie-Anne, maybe it's just routine. She didn't believe that for a second, but closed the robe around her, slowly slid the chain across its slot, and opened the door.

Taggart was smartly dressed in a designer suit, tall with short brushed back black hair and dark eyes. He would be early to mid-thirties. His partner, probably of a similar age, was tall for a woman, with blue eyes and wearing tight fitting jeans and a white polo shirt with a police logo. The polo accentuated her toned, tanned arms. The attractive woman's short blonde hair gave her a slightly masculine look and judging by her figure, she obviously took care of herself. *Maybe she was Miss Policewoman 2020.*

Julie-Anne ushered Taggart and Brown across to the sofa. She remained standing, hoping this would be a brief visit. 'Please take a seat and tell me what this is all about.'

Taggart spoke first. 'I'm sorry to tell you this, but Paul Gao is deceased.'

Her mouth tightened. 'Oh,' she replied diffidently, trying to remain impassive while digesting the revelation. 'That's awful.' Julie-Anne propped down on a stool at the breakfast bar. I'm sorry to hear that.'

'I assume by your reaction that Paul Gao is known to you?'

'Yes, he is.'

'How do you know him?'

She wasn't going to reveal that she had been investigating him at this point. 'He is a friend of a friend of mine. A few weeks ago I attended dinner at her place and he was there also.'

'What's your friends name?'

Julie-Anne wasn't about to reveal Melissa's details either without a darn good reason. 'Let's take a step back first. Why are you really here?' she demanded.

Taggart sat forward and looked Julie-Anne firmly in the eyes. 'Ms Granger, we are investigating a potential homicide and you have become a person of interest.'

She rebounded. 'I'm an investigative reporter and I know that a POI usually means suspect, so is that what I am, and why you're really here?'

'In short, yes and yes, so I would suggest cooperation is in order here, unless of course you would like to take a ride to Marrickville and we can continue our chat there. It's your call.'

That straightened Julie-Anne up somewhat. She could demand the presence of the Daily News' lawyer before answering any questions, but that would have to take place at Marrickville. 'Melissa Wu. She is a social justice lawyer.'

'That wasn't so hard now was it? What's your involvement with the deceased Mr Gao?'

'I told you, I met him at a dinner at Melissa's place.'

'Was that your only involvement with him?'

They wanted a definitive yes or no answer which Julie-Anne wasn't providing. She would deflect. 'Firstly, I would like to know why I am a person of interest in your investigation.'

Brown spoke for the first time. 'Okay, Ms Granger, let's stop dancing around here, shall we?' The female detective pulled a tablet from her bag, tapped on the gadget and stared at the small screen. After a moment she looked up. 'This is why you are a person of interest in our investigation. Take a look,' she demanded. The cute blonde persona had quickly evaporated as she rose to her feet, walked across to Julie-Anne and handed her the tablet. 'Tap the play button when you're ready, Ms Granger.'

She didn't need to. The still image on the screen told her the reason behind the detective's visit. Her heart began beating faster, her hands were shaking and she couldn't draw enough air. She sat on the stool, frozen in time.

'Now, does that appropriately answer your question?' Brown asked, heavy on the sarcasm.

Julie-Anne stared at the screen, unable to find the words she needed to.

'It appears you both enjoyed the dinner party quite a lot,' she added, taking the sarcasm to a whole new level. 'Now, do you want to explain your involvement with him? Other than the obvious, of course, which is self-explanatory, don't you think?' The woman detective allowed a wry smile to creep across her face.

'I can explain.'

'Which part of self-explanatory didn't you understand?' Detective Brown asked.

'Fuck you.'

'I've heard you go both ways.'

That got Julie-Anne pissed. 'You know nothing about me, lady,' she snarled, 'so keep your smart mouth to yourself.'

'On the contrary, Ms Granger, I know rather a lot about you. You are an investigative reporter for the Daily News where you are well regarded. You have written numerous hard hitting features on organised and corporate crime in this city and you have a reputation for pushing the envelope. I guess we can see that for ourselves,' she said nodding at the tablet. 'On a personal level, you used to be in a relationship with an AFP detective until he moved on and then had relationship problems of his own, according to your most recent article. And following that you seem to prefer the company of Ms Wu. Through your investigative work you are well known in police circles, so we were easily able to identify you. How am I doing, Julie-Anne?'

While Brown had regaled her life story, Julie-Anne had used the time to regain her composure. She sighed. 'I was investigating Gao for an extortion attempt against one of the state government's ministers. I was getting close to proving my case, but now I guess that's a dead issue.' She swallowed a chuckle at her unintended quip. 'I'm sure Detective Michael Sanderson from Day Street will vouch for me. He is aware of the investigation and my activities surrounding Gao.'

The female detective smirked. 'All of your activities, Julie-Anne?'

She glared at the woman. 'Which part of fuck you didn't you understand, lady?' she replied angrily. Out of necessity Julie-Anne needed to settle herself. 'No, and I would appreciate it if it remained that way.'

Taggart spoke for the first time in a while. 'We researched

Gao in the COPS database and came upon Sanderson's notes on the case you mentioned. What else can you tell us about that?'

That's more like it, a more conciliarity tone. 'I assume you are aware of the burnt out car, the charred remains found in the trunk and the KALOF Sanderson issued for the getaway vehicle and Gao himself.'

'Yes, we are. When was the last time you saw Gao?'

'When he ran me down in Goulburn Street and put me in hospital last week. I haven't seen nor heard of him since. Do you want me to verify that?' she asked as she slid the robe off her shoulder and revealed a large yellowish bruise.

'I'm sorry, Julie-Anne.' Brown offered.

'I thought you would be aware of that, after all I did provide a statement to the uniformed cops. Although, I didn't realise it was Gao's doing at the time.'

'Exactly what date did he run you down?' Taggart asked.

'Last Wednesday, the third.'

'That's four days subsequent to the date stamp on the video.'

She shuddered at his mention of the video again.

'So what changed in your relationship in the intervening four days?'

Julie-Anne stared at Taggart unwaveringly. 'There was no relationship.' She didn't know if the two detectives were aware that Ben Chandler was the target of the extortion, so she would be carefully opaque with her response. 'I came across some incriminating photos in his apartment that lead me to believe he was extorting a person in a position of authority. I took snapshots of the photos and hurriedly left the apartment. I guess he desperately wanted them destroyed, so he ran me down and stole my laptop bag which contained all my electronic devices. There you have it, detectives.'

'What was so incriminating about the photos that led you to the extortion conclusion?'

Careful Julie-Anne. 'The woman in the photos wasn't the person in authority's wife.'

'And you know that how?'

'I'd seen pictures of the man's wife before,' she lied. She was leaving her friend Sophie out of this.

Taggart wasn't done yet. 'Why don't you simply tell us who the persons in the photos are?'

'That will never happen. You're the detectives, so I suggest you do some detecting.'

'Really? How about we take you to Marrickville, leave you in an interview room for a few hours and give you some time to rethink your obstinance?'

'That would be a waste of time for all of us.' Julie-Anne released an exasperating sigh. 'Look, why don't you speak to Sanderson and let him fill in some gaps for you. I'm sure he can verify my story even if he won't mention the specifics.'

Taggart smiled at her. 'And will he be able to verify the relationship between you and Gao and the reason behind the video?' he asked drily.

'I would appreciate it if you could maintain discretion over the use of the video. It could lead to the destruction of many careers, destroy families, and wreck people's lives, not just mine.'

'You would appreciate that would you? Well I would have appreciated some definitive responses to our questions, but they weren't forthcoming.'

'Rubbish. You most certainly know a lot more about Gao and what might have led to his death than you did when you arrived here an hour ago.'

'You haven't given us anything conclusive that will progress our investigation, so maintaining discretion isn't exactly at the top of my to do list, Ms Granger.'

'Talk to Sanderson.' Julie-Anne rose from her stool. 'Now listen carefully, detectives. This goes all the way up to the Premier of the state and has national and international implications, so I would tread carefully if you value your careers. Otherwise you'll be walking the beat in uniform checking for people wearing facemasks before you know it. Is that conclusive enough for you? Now allow me to get the door for you.'

As they walked out Brown turned to face Julie-Anne. 'If you ever want a change of career I'll be happy to be a referee for you.' she said through a superior smile.

Stay calm Julie-Anne. 'Keep walking lady.'

'I will, although I'm sure we'll be seeing each other again.'

97. Chinese Consulate

Tuesday 9th June

'Yes, Mei Lin.'

'Mr Zhang, the Minister of Education and the Deputy Commissioner of the Australian Federal Police are here to see you.'

'I don't have an appointment in my calendar, Mei.'

'No, sir, they have not booked an appointment.' This was not good. The Minister had never been to meet with him at the Consulate before and now he had a federal policeman with him. Xiao needed time to think.

'Have them take a seat, Mei.' No sooner had he placed the receiver down when his door opened.

Ben Chandler pushed through the doorway and strode purposefully across to Xiao's desk, closely followed by the Deputy Commissioner.

'Gentlemen, good morning,' the Consul General said, hastily composing himself. 'I was just finishing a report for the Ambassador in Canberra.'

'This won't take long,' Chandler replied brusquely.

'Oh, okay. What can I do for you, Ben?'

'Xiao, three weeks ago today you came to see me at my office. The reason for your visit was obvious. You were lobbying me to reinstate the Confucius Institute into the state education system. The meeting was civil, we agreed to disagree and you left. I'm sure you recall that meeting.'

'Yes, of course, Minister, what of it?'

'Well, it seems that you weren't satisfied with the outcome after all and you decided to take matters into your own hands.'

Don't speak unless you can improve the silence. Xiao scrunched up his nose and forehead feigning ignorance.

'Have it your way. I have been the subject of extortion attempts which were designed to intimidate me into reintroducing the program.'

Xiao raised his eyebrows. 'That is just horrible, Ben.'

'Yes it is. I don't suppose you would happen to know anything about that by any chance?' Chandler asked cynically.

'Of course not. Why would you ask such a thing?'

'You know very well why, Xiao. Your Special Emissary, Paul Gao was behind the extortion.'

'I am taken aback by your assertion, Ben. That is not possible.'

'It is not only possible, it actually happened, but you already knew that didn't you? Unfortunately for your Mr Gao, the state and federal police became aware of his illicit activities. In his panic to cover his tracks and avoid detection he tried to run down a reporter and then he murdered his accomplice.'

'This is fanciful, Ben—

Chandler cut him off. 'Cut the crap, Xiao. When you were interviewed by the detectives last week that surely would have rung alarm bells for you. They were getting too close to you and made you realise that your plan was dead in the water. As a result you had to act quickly to eliminate Gao before he was inevitably arrested. You couldn't allow him to implicate you nor the People's Republic of China, so you had an assassin flown in from China and the rest is history. The AFP have a record of the assassin, Yu Dayong, entering and leaving Australia on the weekend. How am I doing, Xiao?'

Xiao sat upright, leaned forward and placed his clasped hands on the desk. 'Gentlemen, you do realise you are sitting in a sovereign facility of the People's Republic of China,' he said.

The DC, John Robertson, spoke for the first time. 'Mr Consul General, the evidence against you for your personal involvement is largely circumstantial. We may have even more when we have the ballistic results from the murder weapon returned. I am more than willing to layout the evidence for you if you so wish. You of course will claim diplomatic immunity, but the publicity will be extremely damaging and highly embarrassing for you and your beloved mother country.'

'You have no evidence. This is just harassment,' Xiao replied, less convincingly this time.

Ben Chandler wanted every moment of retribution he could get and was eager to jump back in. 'I believe a well-regarded reporter, the same one who Gao tried to kill, is currently writing her feature article on Chinese interference in Australia. Apparently you are acquainted with Julie-Anne Granger. Well she has made the link between Sun Jie, Paul Gao and yourself and your failed attempts to blackmail a Minister of the state. I imagine there might be an oblique reference to your link to the assassin in the article as well. It should make for interesting reading. It won't be published until Saturday, so I imagine you will have to read it on the plane to Beijing.'

'This is nothing but harassment,' he replied angrily.

The DC stepped forward. 'Mr Consul General, there's more. My Chief Commissioner has spoken to his boss, that would be the Australian Attorney General, whom I understand has summoned your ambassador for a meeting. To avoid an embarrassing situation the AG will strongly advocate that for the benefit of maintaining stable diplomatic relations between our two countries you should quietly leave the country and he will encourage your ambassador to seek a more suitable replacement.'

'You cannot do this. I am an authorised representative of the People's Republic of China,' he said indignantly. 'This is blackmail.'

'No, that would be your specialty, Xiao. Your name will be added to the Movement Alert List which prevents you from flying within, out of or into Australia for the duration of the ban. In your case that will be for the remainder of your life. To enable you to close out your affairs here in Sydney the ban won't commence until midnight this Saturday. I will call you later in the week and arrange for your escort to the international airport.'

'This is preposterous; you can't do this. I am an appointed representative of the People's Republic of China. My government won't stand for this,' Xiao replied, huffing and puffing.

'You're partly correct. They won't be happy at all. You know better than most that China plays the long game, so they won't want to waste any political currency on a lowly diplomat.' The DC nodded to Chandler. 'If you have nothing else then I think we're done here, Ben.'

'I'm good. Goodbye, Xiao.'

98. Sydney Daily News

Thursday 11th June

Julie-Anne was in an upbeat mood as she drove her electric blue BMW 3 Series along King Street Newtown while singing along to Queen B's monster hit, Ladies. *'Cause if you like it, then you shoulda put a ring on it.'* She was smiling, dancing in her seat and her hair was swaying in time. She turned into Cleveland Street and took the short cut via Crown Street to her office in Surry Hills. It was a cool overcast morning, so she had resisted the temptation to flip the canopy back. She parked in her dedicated bay then grabbed herself a soy latte from the foyer café and as usual made her way up the fire stairs to her cubicle on the third floor. It was her first time back at the office since the incident in Goulburn Street and she was looking forward to feeling like a part of the team again. She woke her desktop, logged in and navigated to the paper's server where she had uploaded her first draft on the Chinese interference investigation. She went to her folder and clicked on the link to her draft. She had commenced the feature by providing the big picture overview of China's attempts to exert their influence across the globe, more specifically throughout South East Asia and recently Australia. She re-read the remainder of her draft to freshen her memory.

The People's Republic of China continues to use its

economic might to bully nations to achieve their political goals. This bullying has a new name: Wolf Warrior diplomacy, which describes an aggressive style of diplomacy purported to be adopted by Chinese diplomats in the twenty first century. Wikipedia states that: Wolf Warrior diplomacy is characterized by Chinese diplomats use of confrontational rhetoric, as well as diplomats increased willingness to rebuff criticism of China and court controversy in interviews and on social media.

Prior to the advent of Wolf Warrior diplomacy, Chinese diplomatic practice had emphasized the avoidance of controversy and adopted the use of cooperative rhetoric. Wolf Warrior diplomacy has become more apparent throughout the COVID-19 crisis as China rails against global criticism of its role in delivering the virus to the world. The Sydney Daily News can reveal that this more aggressive style of diplomacy has now reached New South Wales.

Following concerns of potential propaganda in New South Wales schools, the Department of Education ordered a review into the Confucius Institute in 2019. Hanban, the international arm of China's Education Ministry states that the Institute is designed to provide scope for people all over the world to learn about Chinese language and culture. In addition, the institutes have become a platform for cultural exchanges between China and the world as well as a bridge reinforcing friendship and cooperation between China and the rest of the world.

Of primary concern to the state government was that the Confucius Institute program, previously run in thirteen state schools, had been paid for by Hanban, and employed teaching assistants that were vetted by the Chinese government for "good political quality" and a love of "the motherland". As a result, the Department found that there was a perception that "the Institute is or could be facilitating inappropriate foreign influence, and that New South Wales is the only government department in the world hosting a Confucius Institute". The review said the arrangement placed Chinese Government appointees inside a New South Wales Government department. Due to these concerns of potential foreign influence, the state government removed the Confucius Institute from their high schools and colleges in late 2019. This was not well received by China and in particular, the Chinese Consul General to New South Wales, Zhang Xiao, who wrote at the time:

On the so-called political influence through Confucius Institute programs, China has always been committed to developing relations with other countries based on principles of mutual respect and non-interference in each other's internal affairs. It is noted that the relevant review by the NSW Department of Education found no evidence of actual political influence through its Confucius Institute program. We hope relevant parties will discard their ideological prejudice and view China's development and foreign policy in an objective and rational manner.

In August 2019 the Global Times, a mouthpiece for the Chinese Communist Party wrote: The NSW education department should deliberate on the negative influence this could bring to educational cooperation between the two sides, and the Confucius Institute reserves the rights to make further measures to protect the institute's legal rights, the institute said in a statement.

It appears the Chinese Communist Party wasn't tardy in enacting their "further measures".

Following an exhaustive investigation into potential Chinese interference, this journalist can confirm that China didn't take the decision to remove the Confucius Institutes lightly. The Consul General has been actively lobbying the state government to have the Institute reinstated. That continued lobbying proved unsuccessful. Not satisfied with the rejection they faced, it seems that certain officials with close ties to the Chinese Consulate in Sydney have resorted to less than honourable methods to achieve their ambition. This is where the Wolf Warrior diplomacy is relevant.

The Sydney Daily News can reveal that a high ranking state government minister has been the subject of brazen extortion attempts aimed at having the Confucius Institute reinstated. These alarming attempts at overturning the state government's decision were undertaken by a Special Emissary of the Chinese Consulate in Sydney.

This journalist met the Special Emissary, Paul Gao, at a social function, and subsequent to that fateful meeting certain incriminating information came into her possession. That information was provided to the Australian Federal Police who immediately established a joint taskforce with the state police. In conjunction with state and federal police, the Sydney Daily News uncovered links between the perpetrators of the extortion and the Chinese Consul General to New South Wales.

Gao had engaged the services of an ICT technician, Sun Jie, to undertake the technological aspects of the extortion attempt and subsequently, the investigation established a direct connection between the two agents.

Given Gao was employed directly by the Consul General it stands to reason that he was fully aware of his emissary's activities.

In a shocking turn of events, undoubtedly precipitated by the investigation, the charred body of Sun Jie was found in the trunk of a burnt out motor vehicle in an industrial estate near Silverwater. It is believed that the demise of Jie was at the hands of Gao. Four days later Gao's body was found at his apartment in Camperdown. The crime scene had been laid out by the perpetrator to imply the appearance of suicide. Subsequent testing by NSW Police Forensic Evidence and Technical Services specialists revealed that Gao hadn't died by his own hand. He had been assassinated. The assassin is known to have entered Australia through Sydney International Airport on Saturday sixth of June and departed the following day. Given Australia's strict border controls and the brief time the assassin spent in Sydney, the Sig Sauer P226 pistol used in the assassination would have been obtained locally. Someone living in Sydney with a connection to the suspects in this case had provided the murder weapon. The Consul General has denied any knowledge of the events detailed within this article. Written requests for an interview with the Consul General were ignored. Instead a statement was released on his behalf. The statement read:

"It was in Beijing's interest to recognise its robust interactive relationship with Australia's most populous state was mutually beneficial because the two-way trade between the countries had also been of great benefit to China. China valued this relationship and its representatives would not be involved in any activities that undermined that relationship."

Julie-Anne had just finished reading her first draft when her mobile rang. 'Good morning boss, how are you?'

'I'm fine, but more to the point, how are you feeling?' asked her editor.

'Yeah, much better and I'm back at my desk. I've just reviewed the first draft of my feature.'

'That's what I wanted to discuss with you. Seeing as how you're in the building would you mind coming up to my office?'

'On my way, boss.'

Wanting to get her daily steps up after her hospitalisation Julie-Anne entered the stairwell and as usual her long legs took the stairs two at a time as she bounded up to the top floor. She was in a buoyant mood now that she was finally back at work and surrounded by fellow journalists banging away at their keyboards. 'Good morning, Chris,' she said cheerily.

'Take a seat, JA.'

'That sounds ominous, what's up, boss?'

'Your feature. It's lacking in detail,' he replied, getting straight to the point.

She already knew where this conversation was heading and had expected to be forced to defend her decision to omit the names of two key people in the investigation. 'You want names, don't you?'

'If it's not too much to ask, yes. We are a newspaper and we report the news. Your feature reads well, but lacks specifics. Detailing names will give it the grunt it requires.'

'And ruin people's lives, Chris.'

'We're not some sort of societal moral arbiter here, JA. We simply report on the findings of our investigations. We didn't force these people to leave their morals at the door when they decided to become entangled in an affair.' Her mind drifted back to when she had recently parked her own morals for the benefit of a story.

She harumphed. 'Really, Chris? Since when have we joined the ranks of the tabloids, the online media behemoths, the after dark media and felt the need to include the salacious details of people's lives in our articles to satisfy our readership? We're not the Mirror or the Mail for chrissakes.'

'Explain your rationale for omitting the names of the people involved then,' he demanded.

She was becoming indignant now. 'Do I really have to explain that to my editor?' His pointed stare answered her question. 'Okay. Ben Chandler has a family, a life and a career, all of which will be destroyed and he will be relentlessly trolled online if we name him. So will the woman who he had the affair with. That's not in the public interest, Chris,' she sighed. 'The Minister was being extorted, so irrespective of how that came to pass, our readers don't expect us to destroy his life, especially just for the sake of adding some *grunt*.'

'Don't push it, JA. What about the hotel? You haven't named it either.'

'The hotel chain has four hundred hotels in China and you know there will be a backlash against them by the Chinese government if they are suspected of cooperating with an investigation that has implicated one of their diplomats.' Russell gave her a blank stare that she interpreted as; *really, JA?* 'Alright. The GM was more interested in protecting his brand than showing any concern for Ben Chandler anyway, so I'll name the hotel if that appeases you.'

'Yes, it does, and I would like a comment from the hotel about how there was such a lapse in their security that the privacy of a senior government minister was so easily compromised. If they refuse then I suggest you might want to be more specific in your article about the gaping holes in their security. Now about the woman involved. What do we know about her?'

Julie-Anne was hoping that might slip his mind, but he was a stickler for details. 'She's a friend of mine.'

'Of course she is. Well, that at least explains why she has remained anonymous throughout this whole messy affair. The last time it was the detective, Jack Wagner and your new bestie, Melissa Wu who were turning you upside down. Who are you dating now? I can't wait to see what their involvement will be in your next investigation,' he said.

Stay calm, Julie-Anne; you're almost through this. 'That's hardly fair, Chris. Sophie was the woman who was being threatened with her family's safety by Li Qiang earlier in the year. She gave me his name in the first instance and that was the kicker I needed to progress my money laundering investigation. I, *we*, owe her something for that, surely.'

'I'm sorry, JA, but we are in the middle of a hostile takeover at the moment, so we need to put our best foot forward editorially and that means showing our shareholders that their interests are best served by staying loyal to us. To do that we need to publish quality journalism and having a feature article without definitive information diminishes our reputation.'

'Surely exposing China's attempt at influencing government ministers through brazen extortion is definitive enough,' she groaned. 'Why do we have to impugn the name of an innocent young woman who's trying to get her life back on track?'

'Alright, alright.' Russell sighed. 'Let me think about it.'

99. The Winery

Friday 12th June

When Julie-Anne was in the middle of an investigation she kept her calendar free just in case she needed to react to a sudden development, as often happened. As a result, now that the investigation was complete she found herself with some free time. With nothing planned for tonight, Julie-Anne would walk around the corner to The Winery and treat herself to a celebratory drink. She liked this laneway wine bar with its stylish bohemian décor and modern Australian food. She perched at the bar and ordered the Wild Rocket and Pecorino Croquette with Sundried Tomato Mayo. She would wash it down with an Aperol Spritzer. There was an added reason to celebrate. Chris Russell had called her back up to his office late in the day and confirmed that she could leave Sophie's name out of the story. Julie-Anne had thanked him, but they both knew her name was never going to be included.

Julie-Anne's mind was wandering and she was thinking about an inquest that would undoubtedly be held into Gao's death. If that happened, as it most likely would, then she would surely be called as a witness. She imagined one of the key questions the Coroner would ask. *"And Ms Granger, exactly how did you manage to have the photos in your possession?"* She had studied Section 126k of the Evidence Act 1995 intricately and particularly the subsection that dealt with protecting the identity of an informant through journalistic privilege. In this case she conveniently considered herself to be the informant. *That will be an interesting legal argument.*

Her musings were interrupted by a voice from behind. 'Fancy seeing you here, Ms Granger,' the bubbly voice chirped. Julie-Anne turned her head in time to see Detective Amanda Brown plop down on the adjacent stool.

Julie-Anne felt her eyebrows rise in surprise. 'Well, if it's not Miss Policewoman 2020 herself. I suppose you're going to tell me this is just happenstance,' she replied.

'Of course, I adore this place and come here often, especially on a Friday night. I love Crown Street and its bars and restaurants.'

'Yeah, sure, pull the other one it plays Jingle Bells. You're a detective and I'm an investigative journalist, and as such, neither of us believes in coincidences.'

'Think what you like,' Brown responded dismissively. She looked at Julie-Anne's colourful drink and ordered one for herself.

'Oh, I will, don't worry.' Julie-Anne ignored the woman while sipping her drink and tucking into her croquette.

Eventually Brown broke the silence. 'I spoke to Sanderson and he confirmed your version of events.'

'Well, good for you, detective,' she replied. 'I thought you and Taggart might be walking the beat by now.'

'Amanda, please.'

'Well, good for you then, *Amanda*.'

'He cleared you of any involvement in Gao's death although he wouldn't divulge details of the extortion and various documents in the case file were either redacted or password protected.'

'So, does that mean I'm no longer a person of interest then?'

The detective cast an alluring glance. 'Well, not to the New South Wales police anyway.'

Julie-Anne picked up on the nuanced response, turned away and immediately reverted to the topic. 'I told you it was a sensitive case, so you shouldn't be surprised that you couldn't access the files, *Amanda*.'

'You know you can tell me what happened "off the record",' she said while curling her fingers into rabbit's ears.

Julie-Anne swivelled on her stool to face the woman. 'Are you kidding. There are only four or five police officers in this world that I trust and none of them are sitting next to me.'

'Oh, that hurts,' Brown replied while exaggeratedly pouting.

Julie-Anne almost smiled at the routine. Miss Policewoman was trying her darndest to ingratiate her, for what specific reason she had yet to ascertain. 'Oh, stop it. You look like Posh Spice with that pout.'

Amanda gazed into her eyes. 'That was some performance of your own.'

Julie-Anne turned away and stared down into her drink, knowing precisely what the woman was referring to. She sighed ruefully. 'It wasn't my proudest moment.' She felt the woman's eyes still on her.

'Well, for what it's worth, you were just spectacular. You should have seen yourself, particularly when your body was at full stretch. You looked like a goddess.'

Now, where have I heard that before? Julie-Anne turned to face her. 'Is there a sign on my forehead that states, "I'm available, so feel free to chat me up"?'

'Sorry, I was just paying you a compliment,' Amanda said.

'Yeah, well, that's not the sort of flattery that I want, nor need for that matter, so keep your thoughts to yourself.'

'Just for tonight, how about we agree to a truce?' Brown suggested in a soft, warm voice.

Julie-Anne looked fixedly at her. Amanda's sultry gaze was projecting back at her. She finally had it confirmed where this interaction was heading. *That's all I need, another complication in my life.* She placed a fifty dollar note on the bar and slid off of her stool.

'It's been interesting. Goodnight, Amanda.' She started towards the exit then abruptly stopped. Turning back to face Brown, she said, 'by the way, if you're going to tail someone you might want to brush up on your concealment techniques. I spotted you in the reflection of a shop window seconds after I left my building. Bye.'

100. Sydney International Airport

Saturday 13th June

Jack and Michael Sanderson were in Jack's mustard coloured 1971 MGB-Roadster parked up on Shep's Mound adjacent to the main north-south runway at Sydney's Kingsford Smith Airport. The Roadster was a soft-top convertible that Jack had lovingly restored over time with the help of his father. The two detectives were in a celebratory mood drinking midnecks of One Fifty Lashes and looking up into the azure sky on a surprisingly pleasant, twenty degree, June day. The occasion for their celebration was that Zhang Xiao would be aboard Cathay Pacific flight CX 100 which was due to depart for Hong Kong at three forty five this afternoon on the first leg of his one way flight to Beijing. Jack had arranged for two of his fellow AFP officers to escort Xiao to the airport, so that he and Sanderson could celebrate their minor victory together. Sanderson was quiet and listened while Jack spoke to his colleagues inside the terminal. 'Okay, thanks, good job.' He disconnected the call. 'He's on the plane and the last door has been closed.'

'It feels quite strange really, Jack. We solved the case without ever actually charging anyone with any offences. That's what we're supposed to do,' Sanderson lamented. 'I have no doubt that had we had access to Xiao's encrypted phone we could have directly linked him to the assassination. But, that's all water under the bridge now.'

'I know, but none of Xiao, Gao or Sun Jie will be able to cause any harm to anyone in this country again, so that's a big win. Although unfortunately, in reality, it's only a minor setback for the Chinese, as I'm certain all three will be replaced in the near future. They won't take this lying down.'

'If it wasn't for Julie-Anne somehow obtaining those photos we wouldn't have gotten to first base. Have you asked yourself how she came into possession of the photos, Jack?'

'Many times, and I've asked her on numerous occasions too, but I get the same response every time, which of course, I don't believe for a second. JA's an intelligent, shrewd and resourceful reporter, so whatever she did to obtain those photos, she's keeping her own counsel.'

Sanderson knew the answer to his own question. Taggart and Brown from the PAC in Marrickville had shared the video with him under the guise of confirming the identity of the two participants. Even though he and Jack had now become firm friends as well as colleagues, he wasn't about to reveal Julie-Anne's secret to him. Jack would be furious if he found out that he had known and hadn't told him. That could breach their trust and lead to the end of their friendship. Trust was everything to a cop. That wasn't the primary reason he had avoided telling him though. Julie-Anne would have enough of her own demons to deal with following her amoral behaviour without incurring Jack's inevitable wrath. Sanderson would stay mum. He hadn't watched the entire video, just enough to identify Gao and Julie-Anne. It had been tempting though, given Julie-Anne was an alluring woman with an incredible figure, but his carnal desires were overridden by his obligation not to breach her privacy. He hoped his fellow colleagues at Marrickville felt the same otherwise her life and career were toast.

'Here we go, buddy.' Jack had been checking for Cathay Pacific flight CX 100 on the Flight Radar app and it now showed the Airbus 350 slowly heading south down the main runway. 'Here she comes.'

The men raised their beers to the giant plane. 'Goodbye, Xiao,' Jack called out while flipping the bird.

'Good riddance, Mr ex Consul General,' Sanderson whooped.

Jack placed his empty beer bottle in the cup holder. 'Well, I suppose that's it then. The Consul General's left the country never to return and Wie, Yong and Danielle are all on remand for various drug related offences which carry significant prison time. And just like the extortion attempt we never even came close to nailing the kingpin of the drug importation in China. Someone with balls of brass will assumes Wie's position in Chinatown and we'll be on the merry-go-round all over again.'

Sanderson turned to his partner. 'What comes, when it comes, will be what it is, Jack.'

'You and your life quotes.'

101. Coogee Pavilion

Saturday 20th June

Julie-Anne's feature published a week ago today had been well received, circulation and clicks for that edition had skyrocketed and there was even talk of a Walkley nomination. She had been in a wonderful headspace all week. It was forecast to be a warm twenty five degrees in Sydney, so she intended to make the most of it. She was heading to the Coogee Pavilion for lunch with her two besties. The Beemer's canopy was stowed, her locks were freewheeling in the wind and she was singing along to the Beach Boys classic Good Vibrations as she accelerated up Alison Street past Randwick Racecourse. She glanced down at her summer attire. Talk about synchronicity. The song could have been written for this precise moment in her life.

I love the colourful clothes she wears
And the way the sunlight plays upon her hair
I hear the sound of a gentle word
On the wind that lifts her perfume through the air

Julie-Anne was still singing to herself as she walked up the stairs to the rooftop. *'I'm pickin' up good vibrations oom bop bop'*. She strode confidently across the dining room towards the balcony and heads were turning. She was wearing a black long sleeve, yellow floral patterned blouse tied above the waist and matched with a pair of rich yellow shorts and black heels. Having bemoaned her fading tan she had topped it up courtesy of Bondi Sands.

'Shorts, Julie-Anne? Really?'

'This unseasonably warm winter's day will undoubtedly be the last for ages, so I am making the most of it. Don't you like the look?'

Melissa stepped forward, reached out and undid another button on Julie-Anne's blouse. 'I like it a lot better now.'

'You are incorrigible. Have I told you that?'

Melissa, as was her tradition, was predominantly in red, wearing a white flowing maxi dress adorned with large red roses and turquoise leaves. And she wouldn't be Melissa without the fire engine red Jimmy Choos. 'You are definitely a woman of colour.'

'Nice double entendre.'

Julie-Anne's hand jerked to her mouth. 'Oh, no, I just realised what I said, sorry.'

'Chill out girlfriend; it was funny.'

'You managed to get a window table with a view.'

'Of course, I booked early. Here comes Sophie.'

Their friend was wearing a white daybreak dress with silver sequined overlay, frilled hem and scooped neckline. The outfit was complemented by a pair of white strappy sandals. She looked like summer itself. 'Shorts and now a mini. I feel overdressed. Aaargh,' Melissa groaned.

'You look fabulous as always,' Julie-Anne replied as she turned to greet Sophie. 'You've dressed for summer as well.'

'We're already well into the first month of winter and I can't believe it's twenty one degrees so, I dressed accordingly. The last time for a while I imagine. The downside is that it's as flat as a tack out there, so I couldn't even bodysurf this morning,' Sophie lamented. 'It does look spectacular though,' she said while admiring the cerulean sheen below the balcony.

Julie-Anne smiled mischievously. 'You are such a thalassophile, Soph.'

'A what?'

'A thalassophile. Someone who is magnetically attracted to the ocean. It's you to a T.'

'And you are such a journalist, girl.'

Over a platter of Sashimi and a bottle of Italian Prosecco, the women were discussing their wretched run of luck with men lately. Paul Gao, Ben Chandler and Jack had all caused the women varying levels of pain and anguish over the past few weeks.

'You shouldn't include Jack in that group, he's a really kind, considerate guy,' Melissa said.

That surprised Julie-Anne. 'Where did that come from?'

Melissa realised all too late how that sounded. 'What?' she blurted out defensively while nervously twiddling her bangle.

'Later, girlfriend,' Julie-Anne said coolly.

Sophie broke the tension. 'Ben's a really good guy. If anyone's to blame for our demise it's me, after all I went back the third time fully understanding the expectation.'

'I don't believe in perpetuating victimhood, but in your case there's two victims, Sophie. And more if you count Ben's family.' Julie-Anne noticed her friend's uncomfortable expression. 'Sorry, I shouldn't have said that.'

Melissa rose from the table and made her way to the bathroom.

Julie-Anne stood also. 'I'll be back in no time, Soph. You'll probably be swept off your feet while we're away.'

'Yeah, I wish. That's all I need at the moment.'

'You slept with Jack,' Julie-Anne said indignantly as she burst into the ladies room. 'Really, Melissa?'

'Let me explain.'

'This will be good.'

Melissa felt her face flushing with anger. 'Don't you take that sarcastic tone with me, woman. You haven't exactly covered yourself in glory recently. In fact you've carried on more like a sl—' She stopped herself short, immediately regretting what she was about to say.

'Go on, you can say it. I know what I did and I will have to live with that. But, what about you sleeping with my ex? What's your excuse?'

Melissa sighed. 'On the night that I found out that Paul had died I was obviously upset, confused and more than a little vulnerable. Jack was very kind, considerate and empathetic throughout. I didn't want to be alone, so he suggested that I stay the night. Nothing happened, Julie-Anne. Nothing.'

Now, Julie-Anne sighed. 'You and Jack have always been attracted to each other and you both lingered slightly when you hugged at the hospital. I thought maybe that—'

Melissa grabbed her besties hands. 'Nothing happened.'

Both women were silent while regarding each other in the vanity mirror. Melissa broke the silence. 'There's still one thing that's bugging me though. How come I had to read your article to find out that Paul didn't actually commit suicide, but rather he was assassinated?'

'Who said he committed suicide?'

'Jack told me outside Paul's apartment the night he found the body.'

'Would that be the same night that you stayed over? Oh, of course, silly me.'

'Enough with the sarcasm, Julie-Anne, it doesn't suit you. I've very clearly told you that nothing happened. Now, how about we just park it and move on?' she pleaded. 'Agreed?'

'I've harmed the relationships of three of my friends with

my latest investigations, so I suppose that's only fair,' Julie-Anne acknowledged ruefully.

Melissa eyed Julie-Anne's wistful expression. Time to lighten the mood. 'Okay, now let's go and rescue Sophie. No doubt she'll be surrounded by men, particularly given what she's wearing.'

'Yeah, I know. She looks fabulous as always and she's a lovely girl.'

'Yes, she is.'

'I've been thinking that we should give our little group a name. What about Victorious Secret?' Sophie suggested when the women rejoined her. 'Even with everything that's been thrown at us this year we're still here. We've emerged victorious. And I'm certain we each have some juicy secrets,' she said.

Melissa looked at Julie-Anne and thought back to their bathroom conversation. She broke away from her bout of reverie. 'Yeah right; I'm not even wearing a bra, but I like it,' she said.

'Me too, pun intended,' replied Julie-Anne. 'Victorious Secret it is.'

Sophie was now staring out at the shimmering blue water and Julie-Anne noticed the contemplative expression on her friend's face. 'A penny for your thoughts, Soph.'

'I'm thinking about giving it another go with Ben,' she replied. Neither Julie-Anne nor Melissa responded. 'Okay, I see that went down well, ladies.'

Julie-Anne broke the impasse. 'We only want you to be happy, so please be careful. Maybe you should wait awhile until the inevitable media storm abates. That might afford you guys some quiet, quality time together and provide your relationship with the best chance of success.'

'I know and I won't be rushing into any relationship in a hurry. I knew it was wrong in the first place, but he was so charming, considerate and witty that after the second booking I just decided to go with the flow so to speak. He was a breath of fresh air after that horrible Li Qiang. If I do give it another go I'll be taking my time and being very cautious, don't worry ladies.'

'Good luck, Sophie,' Melissa said as she embraced her friend.

Sophie grasped Melissa's hands and looked sympathetically into her eyes. 'Anyone of interest on the horizon?'

'No more men in the immediate future for this girl. Once my friendship with Paul ended I decided to refocus on my practice. I'm actually already in the middle of compiling a new class action for the residents and families of Agnes Waters Lodge. They are seeking an explanation and compensation over the loss of their loved ones during the coronavirus outbreak. So, that's my focus for the next few months.'

'Good for you. That's a wonderful cause.'

Sophie turned to Julie-Anne. 'And what about you, girlfriend?'

Melissa was looking intently at her and Julie-Anne wondered why. Throughout the dinner and especially during their escapade in the pool Melissa had been openly flirting with her and they had kissed, caressed and fondled with abandon. Was that a sign that she was hoping to rekindle their relationship. 'Nothing to tell here, Soph. I'm already on the lookout for my next investigation.' An idea popped into her head. 'Hey, Melissa, maybe I can have a look into your class action. Do you need an investigator by any chance?'

'Actually, I haven't engaged one yet, but I will have to eventually. Do you think you could manage it with your workload?'

'Of course. That's what I do anyway. You would get a trustworthy investigator and I might get a juicy story out of it.

I'll have to clear it with my boss though, but I think he'll go for it.'

'Okay, that sounds like something worth exploring, albeit on another day when we're not into our second bottle of Prosecco. Cheers, ladies,' Melissa toasted.

'You're kidding,' Julie-Anne blurted out in astonishment. Melissa and Sophie's heads turned in unison to see what had surprised her. 'Is that Jack over there having lunch with that woman?' She recognised the woman, but where from? Suddenly it came to her. 'Oh, my god, it's Lucie Chan.'

'Who's Lucie Chan?' the other women hollered in chorus.

'She was the dealer who revealed to Jack the location of the cocaine storage locker which eventually led to the demise of Danielle and Wie Ping Lie. I can't believe it.' She looked at Melissa and again thought back to their conversation in the bathroom. She was still twiddling her jewellery. 'I'm going over there,' Julie-Anne said.

She strode purposefully across to the table flicking her hair for effect as she went. 'Well, hello, Jack,' she gushed theatrically. 'Fancy seeing you here.'

'Hello, JA.' He stood and greeted her. 'You've met Lucie before, I believe.'

'Yes, I have. Hello, Lucie,' she replied aloofly. Chan stood and offered Julie-Anne her hand in greeting. She was wearing a long sleeve, gold sequin, bodycon mini dress and matching gold pumps. Julie-Anne knew exactly why Jack was having lunch with this woman and she hated that the woman looked fabulous.

'I'm going to powder my nose and will leave you two to chat. I'm sure it will be extremely entertaining,' Chan said, heavy on the irony.

'Oh, Jack, what the hell are you doing? Lucie Chan, really!'

'It's nothing. She invited me to lunch and I thought, why not? There's not much else going on in my life these days.

Anyway, you know what they say, keep your friends close and your enemies closer.'

'Yeah, sure, Jack. Pull the other one; it plays Jingle Bells.' Julie-Anne laughed to herself at having used that decades old expression twice in a week.

'Too funny as always, JA.'

'This is not funny, Jack' She furnished a dark look. 'You need to be careful around that woman. Somehow she's gone from being a target of our investigation to suddenly having lunch with the detective who very nearly sent her to prison.'

'She's turned over a new leaf. Anyhow, it's just lunch, JA,' he replied.

'Yeah, sure. I know you better than that. Anyway here comes Ms Dial-A-Dealer now, so I'll leave you two to discuss her newfound interest in horticulture.'

Jack's brow furrowed. 'Horticulture?'

'Work it out, detective.'

'I like the blouse, JA,' he observed as his eyes drifted south.

'Your Lucie's got a great rack too; you'll be fine, Jack. Bye.' Julie-Anne turned on her heels, flicked her hair for effect again and sashayed exaggeratedly back out onto the balcony.

'What's with all the cavorting and strutting?' Melissa asked.

'I was just having some fun and reminding Jack of what he lost. Julie-Anne topped up their Proseccos. 'It's been an interesting and challenging three months ladies and we've come out the other side unscathed. Well mostly. Here's to a quieter time ahead. Here's to Victorious Secret.'

'To Victorious Secret,' they chorused.

Epilogue

Friday 3rd July

Julie-Anne's feature article on Wolf Warrior Diplomacy was published on Saturday 13th June and that day's circulation for the print version of the *Sydney Daily News* increased by fourteen percent and the online clicks by a whopping twenty one percent. Her boss was so buoyed by the success of her feature that he granted her two weeks paid leave. She had used the time to heal her body and rebuild her strength in the gym following her brush with death in the CBD exactly one month ago to the day. Her mind and body had recovered quicker than anticipated and she felt rejuvenated and back to her old self. Wearing jeans and a red colour block rugby top, and with a throw blanket covering her legs, Julie-Anne sipped her home made latte and savoured a draw of her first and last cigarette for a while. She was about to dive headlong into a very different and challenging investigative role which, even more than usual, would require her undiluted focus. This would be the last day of her sabbatical. With the saturation coverage of the COVID-19 pandemic still dominating the headlines Julie-Anne flopped the paper down on the patio table and allowed her mind to wander. She pondered the events of the past six weeks.

The video of her indefensible conduct had apparently been circulated among a small group of male detectives from Inner

West Police Area Command at Marrickville by Thomas Taggart. Amanda Brown was disgusted with the boy's club behaviour and reported the matter to the PAC's Superintendent. As a consequence, Taggart was reported to be slowly coming to terms with his career ending posting to the regional town of Albury down on the Victorian border. Detective Amanda Brown had been transferred to the Eastern Suburbs PAC at Waverley. Detective Michael Sanderson had heard from a colleague, that while Brown had taken the honourable course of action, her fellow detectives at Marrickville had refused to work with her. *It doesn't pay to be a whistleblower in the New South Police Force apparently.*

Melissa Wu, true to her word, was already heavily engaged with potential plaintiffs who were seeking to take legal action against the Agnes Waters Lodge aged care facility. The plaintiffs were alleging that as a result of their loved ones entirely preventable deaths, families had suffered acutely from depression and anxiety and experienced profound grief. Provided there was a feature story for the Sydney Daily News, Julie-Anne's boss, Chris Russell, had agreed that she could act as Melissa's investigator. Her primary role would be to seek out evidence to support the plaintiff's claims against Agnes Waters. Julie-Anne was intending to use the weekend to conduct her own preliminary research before diving into the role on Monday.

Ben Chandler and Sophie Zhao's affair had somehow managed to avoid scrutiny from the tabloid, after dark media and online trolls thus far. Ben had moved out of the family home and rented a three bedroom house through Airbnb in nearby Pearl Beach. It was close by the ocean, had plenty of space for his boys to stay, and far enough from Woy Woy that he was unlikely to encounter his still very disillusioned and angry wife. He was desperate to see Sophie again and had been persistent in his pursuit of her. Sophie had finally agreed to meet with him, but definitely not in public. And she was never going back to that hotel again. No way that was happening. With seemingly few options available to them, Julie-Anne had conceived a plan which both of them were comfortable with. She would go and stay overnight with Melissa and they could make use of her apartment. It was located in a quiet, secluded, tree-lined street far from where both of them lived, so it was unlikely Ben would be recognised. Sophie was adamant that she would be taking it very slowly the second time around. If there was a second time. Just in case, Julie-Anne had refreshed the bed linen, laid out scented towels, and left heart-shaped chocolates on the pillows. She had cooked them a hearty minestrone soup and a chicken lasagne and left a bottle of her favourite red on the benchtop. She had smiled to herself as she headed out the door.

Under increasing pressure from Australia's Attorney General, the Chinese Ambassador to Australia finally released a statement regarding the Consul General to New South Wales unscheduled departure from the country. Zhang Xiao's mother had been diagnosed with a terminal illness. In China, family was regarded as the most important facet of an individual's life and the People's Republic of China would honour his wish to be with his family during this difficult time, the statement read. Given the importance of the bilateral relationship between the two countries a high-ranking replacement would be sought as a priority. China expected to announce the appointment in the near future. *And then life on the interference merry-go-round would continue,* Julie-Anne thought.

During their lunch at the Coogee Pavillion Lucie Chan had revealed to Jack that in her early twenties she had graduated from Sydney University with Bachelor of Advanced Computing and Bachelor of Science degrees. Julie-Anne had once told Jack that Chinese students were often considered more well-suited to the technology and science fields due to the emphasis placed on STEM subjects in their curriculum. Whilst she was actually Eurasian, Jack had always known that Lucie was more intelligent that she had chosen to reveal at times during the interview process. The degree revelation had surprised the hell out of him though and an idea had germinated in his mind. With her degree and obvious street smarts she would quite possibly make a damn good intelligence analyst. Julie-Anne knew Jack well enough to know that he was thinking with his other brain. Nevertheless, Jack had canvassed the idea with his DC, but John Robertson was still smarting from being completely blindsided by Danielle Mortimer's deception, so he wasn't having a bar of it.

Despite the eradication of the Chinatown Triad head Wie Ping Lie and his crew, Michael Sanderson knew that it would only be a matter of time before they were replaced. With the ridiculously high price of cocaine in Australia there was simply too much money to be made. Even more so if the syndicate continued to bring in the high purity cocaine that the eastern suburbs elite were addicted to. Whomever the head of the syndicate was in China, they would be desperate to source a suitable replacement. And with the combination of her obvious intelligence, street smarts, and good looks Sanderson knew precisely who would be at the top of their list.

Now fully recovered, Julie-Anne was tonight going on her third date with the charming and persistent Jordan Doherty. She was looking forward to enjoying his company again, although her role with Burwood Legal Services was vitally important to both her and Melissa, and that would be her sole focus for the immediate future.

Julie-Anne looked up at the leaden sky dominated by large gunmetal grey cumulus clouds drifting in from the south. As if on cue it started to pour. Winter had well and truly arrived. She would miss the warm weather, but with her dual role, she had a lot to look forward to, and be grateful for. She smiled. Life was good.

Teaser for Deadly Waters

Chapter One

Her name badge read Sue Levy – Head Nurse. She had trained as a radiographer, but somewhere along the way her management skills and knowledge of the broader health industry had been identified and her career had morphed into her current role at Agnes Waters Lodge. Up until the onset of the Coronavirus pandemic she had thoroughly enjoyed the role itself, the challenges and the immense job satisfaction it engendered. Then everything had changed. The father and son ownership team of Maxwell and Jordan Doherty, instead of increasing medical services and employing the appropriate COVID-19 protocols, implemented a regime of drastic cost cutting that further exacerbated the decline in health services to Agnes Water's aging residents.

The blood curdling shriek from the opposite end of the corridor brought her out of her moment of reflection. A woman was running erratically towards her. 'What's happened Teresa?'

'It's Mum, she's not breathing.'

Levy reached under the counter and grabbed an Ambu Bag. The two women dashed along the corridor to Teresa Minchin's mother's room. 'How long has she been like this?' Sue asked.

Teresa had immense respect for the Head Nurse, who she knew had been doing her best under trying circumstances, but that question infuriated her. 'Shouldn't I be asking you that exact same question?'

Sue Levy blushed, knowing that the distraught daughter was correct. 'Let's focus on your Mum for now. Call an ambulance then I'm going to need your help.' She saw the enraged expression on Teresa's face. 'I can't do CPR and administer oxygen at the same time.' Sue tore open the plastic bag and unpacked the oxygen mask. 'Is the ambulance on its way?'

'Yes.'

'Good. Now you need to hold this mask on your mother's face with one hand and the oxygen bag with the other. When I tell you gently squeeze the inflated bag twice. Okay?'

'Yes.'

'I'm going to start chest compressions now, Teresa.'

'Be gentle, she's old.'

'I will.'

Mrs Beardman wasn't responding to the compressions, so Sue instructed Teresa to squeeze the bag. 'Okay, now do it again, gently.' Sue stared in hope at Mrs Beardman's chest. She was praying that the administered oxygen would generate a response. It didn't.

Just then a masked-up, female paramedic entered the room followed by her male partner. The uniformed woman placed her PRK Kit on the floor and checked the patient. 'How long has she been like this?'

Teresa projected am angry glare at Levy.

'I don't know,' the women replied in unison.

'Alright, stand back.'

The women watched on as the paramedics went to work. Teresa with tears streaming down her face and Sue's expression was awash with guilt. The aim of CPR was to circulate oxygen and blood throughout the body to keep vital organs and the brain alive. Minutes ticked by and the lack of rise and fall in Mrs

Beardman's chest was telling. Sue was acutely aware that without oxygen brain damage can occur after about four minutes. The longer the brain was deprived of oxygen, the more likely and severe the damage to be. She checked her watch. Nine minutes.

Teresa began to sob and Sue pulled her into an embrace.

'I'm sorry,' said the female paramedic as she stepped back from the bed. 'There's nothing more that we can do.'

Hearing the finality in the paramedic's words was too much for Teresa. Her grief and anger bubbled to the surface and she aggressively pushed Sue away. 'You did this. You're responsible,' she bawled.

'I'm sorry, Teresa. I really am.'

'Well, sorry just doesn't cut it. My mother was healthy before she was admitted to this hellhole.'

Sue knew that Teresa's mother should have been transferred to a hospital for treatment days ago. The Dohertys, in fear of instigating a mass exodus of residents, had resisted implementing that protocol. And now it had seemingly cost another human life. The Head Nurse endeavoured to apologise again, but it was in vain. Finally, she excused herself and made her way to the nurse's station from where she would call the doctor to attend and issue the death certificate. Sometimes she just hated this job.

Acknowledgments

A special thank you to Jochem Groeneveld, the most enthusiastic and voracious book reader I know, for providing his valued feedback on the first draft some three years ago now.

To my beta readers, Kat Todd and Ramona Schick, from opposite coasts of this vast land, for keeping me on track, especially with my portrayal of the female characters in the book.

It would be remiss of me not to acknowledge celebrated author, Tara Moss, who's dynamic character, Makedde Vanderwall, provided the inspiration for Julie-Anne Granger.

A special thank you to Alana Lambert from Book Burrow for her support, sage advice and technical expertise, but mostly for her patience and understanding. It wouldn't have been possible without you.

And I am eternally grateful to all those people who purchased my first book, *Uncharted Waters*, and especially to those of you who provided reviews on Amazon and Goodreads. Bless you.

About the Author

Peter has been an avid reader of contemporary fiction for many years. He has read in excess of five hundred books in the past decade particularly from such globally successful authors as James Patterson, Lee Child, David Baldacci, Tara Moss and Stella Rimington. In early 2020, being semi-retired, and with Melbourne plunged into lockdown, Peter needed to discover new activities to occupy his time and maintain his sanity. He decided to challenge himself, put pen to paper and embark on a new journey as an author. *Uncharted Waters* was his first book along that journey. *Uncharted Waters* was published in September 2022 and has received numerous positive reviews (see Goodreads). It was also nominated for the Miles Franklin, University of Queensland and New South Wales Premier's literary awards. *Duplicity* is Peter's second book.